THE
TAIAHA
CONNECTION

IAIN CLARK

For Cathy & the family – with love

PART ONE

Glasgow, Scotland. December 1971

It was cold. He could feel the cold air on the tip of his nose. He smiled to himself and stretched lazily. The rest of him was snug as a bug in the eiderdown sleeping bag. He'd begun the habit of sleeping in it after chatting to Euan, one of the young students in the downstairs flat. Evidently, they were all finding sleeping bags the answer to combating the Scottish climate. He chuckled as he recalled Euan telling him that when you got into a bag with a girl, the temperature rose ten-fold but that it could get a bit claustrophobic. And then, in all seriousness, he had added that the answer was to get a second bag and zip them both together.

Thinking of students, he was suddenly aware that the building was abnormally quiet. He could hear the traffic down on Byres Road and the occasional car moving off in Cranworth Street, but not a sound from the half dozen student flats scattered around the four- storey tenement. Usually, they didn't stir too early in the morning unless some of them had early lectures or it was the frantic run up to exam time. But, of course, they'd all be away by now for the Christmas break. The buggers could be noisy enough at other times, inevitably in the small hours of the morning. Not that they bothered him. Having a top-floor flat in the sandstone edifice was still a delight to him, even after eighteen months of living there.

Sean opened his eyes. The curtains in the bay window recess were wide open and the faint glow from the street lights dimly illuminated the room. It was the twenty-third of December. It may have been the season of cheer and goodwill to all men, but a dark and damp Glasgow December morning would greet all citizens venturing forth.

He twisted round to check the small alarm clock on the bed-side table. It was just after eight. Jeez he'd have to get a move on. He had to be at Glasgow Central for two. He'd still to sort out his gear and pack. And he'd better give the flat a quick tidy up. After a few pints at the Aragon last night with Jim and Lynne, he'd come home with a fish supper, scoffed it in the kitchen and made straight for bed. Bracing himself, he counted to three, pulled the side zipper and clambered out of his cosy cocoon. Goose pimples started to multiply as naked, he nipped into the bathroom to turn the shower on and then popped through to the kitchen to fill up the kettle and flick on the switch. An after-thought had him scurrying through to the bedroom studio to put on the gas fire.

Shaved, showered and dressed, he was carrying a black coffee and a plate of toast and honey through to the fireside when he noticed a pile of mail on the lobby floor. Old Mr MacPherson, his neighbour on the top landing, had obviously collected it from the downstairs box. Kind old guy, thought Sean as he balanced coffee and plate in one hand and bent down to scoop up the letters.

Putting his breakfast on the hearth, he sat on the rug with his back against the sofa. Sifting through the mail he suddenly paused. His pulse rate quickened. The envelope had an airmail sticker. A brightly coloured New Zealand stamp was affixed to the top right-hand corner. And he was pretty sure he recognised the writing. Slowly he turned the envelope over. The sender's address was there. It was from Marama.

Sean clutched it to his chest and closed his eyes. He could feel his heartbeat increase. He forced himself to inhale and exhale slowly, in an effort to calm an involuntary tremor that was beginning to course through his body. He eased the bottom of the letter flap up with his thumb nail and then worked around it until he was able to lift the whole of it up in one piece. He took the card out, and as he raised it to look at the Christmas greeting super-imposed on the picture of a pohutukawa tree, something fell onto his lap. Gently he lifted it up. It was a photograph of Marama and a beautiful little girl. He gazed and gazed at the photo and his eyes began to fill with tears.

2

Applecross, Scotland. 1930

Murdo MacLean maintained his steady pace up the ancient track that had been cut into the hillside above Applecross Bay. He paused near the top where the track disappeared behind a large overhanging rock and his eyes swept across the one hundred and eighty degree vista that was so familiar to him. Below, a low autumnal tide had exposed the sands of the bay for around four hundred yards, out to the point where the dark blue waters of the Sound of Raasay lapped at its entrance. Directly across from him, peat and wood-smoke rose lazily from the row of cottages that made up the village's main street whilst above and beyond, the mountains of the Bealach na Ba (the Pass of the Cattle) loomed hazily and fortress-like in the late afternoon sunshine. To the south-west, the Cuillins of Skye, dusted with the season's first snowfall, stood regal and tall and across the Sound a rapidly sinking sun was beginning to paint the sky over the isle of Raasay in various hues. 'God's own country,' muttered Murdo to himself as he turned and strode round the rock outcrop, quickening his pace along the now levelling out track.

It was twilight, the gloaming time, when he arrived at the hamlet of Lonbain. He descended the pathway leading to the old croft house, home of his mother's family and now of Calum, the last of the siblings still alive. Murdo knocked on the door and entered, lowering his head below the ancient lintel. A couple of burning peats gave a low red glow to the hearth but did little to illuminate the surrounding darkness. 'Uncle Calum,' he called out and was rewarded with a grunt followed by a series of coughs, splutters and a croaky 'bugger' from the vaguely outlined settee that sat adjacent to the fire. Murdo set his rucksack down and stepping over to the mantelpiece, felt for the matchbox lying on the shelf beside the oil lamp and set it going. As the flame rose, he took in the scene before him.

The old fellow was lying out on the couch, apparently fully dressed but his bottom half covered by an old blanket. His thick woollen jumper barely concealed the thin scrawny neck but not the gaunt face and sunken cheeks. A few days' growth emanated from his chin, complementing his straggly moustache.

'Ciamar a tha thu? How are you, Uncle?' asked Murdo speaking in their native Gaelic.

'Damned near dead,' croaked Calum hoarsely as he sought to prop himself up against the sofa's back. 'I take it that that quack Ross gave you my message?'

'Yes, I was speaking to Doctor Ross this morning and he said you wanted a word with me.'

'I do. But I've not asked to have you here so as I can

complain about my bloody health. Poke at these peats, boy, and stick another log on the fire. I have something I want to talk about.'

When Murdo had tended the fire and moved to sit down beside the old man, he paused. 'Wait a minute Uncle, I've got fresh scones just made by Catriona this afternoon. Will I not butter some and make you a wee strewpag?'

'Bugger the scones. There are more pressing things on my mind,' snapped Calum. Then softening his tone somewhat, he added, 'Ach, sorry, Murdo, I'm a crabbit old bastard. We'll maybe have the scones and tea later. Now before you sit down, get yourself a glass and pour us both a dram,' he said gesturing to the bottle of malt whisky, jug of water and empty glass sitting on an upturned crate in front of the settee.

Murdo did as he was told, quite taken aback by the fact that the bodach, the old fellow, had actually apologised to him. This was quite out of character. He seemed to have something he wanted to get off his chest and Murdo felt his interest quicken.

A sizeable slug of whisky in each glass, with a small dash of added water, saw Murdo's task completed. He handed the dram to his uncle and went over to sit on the wooden chair on the other side of the fireplace. Raising his glass he said, 'Slainte, Uncle.'

'Slainte,' Calum replied.

Calum sighed. Cupping the glass in both his hands, he looked straight at his nephew. 'Murdo, you know I am not a religious man. I never have been. I had enough Free Church doctrine thrust down my throat as a child and young man. But for all that, I have had plenty of time over these past years to think about the life I have lived. We all have regrets in life and I am no exception. Most of my regrets I can shrug off for the past is past and there's nothing we can do about it. But there's one that I have carried with me from the time I was a young merchant seaman. I have possessed a guilt for the past sixty-five years and, for all I know, maybe a curse as well. I have never spoken to anyone about this before, but I feel a need to tell my story to someone before my time comes to an end.' The old fellow put his hand out to lift a piece of folded material that lay on the settee beside him. He placed it on his lap and opened it out to reveal a carved wooden object.

His nephew looked at the object with interest and then to his uncle who was staring intently at the carving. 'You know,' began Calum, 'I brought this back from New Zealand. No, that's not true. Rather, it would be more accurate to say, it *came* back with me. It belonged to a Maori chief.' Calum sighed as he turned it over in his hands, lost in reverie. And then he began to talk.

'As a merchant seaman, I was in Sydney, Australia, with our ship The Isa awaiting company instructions for our next trip. When the orders did arrive, it transpired that we were bound for Dunedin, in the South Island of New Zealand, with passengers, supplies and equipment. It was 1862 and the population in Dunedin, the main town in the province of Otago, was growing by the day. Gold had been discovered at a place called Gabriel's Gully and that, along with other discoveries in inland Otago, had put the town and province firmly on the world map. Swarms of prospectors were flocking there.

'When the ship docked at Port Chalmers, Dunedin's seaport, the passengers – most of them seasoned veterans of the Australian goldfields – disembarked and promptly made for the town. Whilst on leave in Dunedin, I got caught up in the gold fever. Everywhere you went there was talk of gold discoveries and people making fortunes. I came across an Irish prospector in one of the town's hostelries........'

Calum's Story

The public bar was awash with humanity. Perhaps it was the heat, excessive for a Dunedin January day, that had driven them all indoors seeking shade and drink to quench dry and thirsty throats. Little light from its high-set windows filtered into the dark cavernous interior, necessitating the glowing oil lamps suspended above and around the crowded bar. Shade there was aplenty but the inside temperature equated with that outside and a multitude of smoking pipes and cigarettes contributed to the thick fug and blue haze over-hanging the noisy clientele.

At Calum's nod, a bar-tender replenished his glass with more whisky. Without thinking Calum responded, 'Tapadh leibh' (Thank you).

'Tha Gaidhlig aig thu?' (You have the Gaelic?)

Calum's attention was drawn to the voice speaking in his native tongue but with an Irish accent. It was the bearded stranger standing next to him. He replied, 'Tha, Albannach.' (Yes, Scottish).

He had noticed the big fellow when he arrived, sipping his drink and gazing directly ahead at his morose reflection in the mirror below the bar's gantry. Given his demeanour, Calum had refrained from engaging him in conversation.

'You off to the fields?' said the stranger.

'No, I'm just off my ship. We docked at Port Chalmers and I've got a few days to have a look around before we head back to Sydney.'

'Ah, a sailor boy then.' The Irishman looked at Calum thoughtfully. 'And ye'll no doubt have some money to spend whilst you're ashore. Well, there's plenty of flesh spots and drinking dens here for sailors to spend their hard-earned wages on.'

'Not me. I'm a quiet-living man. Sure, I like a bit of a drink but I won't be blowing all my wages on wild women and the like.'

The bearded one let out a roar of laughter and slapped Calum on the back. 'Spoken like a true Scotsman! So, what are you going to do then with your gotten gains?' But before Calum could answer, a large ham of a hand was stuck out in front of him, 'Thomas O'Neil of Kilkenny, Ireland. Most folk call me Beardie.'

'Calum MacLean of Applecross, Scotland,' answered Calum wincing slightly as the massive paw squeezed his hand.

'I was just going to say, if you're a sensible fellow who doesn't throw his money around then there's ways here to capitalize on it, to make a fortune in fact.'

'I thought that hunting for gold was the way everyone here plans to make their fortune.'

'Ah, gold! Yes, everyone hopes to strike it rich. Mind you, a lot of the ones making their fortunes are the suppliers of the supplies, if you take my meaning. But there's no two ways about it, there's gold in those hills if you know where to find it.'

'Och, I'm no prospector. I don't know the first thing about the business but I do know that whilst there are fortunes to be won there are also fortunes to be lost.'

'True my friend, true. But if you know how to go about it, or if you know someone who knows how to go about it then you're half way there. Take me for instance. If you accompanied me on a trip you'd be in safe hands. You're a fit looking fellow and you don't look as if you're afraid of hard work. Follow my guidance and you'd be fine.'

The stranger's enthusiasm had pricked Calum's interest and the cautious Scot asked, 'Are you looking for someone to accompany you to the goldfields?'

Beardie gave a wolfish smile and turning to the counter shouted, 'Here, barman, fill this man's glass up and leave the bottle with us.' Then putting a hand on Calum's, he said, 'I am indeed looking for a partner. But I need someone sensible, someone like you. Now I'll lay my cards on the table. I'm a bit down on my luck just now. I came over from California and I've been up to Gabriel's Gully. Was working up there with another Kilkenny man. Found some gold too. On our journey back, we were dry-gulched by some Aussie bastards. My partner was shot and I was left for dead. I survived though. Took my equipment and mule back here to Dunedin. Had to sell some of it to get by.

'Now,' he leant over and dropped his voice to a whisper, 'I've got first-hand knowledge of where to find the gold stuff. And it's not up Gabriel's Gully way.' Putting his finger alongside his nose he added, 'I'd be willing to bring you in as a partner. But it would mean you coughing up a chunk of your hard-earned wages. Got to speculate to accumulate, my friend. But your speculation will be based on a rock-hard certainty.'

Thomas O'Neil's enthusiasm and the substantial consumption of John Barleycorn had sparked in Calum a spirit normally suppressed by an outlook borne of cautious and frugal upbringing. Sobered, but excited by his uncharacteristically wild decision, he found himself the following day sweating under a hot sun and leading a pack-horse behind O'Neil as they made their way northwards along the cart track leading out of the town.

O'Neil had persuaded Calum to spend his wages on rations and additional equipment. From the pub, they'd adjourned to a nearby store that sold pretty well everything a prospector might need. There, Calum was able to include in the purchases, clothes suitable for the journey.

'Yes, Calum Boy,' said O'Neil as they walked up the steep track north of Dunedin known as the Kilmog, 'we're going to strike it rich. It was your lucky day the day you met me. All these fools you saw in the town will be heading south and then inland. But we, me boy, are heading north and inland. North to Palmerston and then inland up the Pig Root to a special spot that hardly a soul knows about yet.'

Calum listened to the Irishman as he prattled on. 'I was lying in a bunk-house a few nights ago. Had a fair shot in me if truth be told, but not so pissed that I didn't have me wits about me. And there were these two fellows whispering to each other in bunks next to mine. They thought I was out for the count and I didn't let them think any different. It's surprising what you can pick up when pretending to be asleep – nuggets of information. Nuggets that might just turn into gold!

'Turned out they were just back to get more supplies but I was able to work out where they were prospecting. Seems there's no-one else there at the moment. This is your big chance, Thomas, I told myself. All I need is a backer to help with the supplies. Someone steady. Someone reliable. And there you were, Calum MacLean. The answer to my dreams, and I to yours. We'll make a great partnership.'

Calum smiled and thought to himself, Well Beardie, if you can prospect half as well as you can talk, I'll be in very good hands.

Jumping ship hadn't bothered Calum too much. In the merchant navy this was a common occurrence and there were always boats you could pick up to work your passage home if things didn't turn out the way you hoped they would. No, he'd never done anything like this before. O'Neil's talk and promises had excited him. He was young and single. Here was an opportunity. He had nothing to lose.

3

Calum and Beardie lifted their bottles of ale and glugged at the contents greedily to quench their raging thirsts. Beardie was first to finish his and slapped the bottle down on the counter. Calum was not far behind him.

It had taken them two days to arrive in the fledgling township of Palmerston, tired and foot-sore. Having found a suitable spot by the river to set up camp and feed and tether the horses, they headed for the nearest watering hole they could find. A one-horse town Palmerston may have been at that time but as an alternative route and stage point into Central Otago, there was no shortage of drinking dens. They were soon ensconced in a make-shift saloon comprised of wood and calico.

'Right, MacLean,' said Beardie pushing a glass of whisky across to Calum and raising his own in the air, 'here's to tomorrow! Tomorrow, we reach the place where our dreams begin.'

Calum raised his glass in acknowledgement. Beardie tossed the contents down his throat in one fluid movement then gasped and cursed, 'Be-jasus, barman. Where in the name of God did you get this stuff? It's bloody firewater!'

'Finest Scotch, my friend. Well, an Irish version in fact. And you being from the Emerald Isle will no doubt appreciate its qualities.'

'Qualities! It's the nearest thing to poteen I've tasted. Sure you've not got some fellows brewing this stuff up in the hills there?'

Calum gasped at his first sip, feeling the fiery liquid hit his throat and then the burning sensation of it as it moved downwards and spread outwards into other cavities. 'My God, Beardie, it's strong stuff indeed.'

Keen to appease his customers and encourage them to further imbibe, the barman added, 'Here, gents, try another. This one's on the house.'

Apart from adjourning to a nearby canteen for a plate of rather doubtful looking stew and several hunks of bread, they continued to consume jugs of beer and shots of the firewater that the bar-tender avowed was Irish whisky. The late afternoon turned into evening and the bar became busier. O'Neil became more garrulous and louder with it, laughing raucously at his own jokes and bending the ear of any listener he could engage in conversation.

As O'Neil became louder Calum grew quieter, drawing into himself. Though he had consumed a lot, his sensitivities were not dulled to the extent that his companion's noise and bluster didn't cause him embarrassment. He became alarmed when O'Neil began to intimate that they were heading for a new prospecting spot that would yield them a fortune, not a wise move in frontier areas where gold fever gripped the populace. His embarrassment was further added to when O'Neil began to show an interest in some Maori women who were drinking nearby with a group of prospectors. Beardie had gone over a number of times and tried to persuade the females to come and have a drink with him and his friend. A few lewd comments had the men laughing but he had no success in enticing the females to join him.

Near to midnight, bleary-eyed and inebriated, they decided to head back to the camp site. A thin mist was rising off the water, chilling the night air. Swaying along the river path with O'Neil roaring out the chorus of an Irish ballad, they arrived near to where the tent was pitched on a grassy level close to the water's edge. A scurrying figure appeared along the path from the opposite direction. It was a young Maori girl who looked to be in her mid-teens. O'Neil grabbed her by the arm and she cried out, 'Please, let me go. I look for my cousin. She should be at home with her baby. I think she drink with the pakeha.'

'You hear that Calum boy, there's another one too. This could be your lucky night,' laughed O'Neill scooping the girl up as though she were a bag of flour and holding her over his ox-like shoulder.

The girl's screams jolted Calum out of his alcoholic haze and he suddenly became aware of what was happening. Staggering close to O'Neil he shouted, 'For God's sake man, let the girl go. Come on Tom, she's little more than a child, let her go on her way.'

'Child my arse,' snarled O'Neil. Feel the tits on her. They're big enough, so as far as I'm concerned she's old enough.'

'But what are you going to do with her?'

'Do with her? I'm going to shag her silly.' O'Neil had the wailing girl on the ground in front of the tent with her flaxen skirt thrust up to her midriff. 'And if you want some, you're going to have a bloody long wait.' The now almost hysterical girl struggled to escape and he brutally struck her across the side of her head, momentarily stunning her. As he sat astride her, he began to slide the braces off his shoulders and to tug at the waistband of his moleskin trousers.

Calum was frozen to the spot, too scared to move. He knew he should make an effort to help the girl but was too terrified of the brute in front of him to do anything. Futilely he cried out, 'O'Neil, for God's sake please stop.' But before he could utter another word, there was a loud roar and a sudden force hit him, knocking every bit of air out of his body and propelling him sideways and onto the ground. This was followed by a resounding swish and an enormous crrr-ack that seemed to linger in the air. The flat blade of a Maori taiaha had just connected with the back of O'Neil's head. Such was the force, the staff broke, leaving the spear end and a small piece of the shaft remaining in the hands of the attacker.

He was a fearsome sight. The fellow was wearing a cloak but not much else. His face and body were covered in the raised tattoos, the moko, of a Maori warrior. He looked lean and muscular. His face was distorted with anger and loathing as he looked down on O'Neil lying prostrate on the ground.

As Calum lay winded, he watched in awe as the rescuer

rolled O'Neil away from the sobbing girl with his foot. Discarding the weapon end, he gently lifted her up by the arms. Softly he spoke to her in their native tongue and the young girl, still weeping, nodded and ran off back along the path. As the warrior bent to pick up the broken flat-bladed part of the taiaha, Calum became aware that this was not a young man though he appeared to have the body of one. Indeed, he must have been near to sixty if he were a day.

O'Neil groaned and shook his head. Unsteadily he pushed himself up on to his knees to discover what had hit him. The Maori looked at him with disdain, and uttered a string of words in Maori. He then said in English, 'The pakeha has been made welcome in our land. We welcome the pakeha who has honour. We despise pakeha like you. I am a chieftain of my people. That girl is my daughter. If you had dishonoured her, I would have killed you. Go from here. Go now!'

Calum watched as the old chieftain turned from O'Neil and began to walk off. A clicking sound drew his attention back to O'Neil. He was on his knees and cocking a revolver that he'd pulled from his waistband. Later he would recall that he had time to stop O'Neil firing but had felt rooted to the spot, unable to move. He just managed to yell out 'No-oooo!' as he watched O'Neil shoot the chief in the back. The chief's body jerked upright, then seemed to stiffen. Slowly he turned around. The staff was still in his right hand. O'Neil made the mistake of lowering the pistol. The chieftain uttered a final battle roar, sprang forward with the weapon now in both hands and smashed it down on O'Neil's cranium.

O'Neil fell to the ground, whether senseless or dead Calum couldn't tell. The chief had also fallen and lay on his back.

Trembling, Calum looked around and then scrambled across to where the old warrior lay. His eyes were closed and his breathing shallow. 'I'm so sorry,' Calum whispered. Then he got to his feet. Heart thumping wildly, he looked across to O'Neill's inert body. He felt panic-stricken. The same fear that previously had him rooted to the spot, unable to do anything, was now sending urgent messages to his brain to flee. All that was in his mind was getting as far away from the place as possible. The urge for self-preservation overcame any other rational thought.

Feverishly he lifted his saddlebags that lay open near where the chieftain had fallen. Throwing them over one of the horses he then hastily saddled up. Untethering the animal, he got on his mount and galloped off. As he rode into the night, sheer terror spurred him on. But he also felt himself enshrouded in a cloak of shame and despair.

Calum rode steadily south and into the dawn of the new day, making short stops to rest and water the horse before pressing anxiously on. He arrived in Dunedin late in the afternoon. Even there, forty miles or so from Palmerston, he felt a fugitive and was anxious to catch a ship, any ship, and to flee the country. He did not know whether the old chieftain would live or die or if O'Neill was dead. Whatever the outcome, he was sure there would be a search for him as a witness, or even a possible accomplice, to what had happened. Once rid of the horse, he felt a ray of hope when he learned that The Isa was still in port and due to sail in the morning with the six o'clock tide. With saddle bags slung over his shoulder he reached Port Chalmers just two hours before the Isa's departure. The bosun was organising the taking on of some last- minute cargo and informed him that it was generally understood he'd jumped ship. He said, however, that given the crew complement was understrength, he could resume his place on board. Eyes moist with relief, Calum thanked him and wearily clambered up the gangway.

The Isa set off at high tide, making for Sydney from where it would eventually be heading for its home port of Southampton. Though totally exhausted, he had to fulfil his duty watch before going below decks to snatch a few hours' sleep. When he awoke, he took the saddlebags and began to transfer his belongings to his old sea chest. His heart almost stopped beating when he discovered the broken head of the Maori weapon in one of the bags. Somehow, it had fallen into the bag from the chieftain's grasp. He quickly wrapped it up in a piece of sail cloth and furtively stuck it underneath the belongings in the chest.

Several months later, he was back in the family home at Lonbain. He had no inkling as to how things had unravelled back in Palmerston and thus had a constant worry in his mind that events might ultimately catch up with him. With the rest of the family long gone from the croft, he had returned to his roots and to the daily grind of eking out a living from fishing and crofting.

Slowly and then more quickly, the years began to spin by. Occasionally when he thought of his journeys and travels, he would go to the sea chest and take out the spear head. He didn't find it pleasing to look at. Indeed, the carved face seemed to him to exude a certain malevolence. But he felt a compulsion to keep it, a responsibility, though for what purpose he did not know.

4

'Pit – loch – reee!' shouted the station porter as the Glasgow – Inverness train came to a halt and disgorged more of its festive season passengers. As carriage doors slammed, guards' flags waved and whistles blew, the train drew slowly out of the station.

'Say buddy, sorry to disturb you, but am I right in thinking that you're the author of this book?' asked the bearded American sitting opposite Sean.

Sean looked up from the Herald crossword he'd just begun to tackle and across to the man holding a paperback up to him. The numbers in their compartment had reduced to the two of them and a tweed-suited old fellow propped in a corner beside the door leading to the corridor. The old guy was totally dead to the world and emitting occasional huffs and puffs of whisky fumes powerful enough to intoxicate anyone nearby.

The train had been packed when it left Glasgow. Well before Stirling, Sean had fallen into a deep sleep, oblivious to the noise and high spirits of the shoppers and those citizens heading home for Christmas. As the train trundled on, it picked up a few passengers at its statutory stops but off-loaded many more. It was only at Pitlochry that Sean awoke and sleepily took in his surroundings. Considering he hadn't even noticed that the American was reading his, Sean's book, reflected on how dozy he'd been.

He smiled and nodded to his companion, 'Yes, you're right. But how did you guess?'

'Well, I was watching television in my hotel room a few nights ago and they were doing that little interview with you before showing the first episode of your serial. I thought it was excellent. That's why I went out and bought your book. I guess with my touring around it's unlikely I'll get to see the other episodes and I'd really got hooked on the story. I'm Will Gates by the way,' he said leaning forward to shake hands with Sean.

'I'm delighted you're enjoying the book.'

'Say, Sean – you don't mind if I call you Sean?'

Sean laughed and shook his head, 'Not at all.'

'Thanks. Would you mind signing this copy? I'd like to pass it on to my son when I get back to the States. He's really into reading thrillers and this sure fits the bill. I don't want to be a nuisance. I guess guys like you get fed up being pestered by folks wanting their autographs.'

'I've had very few requests for autographs so far, Will. I very much doubt that many people know of me. But it's good to get feedback from a satisfied reader.' Taking the book, he added, 'Now what would you like me to write for your son?'

Sean and the friendly American continued chatting as the train began its steady climb into the snow-covered hills before they each returned to their respective reading.

Putting down his newspaper, Sean gazed through the window. Despite the outside darkness and the light from the carriage, by resting his forehead against the window and cupping his hands round his face, he could make out the winter landscape – stark and bleak, but impressive. The scene stirred something deep inside him. He was approaching home territory. Tonight he'd stay with a teacher friend in Inverness. Tomorrow he'd catch the Kyle of Lochalsh train to Strathcarron. And then it would be over the hill to home, by car if the snow plough could keep the road clear, otherwise on foot.

He leant back on his seat and closed his eyes. He thought about Marama. How long had he been back from New Zealand? Was it really almost three years? It seemed like yesterday. And it still hurt. A lot had happened for him since then. A lot must have happened for Marama too, especially with the baby. He hadn't communicated with her, not directly. But Bryn had kept him informed about how she was doing. It had been Bryn that kept at him to write to her. He'd never been able to get her out of his mind and one night several weeks ago, after a few drams and against his sober judgement, he'd sent her a Christmas card. Later he'd regretted it. He'd felt foolish. But how did he feel now, now that he'd received a card from her? And a photograph. And three words – *All our love*. What did they mean? Could he read anything further into these words? Should he? He knew that he wanted to.

Sean turned the switch of the convector heater up to full and then returned to his desk. It was one o'clock in the morning. Outside, a star-studded sky ensured the continued presence of the hoar frost covering the ground, plants, trees and buildings.

Lifting up the wooden carving in his left hand, he absently traced the patterns with the fingers of his right. He wondered about its origins. He knew from Murdo that it had come from New Zealand in the 1860's and from his own knowledge of Maori history and culture, he recognized it as being the spearhead end of a weapon, probably a taiaha. It was a beautiful piece of work. Scary but beautiful. The riveting gaze of the paua shell eyes commanded attention. The protruding tongue emanated defiance, challenge and aggression.

He thought about his meeting with old Murdo MacLean two days into the New Year. Murdo, now eighty-four years old, was living in a rest home in Inverness. He had heard from his niece about Sean's writing successes and of his New Zealand work experience. Learning that Sean was staying with his mother over the winter break, he had wanted to meet up with him. His niece Shona had taken him over to Applecross for the day and left him with Sean whilst she visited nearby relatives.

He recalled their conversation clearly. Murdo had first produced the carving and handed it to Sean, 'What do you make of that, Sean?' he had asked. 'Do you know what it is?'

Sean had turned it around in his hands. 'It's a Polynesian spearhead, I think. It looks like it's been broken off from, say the shaft of a taiaha, a weapon used in warfare and on ceremonial occasions. How do you come to have it?'

'Well, there's the thing, and that's why I have come to see you. My old Uncle Calum gave it to me. He thought that one day I might find someone who could have it returned to New Zealand.' And then Murdo had commenced to tell him Calum's story.

Murdo's tale had startled him. The story in itself was fascinating enough. But the fact that it had involved the area in which he'd been working, and he'd grown to know and love, seemed almost too much of a co-incidence to be true. Sean had asked Murdo why he'd brought the carving to him and Murdo had replied that with Sean being a writer and having New Zealand connections he was hoping he might be able to have the head returned to somewhere appropriate in its country of origin. 'And who knows,' he had added with a smile, 'it just might give you inspiration for another tale.'

And it was some story indeed, thought Sean as he reflected upon Calum's adventures.

He laid the carving down, pushed his seat back and rested his feet on the desk top. Putting his hands behind his head he closed his eyes. In an almost dream-like state he imagined himself transported across the oceans back to the place that had become his other home. There was something else in Murdo's story that had struck a chord with him. Something to do with the old chief. But what was it?

He thought of Calum's account of the taiaha. His senses quickened. Old Murdo was right. There certainly was material for a story here. There was scope for keeping it in its historical past or bringing it up to the present day. Apart from the historical aspect, the tale leant itself to the mystery genre he was used to writing in. Either way, there was an opportunity for him to have a reason, a justification, to travel back to New Zealand. He had always felt he needed an ostensible purpose for going back. An outward purpose. But in his heart, he knew his reason for a return was always going to be Marama.

'I knew you weren't asleep, Sean,' said his mother bringing in a cup of cocoa.

'Thanks Mum,' said Sean taking a sip of the hot drink. 'I was asleep earlier but now I'm wide awake.'

'Still having bad dreams, Son?'

'How do you know about that, Mother? I've never mentioned such things, have I?'

'Not really. But sometimes late in the night I've heard you tossing and turning and talking away to yourself in your sleep. Mind you, it had improved for a while, but since you've been back for Christmas, I believe you've become more restless again. I used to think it was all about you having such a vivid imagination and all the time you spend writing, but there's something else isn't there?'

'Aye.'

'Something happened in New Zealand, didn't it?'

'Aye. It's not something I've wanted to talk about for they're not pleasant memories. There was a terrible accident and I was partly involved in it, though it wasn't my fault. But the outcome was that someone I cared about very much was emotionally hurt as a result. I felt I could have done more to help this person.'

'Sounds like there was a girl involved.'

Sean opened the desk drawer and took out Marama's card and photograph which he handed to his mother. He then began to tell her about the accident and Marama and why he had returned to Scotland, why he felt forced to return earlier than planned – something he'd refused to discuss with anyone. He admitted that the fact that she would be expecting a child by another man had also swayed him to leave. Yet, since then, he'd thought how selfish he had been in not thinking of the trauma she might face in being all alone when he could have been there, if only as a friend, to support her should she require it.

'I still love her very much, Mother. There's not a day goes by when I don't think about her. It's not that I've lived like a monk. I've been out with other girls in Glasgow and enjoyed their company. But none seemed to measure up to the way I feel about Marama.'

'Well, Sean, if that's the way you feel about this girl, my advice is to go back to New Zealand and see if there is any chance of you both getting back together again. You've been back here, what, almost three years? You still miss the girl. If you don't at least go out there to see how she is and how she responds to you, you might live with the regret for the rest of your life. And the card, is this not some kind of encouragement?'

'I don't know. I'd like to think so but maybe it's just her sending a polite reply.'

'I don't think so. Sending a card to you is one thing. But

why would she also send the photograph?'

'Her daughter's a wee beauty, isn't she?'

'Yes, but looking at her mother it's easy to see where she gets her looks from. Go, son.'

'You're right. I might have kept this all to myself for a long time but I'm glad I've talked to you about it at last. I need to go back and see if there's any hope of a future with Marama. And just before you came in, the perfect opportunity to go back to New Zealand suddenly dawned on me.'

He then explained his ideas for a novel based on Calum's story and added, ' I should have my present work with my publishers all wrapped up by the end of February and I'll tell them I plan to take a month or two out to research a story set in New Zealand.'

'That sounds ideal. I take it that other than the card, you haven't heard from Marama since you've come home?'

'Not directly. But Bryn keeps me informed in his letters about how's she's getting on. He does tell me that she often asks about me and seems genuinely pleased about my writing successes.'

'And what about her baby?'

'She's called Kirri. She'll be around two and a half to three years old by now.'

'Well, Son, I think you're doing the right thing. This girl Marama sounds very special. I'll be keeping my fingers crossed for you.'

'Thanks, Mother.'

5

A frantic six weeks ensued and saw Sean's current manuscript completed and delivered to his Edinburgh publishers. Preparations for his story research included sending letters of introduction to the two Dunedin newspapers, museums and university history department. Telephone calls to New Zealand established that his old cottage in Glenbeg was empty and would be his for a nominal rent. There was an assurance from Bryn Jones, his head teacher colleague, that all and sundry were looking forward to his return.

After a final visit back to Applecross, Sean stopped in Inverness to meet up again with Murdo and gather further information about his sea-faring Uncle Calum.

It was on the twenty- first of March at five o'clock in the morning when Sean left a moist and chilly Heathrow airport, courtesy of Air New Zealand. He was going back.

The rush of trip preparations in addition to tasks to be completed, ensured that the past few weeks had gone by in a blur. It seemed he'd been constantly on the run since the fateful night when he'd decided to return to NZ. Despite an early bed in the Hilton Heathrow Hotel, he'd spent as much time looking at his alarm as he had dozing. Having to rise at the ungodly hour of three o'clock to ensure he met the check-in deadline, resulted in him being quite exhausted by the time he had settled into his window seat just behind the wing. With belt fastened and seat in the upright position for take-off, he managed to keep his eyes open and just about focus on the Air New Zealand stewardess as she took the passengers through the airline's safety procedures whilst the Boeing 707 taxied along to its take-off position. But much to the amusement of the young Swedish student seated beside him, he was already fast asleep when the huge aircraft's engines roared to a crescendo and it began its charge down the runway.

He woke to the tantalizing smell of freshly cooked bacon and the subdued hum of the engines. He glanced to his right. The young Swedish guy was getting tucked into a warm bacon roll. Other appetizing eats were on the tray in front of him. 'Ah, you are awake. Feel like some breakfast? It's good!'

The food aroma was reminding Sean that he hadn't eaten since the previous evening. He raised his hand as a smiling stewardess approached and was soon tucking into a breakfast tray identical to his companion's. He knew he needed more sleep but couldn't resist ordering a pot of coffee with his meal. He reckoned it would take an enormous amount of caffeine to keep him awake and had no fears about finding difficulty in returning to the land of Nod. As he ate, he felt a knot of excitement tinged with some anxiety.

With breakfast over and the tray dispatched, Sean put

his seat into a gentle recline position. He closed his eyes. He thought back to his working holiday in New Zealand and his teaching post in the small rural community of Glenbeg in the South Island's province of Otago. Scenes and events from the past came flooding back. The adventure had started off so well. Head teacher Bryn was a friend and inspiration right from the start. And then there was Marama, a beauty yes but also a delightful, humorous and supportive colleague. The three of them had made quite a team. He'd made many friends both in the village and in the city of Dunedin. And then towards the end of his first year, things dramatically and tragically fell apart.

It had taken all of six seconds for him to fall for Marama Te Kanawa. He loved just everything about her. He couldn't wait to get to school in the mornings to see her and to be near her. She was engaged to Rob Maitland, son of a local farmer. Being fairly reticent, Sean had accepted that that's the way things were. He didn't attempt to flirt with her but he revelled in her company both professionally and socially. Much to his delight, it seemed the feeling was mutual. Marama's parents were dead and she lived with her grandparents, Tama and Mere Te Kanawa. They also became his friends and he became a frequent visitor to their home. In Tama he found a kindred spirit. Both were interested in the historical culture of the other and surprised to find so many similarities in the old tribal and clan systems.

The big 707 droned on, eating up the air miles. Unlike Sean, the Swede sitting alongside him couldn't sleep though he had tried a number of times. His attention was occasionally drawn from his book to the face of the sleeping Scot. He may have been in a deep sleep but it appeared to be a troubled one. Occasionally he would grimace and toss his head one way and then the other, his mouth silently forming words that only the sleeper could hear.

Sean was in the dreamworld, back in time, back to when he was first in New Zealand. Scenes and voices, real and unreal, related and unrelated, appeared and disappeared in his subconscious.

PART TWO

6

Glenbeg, New Zealand. 1969

Sean woke with a start and sat up. Disorientated, he looked around him and noticed the faint glow of light that hailed the imminent arrival of dawn. He felt chilled and hung over. That, along with a growing recollection of where he was and how he'd got there, forced him to clamber off the rock and make his way back along the path. As he reached the point where the river cascaded twenty feet or so to the pool below, he was startled to hear above the fall of the water the revving of an engine. Two beams of light suddenly shot across the pool then began leaping in erratic unison. He saw the source of the lights, a truck careering down the short, rutted track that lead from the back road to the river. Bouncing crazily, the vehicle continued its head-long rush and crashed into the pool. A strangled shout came from the cab and then the front of the vehicle began to sink into the deep waters.

Frantically he ran down the path and across to the pool. The cab was close to being totally submerged with the tail end of the truck hanging almost vertically over the edge of the embankment. He steadied himself against the up-ended side and then his head exploded. Intense pain was momentarily removed as he lost consciousness. He was sinking into an inky blackness. The return of the pain and a need to breathe galvanized his body into automatically swimming for the surface.

The current had carried him further downstream. His head broke through the waters and gasping and choking he managed to pull himself up onto the far bank. There he lay, chest heaving, as he gulped down quantities of air. The pain was excruciating. He put his hand to the back of his head and then held it up to his face. Even in the dim light he was aware that his hand was covered in blood.

What had happened? Then a sense of urgency and anxiety came back to him as he recalled the voice in the cab. He got to his knees and then on to his feet. He could feel himself swaying from side to side before darkness descended once more.

He was aware of an incessant thudding noise but uncertain as to whether it was just near to him or actually inside his head. For sure, he was feeling pain and the ache of it appeared to be dancing in time to the racket.

Sean groaned, mentally willing the noise to stop. Slowly his eyes opened and the room came into focus. Just as he realized that the thudding was at the front door, it stopped. He winced as he turned to check the alarm clock on the bedside cabinet. It was eight thirty. And then a hammering commenced on the bedroom window and a voice shouted,

'Sean….Sean, wake up! Come on lad! Look you, there's been a terrible accident.'

The word 'accident' jolted him into full wakefulness. 'God! Last night…the river, the truck, Marama!' It was coming back to him. He sat up quickly and was aware of the source of his pain. Instinctively he put his hand to the back of his head. His hair felt matted, partly sticky and partly hard. He turned round to see the pillow a mess of dried blood. As the banging and shouting persisted he leant across the bed and lifted the bottom of the curtain. He nodded to the figure at the window. It was Bryn.

He threw the blankets back and got out of bed. Grabbing the dressing gown from the door hook and wrapping it around him, he gingerly walked to the front door and opened it. Bryn stared at him.

'Hells bells, boyo, what's happened to you? There's blood all down your neck!'

'I don't know. Last night I was down by the river and….'

'The river! You were down at the river! Sean, Rob Maitland's dead. His truck was found a couple of hours ago submerged in the big pool. Did you see the truck there? Have you any idea what happened?'

'Rob, dead?' Sean looked at Bryn in disbelief. He shook his head dazedly then flinched at the pain of the sudden movement. 'You'd better come in. I need a strong coffee and a couple of aspirin.'

'God! The back of your head is a mess,' said Bryn following him through to the kitchen. 'I'd say you need a doctor. Now sit down. I'll get the coffee and clean that head up a bit. You can tell me what you remember whilst I fix you up.'

As Bryn bustled about, Sean lowered himself carefully into the chair that Bryn had pulled out from the table. 'Jeez, Bryn, how did I get like this? You're saying that Rob's dead and that it happened down at the river. I was down at the river after the party and I remember a vehicle going into the river. I ran to help and ended up in the water. Oh, and before that I remember some sort of bang and an agonizing pain filling my head. I must have blacked out because the next thing I recall was swimming to the bank. But that's all. I don't even remember getting back home and into bed.

'I definitely didn't see any sign of Rob though he must have been in the truck. The last time I actually saw him was at last night's party up at the homestead. There's something weird about all this.'

'Calm down, lad. What you've said makes sense. But you'll have to report this to the police. They're at the accident scene now. They'll be looking for anyone who's witnessed what happened or can shed any light on this tragedy. I got the news from Dan Munro. I've no idea if Marama knows anything yet.'

'Marama! I have to see her Bryn. Jeez, this is a nightmare. I walked Marama home last night. We went by the river path.'

'Sean, is it possible that Marama has been injured as well? Do you remember if she was with you when you got hurt?'

'No, no. I walked Marama home after the party. Dan

and Gail dropped us off at their place. I remember quite clearly going along the river path to Marama's home. I then went for a walk further up the river. I'd had quite a few drinks at the party but I was fairly sober by that stage.'

'Right, now get this down you,' said Bryn handing Sean a steaming cup of sweet black coffee and two aspirin. He then filled a bowl with hot water and after pouring some anti-septic into it began to gently sponge the back of Sean's head, taking care not to go too close to the wound. 'You'll be needing stitches, Boyo. We'll have to get you into the Palmerston surgery before lunch-time. Remember you're in Kiwi-land and most places are shut on a Saturday afternoon. Otherwise, it'll mean going all the way down to Accident and Emergency in Dunedin. They'll no doubt check you out for concussion too. Mind you, all you Jocks have hard heads!'

Having cleared up Sean's wounds as best he could, Bryn said, 'Sean, I'm going down to the accident scene to explain to the police about your injuries. I'll say that you're quite willing to see them right away but that it's important to get you to a doctor as soon as possible. OK?'

'I guess you're right, Bryn,' said Sean slowly. He closed his eyes against the throbbing in his head and took another sip of his coffee, hoping that the effect of the aspirin would kick in quickly. Then opening his eyes, he added, 'Won't they be suspicious about my presence down at the river, especially given the fact that I can't explain how I ended up at home without raising the alarm?'

'Stop worrying. Just tell them the truth. You didn't do anything wrong. You were injured and undoubtedly concussed. I reckon the doctor's bound to back you up on that. I'm off. Shouldn't be long before I'm back, no doubt with a visitor.'

As he walked away from the cottage Bryn frowned. He was worried about his young friend and the injuries he'd sustained. It was indeed a strange business, he thought to himself. And although he hadn't said anything to Sean, he felt sure his colleague would be in for a grilling from the Law.

Fifteen minutes later, a quick double knock on the door jerked Sean awake from the doze that had him on the brink of oblivion. Bryn entered and was followed by a police sergeant.

'Ha, caught you napping Sean boy! This is Sergeant Braithwaite from Palmerston. Sergeant, this is my teacher colleague and friend, Sean Campbell.'

'How do you do Mr Campbell? Not very well by the look of you.'

'Hello, Sergeant. No, I'm not feeling too wonderful at the moment.'

'Mr Campbell, Mr Jones has briefly explained to me that you were in the vicinity when Rob Maitland's truck went into the river last night. Now I gather you need to go into the surgery at Palmerston. But I would like a quick outline of what happened to you last night and anything you can tell me that might shed some light on what caused this tragedy. Mr Jones can then take you to the cottage hospital. The Dunedin CIB should be up here shortly and they will want a more detailed interview with you. I'm sure that will be done sometime in the afternoon.

'Now, Sir, can I just have a wee look at this wound that

Mr Jones was telling me about? Oh, nasty!' he exclaimed as he looked at the open wound, congealed blood and the dark and heavy bruising on Sean's neck and shoulders. 'You're certainly in need of some medical attention so I'll be as quick as I can.'

The sergeant drew up a chair next to Sean and opening his notebook said, 'Now take me through your movements from say mid-evening last night.'

Sean related the events of the evening from the time Dan and Gail picked him up to go to the party. When he stated that Rob was also present, the sergeant interrupted to ask, 'Would you say Mr Maitland had been drinking heavily?'

'Rob had seemed alright earlier in the evening but was somewhat the worse for wear later on.'

'And his demeanour later on,' prompted the policeman, 'would you say he was happily drunk or otherwise?'

Sean hesitated and then said, 'Well, just before we left, he was actually quite aggressive.'

The sergeant raised his eyebrows and Sean plunged on, 'I was dancing with Marama, Rob's fiancée. Rob appeared and was quite nasty towards Marama.'

'In what way?'

'Well, he grabbed my arm and hauled me away from Marama and then called her a slut. Marama was really upset and everyone around was quite shocked. I should add, Rob normally seems an easy-going guy. His behaviour certainly seemed to be out of character.'

'M-mmm.' The policeman jotted some observation into his notebook.

Sean continued his account, including walking Marama home from Dan and Gail's house. He explained that as it was such a beautiful evening, he decided to walk back up past the waterfall. He described how he'd fallen asleep on a rock above the falls and on waking how he saw the lights, the truck and how he'd heard a cry as it entered the water. He concluded by stating that he had no idea how he eventually got home but could only assume that the memory gap was due to his receiving a bang on the head.

Having requested that Sean go over again the events from the time the vehicle appeared, Braithwaite then asked, 'Is it not possible that you were hit by the vehicle?'

'I don't see how I could have been as it was actually in the water as I was running towards it.'

'Well, Mr Campbell, said the sergeant, 'as I said before, CIB will wish to talk to you later on. I'll give them this interim report in the meantime and let Mr Jones get you to Palmerston. This is certainly a strange and tragic business.' Standing up, he closed the notebook and put it into an inside pocket. 'By the way, are these the clothes you were wearing last night?' he asked pointing to the wet garments lying by the back door.

'Yes, looks like them though I don't recall taking them off.'

Braithwaite picked them up and added, 'I'd better take them. Forensics will want to check them out. It's routine procedure. You don't have any objections? No? Thank you Mr Campbell, that'll be all for now.' He nodded to Bryn, 'Mr Jones,' and let himself out the front door.

'You were fine, Sean. That went alright.'

Sean grimaced, 'Not sure about that. And what about him taking away the clothes, what do you make of that?'

'Well, he said it's routine procedure. Come on! That's your Scottish pessimism coming out. Right, get dressed. I'll just give you a hand to get your shirt on and then I'll have a quick word with Pam and get the car out. Give me ten minutes.'

7

Their arrival at the Palmerston Cottage Hospital proved to be well-timed. There were no patients in the waiting room and Sean was able to be seen straight away by the duty doctor, a cheerful young Aucklander who introduced himself as Mac. The wound was thoroughly cleaned, a number of stitches inserted and a routine tetanus jab administered. Further examination by the doctor led him to conclude that Sean was not totally clear of the effects of concussion.

'Right, Mr Jones, you'll have to keep an eye on your friend Sean for the next twenty-four hours and see he takes plenty of rest. And Sean, under no circumstances should you drive this weekend.'

'OK Doc. But what about my memory gap. I mean the fact that I seemed to get from the accident spot to my home without any recollection of doing so?'

'Not surprising. Concussion provides the simple explanation. You got home on auto-pilot so to speak. Mind you, there's one thing puzzles me. If you weren't hit by the vehicle or by a piece of equipment falling from it, what did hit you? You sure as hell didn't receive these injuries from just falling into the river. Well, fellas, I'm finished for the day and off down to Dunedin for the big match at Carisbrook. Got two tickets, one for the girlfriend and one for me. Hope to see Auckland stuff Otago for a change. It hasn't happened for a long time. Safe journey home.'

Bandaged up like a soldier returning from the battle zone and armed with anti-biotics and pain-killers, Sean followed Bryn out to the car. Driving back to Glenbeg, Bryn was pre-occupied with the doctor's speculation as to how Sean had sustained his injuries. Unbeknown to him, Sean was wondering the very same thing.

When they returned home, Sean was escorted into Bryn's house where Pam had lunch ready for them. Bryn went off to report to the police that Sean was back from the surgery. He was gone for some considerable time, but explained when he sat down to join them at the lunch table that the CIB had just arrived and that he'd opened up the school so that the investigators could make use of the staffroom and facilities. He also told Sean that the senior detective in charge of proceedings would like to speak to him in the school at three o'clock. Pam suggested that after lunch Sean would have time to have an hour's rest on their sofa. He gratefully accepted her offer.

'Ah, Mr Campbell, I see you have been well and truly bandaged up. Are you feeling a bit better?' asked Sergeant Braithwaite as he ushered Sean through to the staffroom. There he introduced his superior, a serious looking individual in civilian clothes. 'This is Detective Inspector Millar.'

Millar, who was seated at the staff table, nodded and gestured for Sean to sit on the chair opposite. Braithwaite sat on a chair positioned slightly behind and to the left of his superior. Again, he took out his notebook and pen from an inside pocket.

'Right, Mr Campbell,' began Millar, pausing to press his hands together as if in a position of prayer. 'A young man, a member of the Glenbeg community, has been tragically drowned. His vehicle ended up in the pool below the waterfall. The vehicle has been recovered from the pool and its occupant, Mr Rob Maitland, has been taken to the mortuary in Dunedin for a post- mortem examination. Our accident team is still searching the site.' Millar placed his hands on the tabletop and began to tap his forefinger slowly on its worn surface.

Sean began to feel uncomfortable. Here we go, he thought, here comes the grilling.

'This may, I say *may*, be just a tragic accident. But at the moment we have too many unanswered questions for my liking. Questions that I intend finding answers to. So, with regards to yourself, please go over again your account of events from the time you arrived at the party with Mr and Mrs Munro.

Sean did as requested. Millar leant back in his chair and looked at him. The finger tapping routine went into operation again. 'Let's establish one thing to start with. Would it be fair to say that after your altercation with Mr Maitland you were feeling some animosity towards him?'

'I couldn't believe he would speak to Marama like

that. Yes, his behaviour annoyed me. And it was totally uncalled for.'

'Do I detect that you personally have feelings for Miss Te Kanawa? Did you resent the fact that she was engaged to Mr Maitland?'

'I was friendly with both of them. I do have feelings for Marama. I care for her well-being. I know Marama much better than I knew Rob because she is a work colleague as well as a friend. And I certainly didn't have a bust-up with Rob at the party. He suddenly appeared while we were dancing and made a bit of a scene. You'll find plenty of witnesses to testify to that. In fact, I didn't so much as utter a word during – how did you put it? – this altercation.'

'Right, let's move on. What made you go for a walk along the river bank in the early hours of the morning? We're talking something like three o'clock aren't we?'

'It was a beautiful mild night. The moon was out. I love the river and its surroundings. In such circumstances, to walk further up-river was a very natural thing for me to do.'

Millar looked at him as though he thought this was a very unnatural thing to do. But he didn't comment. 'You said you heard a shout from the truck. Did you recognize the voice? Did you realize whose truck it was?'

'No. It all happened so fast. The noise, the lights, the yell, the sound of the truck hitting the water.'

'And what about this blow to the back of your head? Are you sure that the vehicle or something carried by it didn't strike you?'

'I'm not sure now. The truck was partly in the water as

I was running towards it. I arrived at the side of the vehicle. It was sticking up in the air and the cab was pretty well submerged. I don't see how anything from the truck could have hit me, unless something fell from the back and down on top of me. It was nearly vertical. Did you find anything at the scene that might suggest this?'

Both policemen looked at one another. Millar didn't answer Sean's query but instead added, 'Sergeant Braithwaite's report states that you have no recollection of how you got from the river back to your home.'

'That's correct. I asked the doctor at the surgery if this was feasible and he told me that a head injury of this nature would certainly explain such circumstances.'

'Yes, the hospital report corroborates what you've just said. That will be all for the moment Mr Campbell. One other thing I'd like you to do just now. Would you mind going down to the river with the sergeant here and showing him the exact spot where you came out of the water?'

Well, it's a rather tall order as I don't know where I came out but I'm happy to have a look.'

'Oh, and one other thing. Are you quite sure you didn't enter the cab of the truck?'

'Definitely not. I told you, it was almost totally submerged by the time I got there and the next thing I knew I was in the water.'

'Very well. We'll need your fingerprints. Millar studied the look of concern on Sean's face and allowed himself a slight smile, 'It's standard procedure, an elimination process if you like. Off you go with Sergeant Braithwaite and then come back here. One of the team will get a prints copy from you. It won't take long.'

Sean, feeling the better of having had lunch and with the effects of the anti-biotics and pain-killers coursing through his body, accompanied the sergeant down to the river. As there was no recognised path on the cottage side of the river, it would have taken some considerable time to search through the trees, bushes and grasses on the bank. The investigating team had been ahead of them, however, and placed stakes connected with tape around an area of crushed vegetation leading up from the river.

'Looks like our task has been done for us,' said Braithwaite. He studied the area closely and drew a quick diagram in his little black book. He then bent down and pointed out to Sean some dock leaves liberally sprinkled with blood. 'Blood donating for humans is one thing, young fella, but giving it to plants is over-doing it I'd say.'

Sean smiled, 'Well I didn't give it voluntarily, that's for sure.'

Sean put down the cup of tea that Pam had poured him after he'd returned to let them know how he'd got on. 'Thanks, Pam, that was grand. I must move. I think I'll go for a lie down.'

'Why not stay here? You'll be coming over for tea anyway.'

'No, really. It's very kind of you. I just want to sleep. I'll get myself something later if I need it.'

Standing up, Sean smiled. 'Thanks both of you. I

certainly needed you around me today. One thing, Bryn, do you think you could accompany me tonight to pop in for a few moments at Marama's? I'd like to see her but I think it might be better if we both go.'

'Of course. Was going to suggest the same thing myself. Wouldn't let you go by yourself in the state you're in anyway. Remember what the Doc said. How about I give you a shout around seven?'

'That's great, Bryn. Thank you both again.'

A cheerful fire gave out a welcoming glow as Sean entered the cottage. Pam or Bryn, he thought. What it is to have caring friends! It was around five fifteen and he was exhausted. He flopped down on the armchair and closed his eyes. He thought about the state Marama might be in. He was desperate to see her. Given the circumstances, he'd thought it more appropriate that both he and Bryn, as Marama's work colleagues, visited her together. He drifted off to sleep.

Just after seven they walked via the bridge and road to the Te Kanawas' homestead. They walked in silence. Sean was worried sick about Marama. He knew she would be devastated by the news of Rob's death. Might she also be blaming herself for what happened between them – between Sean and herself last night?

Mere took them into the lounge where a tear-stained and handkerchief-clutching Marama was sitting curled up on the sofa staring blankly at the television set. When she saw them both she stood up quickly and ran into Bryn's arms, crying and sobbing. Bryn hugged and patted her tenderly. Sean, who was slightly behind Bryn, felt his eyes grow moist. Marama then lifted her head towards him and tried to smile. Then a look of concern came over her as she suddenly became aware of his bandaged head.

'Sean! What happened to you?' She moved towards him as if to embrace him and then stopped suddenly, as if some second thought prevented her moving any closer. Instead, she reached out and clasped his hands with her own.

'I'm not sure. I got a bang on the head and fell into the river. That's all I know. That's all I've been able to tell the police. I saw Rob's truck go into the river, Marama. But at the time I didn't know whose truck it was or who was in it.'

Marama looked stunned. Her eyes opened wide in shock. 'You were there? You were down at the river when Rob's truck went in! Why didn't you help him? What were you doing?'

Bryn quickly interjected, 'Marama, he said in a calm but commanding voice that focused her attention, 'Sean did try to help. Sean was almost killed himself. If you saw the injury below these bandages you would see how badly hurt he was.' And then in a gentler voice he added, 'Marama dear, Rob died in a tragic accident. How it happened we don't know yet. But believe me, your friend Sean couldn't do anything to save Rob.'

Marama raised her head and sobbed, 'Oh I'm sorry, Sean, really so sorry. It's just….the police didn't tell me anything about what happened. They were round this afternoon and told me you said you'd walked me home. But they didn't say anything about you being at the accident. It's all such a terrible shock.'

This time Sean did go over to her. He put his arms around her, tears welling in his eyes. 'It's alright, Marama. It's alright. I understand.'

'Pam and the kids send their love. Everyone does,' said Bryn.

Marama's Nan came in with a hot milky drink. 'Right my girl, we're going to get you off to bed and the doctor's left something that'll help put you to sleep.'

Bryn and Sean said their good nights and departed. As they were going down the road Bryn observed, 'Sean, there's more than just friendship between you two isn't there?'

'Well last night I thought so, Bryn. But now I just don't know.'

'Give it time, lad. Give it time. That girl's going through a lot just now. And she's got a funeral and lots more to face up to in the immediate future. She might well appear distant for the next while. But that won't mean she doesn't need you. Just give her time and give her space. And for the record, Sean, I think you're a grand fellow and I think Marama and you are very right for each other.'

8

Rob Maitland's funeral was held the following Friday at the Crematorium in Dunedin. After the accident investigation and post-mortem, the police had closed the case with a pronouncement of 'misadventure'. Rob was found to have had a huge amount of alcohol in his bloodstream and it was considered that this was what caused him to lose control of the truck and to end up in the river. It was established that Rob and his sister Annette had been taken home from the party by their cousin Michael Maitland. Michael informed the police that Rob had wanted him to drive to Marama's house but that he had taken brother and sister back to the Maitland homestead. Annette said she had left Rob sitting on the steps of the veranda and gone off to bed. It was thought that Rob had decided he would still go to see Marama and had made the fatal mistake of driving off in his old Ford in an extremely drunken state.

A large number of folk from the Valley made the trip to Dunedin and after the service many met up at the nearby Tahuna Park Hotel to pay their respects to the family and share with them in an after-funeral buffet. Marama had travelled down with her own family but at the service sat with the Maitland clan. With the school specially closed for the day, Sean had travelled with Bryn and Pam.

A lavish buffet and an open bar had been laid on for the mourners. Typical of Jack Maitland, Rob's father, no expense was spared. Relatives, friends and acquaintances mingled with the family and indulged in the food and drink. Sean had just finished talking to a parent of one of his pupils when he spotted Jack Maitland coming over to him. 'Sean,' he said, smilingly putting an arm around Sean's shoulder, 'could I possibly have a word with you?' Jack Maitland's requests always seemed to come out more as commands. Sean found himself being propelled towards the open French doors that led out onto the hotel's extensive gardens. When they were around twenty yards from the doorway and clearly out of reach of anyone's hearing, Maitland dropped his arm and turned to face Sean. Sean, who had been wondering what compassionate comment he might come up with regarding Rob's death, suddenly realized when he looked at Maitland that this would not be required. Any warmth he had exuded within the room had vanished from his face and when he began to speak, his tone and words were steely and threatening. 'Right, Campbell, they say Rob's death was an accident. I think that's bullshit. One way or another I think you bear full responsibility.'

'But….,' began Sean feeling lost for words.

'But nothing. I've seen the police report. I've had reports about what went on at the party. If you hadn't been dancing with Rob's girl, and canoodling with her there would have been no bust up at the homestead. And if that had been the case Rob, wouldn't have come out with what he reportedly said. He wouldn't have felt so bad and upset afterwards that he decided to get into that bloody truck and go and apologize to the girl. And he wouldn't have ended up in the bloody river.'

Maitland had become redder in the face. Anger was visibly welling up within him. But he kept in control and kept his voice low. 'And you just happened to be at the river. What a bloody coincidence! But you weren't able to help Rob because you were injured and then concussed. What a load of shit! You had no bloody intention of helping him. Rob dies and you get his girl. I've got you sussed, Campbell.'

'Listen, Jack, I know you're upset and hurting. You've lost your son. But what you're saying just isn't true.'

'True! We'll see what the truth is. I'll be watching you, Campbell. And I'll be watching to see if you go anywhere near that girl. You might work with her but outside of the school you'll keep clear of her. Jack Maitland turned to go and then turned back again and said chillingly, 'They say accidents happen every day. I'd watch my back if I were you.'

Taken aback and shaken, Sean watched Maitland's large frame disappear into the function suite. 'God, is that guy grief-stricken or unbalanced?' he asked himself. 'I hope for my sake that whichever it is that it's temporary.' With heart beating loudly in his ears, he walked to the garden gate that led to the car park. There he climbed into the back seat of Bryn's unlocked car. He lay back and closed his eyes. His mind kept replaying what Jack Maitland had said until he eventually fell asleep. He was in a deep but troubled sleep when Bryn and Pam climbed in for the journey home some considerable time later.

Sean lay on the sofa. He had left the lights off and the room was in comparative darkness. The two sizeable logs sitting on top of some coals had taken well. They were now burning brightly and the flames flickered and darted like the tongues of dancing serpents, their shadows moving in unison on the walls and ceiling of the cottage.

He thought of the party held just two weeks before and how drastically life seemed to have changed in that short period of time. How he wished that the clock could be put back and things returned to how they had been.

The venue for the party had been Dan Munro's old homestead further up the valley. It was hosted by young Nick Munro to celebrate his cousin Neil's engagement to Judy, a teacher at Palmerston High. A large gathering of folk from the Valley, along with some of Judy's colleagues from Palmerston, were already assembled when Sean arrived with Dan and Gail Munro. His carry-out consisted of a peter of lager and a half bottle of gin. The party was in full swing. Folks were spread throughout the house – some smoking and chatting out on the veranda, some in the hall, others in the kitchen inhibiting the movement of wives and girl-friends who were organising the buffet 'eats' for later. Most had gathered in the lounge.

From his time in New Zealand, Sean had learned that the form for parties was for the menfolk to bring booze and the women a "plate", a plate loaded with some culinary delight which might consist of home-made pies, smoked meats, scotch eggs, sausage rolls, savouries, Bluff oysters, smoked eels, multi-layered club sandwiches, spare ribs etcetera …etcetera. For those opting to bring something sweet, rich cream sponges, meringues and the famous New Zealand pavlova were likely contenders.

The large lounge area had been made even more spacious by the removal of armchairs and settees but seating had been provided along part of the room's perimeter with an assortment of dining and kitchen chairs. Against one wall stood a line of trestle tables, borrowed from the village hall. A third of these groaned under the weight of two beer kegs, peters of lager, an assortment of spirit and cocktail bottles and a large bowl of punch. The remaining two thirds were partially piled with plates and cutlery, leaving a large space for the delivery of food from kitchen to table top.

Sean noticed Rob, a little the worse for drink, sitting next to a girl whom he recognised as Lyn the barmaid at the Glenbeg pub. Rob's arm was nonchalantly laid along the back of her seat. Their knees and thighs were close up against each other. A handsome blond-haired guy whom Sean didn't know sat next to Rob.

Sitting at the far end of the room was Marama's brother Hemi, a near-full jug of lager at his feet and a glass of lager in one hand whilst the other nursed a guitar that lay across his lap. Laughing, carefree Hemi of the bulging biceps and continual happy smile was in his element. Typically possessing the musical talent of his Polynesian race, he had been entertaining the assembled guests. Whatever the request, he could usually provide a rendition or accompany the singer and contribute harmonies to boot.

'Where's Marama?' yelled a voice from the back of the room which Sean immediately recognised as belonging to Frank Cleland. 'Come on Marama. Give us Georgie Girl.'

'Yeah! echoed a few voices. 'Georgie Girl, Marama.'

Marama emerged from the kitchen, a partially consumed glass of punch in her hand which she waved laughingly at those around her. 'I'll need a few more of these first, folks.'

Hemi laughed, 'Not you, Marama. Come on. Quit the kidding. If Judith Durham left The Seekers, you'd get the bloody job tomorrow!'

Hemi's comment caused great laughter. But Sean knew, they all knew, that Marama was good. Bloody good! She'd sung with bands in Dunedin before but if she'd gone up north she could have made the big time. Still could if she wanted to.

As Marama wove through the party-goers, she was joined by Joe Rattana who was employed by the local Rabbit Board. Joe had his guitar and as he sat down beside Hemi, they quickly checked that their instruments were in tune with each other and then launched straight into the Geordie Girl intro. Marama burst into song whilst the onlookers swayed and danced along to the music. This was followed by the plaintive Lemon Tree and then the Seekers' big hit The Carnival Is Over. Cheers, whistles and calls for more resounded around the room.

By way of introduction, Marama raised her hands to the audience. As they quietened down, she said, 'Right, folks, we've got another singer here for you tonight. And he's good and all the way from Bonnie Scotland! It's Sean Scottie Campbell!'

Whilst another round of cheering and clapping went up, Marama walked over to the slightly flushed Sean, took him by the hand and pulled him over to the front of the room. Apart from Hemi, Bryn and Marama, no-one was aware of Sean's singing ability. It had only come out after Sean had sat in on Marama's work with the school children when they were preparing some Maori items for a school concert. Sean had learned some of the material himself and had been caught out when Marama came across him strumming the guitar and singing some of the songs in the classroom one evening. It was then that he confessed to having done a bit of band work himself in Scotland.

Sean downed the beer he was holding and said something to Hemi and Joe. He then looked around the room, 'OK people. Here's a wee song they sing in Glasgow when they come out of the pubs on a Saturday night.' After Hemi's chord strike, and with everyone expecting Sean to be singing I Belong to Glasgow, he instead began to sing the Maori action song Pa Mai with Marama on the actions and the three of them providing the harmonies. This went down well. His next song, he explained, involved a big woman called Eli Mae who wished to take up golf – her handicap being that she had a very large chest. This went down even better. He then finished up duetting with Marama in the beautiful Maori love song, Pokare Kare.

After getting a peck on the cheek from Marama and a clap on the back from Joe and Hemi, Sean moved over to the 'bar' to replenish his glass. A deep and unusually cultured voice spoke just behind him, 'Good singing, Sean. I can tell that's not the first time you've sung.'

Sean turned round and the stranger who'd been sitting next to Rob Maitland put out his hand, 'Michael Maitland.'

A flicker of recognition suddenly dawned upon Sean as he took the proffered hand, 'Yeah,' said Michael smiling, 'I'm Rob's cousin. You've probably come across my dad, Grant Maitland, before. He and Uncle Jack are brothers. I've been doing the young kiwi "trip to the old country" thing. Just got back last week in fact. I'm due to start work in my father's Dunedin business on Monday.'

'Think I did hear your name mentioned before,' smiled Sean. 'I can see a faint family resemblance but confess you don't look too much like a farmer,' taking in the casual but immaculate slacks and jumper and the somewhat posturing stance.

'God, I'm certainly no farmer and have no intention of being one. I leave that to my country cousins,' asserted Michael. The business world's the place for me. I've got my degree in law and business studies, I've done my European tour and now I'm set to make a killing in the commercial world. I'll start in my father's Dunedin offices but we're ultimately going to get a foothold in Auckland. After that, the sky's the limit,' said Michael taking a sip of his gin and lemonade. 'And what about you? Are you satisfied to remain in school teaching, primary teaching at that?'

Sean sensed the tone of disparagement in Michael's voice. 'This guy's a bit of an arse', he thought. He was, however, rescued from further conversation by the arrival of Vic, Rob's brother, at the bar.

Vic, if not totally pissed, was certainly more than half way there. 'Well, if it's not Mr Education and Mr Big Business! What are you two pillocks talking about? Come on, I'm going to get you both a drink, a proper drink. What are you drinking Mikey Boy, it's not bloody lemonade I hope?'

Michael escaped quickly. 'Thank you, Vic. But I need to see Marama. I haven't spoken to her since I got back. I'll see you both later.'

'See, Seanie Boy, I did you a favour. He might be my cousin, but that guy's a prick! Now, is that lager or a Dog's Nose you've got? asked Vic eying up Sean's glass.

'It's lager, Vic,' said Sean. 'I don't fancy a Dog's Nose tonight but how about sharing a dram with me?'

'A dram?' asked Vic squinting blearily at Sean. 'You mean a whisky?'

'Got it in one, Vic,' said Sean as he opened a bottle of Glen Morangie and poured a stiff dram into two glasses. What the hell, he thought, I could do with this.' Adding some water to his own he handed a glass to Vic and asked, 'Do you want a spot of water in this?'

'Not on your life. When I drink whisky, I drink whisky. When I drink water, I drink water.'

'The Quiet Man. Maurice Walsh.'

'Whaa ? asked Vic.

'Never mind, Vic. Slainte. Here's mud in your eye,' said Sean raising his glass to Vic.

'Up your kilt, Scottie,' said Vic who had mellowed considerably since his cousin's departure. 'You know,' said Vic nodding in the direction of Michael who was on the other side of the room talking intently to Marama, 'I'd watch old Mikey if I were you. He's Mr Smooth and I don't trust him.' As Vic knocked back the rest of his whisky he added, 'He might act like a bit of a poof but he's a hard bastard.' With that Vic wandered off to bend someone else's ear.'

Sean paused for thought. He'd just poured himself another dram when a voice shouted, 'Gangway! Make a space, grub's on its way!' and a procession of ladies came into the room bearing the eats.

9

The party was going down well with one and all. After a food feast and a quieter time to draw breath and rack up the energy levels, the night became more riotous. More and more folk were up dancing. Most of the men got merrier as the night progressed. Many of the younger women were not too far behind them whilst some of the older matrons, assigned by their loving spouses as chauffeuses for the night, restricted themselves to a couple of Pims Number One's or a Merry Widow along with copious cups of tea.

If not up singing, Marama, Sean noted, was knocking back the punch and dancing with gay abandon. On three occasions she'd dragged Sean up for a dance. Realisation had also come to him at some stage in the evening that Rob and the barmaid Lyn were not in the room. If Marama was aware of this fact, she was choosing to ignore it and seemed to be happily "merry" rather than drunk.

After a couple of malt whiskies and a few beers, Sean was feeling quite mellow. As the inside bathroom was designated a 'ladies' area for the night, he'd headed outside to relieve himself and get some fresh air at the same time.

He went through the kitchen where some of the older ladies were gossiping and washing up. A few quips and suggestive comments about why he wasn't wearing his kilt had them all in stitches and him laughing in unison.

Having made it safely out the back door and adjusting himself to the night light, he could make out one or two couples in the shadows. He therefore walked across the yard to the back of the wool-shed and just beyond to a line of conifers where he released a long and satisfying jet of water into the night air.

Having done up his fly, he turned and nearly jumped the height of himself as a husky voice whispered in the darkness, 'Hi Seanie boy, what've you got there?'

Peering through the dark he could make out the outline of a curvy young female. He suddenly twigged who it was, Annette Maitland, Vic's young sixteen-year old sister. Warning bells began to ring in Sean's slightly inebriated brain. He hadn't directly come across Annette before. He'd certainly noticed her earlier in the evening horsing around with another couple of young guys on the veranda. And he'd certainly heard of her before – the girl with a mature woman's body and an apparent willingness to get astride any passable looking male. At sixteen she was now just at the legal age of consent. Until recently, local males would have referred to her as "jail bait". This along with the fact that she was Vic's sister and Jack Maitland's daughter, put a lot of boys off getting too close to her.

'It's Annette, isn't it?' asked Sean taking a step back as Annette came close up to him, hands on curvy jean-tight hips. Her short white blouse strained to hold in the rounded mammaries. 'Annette, you shouldn't be over here by yourself. Come on, let's get back to the house.'

'But I'm not by myself, Sean, you're here!' He could smell the sweet after-scent of gin on her breath as she boldly moved right up to him, put her left arm around his waist and slid her right hand down to fondle his crotch.

'Jeez, Annette, what the hell are you doing? You're a bloody schoolgirl!' said Sean throwing her arm off and leaping backwards. 'And you've been drinking! What will your parents say?'

'They're not bloody well here, are they? And they won't know, will they? I came with Vic. I like a bit to drink. And I like a good shag. I'm good at shagging!' exclaimed the petulant Annette, annoyed that she obviously was not going to score with Sean. And then as an after- thought she added with a sly smile, 'I could get you into serious trouble, you know.'

'Listen, you silly little bitch, I'm going back over to the house. You'll come over just after me. If I don't see you in the lounge in the next few minutes, I'm going to tell your brothers exactly what's happened.' With that Sean headed back across the yard, hoping like hell that she'd do as she was told. He didn't know exactly where Rob was and Vic was by now unlikely to be capable of absorbing and reacting to any information at all. And as a male teacher, he knew only too well the trouble a young attractive female pupil could cause, if of a mind to do so.

Considerably sobered, Sean arrived back in the lounge

to the strains of Pearly Shells. He headed straight to the bar and poured himself a dram. Taking a swift swallow, he turned around and was relieved to see the totally unabashed Annette smilingly wave across to him before moving towards a drunk young farm-hand in front of whom she began to sway in a seductive hula style.

'Thank you, God,' said Sean offering a silent prayer to his Maker.

The night merged into the small hours of the next morning. A number of folk had already departed and Sean was looking around for Gail and Dan when a hand grabbed him and pulled him once again up for a dance. It was Marama, a little more unsteady on her feet and slightly subdued. Hemi was singing Engelbert's 'I'll Have the Last Waltz', with everyone joining in the chorus. Marama had both her arms around Sean's neck and her head snuggled against his shoulder. Sean closed his eyes and smelt the fragrance of her perfume and felt the softness of her hair tickle his chin. He was rudely brought out of his reverie by an angry shout and a strong arm roughly hauling him away from Marama.

'Campbell, you bugger, that's my fiancée,' said a dishevelled and very drunk looking Rob Maitland as he peered and swayed before Sean. 'And you,' he said looking at Marama, 'should be bloody well ashamed of yourself, you little slut!'

The music had stopped and a sudden and shocked silence momentarily came over the revellers at Rob's outburst. Marama had begun to cry. In a sobbing voice she answered the accusing Rob, 'Well you should know all about sluts!' and ran from the room. To deflect from the situation, Hemi and Joe started playing a couple of Beatles numbers. Sean moved to speak with Rob but Dan and his son Nick each put an arm round him and walked him through to the kitchen, with Dan saying, 'Leave it, Sean. No use talking to him when he's in that state. Time to go anyway, I reckon. It's been a great party but Gail's ready to leave so I think we should go now.'

Sean agreed.

Rob was similarly escorted by Michael Maitland, not to some fresh air but to the bar.

10

Having further congratulated the engaged couple, who happened to be in the kitchen at that moment and having thanked Nick for a great party, Sean and Dan followed Gail out to the yard and around to where the car was parked. Gail and Dan got in the front and Sean into the back. There he found a huddled up and tear-stained Marama. He squeezed her hand and lightly kissed her on the cheek. 'Things will be OK,' he said.'

'Course they will,' said Gail. 'But I thought it best that Marama come with us. Time for bed and a good rest, Dear.' Turning on the ignition she drove down the track to the main road.

Gail drove down the Pig Root. The night air was warm and balmy and a full silvery moon hung above the hills. It seemed to play hide and seek, dancing behind rocks and trees, but keeping apace with the car as it wound its way down the twisting road to the lower valley.

Sean had his arm along the back of the seat. Marama had fallen asleep, her head resting on his shoulder. Her long eyelashes flickered now and again and he could feel the gentle rhythm of her breathing. He sat still, not wanting to disturb her, concerned for her, loving her. His mind flashed back to the scene at the party. What a bloody shambles, he thought. Rob had been a right prat. And what about the talk of him playing around? There certainly seemed to be some evidence of it tonight. Maybe Rob's behaviour wasn't as out of character as folk might think.

Gail turned the car into the cul-de-sac and then swung into their driveway. Dan, who'd slept soundly all the way home, grunted and stretched. At the same time Marama opened her eyes and focused upon her surroundings. Gail opened the car door, 'Do you two want to come in for a cuppa?'

Sean looked at Marama. She shook her head and said, 'No thanks, Gail, I feel like getting home.'

'I'll walk Marama over,' said Sean as he got out and went around to open the door on Marama's side.

Dan climbed out and looked around him somewhat unsteadily. 'Well, kids, it's been some party. Me, I'm off for some shut-eye. G'night,' and he headed for the house.

'Night you two,' whispered Gail softly as she followed Dan to the house.

Marama tucked her arm into Sean's and they walked past Sean's cottage and towards the pedestrian swing bridge that spanned the river at the end of the cul-de-sac. They walked in silence. On the other side of the bridge, Marama looked at Sean and said huskily, 'Sean, walk me along the footpath by the river. We can cut across the hayfield to get to the house.'

Sean croaked in reply, 'OK.' His heart began to beat faster. Was it his imagination or was Marama clinging onto his arm just a little bit tighter?

Despite the alcoholic excesses of the evening, Sean felt his senses heighten. Just as he was aware of the presence and beauty of the girl beside him, so was he also aware of the magical scene that had suddenly enveloped them. The long wistful call of a morepork sounded through the warm night air. Moonlight slanted through tree foliage casting the river waters and its banks in silver light and dark shadow. The river moved slowly, its waters gurgling and chuckling as they encountered projecting rock and stone. They both stopped and gazed at the scene. 'It's beautiful, isn't it?' whispered Marama.

'Yes, it is,' responded Sean in a soft voice – each speaking in lowered tones as though to ensure the magic and tranquillity around them would not be broken.

Marama was standing slightly in front of him. It seemed to Sean that an invisible force was pulling them together, Marama leaning backwards and he forwards until they were within a hair's breadth of one another. And then they touched. She sighed and turned her head, lifting her face up to him. Sean put his arms around her waist and leant over her shoulder to kiss her slowly and then deeply. As their tongues began to probe and explore, Marama turned to face him, responding with a passion. Her fingers dug hard into his shoulder muscles as she pressed herself against him.

As their wanting increased, they simultaneously stopped and hand in hand moved off the path and under the cascading foliage of an ancient weeping willow. Marama laid down the cardigan that had been draped over her shoulders. They knelt facing each other and embraced.

Afterwards they lay on the soft bed of dried leaves and moss, legs, arms and fingers entwined, allowing the beating of hearts and panting of lungs to gradually subside. They listened to the sound of the water and the occasional calls of the hunting morepork.

'Oh, God, Sean. I shouldn't have done that,' whispered Marama, moving from their embrace and stretching to reach for her top. 'It's not fair on you, and it's.......'

'Shshsh! said Sean getting to his knees and wrapping his arms around her. 'I love you, Marama. I think I fell in love with you the first day we met. That was the most wonderful experience of my life! I want us to be together, now and always.'

'I love you too, Sean. But my life's a mess at the moment. I'm supposed to be getting married to Rob next month. Everything's organised and Jack Maitland's paying for this huge wedding. There's going to be all hell to pay if I don't go through with it.'

'The bottom line is, Marama, do you love Rob? If you do, then you must go ahead with things. If you don't, then you're making the biggest mistake of your life. You can come with me. We can go back to Scotland. We can go anywhere we like. Things will blow over. And stuff Jack Maitland, his pride might be dented not being able to put on a big show, but you're hardly marrying him!'

'No, I don't love Rob. I thought I did, at least until you came along. Don't get me wrong, Rob and I got on great at the start. He was good fun. Always ready for a laugh. But there wasn't a lot to him really. We never talked about life and the things that you, Bryn and I have great debates about.

And then there was the "girl" thing. Rob has always had an eye for other females, and not just an eye. I know he's been unfaithful, a bit like his dad in that respect. But I don't think he considers that a big deal. It's as if he thinks that being the man, it's OK to play around and then come back to the little wife at home. Silly bugger!'

'Well, girl, I can't say that I'm sorry he's fallen in your estimation. But I can't understand either how he could behave like that tonight. I know he was drunk but he was way out of line.'

'Oh, he's behaved like that in private before, especially lately. The "hail-fellow-well-met" guy is the Rob folk know outside. But Rob Maitland has a temper and he's not controlling it as well as he used to.'

Sean pulled Marama to her feet. 'Never mind, we'll sort things out. First, we get you home for some sleep. Just as well tomorrow's Saturday. Come on, Marama, no worries!'

And so they walked, an arm around each other, as far as the fence at the corner of the hayfield. They climbed over it and then walked across the stubble to the back gate of Marama's Nan's garden. There they embraced and Sean watched her move to the back door, wave once and go inside.

Sean sighed and hands in pockets walked back down to the river. Dawn would not be long in coming but he believed that sleep would totally elude him whilst his mind was a whirlpool of thoughts and emotions. Marama loved him! Incredulous at the thought, he couldn't stop smiling. He felt more intoxicated now than when he had been imbibing at the party. The smiling lasted all the way back to the swing-bridge.

At the bridge he decided to carry on up river, allowing free rein to his thoughts and dreams for the future. At this point, thick vegetation covered the river bank and narrowed the path to little more than the width of a sheep track. The moon, however, still illuminated enough of the track for it to be followed. About half a mile further on, he passed the waterfall and its deep pool. Shortly afterwards, he stopped and climbed onto a large rock that squatted like some giant troll to the right of the track. He lay back on the hard surface and stared at the moon and the star-studded sky. Gradually his eyelids began to droop and he fell into a deep sleep.

In his dreams he found himself on the edge of an open area of ground. Somewhere voices were chanting in unison. He was aware that the chant was in Maori. It was night-time and a mist swirled before and around him, one minute clearing to give him a glimpse of what lay ahead and the next blanketing his view. He could make out a young girl kneeling at the feet of an older man. Behind them was a Maori meeting house, a whare whakairo. They were in traditional costume. The man had a regal bearing and was heavily tattooed in the mode of an ancient warrior. He reached out his arm towards Sean and uttered some words. Sean found himself able to understand exactly what he was saying – 'Bring it back from across the great ocean of Kiwa, pakeha, bring it back to its rightful home.' Just as the mist began to obscure his view, the girl got up and looked directly at him. It was Marama!

Despite Bryn urging her to take more time off, Marama had insisted on returning to work on the Monday following the funeral. She assured him that she was ready to work and, in fact, felt she needed it to focus her attention. She promised him that if she found she couldn't cope then she'd ask for Jean Donald, the retired teacher who had covered for her before, to take over.

But it was a pale-faced and withdrawn Marama that recommenced teaching that week. Bryn was able to observe her successfully engaging the pupils and immersing herself in the demanding life and routine of the infant classroom. But he was concerned that she was so remote and uncommunicative in the staffroom at break and lunch-times. Indeed, she tended to make her cup of tea and immediately adjourn to her classroom. At the end of the school day, where she would normally have carried on in school till after five o'clock, she instead would set off for home laden down with marking and preparation materials. Initially, he could understand such a pattern, but when there was no change in her behaviour after the second week back, he became more worried. Her communication with Sean was monosyllabic and it seemed that she was purposely avoiding him wherever possible.

Sean, as advised by Bryn, was endeavouring to give Marama time and space. But he was concerned for her and couldn't understand why she appeared to be making a point of almost ignoring him. It was the Friday afternoon of the third week and with school finished for the day, Sean decided that he had to confront her. She was ushering out the last two chattering infants from her classroom when Sean approached her.

'Bye Miss Te Kanawa. Have a nice weekend. Have a nice sleep!' they giggled as she shooed them out the door.

'Marama, I need to talk to you.'

Marama looked at Sean. 'I don't really have time right now, Sean. I need to get home. I'm taking my Nan into Palmerston.'

Sean entered the classroom and closed the door. 'Marama, I have to talk to you. I'm sick with worry about you. I can't sleep for thinking about you. You're in my head all the time. And it's hurting like hell that you seem to be going out of your way to ignore me. I know Rob's death is a tragedy. But what about us? What about the night by the river? It seems now like it was a dream but I know it happened. And I know how I felt and I think I know how you felt. I can wait as long as you like but I need some sign from you that you still feel something for me and that we have a future.'

Marama looked at Sean and shook her head, 'We have no future, Sean. I was drunk when we were down by the river. I'm not blaming you for what happened. What's the old saying – it takes two to tango? I shouldn't have encouraged you, but there we are. And now Rob's dead. I feel it's almost as if someone is punishing me for what I did.'

'That's silly Marama. You have nothing to be ashamed of or feel guilty for. You said yourself at the time that you didn't love Rob. And if he had lived, would things be like this between us now?'

'It's too late to think about what might have been. You know, Jack Maitland told me he thinks you're responsible for Rob's death. I don't believe that at all. But I think, for us, it's just a doubly tragic co-incidence that you were down by the river at the time that Rob drowned. And I feel so guilty. If it hadn't been for me, you wouldn't have been down at the river and perhaps Rob wouldn't have been either.' Tears were beginning to roll down Marama's cheeks. 'One other thing, Sean, I'm pregnant. I'm carrying Rob's child. I still haven't told anyone. I've got enough on my plate, Sean. I don't need any further complications. Go back to Scotland.' Turning away from Sean she choked and added, 'Go back home, Sean. You'll be doing us both a favour.'

Stunned and speechless, Sean left Marama and went through to his own room.

It was the day before the Easter break. The wonderful autumn colours, normally enhanced by clear blue skies, were not in evidence today. Low and heavy cloud had given a greyness to the landscape and the chill wind blowing down the valley heralded the advent of winter. The day matched Sean's mood as he walked along the river bank one last time. Tomorrow he would begin his journey home to Scotland.

With hands thrust deep into the pockets of his duffle coat, Sean leant forwards into the buffeting wind. A great sadness had engulfed him these past few weeks. Marama's words had given him much to think about. He also felt that Marama stating she was carrying Rob's child, had under-lined her wish to bring closure to their relationship. And, he had to concede, this news had created a wider gulf between them. In the end, he had reluctantly written to the Otago Education Board in Dunedin informing them of his intention to terminate his teaching contract from the commencement of the Easter holidays. Prior to that he had discussed his intentions with Bryn, giving his reasons for doing so. Bryn, his friend and colleague, tried to dissuade him but could see that Sean's mind was made up. When told of his decision, Marama had looked sad but only said that she wished him well.

As he approached the bridge, his eye was drawn to a movement behind some rhododendron bushes on the far bank. A flash of fair hair appeared, then vanished, then appeared in full view, as a boy climbed the path up to the bridge. He stopped for a moment to look across at Sean before continuing up to the road above. Sean smiled. He'd guessed right away that it would be Jakob. Jakob, wearing his old brown parka and clutching his drawing pad and pencil. Jakob Zarkov, the nine- year old who didn't speak to anyone outwith the family home, who didn't seem *able* to speak to anyone. But the same Jakob who one day came shyly up to

Sean in the playground and showed him an exquisite pencil sketch of a bellbird. And the skill with which it had been done had made Sean gasp in wonder. Someone else Sean would miss.

The previous evening Sean had answered a knock on the cottage door to find Tama, Marama's grandfather, standing there. 'Tena koe, Sean,' said the old man.

'Haere mai, Tama,' replied Sean. Sean asked Tama in, waved for him to take a seat by the fire and went off to open a bottle of beer. He set a glass down beside Tama, sat opposite him and lifted his own glass, 'Slainte, Tama.'

'Kia ora, Sean,' Tama replied.

Sean had been fascinated by Maori culture, its music, its history and folk-lore. And most of all, he greatly admired and respected the Maori people he had come across since his arrival in New Zealand, impressed by their hospitality, their good nature and humour. Their recent history and treatment at the hands of the land-hungry colonist was good enough cause, he felt, for them to harbour resentment and strong grievance. Shortly after he had arrived in Glenbeg, Marama had invited him to meet her family. Sean had hit it off with them right away. Tama in particular had spent much time with Sean sharing his knowledge of his native culture and history. Sean had also been able to inform him about his Gaelic ancestry in the north-west of Scotland and discuss similarities in its history and folk-lore.

'Well, Sean,' I am sad to hear that you are going back earlier to Scotland than planned,' said Tama.

'Yes, Tama, but I believe it's for the best.'

'Sean, Marama's grandmother and I believe that you may have feelings for Marama. Marama also told us that she urged you to go home. But we do not believe that in her heart that is at all what she really wants. Things have been hard for her of late. I think that, given time, her attitude will change. Normally I would not interfere, but I feel sad for my grand-daughter for I know her heart is sore and I felt I should speak to you about this.'

Sean wondered if Marama had told her grandparents about the pregnancy, but all he said was, 'I love your grand-daughter, Tama. But she has made her feelings clear to me and I believe I should go. I will miss her terribly and I will miss you and Mere. Perhaps I will come back at some future date.'

'I hope you will, Sean. I hope you will my friend.'

It was the end of the final school day. Sean, already packed up from the previous evening, locked up the cottage for the last time and went over to say his goodbyes to Bryn and his family. He was met at the door by a tearful Pam, 'Oh Sean, we'll miss you so much,' she cried hugging him fiercely.

With a catch in his voice Sean croaked, 'And all of you, Pam.'

Endeavouring to add some levity to the scene, Bryn clasped Sean's hand tightly, 'Going to miss you my haggis-eating friend, and your singing Land of My Fathers in that quaint Scottish accent. And now that you know the words, I expect you to join in with my countrymen when they stuff you lot at Murrayfield next season.'

As Bryn embraced him, Sean felt too emotional for a quipped response. 'Thanks for everything Bryn. You and Pam have made me so welcome and I've so loved living and working in this wee community.' He then shook hands with Rhys and Glyn and kissed Ceri on the forehead. 'Take care, kids. I'll write to you all. See and reply!'

Climbing into his little Austin 7, he set off for Dunedin where he stayed the night with his friends the Bells. The next morning, he boarded a plane at Taieri airport and began the long trip back to his family home in Ross-shire, Scotland.

PART THREE

New Zealand 1972

12

Annette Maitland swung her mother's Mini onto the Glenbeg/Palmerston road and put her foot down hard on the accelerator. Her mother grimaced and said, 'Not too fast, Annette. We're not in any hurry remember.'

'Relax, Mother, this little box doesn't know what fast means!'

Annette was excited. It was her birthday and it promised to be the most spectacular one yet. The two women were heading for Dunedin, intent on a day's shopping that included picking up a new car for nineteen- year old Annette and viewing a flat in a newly-built apartment block in the residential area of Maori Hill. The following week Annette was due to begin working in the offices of her uncle, Grant Maitland. Their day out was to conclude with dinner at the Embassy Hotel where Julia had booked them in for the night, followed by a show at the Town Hall where a Scots pop group known as Middle of the Road were performing.

Annette Maitland was a knock-out. Her shoulder-length blonde hair, gorgeous complexion, sparkling eyes, voluptuous breasts, curvy body and shapely legs, were reason enough for her to be fantasized over by most of the boys who came into contact with her. Father Jack adored her. Mother Julia was slightly in awe of her. All her girl-friends were totally envious of her. She was quick-tempered, self-assertive and used to getting her own way. Her parents had indulged her every whim since the time she was a cute and precocious toddler. Thus, in the course of growing up she was, unsurprisingly, a spoiled brat. Annette knew how to manipulate folk, especially men-folk.

Unlike her brothers who had gone to the local primary school and then on to secondary at Palmerston, when her primary schooling was over Annette had been sent to the fee-paying Saint Columba's College in Dunedin. Her parents, aware of her attraction to boys and recalling their own adolescent appetites, thought that the close supervision in the boarding school would do Annette the world of good. The influence of the UK's swinging 60's had permeated the lifestyle of the young in the university city of Dunedin, resulting in Annette "having a ball" as she put it. By the time she was in her fifth form year, night-time escapes to student wool-store hops and parties and clandestine meetings at the homes of other senior high school pupils, rounded off Annette's education to her satisfaction.

'Can't wait to see this flat, Mum,' said Annette. 'I'm really hoping it fits the bill.'

'I still think it might be better if you stayed with your Uncle Grant and Auntie Diane for a bit. It's a big step going to live in a flat all by yourself, Annette.'

Annette thought to herself. 'I'll only be on my own

when I want to be on my own.'

'Mum, relax, I'll be fine. I've loads of friends in Dunedin. A lot of them are at uni and will be in flats just like me. It'll be great!' She smiled to herself as she recalled her last student flat visit. It had been the night after the school prize-giving ceremony. She had told her parents that she was staying over for a party with a friend who was a day pupil at the school. In fact, she had spent the night with a randy medical student called Trev. And good old Trev had found his stamina and prowess quite eclipsed by Annette's insatiable appetite. 'She's a bloody nympho,' he had told his envious flatmates later.

'If you say so, dear,' sighed her mother. She also thought of herself at that age. It may not have been as adventurous a time as the 60's, but they had had their moments. She was under no illusions as to the number of male visitors who might end up at her sexy daughter's apartment.

As they descended the motorway in the final approaches to Dunedin, Annette glanced at her mother, 'Hey, Mum, have you heard that that teacher Sean Campbell is coming back to Glenbeg?'

'Yes, someone mentioned it in the store the other day. Seems strange to me. I didn't say anything to your father as you know how strongly he feels about him. His coming is bound to stir up bad memories. Why in heaven's name would he want to come back?'

'Why indeed! I hear that he's now a writer and quite successful in the UK. They say some of his stuff has been serialized on television. He's supposed to be researching some story that involves the gold rush days.'

'Really? Who told you all this? You seem to have learned a lot about him. I hope you're not too interested, Annette.'

'M-mmm. Well, I heard it from Marama when she was up at the house the other day. She gets all the news from Bryn Jones. I gather they still keep in touch.'

'Interesting. Just hope he keeps out of your father's way. I know he's still very bitter about Rob's death. Being your father, it has to be someone else's fault. He puts a lot of blame on this Sean boy.

'I know, Mum. But we both know what Rob was like. He chased girls all over the place, even after he was engaged to Marama. And at the dance that night – I was there, remember. It was Marama that got Sean up to dance. A smoochie waltz and a wee hug, it was no big deal.'

'And you, girl. Don't be fluttering those pretty eyes at this Scots boy. Keep clear, d'you hear?'

'Yes, Mum,' smiled Annette, 'but he was rather cute, don't you think?'

'Yes, he was rather handsome,' said Julia with just the trace of a smile crossing her lips.

As they turned left off the motor-way beside the Northern football ground, Sean Campbell's car came onto the north-bound carriageway. Neither party noticed the other.

Sean Campbell carefully changed down to third and then second gear, gently braking as he passed the sign that announced 'GLENBEG'. It may have been almost three years since he was last in the place but it felt like it was just yesterday. Nothing new was in evidence as the car slowed down and he turned right, just before the old store and its two pumps. He smiled as he noted the few homes in the cul-de-sac and recalled their inhabitants.

He disengaged the clutch and let the Imp coast the thirty yards to the road's end, then swung the wheel to the right to let the car stop in the grassed driveway of the small wooden cottage that had been his home. He switched off the ignition and sighed. It had been a long trip – plane to London, over-night stop in Singapore, refuel in Sydney and finally an internal flight from Auckland to Dunedin. He didn't feel too jet-lagged at the moment but guessed it would catch up with him in the next twenty-four hours or so.

'It's good to be back,' he thought. He felt a sense of excitement thinking about meeting up with many of his friends in the Valley. But mostly, all he could think about was when he might see Marama again and how she would react to seeing him. Would she be at all welcoming? Would she be cool, or even cold? Or worse still, would she possibly ignore him altogether? He tried to block such thoughts from his mind. He knew they were irrational. He had, after all, got the card from Marama and Bryn had assured him that everyone was looking forward to seeing him. Well, he could think of one or two that wouldn't be too delighted to see him, but what the hell. Maybe Marama was married or involved with someone and Bryn had been keeping it from him. 'Come on, Campbell, get a grip,' he told himself and swung open the car door.

As he got out of the car he paused for a moment, suddenly aware of young voices raised in song. 'Wales, Wales, home sweet home is Wales….' they chorused in unison. The sound, so melodic and plaintive, raised the hairs on the back of his neck as he gazed across to the school directly opposite the cottage. And to any passing stranger, he reflected, this was perhaps unusual music to be coming from a country primary school in kiwiland. Bryn Jones, was obviously still spreading a bit of Welsh culture. Just so long as he doesn't try to convert them to supporting the Welsh rugby team instead of the mighty All Blacks, he thought.

The sound of twigs crackling and the sight of a plume of white smoke rising behind the cottage and into the clear blue autumn sky, drew his attention. With the pleasant smell of wood smoke in his nostrils, he walked round to the back of the small plot fenced off from the field behind and identified the source of the fire.

Forty yards away across the field a man in a Panama hat was forking piles of leaves and brushwood onto a newly lit bonfire. He spotted Sean, waved and thrust the pitchfork into the ground. Then in a slow relaxed movement, he raised a knuckle to push the brim of the Panama up and back from his forehead, before leisurely strolling over to meet Sean.

As he drew nearer, Sean smiled. He guessed Dan Munro would be in his mid-sixties. The tanned and weather- beaten face told of someone who'd spent much of their life outdoors. Despite the loose open-necked shirt and baggy trousers belted at the waist, it was clear that this lean body carried little or no extra weight. Slanted eyes, designed perhaps to combat strong sunlight, did not totally disguise a submerged twinkle that appeared to come closer to the surface with its owner's approach.

Dan chuckled as he reached the fence and stretching out a tanned and calloused hand said, 'Well, if it's not Sean Campbell. G'day Sean you young bugger, how are yah?'

Clasping the strong hand in his own Sean answered, 'I'm fine, Dan. It's great to see you again. And how's Gail and the family?'

'Box of birds, Sean,' replied Dan. 'All great. Katelyn's moved up to Naseby with Barney and they're expecting an addition to the family any day soon. Young Nick's running the station for me and living up in the old homestead. He's still fancy free and playing hooker for Palmerston. So long as he concentrates playing hooker and not looking for bloody hookers in Palmerston, he'll be alright. They say he's got a chance of a trial for Otago but we'll see. Gail's fine. Things are a bit quieter on the farm just now so she's roped me in to do a bit of clearing up around the garden.'

'Great day for it, Dan.'

They chatted on, Dan updating Sean on local news and inquiring about life in Scotland and his switch over to becoming a full-time writer.

'Anyway, young fella, guess you'll want to be getting settled in. I reckon you'll find things much as they were before. The old place has had a lick of paint. Me and a few of the Board members got around to freshening thing up last weekend. No-one's stayed there since you left. Wouldn't say it was top-notch decorating but it's not looking too bad. We did have a few peters and a couple of Dogs' Noses when we finished up. Now that's something we've not done in the old cottage since your departure!'

'Reckon I'll pass on any Dogs' Noses for the moment Dan, but you never know what tomorrow will bring!' Sean mentally grimaced as he thought of previous occasions when a few of the local farmers would arrive at the cottage late in the afternoon with two or three half-gallon jars of beer and a bottle of gin. The old pub had been closed then and the cottage provided an ideal venue for a drink. A Dog's Nose was created when a good slug of gin was added to a glass of beer. This, Sean knew to his cost, could be a lethal concoction. The Glenbeg pub had been closed during his stay, but he'd heard it had recently re-opened, much to the delight of the locals.

'Go and get yourself sorted out, Sean. Door's open and the key's on the wall hook. Gail's got a few things in the fridge for you, bread in the bin and all that – enough to keep you going before you have to go round to the store. We'll see you later about coming along for a meal. Tonight, you're invited to have a meal with Bryn and the family. He said to go over to the house around six o'clock. I'd better keep an eye on the bonfire. With all the dry weather we've been having I don't want the bloody fire brigade from Palmerston arriving with all bells ringing. Leave you to it, Sean.'

Sean thanked Dan and smilingly watched him depart. Great bloke, he thought, and he hasn't changed a bit.

13

It was around four o'clock when Sean, changed into shorts and tracksuit top and running shoes, closed the cottage door and started to jog the twenty yards separating the cottage from the old swing bridge that spanned the slow-moving Waihemo river. His movement across the bridge caused it to creak and groan and slowly begin to sway in response to the rhythm of his stride.

He ran for about three hundred yards through a shaded avenue of autumn-hued poplars before turning right onto the tarred back road that connected a few smaller steadings, the main house of the Maitland sheep station and the road to the Limeworks, before it then swung back across the river to the main Palmerston-Pigroot highway.

The sky was still a clear blue, but the shadows were lengthening and it wouldn't be long before the setting sun sank below the horizon, leaving the valley in total shadow and the diffused glow on the Horse Range tops suddenly vanishing. The temperature had already dropped a degree or two as Sean stepped up his pace and settled into a rhythmic lope that felt invigorating in the lower temperature. His breathing was steady. He felt good.

The road ran more or less straight and level for the next mile and a half before reaching the bend that would take it once more back to the river. Where the road forked, Sean took the left turning onto the gravel surface that began to snake its way in a gradual uphill climb to the limestone quarry nestling in the foothills some three miles ahead. He shortened his stride and slackened his pace. His breathing was a little bit heavier but he felt surprisingly energetic. No feelings of jet lag yet.

Four hundred yards from the top and at the final bend, he checked his watch. He calculated he'd taken some twenty minutes to climb the winding road that lead to the quarry. Once round the corner, the incline lessened and then flattened out before dipping slightly to make the short crossing over a sturdy wooden bridge spanning a shallow gully. Below the bridge a stream gurgled and tumbled its way down to the valley. The road then ran up to the cattle grid with its over-head signpost proclaiming, "Maitland Limeworks." Beyond, sat a group of prefabricated huts and outbuildings. Just before the grid, Sean stopped and did a few stretching exercises then gazed at the scene before him.

Above, a great gaping hole, the result of decades of cutting and blasting, dominated the hillside. The craggy rock face was etched with terraced cliffs and ledges. A rough track, wide enough for one vehicle only, clawed its way around the left side of the quarry up to a level area where a digger pushed and probed at the residue of a recent blasting, great clouds enveloping it and the several enshrouded figures nearby.

He guessed that the driver could well be Hemi but couldn't distinguish anyone in the murk.

After a few more bends and leg stretches, he turned to head back down the hill. The sudden sound of a roaring engine and squealing brakes made him pause and look back up the quarry. A dust-covered and open-topped jeep was coming down the track at a somewhat perilous rate, drifting at the tight bends and rattling and juddering over the roughly-gravelled surface.

It came to a skidding halt beside him. The few days' stubble and a battered bush hat failed to disguise the face of Vic Maitland. The squat and powerful figure shouted at him, 'Seanie Campbell! What the hell are you doing here you Pommie bastard?'

'And g'day to you too, Vic,' replied Sean. 'Guess I'm out for a bit of fresh air. But as I've told you before, it's Scottish bastard, not Pommie.'

'Scotch or Pommie, it's all the same to me,' laughed Vic. 'You should all stay in bloody England. Nick Munro told me in the pub the other day that you might be coming back here. Said something about writing a book.' He added quizzically, 'I thought you were a bloody teacher?'

'Well, Vic, I was a teacher but folk have started calling me a writer, so I guess I'll go along with that in the meantime.'

'Still seems bloody strange to me that you've come all this way to little old Glenbeg, you being a big-time writer and all.'

'I'm going to be researching some stuff for a new book, Vic. That's why I'm here. Who knows, you might even be in it!'

'Yeah, that'll be right. But I just might have to find out more about this story you're writing. Folks round here wouldn't be too happy if you took the piss with all your fancy writing. Be seeing you!' And flicking the remains of his cigarette in Sean's direction, Vic gunned the jeep down the hill.

Sean began running in the same direction, lengthening his stride and free-wheeling down the hillside. Vic, he thought, hadn't been over-friendly. But then, as he recalled, Vic was that way with most people. Unless he'd been drinking, he wasn't particularly talkative. He had heard that when Vic was younger, he had had a reputation for being pretty wild and had not been the best guy to get on the wrong side of.

But as he reached the tarred back road, Sean put all thoughts of Vic to the back of his mind. The sun had dropped behind the western hills and a glorious golden and salmon-pink sky was beginning to fan out above them. A light but cold breeze hit his face and began to dry off some of the sweat trickling down his forehead and cheeks. The thought of a hot bath and food sped him on his way.

As he entered the tree-lined avenue, he slowed to a jog. It was almost dusk but he could make out two figures coming across the bridge. There was a woman and a skipping and chattering infant.

'Jeez, it's Marama,' he said to himself. Walking did not do justice to the way she moved. He would have recognised the sway of that slim, sylph-like figure anywhere. He approached them at a walk, just as they were stepping off the bridge. His heart-beat had increased palpably.

As Marama and the child drew closer, he saw her eyes light up in recognition and the glimmer of a smile appear on her face, for a split second. This was immediately replaced with a more serious expression that, to Sean's eyes, seemed quite close to a frown. She stopped in front of him. The child, a girl aged about three, clearly had her mother's beauty about her. Dark curling hair flowed down to her shoulders. Seeing a stranger, she moved slightly behind her mother and put her arms around the parent's waist.

'Hello, Sean,' said Marama in a quiet but clear voice. Haven't seen you around these parts for a while. You're looking well and keeping fit I see. We heard the other day that you were coming back to stay in the old place for a while.'

'Hello, Marama,' said Sean, aware that his voice was strained with tension. 'You're looking well too. And this little lady beside you must be Kirri. I recognise her from the photo.'

'Yes, this is Kirri. She was born the year after you left.'

Sean mentally flinched but couldn't discern any accusatory tone in Marama's voice, nor did he detect any emotion or expression.

'Now Kirri's a big girl of three,' continued Marama. 'Say hello to Sean, Kirri.'

'Hello,' said the infant shyly, brown eyes studying him curiously.

'Hi, Kirri. It's nice to see you. You look just like your Mum.' And as an aside to Marama he added, 'What a beautiful little girl.'

He noticed a faint flush on Marama's cheeks. But disregarding the remark she went on, 'We're just hurrying home. I told Nan to expect us back by six for tea. I've just had a meeting with Sally MacRae. You won't know her. She teaches the infant class now.'

Perplexed, Sean asked, 'Are you no longer teaching then?'

'I'm working with the middle years now, like you used to do. Tama still talks about you, by the way. He's over Milford way crayfishing with his nephews, but he's due back soon. I'm sure he'll want to meet up with you.' Her eyes softened, 'And Nan will want to see you too.' Looking over to Kirri who was swinging on one of the wire hawsers anchoring the old bridge, she called, 'Right, Kirri, let's go. Say good-bye to Sean.'

'Bye, Kirri. Bye, Marama.' He wanted to say something else but with the emotion of seeing her again, he was lost for words. As he walked across the bridge, he suddenly felt tired and a little deflated. Meeting Marama had happened so quickly and so unexpectedly that he'd almost felt like a shy teenager.

Sean sat with the family in the Jones' kitchen listening to the excited chatter of the three children – Rhys, Glyn and Ceri. A delicious aroma filled the room and even with the window slightly ajar, moisture covered the glass and occasional rivulets snaked down to drip on the sill below.

Pam took the roast joint of lamb out of the oven for Bryn to carve whilst she dished out copious quantities of roast potatoes, kumara, carrots and silver beet onto the plates. A couple of glasses of Speights beer had, if anything, increased Sean's hunger pangs and when Pam placed the loaded plate in front of him, he tackled it with gusto.

There had been great excitement on his arrival at the school house and genuine pleasure expressed at his return. Whilst Glyn, the youngest, had been only five when Sean left, photos along with other correspondence had ensured that Sean would not be dumb-founded over the children's development during his absence. Some novel gifts for the children, including brands of sweets not found in NZ, proved a big hit and equally so, a framed photograph of the Cuillins for their parents.

'That was wonderful, Pam,' said Sean, hands on stomach. 'And that's the trouble with exercise, it makes you want to eat more and more! How about I give you a hand with the washing up?'

'Not tonight, Sean, it's your first night back so we'll give you a break. Besides, we've plenty of willing volunteers, haven't we, kids?'

Groans aside, the family began to clear up whilst Pam ushered Sean and Bryn through to the lounge, informing them that she'd be monitoring homework after the dishes were done.

Sean and Bryn sat facing each other in the armchairs set on each side of the fireplace. Sitting back, Sean sighed and said, 'Seems like I've never been away, Bryn. Well, tell me all that's been happening then.'

'Right, boyo. Quite a bit of water has gone under the bridge since you've been away. But I expect it's a certain person who you really want to know about?'

'Is it that obvious? You're right of course. I've never been able to get her out of my mind, despite being away. I saw her earlier on you know. It was when I was returning from the run. Met her at the bridge. My heart almost stopped beating for a moment. She had her wee girl Kirri with her. She looks as lovely as ever, Bryn. I won't kid you, all this business of me coming back to research a story, well there's a basis of truth in it all, but if Marama wasn't here I wouldn't be either. I think you know that.'

'I know. Well, Sean, things have moved on for Marama. She had a pretty hard time of it after you left. She continued to be pretty depressed and withdrawn almost up to the time she was having the baby. But after that and getting back to work, she seemed to be more settled and more like the old Marama we used to know. And she was always asking me if I'd heard from you and how you were getting on. That's why I kept saying to both of you to get in touch with each other. I used to get so vexed that you both obviously wanted to communicate but didn't feel it appropriate to do so.

But I should warn you, there is a man friend in her life. It's Michael Maitland, Rob's cousin. He's based in Dunedin at his father's offices but he's up here a lot of weekends and Marama would seem to be the main reason for that. I've heard that for the next couple of months he's going to be overseeing the Limeworks operation. So, he's going to be around even more. Can't say I know much about him but let's say he's a bit different to the other half of the Maitland family. I don't know how serious Marama is about him but I gather he's pretty keen on her.'

'I did meet him once. He was at the party that night. I didn't particularly take to him, but that was just first impressions.

'I wish you well, boyo. But look you, my Celtic intuition tells me that you should watch out for this fellow Maitland.'

14

Whilst her Nan was reading Kirri a bed-time story, Marama was walking Turi, her big collie, round the neighbouring field in the fading light. Her mind was totally occupied with meeting Sean and she remonstrated aloud with herself as she walked.

'Marama Te Kanawa, you are one silly bitch. What are you thinking about! Sean Campbell suddenly appears out of the blue and your heart starts thumping like that of a star-struck teenager. Why should you be so excited to see him now? Have you been kidding yourself all this time? You've regularly asked Bryn about him, but whenever he's suggested you contact Sean you've avoided doing so – telling yourself that it was merely a platonic interest and that you didn't want to imply anything else by getting in touch with him.'

Turi ran up to her and cocked his head, wondering who she was talking to, but a sudden rustling under the bushes near the fence had him bounding off to investigate.

'And when you got that card from Sean, what did you do? You sent one back with a photo of Kirri and yourself WITH ALL OUR LOVE! Why the photo? Why "with all our love"? Be

honest, you were wistfully thinking about Sean when you sent it, thinking about what might have been.

And now he's back. Is he back because of the card?

Don't be blooming stupid. You know why he's back. He's researching a story. It's a co-incidence, that's all.

But he told you he loved you and then he left because you told him to. Is it possible that he still loves you? The way he looked at you on the bridge. His eyes were telling you something.

I think your imagination has gone into overdrive, girl.

Jeez, Marama, you're getting yourself tied in knots.'

She lifted a stick as the dog ran towards her and heaved it over his head. She began walking back towards the house. Mentally she tried to get a grip of her emotions and look rationally at her situation. She'd got over Rob's death, she'd got over the trauma of the accident, she'd got over the shock of finding herself pregnant. She'd got over the memories of Sean, and especially of that night. No! That wasn't true. She'd made a conscious effort to try erasing such memories from her mind.

Now, with a beautiful and healthy child and a new relationship, life seemed to be securely planned ahead. Michael, the new man in her life, was tall, handsome and successful. Materially, she and Kirri would not want for anything if she wished the relationship to go further. And yet, was it the insecurity of being an unmarried mother – even in this new 70's decade – that had swayed her to linking up with Michael?

Things had loosened up a lot. There was a lot more tolerance and acceptance of single mothers than there had been in the recent past. For all that, small-town narrow-minded attitudes still existed. Her first priority, however, had always been Kirri. With her grandparents help, she had been able to continue working and thus provide for, and bring up her daughter in, a loving and caring environment. The Maitlands, of course, had wanted to be involved but she tried to keep her contact with them to a minimum.

And what about Sean Campbell? He was different to Michael in almost every way. Sean, the teacher, understanding and patient with the children in his care. Sean the colleague, slightly reserved but a good listener and possessing a quick wit - a great staff member to work with. Sean, the man, kind and caring. Sean, the lover – dare she think it – tender but passionate and fulfilling! God, he sounded like a bloody saint!

Her thoughts drifted to Michael. She recalled how at primary school she hadn't particularly liked him. He'd been three years older than her but in a small school environment she had seen plenty of him. As a young child he'd always demonstrated extreme confidence and high self- esteem. In pupil parlance he was considered a skite – a bit of a blow-hard. He'd also had quite a temper. Some of the children had been a bit afraid of him. Not that he'd ever bothered her. Then again with big brother Hemi around, he wouldn't have dared to try.

Michael hadn't attended Palmerston High, the local secondary school, like the rest of them. At the end of his primary education in Glenbeg, his parents, Grant and Diane, had moved to Dunedin where Grant had already developed a number of business interests. They'd sent

Michael to Fieldings College, the only private secondary school for boys in the town. This, Marama knew from her teacher training and university study days in Dunedin, was down to sheer snobbery, an attitude one couldn't attribute to the average sheep farmer in the Mataura valley. Unlike the UK, New Zealand state schools tended to outstrip their private counterparts in academic achievement. Yes, Michael was different. But as an adult he seemed to have changed. He was very attentive towards her but maybe a little too…what? Possessive? Yeah, possessive, that was true.

And now Sean was back and just a glimpse of him had old feelings stirring again. Not that, as far as she was aware, she'd intimated any of this when they'd met. She pictured him and smiled ruefully. Could Michael be compared with him? No chance!

Jeez, she could do without this, she thought. And, of course, there was the other thing deeply buried within her psyche. And she had resolved that it must remain there, unrevealed, hidden from all.

So, what should she do? At the moment there was nothing she could do. She would just wait and see how things developed. But she didn't want to be under pressure – from Michael or Sean. Kirri was always going to be her number one priority but, blow it, she also had to consider her life ahead. It was a question of making the right decisions. But at the moment she wasn't sure what these might be. Or was she?

Jack Maitland eased his six-foot-two and two hundred and twenty-four pound frame into the armchair rocker. The floor-to-ceiling window commanded a panoramic view of the homestead paddocks and the valley below, but with late twilight almost surrendered to darkness, the appearance of a twinkling star or two in the near cloudless sky heralded the advent of nightfall.

Further down the valley, lights gleamed in the homesteads around the village and smoke drifted lazily upwards from their chimneys. The scene was peaceful and exuded a sense of contentment. But despite the scene and the opulence that surrounded him, Maitland was far from being content. He reached out for the tumbler of single malt on the glass-topped table beside him. Taking a short gulp, he swilled the amber liquid around his mouth and swallowed. Stretching his legs out and crossing his feet, he nestled the tumbler on his stomach and tried to relax his shoulders whilst savouring the after-effects of the whisky.

With the stock all down from the high country, the wethers sold profitably off at the sales and the rest of the flock now on winter pasture, pressing work was done for the moment. He had had time over the past few days to reflect, to reminisce and to dwell on what might have been.

Life had been good for him, he had to concede. He'd built up the station from the modest holding started by his father, an emigrant from Ireland at the turn of the century. It hadn't been easy and he'd worked bloody hard. And sometimes he'd been pretty ruthless. Ruthless, yeah that was fair comment. Buying out small holdings and sometimes having to 'lean' a bit on the owners to achieve his own ends, did not allow for him to be sentimental or too caring. OK, he drove a hard bargain and pressed home the advantage where small-holders were struggling. But that, for God's-sake, was business. No, he didn't have any regrets on that score.

Julia. Now she was a regret. She had been his wife for the past thirty years. They still lived in the same house together but in separate bedrooms. Julia had been drinking fairly steadily before Rob's death, but afterwards she'd gone into a phase of serious drinking. Come to think of it, it was his womanising that had contributed to the widening gulf between them and probably caused her to get into the drinking habit. But he'd always taken the opportunity to get a leg over whenever the opportunity arose. It was something a fella did for God's sake. The shutters really came down between them when she discovered he'd had a regular thing over the years with Mary down at the pub. Almost a year ago, he'd tried to remonstrate with her about her excessive drinking. Her response had been a bitter verbal onslaught that had taken him quite aback. The depth of her feelings regarding his infidelity were, for the first time, fully revealed and railed against him. It was made clear to him that he was in no position to criticize or lecture her on what she chose to do or not do. And so, whilst continuing to live under the same roof and outwardly to demonstrate a husband-wife relationship, their lives had inexorably diverged. Civilities and even pleasantries were observed, but that was all.

Julia was still a fine-looking woman. Her statuesque figure could still turn heads at any social gathering. There were still occasions when he felt the need of her, but to him her bedroom door was now firmly shut, and locked.

And yet he'd noticed a change in her recently. What it was, he couldn't quite put his finger on. She seemed to be much more...what? Alert? Yeah, that was it, alert. Was she off the booze? Hard to tell. Mind you, that wasn't surprising, she was spending so much time up in bloody Oamaru with that sister of Gail Munro's. He hardly ever saw her. God, if he didn't know her better, he'd have suspected she was seeing another joker.

And his sons. What about them? They were like chalk and cheese in many ways. Poor old Vic, even as a kid he was an ugly looking little bugger. Rob had the looks and the personality, but give Vic his due he'd followed his older brother around like an adoring sheepdog. Now that Rob was gone, they didn't see too much of Vic. He came up for the occasional meal but if he wasn't working at the Limeworks or in the pub, he tended to stay put in the old homestead.

He sipped his drink and thought of Rob. A feeling of darkness and despair enshrouded him. Not a day went by when thoughts of Rob did not arise in his mind. God, he missed him. People would often comment on how alike his parents Rob seemed to be, but whilst he might have inherited their looks, on his father's side at least, he did not possess his ruthlessness and resolution. Yeah, everything had been a bit of a laugh as far as Rob was concerned. He could have made it big on the footie field too, with a bit of dedication, but not Robbo, he preferred a few pints and a sheila. A partiality for the sheilas was certainly one thing he'd inherited from his old man – and he didn't seem to have to chase them, they were always wanting to hang around him. And yet

Rob had surprised him, he'd picked Marama as the one he wanted to marry.

Now Marama, she was something else. Smart girl, school teacher, strong-willed. A bit lippy. Very attractive – if you like them slim and neat. Didn't think she'd have been Rob's type, or even that Rob would have been her type. And she was a Hori! Not that he was particularly prejudiced as far as Maoris were concerned. He had them working on the station at shearing times. And he had Joe Rattana keeping the rabbits down. They were good workers. But they were definitely different. Just too laid back. They didn't seem to value material things like the rest of us. Mind you, given Rob's outlook, you'd have thought he was the bloody Maori and Marama the pakeha!

And now there was Kirri, his first grandchild. A beautiful kid and bright and lively, and half- Maori! He frowned and thought, I don't see enough of her. Apart from Julia picking her up from Marama's on a Sunday afternoon, or Marama dropping her off, that's it. She's never actually stayed with us.

His mind drifted and made the link to the bit of land around the ancient Maori burial site. He'd up till now grazed stock on it and considered it his land. He was planning to go into partnership with his brother whose company currently ran the local Limeworks. They'd discovered further limestone- rich land in Hidden Valley, part of the extensive Maitland station and just a couple of miles beyond Jack's homestead. It was an ideal location for further quarrying. An application had been made to extend the company's mining rights to this area. But there had been an anonymous tip-off from someone in planning that there might be a problem with access, given the fact that their planned route ran through part of the old burial site. This rang warning bells in Jack's mind. He thought a diplomatic visit to old Tama Te Kanawa, as the senior Maori elder in the vicinity, might be an astute move.

His mind turned in another direction. He thought of his daughter Annette, off with her mother to check out a flat in Dunedin. She was due to start with Grant in a week's time. She'd been at boarding school over the past five years and he was used to her comings and goings ,but it suddenly struck him that in the future he was going to be left knocking about in this huge house more and more on his own – just like tonight. Yeah, Annette was some girl and no mistake. And some looker. He couldn't imagine her living the life of a nun in Dunedin. But what young sheila would?

He threw back what was left of the malt. As he placed the glass back on the table, he thought of his visit to the pub earlier in the evening. With Julia and Annette not due back from Dunedin until tomorrow, he'd decided to pop down to the pub for a couple of jars. He'd run into Vic and learned that the guy Campbell was back. He thought back to the accident and he thought back to the funeral when he'd told the bastard to piss off. Well, it looked like he'd not got the message clearly. A bit of a reminder might just do the trick and he had a few options about who he could get to deliver the message.

Sean switched off the lamp and pulling the covers up to his

chin, stretched out and gazed at the darkened ceiling. It had been a long day. A very long four days in fact since he'd left his mother's house in Applecross. Incredible to think that he was now twelve thousand miles away on the other side of the world.

He was tired, but his mind kept returning to the meeting with Marama and her little daughter on the bridge. Mentally he tried to replay the sequence of events, recall her words and search in her responses for any tone or nuance that might gauge her feelings towards him, or for him. But he couldn't. Gradually his thoughts became more muddled. For a few moments he hung on to semi-wakefulness. And then he slept. Heavily.

15

'Hello, what can I get you?' smiled the attractive blonde waitress as she approached Sean's table.

'A large hot chocolate please,' responded Sean, 'along with three of your delicious cheese rolls. You know it's nearly three years since I've last been in kiwiland and I've never come across cheese rolls anywhere else, leastways not like they're done here.'

'What, not even in bonnie Scotland?' asked the girl teasingly.

'Especially not in Scotland,' he replied with a grin and added, 'the accent's not that obvious is it?'

'Oh, maybe jist a wee bittie,' she answered, putting on her best Scottish impersonation.

'You've been watching too much Dr Findlay,' he laughed.

'Be right with you,' she smiled again as she moved off to the counter thinking, he's a bit of alright.

Sean looked out onto George Street and the passing traffic and pedestrians. The Troubador, near to the university and popular with students and other academics, was one of his favourite coffee bars. It didn't appear to have changed much since his last visit. At nine thirty in the morning, it was relatively quiet. He was due to meet a Professor Parata, his first point of contact in the taiaha research, at the Otago Museum at ten fifteen.

The waitress arrived with a steaming mug of hot chocolate and equally hot-looking cheese rolls. 'There you are, Dr Findlay,' she said mimicking Janet the housekeeper in the popular TV series. 'Enjoy!'

'Thank you, Janet. I will indeed,' laughed Sean. The cheese rolls looked as delectable as he remembered them. I wonder, he thought, why no-one's produced these in the UK, as he leant over his plate to bite into one of the cylindrically shaped toasted sandwiches. These were created by rolling extremely thin slices of bread spread with specially selected cheese and toasted sufficiently to have the cheese hot and melting its way through the delicate bread walls.

The late breakfast satisfyingly filled a gap in the inner man. Wiping his fingers and mouth, Sean put down the napkin, drained his mug of hot chocolate and went over to the counter to pay the bill. 'That was great,' he said to the girl. 'I will return soon!'

'Glad you enjoyed it, Dr Findlay,' she said, curtseying. 'Just don't make it three years till the next time.'

'That's a promise,' he laughed, as he headed for the door.

There was the threat of rain in the air when he'd arrived in Dunedin on this grey April's morning. He'd found a meter-free park just one hundred yards from the museum and then headed up to George Street, hoping The Troubador would still be there. Now he pulled up his collar, checked his watch and stepped out briskly. He was in good time. He cut down Frederick Street, entering the university campus area, a mixture of academic buildings old and new and countless old wooden bungalows and villas that inevitably had been converted into flats for student accommodation. A cold easterly wind had funnelled its way up from the harbour and was busily adding to the already fallen leaves whirling and dancing over the tree-lined verges.

Sean had allowed himself a couple of days to get over the jet-lag, re-explore the surrounding countryside and sort out his plans for following up on the taiaha story. He had continued with his training runs up to the Limeworks late each afternoon, hoping to catch sight of Marama again but failing to come across her. Bryn had invited him to come over to the school and meet up with the pupils, but he'd thought it prudent to pass on the invitation for the moment. He believed that he needed to give Marama time to get used to the idea he was around and was hoping, hope against hope, that she might take a step towards renewing their friendship, perhaps inviting him round to meet Tama and Mere.

In the museum foyer, he studied the two supporting figures on the wall-mounted coat of arms. He wondered if the sombre expressions on the faces of the kilted Scottish settler and the Maori chief in his traditional costume were due to the seriousness with which they regarded the sentiments expressed below their feet – "MAIOREM INSTITUTIS UTENDO" .... By following in the Steps of our Forefathers.

'Ah, the noble savage and his new partner. What a story that tells us!'

Sean turned to the speaker. A handsome and athletic-looking Maori who appeared to be in his early forties, stood behind him, arms folded across his chest. The dark blue suit, white shirt and sky-blue tie complimented his appearance.

Sean looked inquiringly and asked, 'Professor Parata?'

'Indeed,' Parata smiled. Tupe to my friends, Maori and Pakeha alike. You are Sean Campbell, I take it? Tena koe, Sean.'

'Ciamara tha thu, Tupe,' replied Sean.

It was the professor's turn to look puzzled. Sean smiled and added, 'It's Gaelic, my native language.'

'Ah,' said Parata as understanding dawned, 'then we have things in common. Perhaps like the two on the coat of arms there?'

Sean looked up at the two-dimensional emblem on the wall. 'Well,' he said, 'I come as a humble pupil seeking knowledge from an expert.'

'I like it,' laughed Tupe. 'Come, Sean, my office is this way. He led Sean at a brisk pace along a corridor sign-posted 'Staff Only' which ran off the main foyer area. He stopped at a door with a brass plaque that read, 'Professor T Parata, Polynesian and South Pacific Studies.' Opening the door, he beckoned Sean to follow and waved him to a seat facing a desk that looked remarkably tidy and free of clutter.

Parata laughed as he took in Sean's gaze, 'Tidied up just for you. Wanted to make an impression. I take it your desk looks just like this?'

'You must be joking,' retorted Sean.

'OK, Sean, down to business. But take your coat off and sling it onto that peg on the door.' Taking off his own jacket and fitting it around the back of his chair, Tupe sat down and leant over, elbows on the desk. 'Oh, would you like a coffee or tea just now?'

'I've just had something, thanks.'

'Tell you what, we'll have a chat and later on take a break in the canteen. I've left the rest of this morning free and will try to give you as much information as possible. Now, I got the gist of what you're after when you sent your letter from Scotland, but how about filling me in a bit firstly on this story you have, before I give you what I've discovered to date?'

'Sounds fine,' replied Sean. He then commenced to tell Tupe Parata about the adventures of Calum, starting from the point where old Murdo came to Sean's home in Applecross.

Leaning back in his seat Tupe listened, entranced. When Sean drew to an end, Tupe shook his head. 'What a fascinating story. I can see how this has the makings of a novel for you, perhaps a little different to your most recent one,' he chuckled.

'You've read one of my books! I'm surprised.'

'Well, knowing you were coming I thought it prudent to learn a bit about you. Seemed like a good idea to read one of your novels. In fact, I enjoyed the first one so much that I went out and bought the second one.'

'I'm delighted and impressed. Yes, this potential story would be a bit different. But a blend of fact and fiction certainly could suggest a lot of possibilities.'

'And tell me, have you got the taiaha head with you?'

'I've got it right here.' Sean bent down to lift up the brief-case he'd leant against a desk leg. He carefully took out the carving he'd wrapped in a small hand towel and handed it to Tupe.

The professor handled it gently. Studying it carefully he said, 'This is impressive. This is a work of art and quite old. I would like to spend some time studying it with my colleagues. Would it be possible for you to leave it with me?'

'Of course. I fully expected to do so. You're welcome to hold onto it as long as you choose. Remember, it's old Calum's wish that ultimately it be returned to somewhere, or someone, appropriate. I've accomplished the first step in bringing it back to New Zealand. Hopefully you'll be able to locate a suitable home for it, whether that be your museum or elsewhere. And if you can provide some background for me in doing so, that'll be great. Otherwise,' Sean smiled, 'I'll have to resort to literary licence, a regular indulgence by we purveyors of fiction.'

'Excellent. Excellent,' said Tupe. 'Now, with regards to your original questions. Here's what I've managed to find out:

............Palmerston came into existence as a camp site in 1862 as the beginning of a route via the Waihemo Valley to the Central Otago gold diggings. It was not actually officially named as such until 1864. As you perhaps already know, archaeological digs give conclusive evidence that settlement around the Waihemo estuary goes way back to the time of the Moa hunters. But there has been Maori settlement near the river estuary over the past few hundred years. It is believed that the peoples would have greatly depended upon the rich sources of fish and shell fish that the coast afforded. And, seasonally, they would have ventured inland to hunt duck and fresh-water fish. They would also have made longer excursions to the west coast to collect the much-prized greenstone, pounamu, which they traded with visiting tribes from the north.'

Warming to his subject, the professor continued, 'In the early nineteenth century, coastal Maori worked with whalers and, indeed, intermarried. And there was an established kainga, or village, a mile or so from the river mouth at the time your countryman stopped here with his mining partner. There's no reason to doubt that the event took place just as he says. But whilst there are a few fishermen's homes near the site of the old village and the local meeting house is still used by the community, I haven't been able to find any record of the event. I did travel up there to interview a couple of old folk who were born in the 1880's, but they couldn't recall any story about the incident.'

Seeing Sean's look of disappointment, Tupe lifted his hand, 'But wait a minute, they did mention a Tama Te Kanawa whose home is in Glenbeg as being the best authority on local history. That's where your staying isn't it?'

'Tama!' exclaimed Sean.

'You know him?'

'I know him very well. In fact, he's a close friend. But I haven't come across him since I arrived back last week.'

'Well, maybe your answers are much closer to home

than you thought. When I tried to get hold of him, I was told he was over at Milford Sound crayfishing.'

'Well, I'll be blowed. I did meet Tama's grand-daughter the other day and she said he was due back from the west coast any day soon. I'll certainly look him up.'

'Hopefully he might know something of the incident.'

'What about the chief. If he had died, surely there would be some record of this? And where would he have been buried?'

'Well, first of all, we don't know if he did die. It's also possible that he didn't come from the area and was perhaps visiting friends or relatives. At that time, burials tended to take place on a headland site quite close to the river mouth. Centuries before, I believe that high-ranking dead were sometimes buried in caves near Glenbeg, but I have not visited that site.'

'I know the place. Tama had mentioned it to me before. He said it's a tapu area. It's on land owned by one of the farmers I believe.'

'That's rather strange. Huge amounts of land were bought up by the government from the nineteenth century onwards. In fact, the colonial government insisted Maori land could only be sold to the Crown, and they then sold it on to the settlers at a substantial profit – but that's another story and one which I've got a bee in my bonnet about. But what I meant to say is, that the selling of any land sites that were sacred or tapu just wouldn't have happened. The Maori elders would have been adamant about that and the Crown would have had to go along with it. I'd be surprised if the particular piece of land you are talking about would have been part and parcel of the land deal at the time.'

'That's interesting. I must ask Tama what the story over the ownership is. I expect he'll know. But listen, I fully understand why you'll have a "bee in your bonnet" over land issues. I'm under no illusions as to what the British colonial powers got up to in the past – I've studied a bit of history. And I know fine that the Maori people, like other indigenous folk, would have been taken to the cleaners where the purchase of land was concerned.'

'Look, Sean, it's just after eleven. Let's go over to the canteen and grab a cup of coffee. We can continue our conversation there.'

As they climbed the stairs leading to the first floor where the café and restaurant were located, Tupe continued, 'You know, the whole business of Maori land ownership is a mess. Illegal sales of land in the past have to be looked at. There is a growing concern, particularly amongst our young educated and socially aware Maori, that this subject is not being addressed forcefully enough. But I believe this issue is something that is going to grow and grow in the years to come. I've a cousin who is a lawyer up north and is very much involved in investigating rights of ownership. He's going to be in Dunedin next week. If you like, I'll ask him about the Glenbeg burial site.'

'Yeah. Thanks. I'd be interested to know about that, Tupe.'

The two resumed their chat over cappuccinos. Their conversation ranged from Maori culture and its future in twentieth century New Zealand to the way their personal careers had developed and their hopes and aspirations for the future. Each found a natural rapport with the other.

Shortly after twelve o'clock, Tupe stood up. 'Sean, it's been great meeting you. I hope we will meet again soon. Keep persevering with this story research. I'm sure you'll learn more in due course. I'd be delighted to see you any time you happen to be in town. And thank you for bringing the taiaha back to Aotearoa.'

'That's very kind of you, Tupe. You've been a big help and given me quite a few leads to follow up on. It's been a real pleasure meeting you. I will keep in touch. Good-bye for now,' said Sean warmly shaking the professor's hand.

'Haere ra, Sean. Haere ra.'

16

At around one forty-five, Julia placed her shopping alongside the case in the boot of her Mini and laid the colourful bouquet carefully on top. Closing the lid, she then took off her coat, climbed into the car and laid the coat on the passenger seat. Glancing up at the rear vision mirror she smiled approvingly. At fifty-four still looking not too bad, she thought. And she felt good, really good, far better than she'd felt for years. She'd always been pretty fastidious about her appearance, apart from the bad dark times that followed Rob's death. But they were all behind her now. New horizons had opened up!

She pushed the gearstick into first, signalled and pulled out from the kerb. A makeover at the hairdresser's and a quick bit of shopping completed, she was on her way this Friday afternoon to Oamaru, the blustery wind and grey skies failing to dampen her high spirits. As she crossed the thirty speed limit, she accelerated and rapidly left the town of Palmerston behind her. She was excited. The opportunity for a new challenge lay ahead and after much thought she'd decided she was going to go for it. Much thought? That was not really true. Having the chance of a new motivation and sense of purpose in her life didn't take much deliberating over. And, by God, she was going to take it.

Briefly she thought of Jack. She wondered how he would react. Did she feel guilty at not having discussed anything with him? Not bloody likely. When did he last show any interest in what she was doing, where she was going or what she thought? A marriage of convenience is what they had – very bloody convenient for Jack bloody Maitland, that is. But things were going to change and change in a big way.

She'd first met Jack when she was working part-time in her parents' florist shop in Dunedin and studying at the Art College. He'd been very attentive way back then and very randy. She'd managed to fob him off during their early dates but it wasn't long before she succumbed to his passion and seemingly insatiable sexual appetite. Twenty-four year old Jack, good-looking, cocky and confident, swept her off her feet. His weekend trips down from the sheep farm to Dunedin proved insufficient for both of them. Much to her parents' disappointment, Julia packed in her college course, married Jack and set up home on the farm. Jack's father was ready to sit back, enjoy his wife's baking and let his son build on the success he had made of the farm from his own labours. He handed over the reins to the ambitious Jack who had plans to greatly increase the amount of land and stock.

And yes, she had to admit, Jack had certainly developed the sheep station into one of the biggest in the South Island. He'd bought out other small-holders, introduced more stock, taken advice from Ministry of Agriculture experts and become extremely successful and correspondingly wealthy. And during that time, she had borne him three children and fulfilled the role of the sheep station wife – feeding hungry gangs at shearing times, tending to the needs of her growing children, socializing with other farmers' wives and attending agricultural functions and social events. But it all seemed to be one-way traffic. The person she had been before had all but vanished. She never seemed to have time in these early days for herself. There didn't seem to be any time to rekindle or cultivate any of her previous interests such as her art work. And no-one, least of all Jack, gave her any encouragement to do so. She was the wife and there to satisfy Jack's needs and ego. Oh, she still had retained her looks and would draw envious stares at the annual Farmers' Ball in Dunedin. She looked good on Jack's arm as he proudly showed her off. But she more and more came to realize that, perhaps unwittingly, Jack was regarding her as a prized possession or trophy, which he undoubtedly loved in his own way but saw in the same light as a prize heifer or highly priced ram.

Yes, there had been good times, good family times, with the kids and with Jack. She'd always known that Jack had an eye for the women but it had still come as a shock to her when just after the birth of Rob she became aware that he was sleeping around. When confronted he'd just laughed and said it was a 'fella thing' and nothing serious. She'd warned him that she'd leave him if it happened again and he had promised to mend his ways. In the end he hadn't, but by that time Vic had arrived and with the children's needs to attend to she knew she wouldn't leave, couldn't leave. But

Jack Maitland lost something of her then and lost more in the years that followed.

With the boys grown up and Annette off to boarding school, Julia began to feel aimless. That's when the serious drinking had started. The afternoon tipples increased both in measure and quantity. With Rob's death, her drinking seemed to go into over-drive. If it hadn't been for Gail Munro, God knows how she might have ended up. It was Gail who'd got her to spend time in Oamaru with her sister Rose. Rose had her own florist business there and had got Julia involved in helping her. It took Julia back to the time that she used to work in her own parents' flower shop in Dunedin. She'd always enjoyed working there. Rose had said she was a natural. And it was true that she'd an eye for arranging and floral decoration.

As she arrived in Oamaru and headed for Rose's house she smiled and spoke out loud, 'Gail, what would I have done without you? You got me through the bad times and introduced me to a wonderful new friend in Rosemary. And at fifty-four I've now got the chance of a new life!'

When Sean left the museum, he had gone back to the Troubador for a light snack. The friendly waitress was no longer on duty. As he left the café, a watery sun was doing its best to glint through the clouds. The wind had not lessened, however, and he met up with it at each of the intersections as he strode along George Street. He smiled with appreciation as he noted old familiar land marks, the sign depicting the wee guy on horseback above the Arthur Barnett department store, The Little Hut and other various cafes popular with university and senior high school students. When he arrived at the town's unique centre point, the Octagon, he stopped to identify further landmarks – the massive frontage of the Town Hall, the Octagon and Regent cinemas, the Star fountain and the statue of Rabbie Burns significantly positioned with its back to the imposing Anglican church and, of course, facing across to the Oban pub below. Sean smiled and said to himself, 'Aye, Rab, you're facing the right direction but I'll bet you'd be just a wee bit proud of the fact that your nephew Thomas Burns was Dunedin's first minister!'

He cut across Princes Street and over to the Octagon cinema. Passing it, he moved up Stuart Street and then took a left walking down Upper Moray Place until he arrived at the Public Library. He checked his watch. He had about forty minutes to kill before his next appointment.

As Julia Maitland was heading out of Palmerston, Sean Campbell was entering the premises of the ODT, the Otago Daily Times, Dunedin's daily morning paper. There he was due to meet with Bill Speirs, a retired sub-editor who on a part-time basis dealt with the newspaper's archives and filing sector. He had written to the newspaper offices before leaving for New Zealand, briefly explaining that he was coming over to research material for a novel and to say he would telephone to request access to their files after he arrived. He'd phoned the previous week and been put in touch with Bill Speirs. An appointment had been arranged and when Bill asked him if there was anything he wished him to locate before then, Sean said he'd be interested in any material relating to an incident in Palmerston in 1862, concerning a certain Irish prospector known as Beardie O'Neill. He also asked for verification that a ship called "The Isa" had been in port that year.

Sean crossed the foyer to the girl at the reception counter. 'Hello, I'm Sean Campbell. I've an appointment to see Mr Bill Spiers.'

She smiled pleasantly and pointed to a figure stretched out on an easy chair just to the right of the entrance way. 'That's him. It's a wonder he doesn't wake himself up with his snoring. Hey Bill, wake up! There's someone to see you.'

Bill opened his eyes. 'Wasn't sleepin', Suzie, just restin' the old peepers,' croaked the near horizontal figure. Clearing his throat and getting up stiffly from the armchair, he hobbled over to greet Sean. 'Sean Campbell, g'day mate, a pleasure to meet you,' said the burly and grizzled news veteran stretching out his hand.

Shaking his hand Sean responded, 'Hi there, Bill, but how did you recognize me?'

'Well apart from hearing you give your name to Suzie – see, Suzie, I wasn't dead to the world – I've read your books and your picture's on the back. Bloody good read too, I might add.'

'Thank you.'

'Come on, boy, I'll take you up to the library and see what we can find. Suzie, see if someone will rustle us up some coffee. Oh, and some fancy biscuits wouldn't go amiss.'

'They will if they go anywhere near your belly, Bill Speirs,' quipped the girl laughingly.

'Cheeky sheila,' said Bill. 'Just can't get decent staff these days, Sean. See what I have to put up with.'

'Don't you believe it, Sean,' said Suzie. 'We spoil him rotten.'

Bill led the way upstairs to the Library and Archives room. Sean was surprised at the size of the room. As the sun was on the other side of the building, the room was comparatively dark despite the light coming in from the three large casement windows overlooking the street below. Bill flicked on a light switch which brought the room into greater detail. Whilst its dark wood-panelled walls would have given it an air of dignity and history in the past, much of this was now hidden. Shelving units projecting from the left-hand wall and separated by access aisles, were stacked with labelled box files. An extensive reference section occupied the shelving on the remainder of the wall opposite the doorway. And in front of the windows, two long mahogany tables, around which half a dozen chairs were scattered, gleamed under the strip lighting.

Sean noted some folders and rather ancient looking newspapers at the far end of one of the tables. Bill motioned him in that direction, 'Take a seat, Sean. I've got some stuff to show you, but firstly let's hear your story to date. Suzie will arrive any minute with the coffee. You mentioned in your letter to me that it's got something to do with an old seaman fella from your part of the world.'

'Thanks, Bill,' said Sean depositing his briefcase on the floor and putting his coat around a chair back. Pulling the seat out, he sat back, legs out-stretched and arms folded. Bill sat himself down on the other side of the table. Sean once again told his tale of Calum's adventure.

'Strewth, that's a helluva story,' said Bill shaking his head when Sean finished.

'It certainly is,' added Suzie who'd appeared with the coffee and biscuits, filled the cups and then, sucked into Sean's account, had ended up perched on a nearby chair listening to the rest of the tale. 'But is it really true. Did this all really happen?'

'Even if it didn't, it's the basis for a great yarn,' said Bill.

'I agree with you,' said Sean. But it's all totally true, as far as I know. I was given the taiaha head by Calum's nephew and I've left it with Professor Parata at the museum. And I suppose it's especially believable as it's a confession really. Old Calum kept this event to himself all of his life, and so did Murdo for that matter. Obviously, I can see some possibilities for a new novel but I'd really like to follow up on the story and see what else I can find out.'

'Spoken like a true newspaper man!' said Bill. 'Investigative journalism, it's in my blood and I think it's in yours too.'

'Your wife says it's not blood but black news ink that runs through your veins,' said Suzie getting up. 'That was really interesting, Sean. Hope you didn't mind me staying to listen.'

'Not at all, Suzie, but maybe you could keep the story to yourself in the meantime. If it reaches the book stage, I'll send you copy, if you want it!'

'That would be great. Thanks Sean. I'd better get

downstairs. Mag's will be wondering where I am.'

'Right, Sean. Down to business. You'll see I've collected some material for you that I hope will be relevant. First let me say, I haven't come across any articles relating to your incident, but I haven't gone through everything with a fine tooth-comb. When you wrote to me from Scotland, you did say that the period you were interested in was January, 1862. Our own paper commenced production in 1861 and we've also got copies of The Otago Witness, a weekly that began about ten years before us. So, what I've done is located all the editions for that month. The first half are all already on microfilm and you'll find it on that table by the door with the viewer. We've begun to put archive material on microfilm but it's going to be a long process which I doubt I'll see the end of. The rest of the news sheets are beside you. I've also had a friend check out the shipping records for me and there's a list there you can keep. It's of ship arrivals, departures, cargoes etc. And, don't worry, the Isa is there alright!

'Now, don't despair if there's no record of the event up Palmerston way. Remember there's a lot of stuff relating to gold discovery around MacRaes Flat that might be useful.

'That's great, Bill. It'll give me a fuller picture to work on. But surely there might be some record of the event. What about Beardie's body, if he was indeed dead?'

'Chances are he was dead, Sean, otherwise he would definitely have been discovered and maybe able to give a damning report on the old Maori, or even his partner. Could be that the Maoris came back, removed his body and buried it somewhere. Look at it from their perspective, it wouldn't have been wise to report anything to the authorities. Don't think they'd have been too trustful of the pakeha believing their side of the story. I think it would have been in their interests to dispose of Beardie. As for the tent and equipment, it wouldn't have been of any interest to them. But remember, prospectors and opportunists would have been passing through this area all of the time. Someone would be bound to walk off with anything that seemed to be abandoned. OK, boy, it's all yours. Take your time and have fun!'

'Many thanks, Bill. I'd like a couple of hours if that's alright?

'No problem. You can come in here any time you like. Just say I okayed it.'

'You're a champ.'

'No worries. I know you'll want to keep your investigation under wraps for now, but this would be a great human interest story for the readers, so keep it in mind. I'd also like to do a full feature on Sean Campbell, Scottish novelist and rising star in crime writing. Would you be up for that in the near future?'

'Least I can do after all your help. Will ring you when I'm next coming down and do it then if you like.'

'Good-oh. I'm for offski.' With a vigorous handshake Bill ambled off.

Sean took out a notepad and got down to business.

17

It was getting on for five o'clock when Sean left the ODT. He had planned to look up Alex MacRae, a distant cousin of his father's, who lived in Mornington, and then travel up to Glenbeg. When he had phoned from the newspaper offices, however, it transpired that Alex and his wife were not at home. Sean therefore decided to drop into the Criterion Hotel to see if there were any of his former football acquaintances around. Although it was the football season, he was aware that there was an inter-provincial game on the following day which meant that there would be no local club games played and therefore the possibility that one or two might have dropped into the pub for a beer.

He entered the Criterion's public bar to a hubbub of noise and laughter. Friday evening, he knew, was the end of the week for the majority of kiwi workers. He also remembered that with shops closed over the weekend, Friday night shopping went on until nine o'clock. Many office and factory workers endeavoured to finish at five sharp and to adjourn to their favourite watering holes for a jug or two before heading home. Through the haze of smoke, Sean suddenly spotted two familiar faces in conversation.

Making for the tall table they were standing at, their jug of lager and glasses sitting atop, he placed a hand upon the shoulder of each and exclaimed, 'Well I'll be blowed, only in kiwiland will you see a Glasgow Rangers and Celtic supporter drinking in harmony. Hullo the Glasgow Keelies!'

'Seanie Boy, I thought you'd buggered off back to the Heilan's of Scotland,' said Andy Bell shaking Sean's hand, a welcoming smile upon his rugged face.

'Sean Man!' acknowledged Alec MacKay, the second fellow Scot, 'Great to see you. You're looking good. That west coast snow and pissing rain must agree with you. How's life?'

'Doing great, boys. Just arrived back in NZ last week. I've got a wee assignment that's taken me back to Glenbeg. Was down here on business today and thought I'd pop in on the off chance of seeing some of the old team. And I couldn't have met up with anyone older than you two reprobates.'

'You cheeky young bugger. Alec, put the heid on him while I go and get another jug. A drouth like him and our jug won't last five minutes,' said Andy moving off towards the bar.

'I thought you guys would be playing for Otago tomorrow,' said Sean, recalling the skill and strength of the ex- Dumbarton and Queen's Park players.

'Nah. Andy and I are still playing for Southern but we've retired from the provincial scene. It's up to the younger ones to take their chances now. We've had a good run.'

'Well, I'm sure you could both be holding down your positions there if you wanted to.'

'Aye, maybe Sean. But we're quite happy. Anyway, what

about you. You're famous! The wife's read both your books and says they're great. She can't wait till Kiwi telly shows your serial. You must be very proud, son.'

Andy returned with a full jug and another glass. The trio toasted each other and spent the ensuing hour catching up on news and reminiscing. Both were interested to learn about Sean's reason for returning to NZ. Sean played things pretty low key but did say there was a story he was researching that could well provide material for a further novel

'So, what are your plans for the weekend?' Andy asked.

'Nothing really. I'm just down for the day and will head back up tonight.'

'But you don't need to be back?'

'No.'

'Why the hell didn't you give us a phone?' said Andy. Cara will be wanting to see you. And hey, there's a dance on tomorrow night. You can stay with us and come out to the do. How about it?'

'Och, I'm not going to impose.'

'Listen to him Alec,' said Andy with a wink. 'The bugger "imposed" on us plenty before when he was down in the big smoke looking for talent. What d'you reckon?'

'Great idea. You got any other gear with you, Sean?'

'As a matter of fact, I do. Coming down to Dunedin I always sling some extra clothes into the car just in case. But I still don't want to put Cara out.'

'Listen to yourself! You're not putting anyone out – you'll be sleeping on the bloody floor anyway.'

'Suits me.'

'Settled then. I'll away and phone her to expect you.'

As Andy made for the foyer, Alec said, 'That's grand, Sean. The folk'll be delighted to see you, well the women anyway. I think Liz has got a secret yen for you.'

'Aye, that'll be right,' laughed Sean.

As they left the pub Sean informed Andy he just had a couple of messages to get before heading up to the house. After a quick visit to the off-licence and then to the shops to purchase chocolates for Cara and some sweets for the children, Sean drove out to the beach suburb of St Clair and up the hill to the Bell's home. He parked beside Andy's Volkswagen and as he climbed out was warmly greeted by Cara, carrying two-year old George and accompanied by five-year old daughter Jill.

Rosemary took the cigarette out of her mouth as a car horn gave three sharp blasts, 'Julia,' she yelled, 'that'll be Merv. Come on girl, shake a leg.'

'Coming,' called Julia as she gave her reflection in the hall mirror a final appraisal and headed for the front door. 'Right, Rose, that's me off. Shouldn't be late, but don't wait up.'

'You lucky sheila. A meal out tonight and another one tomorrow,' exclaimed Rosemary from her chair by the fireside. 'And with the best- looking fella in town! Now don't do anything I wouldn't do!'

'That gives me a pretty free hand. Anyway, must dash. See you.'

'Have a good time, girl,' said Rose waving her half-smoked cigarette in the air. The door slammed and Rose smiled to herself. Turning to the large Persian cat hunched up beside the hearth she whispered, 'What d'ya reckon, Puskas?'

As Julia came down the veranda steps, Mervyn MacLean got out of the Holden estate and came round to open the passenger door. 'Hi, Julia, how are ya? You're lookin' great.'

'Thanks, Merv, you're not looking too dusty yourself.' And as she drew nearer, she sniffed, 'And is that Old Spice? I'm honoured!'

'Always try to impress my clients,' laughed Merv closing the door. Climbing into the driver's seat and putting the column stick into first he swung the car round to face the way he'd come in. 'Right, we're off to La Boheme, the new restaurant out by the Kurow road. It's supposed to be really good. So how was the run up?'

'Good. Not too busy,' smiled Julia glancing at the profile of the handsome banker. 'What about yourself, busy day?'

'Yeah, not too bad. Typical Friday, getting things tidied up before the weekend. Anyway. What's the verdict? I'm dying to know!'

'Well, Mr MacLean, we don't want to rush things. Let's wait till we get our table,' said Julia smiling.

'God, woman, you've had two bloody weeks to think about it. At least tell me you've reached a decision.'

'I've reached a decision, Merv.'

'Well at least I'm going to know one way or another.'

Five minutes later they were seated at a table for two, tucked neatly and cosily in a window alcove of the new restaurant. A gently flickering candle placed inside a translucent cream vase added to the cosiness of their table location. Taking out his spectacles, Merv began to peruse the menu.

'Lovely place, Merv,' said Julia approvingly as she took in the surroundings. The large room was beginning to fill up with customers. The tables were strategically placed to allow the diners space and privacy. Through the chatter and laughter, Julia could hear the light strains of Moon River and spotted its source, a pianist at a grand piano positioned just inside an archway on the far side of the room.

'You not going to look at that menu, girl?' Merv asked.

'No, Mr MacLean, I'm leaving it to you to choose for both of us.'

'Well, you might be taking a chance,' grinned Mervyn as he nodded towards the dining room manager who winked and waved to a young waiter. In seconds the waiter appeared at their table with an ice bucket and stand. He lifted out the champagne for Mervyn's approval. Given the go-a-head he deftly opened the bottle and filled both their glasses with the bubbly.

'Why, Mervyn, this is a surprise. That stuff is expensive! Just what are we celebrating here?'

'That's for you to tell and for me to find out. But, what the hell, if it's not a celebration you've gotta admit, it's going to be commiseration with style. So, what's it to be, Julia?

18

It was just before half past eight on Saturday evening when Andy, Cara and Sean were dropped off at the Zingaree clubrooms by Peter, the boyfriend of their baby sitter. Although it was the soccer league's annual dance, it was the large rugby club venue that had been hired for the event. Everyone was in high spirits, these being aided by the fact that the Otago provincial team had soundly thrashed their arch rivals Canterbury by four goals to nil.

When they entered the hall, they could see the dance was in full swing. Alec MacKay popped up in front of them and said, 'Right, folks, got a table and seats booked for you all. There's Liz waving for you. Cara, you take Sean over and introduce him while Andy helps me get the next round in. Don't worry, Seanie boy, there's a kitty. We'll be raiding that Highland sporran of yours shortly.'

As Sean followed Cara over, he had a feeling of déjà vu. A female vocalist, Maori by the look of her, was belting out Georgie Girl. And she was good – not any better than Marama, but definitely good.

Cara and Alec's wife Liz, had just finished introducing

Sean to the rest of the folk at the table, some of whom he'd met before, when Andy and Alec arrived back with the drinks. The band had just finished a Seekers bracket and a minute later launched into Credence Clearwater's Bad Moon Rising. The dance floor was suddenly mobbed. Liz grabbed Sean and pulled him on to the floor before he had time to take a mouthful of his whisky. But the few drams he'd had back at Bell's had put him in the mood. With all and sundry he was soon shaking and swaying.

A good hour and a half of dancing, drinking, chatting and reminiscing flew by before the band stopped and announced to one and all that supper was served in the adjacent room. Folks went through in groups to pile their plates with a huge assortment of mouth-watering eats and then take them back to their tables in the main hall.

Sean was just lifting a chicken leg onto his plate when a familiar voice exclaimed, 'Sean! What are you doing here?'

'Marama! I could ask you the same thing,' replied Sean, initially surprised but, emboldened by drink, not abashed about replying. 'I didn't think soccer was your and Michael's thing.'

Marama flushed slightly, realizing that Sean was aware of her association with Michael Maitland. Just at that moment Maitland appeared on the scene holding a plate in one hand but proprietorially putting his free one around Marama's waist. 'Sean, what a surprise. How are you, and how do you come to be here?'

'I was just asking Marama the same question, Michael. I ran into some football friends yesterday in town and they insisted I stay for the weekend. And here I am.'

'Soccer friends, Sean. Football here means rugby. Anyway, come on Marama, there's someone very important in the business world I want you to meet.'

Rather to Sean's surprise, Marama gave him a quick smile and dutifully allowed Maitland to lead her off.

'Who was that prick, Sean?' asked Andy who'd been standing just behind him and observed the exchanges. 'And more importantly, who was the wee honey you were talking to? She's a real cracker. And I tell you, your Uncle Andy observed some electricity there, and it wasn't between big po face and the wee lassie.'

'I wish,' said Sean.

'Come on, Seanie boy,' that guy's no competition to someone like you. Hell, if I wasn't married to Cara I'd fancy you ma'sel,' laughed Andy, lightly punching him on the shoulder.

Sean smiled, 'Well, much as I like you Mr Bell……' and laughing, both headed back to join the others.

As the evening wore on the band, a local group called the Playboys, varied the numbers switching from some really live wire stuff to a few slow smoochie dances. A modern waltz had just been announced when Alec MacKay leant over towards a slightly sleepy Sean and said, 'Hey wake up, Sean, Miss Dynamite's heading your way.'

Sean looked over to where a curvy female was walking straight towards him. As she drew nearer, he did a double take. It was Annette. The curves, the legs, the breasts were all there, but gone were any puppy features. The half- girl half-woman had gone, the full woman had arrived. She looked class in a glass and she knew it.

'Hell, Campbell,' said Andy out of the side of his mouth, as he eyed up the approaching apparition, 'what is it with you? You and George Best have definitely got something in common.'

'Come on, Sean,' said a smiling Annette as she stretched out her hands to him. This is my dance.'

A slightly dazed Sean got to his feet. As the strains of Engelbert Humperdink's There goes My Everything welled up, he was suddenly aware, very aware, of Annette's body melting into his. She immediately rested her head on his shoulder, her perfume was heady and the gin-scented breath he'd been aware of all these years ago, titillated his nasal passages.

Sean's natural sense of rhythm blended automatically with Annette's. The music was slow and their bodies moved as one in time with the tempo. 'My, Sean Campbell,' she murmured as she moved her hands around his muscular back, 'have you been working out? You do feel so ha-ard!'

Sean tried to move his body slightly off Annette's. But she clung to him like a limpet. Bloody hell, yes, he did feel hard.

'Remember Annette, to me you're still a school girl and you're nine years younger than me.'

'Pull the other one, Sean. I sure ain't no school girl. And none of these guys staring at me at the moment think so either. Interesting that you've got my age worked out though. That's promising!'

It suddenly dawned on Sean, as they changed direction

and Annette stumbled slightly, that she was more than a little under the influence. It wouldn't have surprised him, however, if she'd drunk more than he had. Some kids these days were no lightweights in the drinking stakes and he reckoned Annette fell into this category. If so, she was holding it pretty well. Not that he was exactly sober himself.

As the dance bracket ended, Sean broke away from Annette and began to thank her for the dance but she hooked her arm through his and said, 'Come on, Sean, introduce me to your friends,'

'But what about your friends?' began Sean, looking for a way to extricate himself.

'They're fine. They can look after themselves. They're all big girls.'

'But, I mean, are you not with someone?'

'Oh, you mean a bloke? Nah! We were all having a few drinks in the flat. We knew there was a dance on tonight and had decided to gate-crash it. We quite often do this. They always let us in. A crowd of good-looking unaccompanied sheilas, who's not going to welcome us into a dance? There's always going to be some unaccompanied guys. We usually have a bet on who's going to pull first. And guess who I got!'

As they were talking, Annette had been manoeuvring Sean back to his table group. Before he got a chance to respond, Annette introduced herself. 'Hi, folks. I'm Annette, a girl from Glenbeg and Sean's secret past.'

To Sean's slight embarrassment this was met with some whistles and calls from the other males.

'Well Campbell, you sly dog, you kept that a big secret,'

laughed Alec.

'Hear, hear!' added Andy. 'Now we know the real reason for the times you said you were too busy to come down and see us,' he teased.

'Listen, boys,' replied Sean who'd sat down on one chair with Annette promptly placing her pert butt on his knee and arm around his neck, 'Annette was just a wee girl back then. She's still just a young friend,' he added, trying to pull Annette's hand away from fondling the nape of his neck.

This was greeted with further calls and laughter. And so, Sean found himself stuck with Annette for the rest of the evening. Not that he was particularly dismayed. Annette was certainly popular with one and all and had a dance or two with some of his friends. And that provocative body of hers was compelling viewing.

Sean didn't see any more of Marama until the end of the evening. He was up with Annette for the last dance. The female vocalist was belting out Release Me, possibly Englebert's greatest chart success. Most of the younger couples were shuffling around in romantic clinches. With Annette clinging to him more closely than the material of the tight dress hugging her shapely figure, Sean was scanning the crowd, searching for a glimpse of Marama. As he made a slow turn to the left, he momentarily had direct eye contact with her across a space that had briefly appeared among the dancing couples. Her head was leaning against Michael Maitland's neck. As she looked over his shoulder, she seemed to be staring at him with an intense and worried frown, before disappearing from view.

Rose looked at Merv and smiled, 'So, Merv, your client is now a partner!' It was Saturday night in Oamaru and they'd all just finished eating.

'I take it that's a rhetorical question, Rose!' laughed Merv. 'But you're right.' Then standing up he took a teaspoon and lightly tapped the stem of his wine glass to draw the attention of the rest of the group seated around their table. 'Right, folks, I want you to join me in a toast to two of my favourite people. Some of you might already know that Julia is taking over Rose's business, so we're going to have the pleasure of seeing a lot more of her in Oamaru in the future. I know she's quite excited about the venture and has plans for some other interesting developments. And Rose tells me she has plans to take things a bit easier and although I'm sure we'll be celebrating her retirement at a later date, I'd like you all to raise your glasses and wish all the best to…. "Julia and Rose".

"Julia and Rose," the voices echoed in unison.

'Speech! Speech!' said Tony Skinner, one of two retired sheep farmers in the group.

'Yeah, come on Rose. Come on Julia,' said a few voices encouragingly.

'Not me,' laughed Rose. 'I'll have my say later. Julia, over to you.'

Julia got to her feet. Speech making was not her thing, but the excitement of the moment and the fact that she was among friends, boosted her confidence. 'Well, thanks for that Merv. Yes, I am looking forward to taking over from Rosemary. I used to work with Mum and Dad in their florist shop in Dunedin, but that was a long time ago. It was Rose that really got me thinking about taking over her flower business. At my advanced age…..'

'Get away, you're just a youngster,' shouted Rosemary.

'Thanks for that Rose. But seriously, it has been a big decision for me to make but now I can't wait to start and I've got Rosemary to keep me right when problems arise. I should say too, that I can't thank Merv enough for his professional guidance and help. He, in fact, will be a sleeping partner in the business.'

'You should've bloody well asked me,' interrupted Tony, 'I'd sleep with you any day of the week,' he added to howls of laughter around the table and two sharp digs in the ribs from his amply- built spouse.

'Not that kind of partner, Tony,' smiled Julia, at the same time feeling a slight flush arising around her neck. 'Anyway,' she continued, 'here's to seeing lots more of you all, especially in the shop! Cheers!' she added as she raised her glass in salute.

'Cheers!' replied one and all.

'Well, folks, it looks like everyone else has adjourned to the lounge whilst the staff gets the room ready for the dance. I suggest we do the same,' said Merv.

Replete and in good spirits, the party left the dining room.

After a taxi drive back to Rosemary's and the three of them enjoying a nightcap together, Julia had escorted Merv out to the veranda. 'That was a great night, Merv.'

'All the better for you being there, Julia,' said Merv softly. Then hesitantly he added, 'There's another nightcap at my place if you fancy walking up the road.'

'Thanks, Merv, I'll pass for now.' Raising her head she looked at him directly and said, 'But maybe next time.'

He smiled, 'That'll do me, girl,' and kissed her lightly on the cheek. 'Night, Julia.'

'Night, Merv.'

Julia watched as he walked down the front path, his movement lithe and youthful looking in the dark. Heading along the pavement he turned and waved. Putting her hand to her chest she felt the beat of her heart. 'Lord, I feel like a school girl,' she thought. She sat down on the old veranda sofa. She didn't feel like sleeping. Her mind was much too active. She felt exhilarated. There were her plans for the shop and the addition of a picture gallery and framing section, not to mention the possibility of running some local art classes. Ultimately, she would have to think about moving up to Oamaru permanently. Where would that put her relationship with Jack? Deep down she already knew the answer to that but for now she wasn't going to think about it.

Initially, however, she planned to be in Oamaru three or four days a week, staying with Rosemary. The two girls who worked part-time, were more than capable of running things when she wasn't around. Jack wasn't going to be too thrilled about the arrangement. But he'd get used to it. He wasn't going to have any choice.

Then she thought of Merv. She'd known him for quite a while now, a delightful guy. It was Rosemary who'd put her in touch with him after she'd gotten Julia to seriously think about taking over the shop. As manager of the town's bank,

Merv's expertise had been invaluable. And then she'd gotten to know him socially. She'd learned from Rose of the tragedy that had struck his family when his wife was killed in her car at a level rail crossing and how he'd had to support and bring up a fourteen-year old daughter and son of ten. And, despite his grief and devastation, he'd held the family together, lovingly strengthening the bond between them. He'd continued his role as bank manager to the townsfolk of Oamaru where he was popular and well-liked by his customers and staff. His son was now a third- year medical student in Dunedin and sharing a flat with his sister, a qualified pharmacist.

Merv hadn't married again. Good looking and successful, he would have been a catch for many single females. But although he'd had a few dates over the years, he hadn't seemed to find, or want to find, anyone to replace his late wife. Julia knew he liked her and was attracted to her, as she was to him. And it wasn't just physical, although dancing with each other tonight there was no doubting the electricity flowing between them. And they seemed to have so much in common, sharing similar outlooks on life. Just the other day, Rosemary had looked at Julia through the wreaths of smoke wafting from her habitual cigarette-holding hand, smiled and said, 'You know, Jules, this business move is just about the best thing you could do for yourself, but one thing that'll be even better is getting in tow with Mervyn MacLean.'

The more she got to know him, the more Julia thought Rosemary might be right.

19

'Listen, Mike, I'm a bit bloody concerned about the plans going through. If this tip-off is right and some smart arse gets onto the case, we could have trouble,' said Jack Maitland.

'Can't see any problem, Jack. Our contacts promised to keep the access road bit as low key as possible and it looks to me as they've done that. No-one's raised objections so far and the final decision is just a fortnight away. And if nothing's happened so far, chances are it'll be too late for anyone to do anything anyway.'

'All the same, it's got me uneasy, I don't like it when things are out of my control.'

It was Sunday afternoon. Michael Maitland had dropped Marama off at her home and gone up to Jack's. He was meeting with his uncle to further discuss their plans for the quarry development. Their armchairs were facing the lounge window overlooking the valley. Michael had a mug of tea on the coffee table beside him whilst Jack had a glass of beer.

'All the same, Mike, I think I'll have a word with old Tama about what's going to happen.'

'Do you think that's wise. It might give the old bloke ideas that there's something amiss. In fact, don't you think it's going to focus him on the issue if he hasn't already picked up on it?'

'That's the thing, I don't know if he's aware of what's going on or not. He's been away for about a month, and just arrived back. I feel I'd rather find out what the old bugger knows and ferret out of him whether he's likely to have any objections about the road. Don't worry, I'll not go in cap in hand to him. I'll brush over the whole thing pretty quickly. But I've got to know, Mike.'

'Well, whatever you think, Jack, I just hope you're not stirring up a hornets' nest.

As he approached Evansdale and the long hill climb known as the Kilmog, some twelve miles north of Dunedin, Sean signalled right and changed down a gear. The east coast highway would take travellers all the way from the Scottish-based settlement of Dunedin up to the Anglican settlement of Christchurch two hundred miles further north, and ultimately to the top of the South Island in the province of Nelson-Marlborough. But on this bright and sunny Monday morning, Sean was determined to enjoy the more scenic coastal route on his trip back to Glenbeg.

He could smell the sea, well before the rolling breakers of Warrington Beach came into view. After passing through the small settlements of Warrington, Seacliff, and Puketeraki, he finally pulled over onto the grass verge on the far side of Karitane and switched off the engine. Taking his jacket from the passenger seat, he got out of the car and inhaled deeply. The salty tang brought a smile to his face and he momentarily closed his eyes, feeling the slight warmth of sunlight. Pocketing his keys, he pulled on his jacket, flicked up the collar and walked across a couple of low sand dunes before cascading down a small drop to the beach below.

There was only the faintest of breezes. He trudged across the soft white sand until he reached the firmer dark surface uncovered by the receding tide. He began to stride out, relishing the solitude of the deserted beach. Screeching gulls wheeling and diving just beyond the breakers and the surf lifting, crashing and then hissing towards the shore line, were the only sounds to be heard.

He thought of the weekend. He marvelled at the fact that after all his time away, it had been so easy to slot into life with his friends again. Meeting up with Andy and Cara had been delightful and he had left them promising to keep in touch and to let them know the next time he was in Dunedin.

The dance had been a great night out too, though not without its potential for a fall from grace. He thought of Marama. His heart ached with longing as he imagined walking hand in hand with her in this beautiful landscape. And his heart had begun to beat faster when he saw her at the dance. Was it his imagination or had she seemed to be almost annoyed to see him there? Was it because she was with Michael Maitland? Could it be that she didn't want him to see her with the guy? She seemed to be a shadow of the vivacious laughing Marama he had known before. He had been surprised at how docilely she had moved at Maitland's bidding. Where was the feisty girl he had got to know and to love? It was almost as if the guy had some sort of hold over her. Sean couldn't figure it out.

'One thing's for sure, Campbell,' he said to himself, 'seeing her makes me realize why I came back. But what I can do about getting closer to her I just don't know. It would seem that patience, Seanie boy, is definitely called for.'

From Marama his mind switched to Annette. He smiled. Yeah, Annette was some girl, and no mistake. He liked her. She was as daft as a brush but she had a sense of humour. And she had a body to die for. But hell, she was only nineteen - going on forty admittedly. Thank God he hadn't ended up sleeping with her. But it had been a close-run thing. If Annette had had her way , she'd have had him in the sack and no doubt have shagged his brains out. And, come to think of it, fantasizing over the image was rather pleasurable! But there was Marama to think about, not to mention Annette's father, Jack Maitland. No, he didn't want to go there!

Annette had insisted he see her home. The fact that he'd spent half the night with her, he'd felt obliged to do so and also a little responsible. Fortunately, when they'd got back to Annette's new flat, courtesy of her friend Sharon who was driving and not drinking, he'd managed to persuade Sharon to come in to the flat too. Annette hadn't appeared too thrilled at the arrangement. They'd just got into the apartment when the doorbell went, hailing the arrival of an inebriated and party-seeking group of Annette's social circle. As drinks began to be poured and music volume increased,

Sean managed to slip out without being noticed. He knew Annette would be more than a little peeved at his departure but he'd decided he'd find some excuse to appease her in the future. He'd felt like clearing his head in the cool night air. The long walk from Maori Hill to St Clair certainly had achieved that.

His train of thought switched yet again, this time to his meeting with Tupe Parata. Not only had he learned some valuable information but also, he felt he'd met with a new-found friend. He began to focus upon story potential. Could he make a link between the taiaha's past and the present day? What had befallen the chief who'd been shot by Beardie O'Neil? Had he survived? Had the event been documented? If not, why not? Did the Maori tribe feel they'd had to hide the chief after a pakeha had been killed? Would the chief have received an unbiased hearing in a colonial court? Did O'Neil actually die and if he did what became of his body? And where was the staff of the taiaha – did it still exist? For his own satisfaction he would like to discover the answers to these questions. As a novelist, however, he didn't need to have the answers. He had the licence to create his own story. But fact, as the old adage said, was often stranger than fiction. And thus, all the more fascinating.

And what about the old ancestral burial caves? Surely they must feature? But to write with some authority and credibility on such a subject, he would have to have expert advice. He would need the input of people like Tama and Tupe.

Sean turned round. The south-easterly breeze had increased perceptibly. Though invigorated by the walk, he could feel the wind chill and stinging grains of sand on his face as they were swept and driven along the shoreline. Lowering his head, he broke into a light jog and headed for the car.

Things hadn't gone too well when Jack had broached the subject of the access road the following afternoon. As it turned out, Tama was unaware of the proposed road-build due to the fact he'd just arrived back from the west coast. But it was clear that he definitely was not in favour. Jack was becoming increasingly frustrated.

'Look, Tama,' said Maitland, leaning forward in his chair, 'I've not come down here to ASK you if we can take a road up by the old burial site. I've come to TELL you that that's what we bloody well intend doing. This is just a courtesy visit on my behalf. Having said that, we'll go out of our way to cause minimum disruption, not that I think there's much there to disrupt in the first place.'

'Well, Jack, you don't sound too courteous. And we both know, that land is not yours. It is Maori land in Maori ownership. It belongs to the "tangata whenua", the people of the land. And in this case, that's the descendants of the Maori who lived in the Waihemo area.'

'All due respect, Tama, that's an old wife's tale. I think you'll find it very hard to prove that sort of ownership. And what sort of ownership do you call it when it's supposed to belong to a whole lot of descendants? Hell, if the land did belong to them, how could someone like me buy it unless everyone of these living descendants was to agree to the sale?'

'That's the whole point. The land in question is part of our culture and heritage. It is not for sale. It belongs to us all. And this particular piece of land is an ancient burial site. It is to be respected. To us it is tapu, sacred. When the government bought all the land in the Makarewa area from our forefathers, any tapu sites or areas of historical importance to the native peoples were excluded from the sales. There will be records of this.'

'I doubt it,' said Jack shaking his head. 'And listen, Tama, we're not going to greatly disturb your site. The road will keep, as far as possible to the edge of the area. And it'll be no closer than twenty yards to the cave entrances. Work is due to begin in a month's time.'

They were sitting out on Tama's veranda. Jack Maitland had decided he'd better give the old fellow personal warning of the plans he and his brother had for extraction of more limestone on the other side of Hidden Valley. The Ministry of Works Planning Department had already given statutory notice to the Palmerston County Council, and the local press, of the application by Maitland Holdings to extend the existing quarrying operations to a further development on the far side of the old burial site. Whilst the quarry would be on Jack Maitland's land, the access road involved going through an area, the ownership of which, was potentially controversial. No mention was made of this in the application. Press publication indicated that plans could be perused by any interested members of the public, but at the Maitlands' request, the whole thing had been kept exceedingly low key. The Maitlands were hoping that when the general public became aware of the project, the creation of further employment would be enough to secure universal approval.

'Why can't you access your new site from the old quarry?'

'Come on, Tama, be reasonable, it would cost a bloody fortune. That would mean an extra three miles of road, not to mention having to bridge a couple of creeks. Have you been up to the burial site recently? There's virtually no sign of past settlement, just a rocky hilltop and caves.'

But the niggling at the back of Jack's mind that the access route to the quarry site just might cause a problem, seemed to have been justified. The old bastard was not going to take this lying down. Jack's livestock had grazed on the adjacent land and sometimes quite close to the site. The fact that there was damned all grass around was the reason the animals tended to avoid the place, not the fact that it was tapu! This common Maori ownership business did bother him and land rights were beginning to become an issue all over the country. The last thing he wanted was any legal battle. God, the buggers never made any use of the land there. It was just a pile of bloody rocks and some holes in the ground.

Maitland tried one further piece of persuasion, 'Tell you what, Tama. I hear they're trying to raise money for a new community hall down at the old pa. How about Maitland Holdings make a donation towards the funds, say five thousand dollars, would that help persuade the tribe to turn a blind eye to this bit of road development?'

'It's not for me to say. I will talk to the elders, but I'm sure that like me they will not agree to any road being built on the site.'

Standing up and moving off the veranda Jack retorted, 'Well, don't just talk to the elders. Talk to the young folk too. It's their bloody future. Maybe they'll see things differently.'

20

Myriads of stars were twinkling in a black velvet sky as Tama walked along the back road. It was cold and the visible puffs of his breath in the night air indicated the likelihood of frost before morning. He was making for his young Scottish friend's cottage. He hadn't seen him since his departure three years previously. As he walked, his head buzzed with thoughts of the implications that the road development had thrown up. Jack Maitland's visit and news about the access route had caught him by surprise He thought it might help to air his concerns with Sean.

He was warmly greeted by Sean and shown to the fireside. Sitting there he looked at Sean and said, 'You know, Sean, it only seems like yesterday that you were leaving to return to Scotland. It is good to have you back with us again.'

'It's nice to be back, Tama. And how are you and Mere and the family?'

'Mere and I are fine, Sean. We are not getting any younger but, so far, we have been blessed with good health. Hemi seems to be his usual happy self and little Kirri is a great source of joy to us all. As for Marama, well, I'm not so sure. You probably know she is quite friendly with Michael Maitland. I don't really know the boy, but he is not someone I find easy to take to. However, it is up to young people to make their choices about who they wish to share their lives with, not us. Marama keeps things pretty close to her chest. She was very unhappy for a long time after you had gone, and, no, I don't think it was Rob's death that prayed on her mind so much as the fact that Sean Campbell had left.

'Things changed, of course. With her pregnant and the birth of Kirri she had other things to focus on, other priorities. Kirri is a lovely child and the light of Marama's life, and ours. Kirri, I believe, is what drove Marama to keep going. She is still Marama's first priority in life. But both Mere and I believe Marama has to have a life beyond that and I think she knows it too. I am glad you came back at this time. I think Marama will soon have to make decisions about her future and I believe, and hope, that your presence might have some influence on what she might ultimately do.'

'Thank you, Tama. It is very kind of you to share your thoughts with me.'

'Anyway, Sean, I would also like to talk to you about other things.'

'This might surprise you, Tama, but I have other things too that I need to talk to you about. But let's tonight discuss what might be on your mind. I can wait!'

Tama proceeded to relate to Sean what he had heard about the new quarry development and about Jack Maitland's visit to him some hours before. 'Part of the land they wish to cross to access the new quarry development is definitely

Maori land. I know this for a fact, although I do not know if there is any current proof of it on record. But to our people, this land is sacred, it should not be defiled in any way. I'm sure Jack Maitland is aware of this. But I believe he came to see me hoping that with the years that have gone by, we might take a more relaxed view about this access road.'

'I actually assumed Jack Maitland owned the land that the site was on. But strangely enough I was talking to someone last Friday and the subject of the burial site came up. He assured me that such land would not have been available for the pakeha to purchase. But surely there's another route to get to the land they want to excavate?'

'Indeed. But it means taking a longer route and building a couple of small bridges. This means more money and big businesses like Maitland Holdings are not keen to part with money where they can avoid it.'

'Well tough, Tama. I'm sure they can afford it. Now here's a weird coincidence. I'm just back from Dunedin where I've been investigating information for a book I hope to write. In fact, I learned that you might be able to supply me with some of the facts I need. Forget about that in the meantime, however. The strange thing is, the subject of your cave burial land came up. You see, I'd an appointment to meet a Professor Tupe Parata at the Otago Museum. I don't know if you've heard of him?'

'I know there are quite a few Paratas living in Dunedin but can't say I know the family.'

'Well anyway, the subject of Maori land rights arose. The burial site in Glenbeg was mentioned and he right away expressed surprise when I said I thought the land belonged to a local farmer. He stated that this was highly unlikely. He also told me that he's got a cousin who is a lawyer up north and a specialist in this field. He will be in Dunedin next week. After hearing what you've been telling me, I think it would be worth your while having a talk with this lawyer.'

'Sean, I've a feeling that expert legal advice might be very useful at this time. Of course, I will have to speak to my people living in the vicinity of the old pa. But if I have some specific facts to go on in the first instance, that would be very desirable.'

'Right, Tama, leave it with me. I'll telephone Tupe in the morning and arrange a meeting for as soon as possible. And, in fact, I'll go down with you if that's alright.'

'Excellent, Sean. But what about this information that I might be able to help you with?

'Well, time is getting on and I know that you're an early riser. Perhaps we will leave it to another day.'

'I always have time for my friends, Sean. Tell me what is on your mind.'

Sean placed another couple of logs on the fire and began by explaining how he'd been motivated to return to New Zealand. He described his meeting with Murdo MacLean and then recounted Calum's story. He also outlined what he'd managed to discover on his recent visit to Dunedin.

Tama listened intently, a nod of the head and an occasional lift of the eyebrows being his only visible reaction to Sean's narrative.

'So, Tama,' Sean rounded off, 'that partly explains why

I'm back in Aotearoa.'

'Amazing, Sean. I can see why you've come back to further research your story. Mind you, I guess you could have stayed in Scotland and let your imagination take you where it would.'

'True. But I genuinely wanted to follow up on old Calum's story. And I confess I was looking for some justification to return.'

'Ah, justification.' Tama nodded and smiled. And do you feel justified?'

'Totally,' said Sean returning the smile. 'But come on Tama, I feel you're teasing me. Was Tupe right to say that Tama Te Kanawa might well hold the key, or at least have some answers, to my enquiries?'

Tama sat still for a moment, gazing into the flames of the fire as they took hold on the new logs. Clasping his hands together he looked steadily at Sean for a moment and said, 'I do know something, Sean. And I will tell you, but it is difficult for me. In telling you, I will be breaking a promise, indeed an oath, that I made many many years ago. And yet, listening to you, I feel it appropriate to reveal what I know. But I will tell you with the proviso that you promise not to pass on this information to anyone else. The knowing of it will help your understanding but the knowledge cannot be released to any other party. Do I have your word on this?'

Sean felt strangely excited, but he answered sombrely, 'You have my word, Tama. But I do not wish you to feel pressured into telling me something you would rather not reveal.'

Tama smiled. 'In the circumstances I think I can say I feel *justified* in telling you what I know. You will not find anything about the Maori chief in any newspaper records,' Tama continued, 'but I can tell you now that he did indeed exist. You see, there is the story told by your countryman Calum and there is also a story, similar in part, told by Takurua Potaka. He was the warrior the Irish miner shot.'

'Then he lived after all to tell the tale?' asked Sean excitedly.

'Well, he lived long enough to recount what had happened. But sadly, despite the efforts of our people to remove the bullet and nurse him back to health, he died a week later. He was my great grandfather's friend. He was fifty-eight years old when he was shot by the Irishman. As a young man he had moved to the north island and married the daughter of a chief of the Ngati Kahungunu tribe in the Hawke's Bay district. Sadly, she died of a disease brought by the pakeha, measles I believe. Too grief-stricken to remain in the north, Takarua returned to his home in Waihemo. And strangely, in the timing of his return the title of chief was passed to him. He also brought a daughter with him. Her name was Marama.

Sean gasped. 'Is the girl in the story related to you?'

Tama smiled, 'Yes, you're right to make the connection with Marama. My grandfather, Tama Te Kanawa, married Marama Potaka.'

'Then you and Marama are named after them.'

'That is true.'

'But what of Marama's parents?' Sean paused then

added, 'Forgive me, Tama, I have no right to ask such a question.'

Tama raised his hand and shook his head. 'No, Sean, it was a long time ago, though the grief and pain I recall only too well. My son Kahu and his wife, Ani, Marama's mother, along with my other son Witi were drowned when on a trip to Stewart Island. Marama and Hemi were staying with us. They were very young. It was a time of great grief and hardship for us all.'

'What a tragedy. Marama has never mentioned anything about her parents and I never liked to ask.'

'Well, there you have the story of a family's origins. But I have not yet told you what happened after the shooting.' Tama continued, 'It was decided by the elders that the incident should not be reported to the pakeha authorities. The Maori did not have any great faith in them at this particular time and believed that if any blame was to be attached, it would not be to the pakeha involved. And it was also decided that rather than drawing attention to the death and using the burial ground near the pa, Takarua would be buried secretly in the caves where our ancestors had been buried at Glenbeg. So Takarua Potaka would be the last person to have been buried in the caves. Many years later my grandfather told the story to my father and he to me – each exacting a promise that we only pass the story on to our children. At seventeen my grandfather did not take part in any of the ceremony, but he was used as a look-out near to the burial site so that he might give warning of any people appearing in the vicinity.

'As for the Irishman, some of the men took his body up

into the hills. I believe he was buried somewhere near the caves above the present Limeworks site. All the other belongings in the camp they left, knowing that other travelling prospectors would likely pick them up.

'In the long ago when our people used caves for burying the dead, the passage ways or chambers where the body was laid to rest would be blocked up with rocks and stones. One thing I do know, Sean, the staff of the taiaha was buried with Takarua. It would have been good if the spear head could have been placed with him. But if nothing else, Sean, it has reunited you with us. And as far as I am concerned, that is a good thing. And now I must bid you good night.'

'Thank you, Tama. I feel privileged to have given this information by you. I promise not to divulge any of it to any other party. As to the spear head, perhaps we can discuss with Tupe what you might wish done with it. I am just grateful that it has given me cause to be here with you all again.'

21

It was early Friday evening and the end of the working week. Vic Maitland was in the public bar having a drink with Hemi and Frank Cleland. Despite a quick brushing down, their overalls, heads and boots still bore remnants of the white dust that daily enveloped them during their working hours. Much to Vic's relief, his cousin Michael had left for Dunedin just before midday. He'd found a week of him overseeing operations more than a little trying. Vic was a hands-on guy. Michael was a figures and plans man.

'Thank God that bugger's away for the weekend, he's been driving me up the bloody wall!' exclaimed Vic as he set his glass down on the table.

'Go on, Vic,' grinned Hemi, winking at the others, 'I'll bet you're full of your cousin's suggestions. You just can't wait till Monday to try them out. See, Mick's been to uni. He's got a degree and has big plans for the future. I think you should listen to him old son.'

'That'll be the bloody day. He's full of bull. I run this place fine, with a bit of help from you rat-bags, of course. Mind you, this new development could result in a few changes.'

The others looked blankly at him.

'What development's that, Vic?' asked Frank.

'What the hell, I know you guys haven't heard yet, but an application for planning is already out, so I reckon it's no big secret. See, the Maitlands – that's Mike and my Uncle Grant along with my father– are planning to open up another quarry over behind the old burial site up Hidden Valley.'

'Really?' asked Hemi. 'What about over-production? Can they sell more of the stuff?'

'Yeah, that's just it. Evidently there's going to be a bigger demand than ever for good quality lime in the farming industry and the government's going to continue subsidising farmers to use the stuff.'

'Well blow me,' said Frank. Looks like there's going to be plenty of work. I thought the way the old quarry's going, they might be forced to get shot of some of us.'

'No problems there. Likely be a few extra jobs going.'

'Yeah,' said Hemi, 'but when will the quarry be up and running? 'It'll take a bit of time to build a road from the works over to the valley. And there's at least a couple of creeks to cross.'

'I think they're planning to go alongside the old burial ground.'

'Can't do that, Vic. It's Maori land. Tapu.'

'That's what I thought. But they reckon it's Maitland land. 'What's Tama going to say about this?'

'He'll, say it's Maori land. Ever since we were nippers, we were always told that while that site was Maori land, it was also tapu. We weren't allowed to go near it. The old folk seriously look at it as a sacred place. Gee, Vic, I can see this all causing trouble.'

'Well, boys, it's got nothing to do with me. I'm just telling you what I've heard. Might be the Maori Wars all over again. You going to eat me, Hemi?'

'Not bloody likely. You'd be too tough. Now little Frankie here, he might be a tasty morsel.'

'Well, boys, I'm for off-ski,' said Vic downing the last of his drink. 'Gotta get some grub. Might see you down here later, Hemi?'

'Could do, Vic. Come on Frank, I'll give you a lift to the corner.'

As Vic and his workmates went out of the public bar and into the car park, Jack Maitland was entering the lounge bar from the other side of the building. Julia was away to Oamaru for the weekend and he'd decided he'd pop down for a jar or two. He was also feeling horny.

Of all the women Jack had played around with during his marriage – and there were quite a few – Mary, owner of the Glenbeg Arms hotel, had been a constant in his life. They had come to an understanding long ago. Jack wanted sex without complications and Mary seemed happy enough to go along with that. Each liked the other and each loved what the other brought to the bedroom. Jack knew that when Mary was up for it, she was sensational in bed and it took him all his time to keep up with her. Mary, on the other hand, was under no illusions about Jack's promiscuity, but with it he brought experience and an organ commensurate with his other substantial statistics. Jack was a big man.

Jack was in good humour. A couple of jugs and a romp with Mary would make for a very satisfactory evening he thought. 'Hi Jack, what's it to be?' asked the chestnut-haired beauty behind the bar.

'Hi Lyndy-loo. What you off'rin' me?' smiled Jack.

'Why, Jack, anything you see here is available – at a price,' said Lyn, Mary's twenty-year old daughter, eyes sparkling as she pushed her tight skirt down over her barely-concealed thighs.'

Jack laughed, 'You're a right tease, Lyn.'

'Why Jack, I'm sure I don't know what you mean,' said Lyn pulling a totally innocent expression.'

'Anyway, for now I'll have a jug of lager and a double malt, that fifteen- year Glenfiddich up there will do fine. Where's Mary tonight?'

'Mum's doing her books in the back office at the moment. She'll be through later when things start to hot up. Will you be here when things start to hot up Jack?' asked Lyn provocatively leaning across the counter and providing Jack with an eyeful of ample cleavage as she poured out the golden amber.

'You tell your Mum I'll be here later on,' said Jack as he carried his drinks over to a corner table on the other side of the lounge.

'I'll tell her, Jack.'

Jack had downed his double malt in two sizeable gulps. He had almost finished his lager and was placing the glass on the table when a figure loomed in front of him and said,

'Hello Mr Maitland, remember me?'

Jack looked up and studied the speaker for a moment, 'Hell, Tonto, I could hardly forget you.'

The speaker, a Maori with shoulder-length hair held back from his forehead by a bandana, grinned and said, 'I like it Mr Maitland but na-ah, it's Sonny, Sonny Te Hurinui. I worked for Billy Potaka's shearing gang last season up at your homestead.'

'I remember you. You were the young bugger that caused the rumpus down at the bunkhouse. You put one of the boys in hospital.'

'Nah. I just busted his nose and broke a few ribs. He was OK.'

'And what the hell did you do that for?'

'He said he didn't like my moko.'

'Jeez, and you busted his nose for not liking your tattoos. Hell, it's just as well he didn't insult your sister!' Anyway Son, Sonny, what can I do for you?'

'I think I might be able to do something for you Mr Maitland, or can I call you Jack?'

'Mr Maitland will do for the moment.'

'OK Boss. How about Boss then?'

'Boss'll do fine,' said Jack with a smile. He was feeling mellow. 'Here, take this,' he said handing Sonny a five dollar note. 'Get another jug and bring another glass over.' He watched as Sonny swaggered over to the bar, tight black jeans and black T-shirt that emphasized his well-developed body. He was only around five-nine in height, slightly chunky but all muscle. Clearly worked out a lot. A cocky young bastard and no mistake, thought Jack.

When Sonny returned, no doubt having charmed Lyn at the bar with his come - hither brown eyes and pretty boy face, he took a seat opposite Jack, topped up Jack's glass and then filled his own.

'So, Sonny,' began Jack, 'to what do I owe the pleasure?'

'Well, Boss, Mr Maitland, I was sitting in the public bar having a drink with my mate – you know, in the alcove where there's that glass partition, and I was listening to some boys from the Limeworks talking. They couldn't see me because they were on the other side of the glass and all, but I recognized two of the voices. One was Hemi Te Kanawa's and the other was Vic's. I didn't know the third guy but he was called Frank. They were talking about another quarry being developed.'

Jack's ears pricked up but all he said was, 'So?'

'Well, you obviously know a whole lot more about this than me, but it seems you and the other blokes involved want to put a road in alongside the old burial site. Hemi was telling Vic, though, that you can't do it because it's Maori land.'

'It's my bloody land,' retorted Jack.

'Well, you could be right, Boss, but I wouldn't like to bet my life on that. We all know that most bits of Maori land like that were not sold in the past to the farmers, but kept by the tribe.'

'They're going to have to prove that, and between you and me, there's no written record of them having it.'

'That might be right, Jack, but – is it alright for me to call you Jack?'

Jack waved his hand impatiently. 'Yeah, yeah. What's your point?'

'Point is, Jack, do you have written proof that that particular piece of land is yours? Maybe it doesn't expressly say so in your deeds,' Sonny looked at Jack and when he didn't respond continued, 'Could be that this will go to court.'

'We'll still win the case.'

'Maybe, maybe not. But this will all take time. And to you business folk, time is money. Am I right?'

'You've got a point,' conceded Jack, 'but I don't know where you're going with this conversation.'

'Well, if the land ownership is to be contested, why not go for a second option and buy the land.'

'I've already sounded out old Te Kanawa. He wouldn't wear it, not a bloody hope.'

'But, if the land does belong to the Maori, and I think it probably does, it belongs to the whole community, not to old Tama. They would all have a say on whether the bit you need could be sold off.'

'He'd talk them round to it and no mistake, all this bloody tapu business.'

'He'll talk some of them round to it. But I can persuade quite a few of the younger ones to go the other way. And there'll have to be a vote. And there might be other ways of persuading some people not to vote – if you get my meaning,' said Sonny with a sly smile.

'Interesting. And if this all did happen what's in it for you?'

'Well, Jack, think of what you have to pay to the

community as part of your payment. What you pay to me and the friends I need to help me is the other part.'

'And how much would that be?'

'Oh, it'll be negotiable. But it'll be a bloody sight less than what you'd have to pay to take the road the long way round.'

'OK, we're talking hypothetically at the moment. But I'll grant you, you've got me interested. Another thing, this conversation never took place. We keep everything hush- hush.'

'My lips are sealed.'

'So, how do I get in touch with you, Sonny?'

'Just ring the Royal in Palmerston and leave a message for me to get back to you. It's my regular watering hole. But I'll need your phone number.'

'Right, here it is,' said Jack taking out a pen and scribbling it on the edge of the newspaper he'd been looking at. He then tore off the scrap and handed it to Sonny. 'By the way, I might need someone shortly to use a bit of muscle, so as to speak, on someone who's beginning to get on my tits. You seem like you might be into the persuasion business.'

'No problem, Jack. Just let me know what you want and when you want it.'

'We understand each other. You want another beer?'

'She's right, Jack. There's my mate over there,' said Sonny, pointing to a leather clad biker standing at the door. 'I'll grab my jacket. We're off to a party. Wanna come?'

'I'll pass, Sonny. See ya.'

'See ya, Boss,' said Sonny, his face splitting into a big grin.

22

'We're back, Gran,' shouted Marama as she and Kirri entered the house.

'And I got some lollies for being a good girl,' squealed Kirri as she ran into the lounge where she stopped abruptly on seeing Sean sitting at the fireside with Tama and Mere.

'It's alright Bub, it's Sean. You met Sean with your Mum, remember?'

'Hi Kirri, how are you?' said Sean with a smile. Your Gran tells me you were at the dentist.'

'Sweets are not perhaps the best thing to be giving a child after a visit to the dentist,' said Marama as she walked into the room. 'Hello Sean, how are you?'

'I'm fine thanks, Marama. Yourself?'

'Oh, just the usual. Are you staying for supper?'

'Well....'

'He sure is,' said Mere. 'Sean dropped off some information to your grandfather earlier and I told him to come back for a meal after his run. So, Marama, would you like a drink? As you can see, we're all enjoying one.'

'I'll go and set the table, Nana.'

'Relax, girl. Sit down. Everything's been done. Pour yourself a drink. Kirri, go and get your Squirrel Nutkin book and Nan will read you a story.'

'I'm just going up to my room, I'll be down shortly.'

Sean tensed his leg muscles, sensing Marama's coolness. Tama, aware of Sean's discomfort, winked at him and said, 'You relax too, Sean boy, consider yourself at home.'

Kirri came in with her book and climbed on to her great gran's lap. Thumb in mouth and wide-eyed, she listened intently as her gran softly read to her, occasionally adding a comment of her own to the narrative.

Tama continued, 'You were saying that Tupe Parata's cousin can see us next week?'

'Yes. He's available on Tuesday morning at eleven o'clock. We can meet in Tupe's office at the museum. It sounds like land rights are something he's really expert on. Hopefully he'll be able to keep you right on the legalities.'

'Sounds good, Sean. We'll go down in the old jeep. I've got some stuff to collect at the Farmers' Co-op. Will pick you up at say nine? Can get a cuppa before we meet up with them.'

'Fine with me.'

The back door opened to the strains of Tom Jones' Delilah. It was Hemi back from work and the pub. 'Sean, my friend, Tena koe? Long time no see.'

'Kia ora, Hemi,' said Sean rising to shake hands with Marama's brother. 'Yeah, it's been quite a while. You just finished work?'

'You must be joking,' interrupted Marama following

Hemi into the sitting room. 'Can't you tell? He smells like a brewery. He's been down the pub.'

'Would do you good to be there too, Sis. Anyway, a man works all week, surely he's entitled to a little drink or two at the end of it? But listen, people, I'm off for a bath. What's for tea, Nan, puha and pakeha?'

'No pakeha tonight, boy! But we've got crayfish pie in a cheese sauce along with some roasted kumeras and yams and some silverbeet to top up your vitamins. Pudding is a surprise.'

'Sounds good, Nan,' said Hemi heading for the bathroom.

'Dinner's in the oven,' called Mere after him. You've got fifteen minutes, Hemi.'

Twenty minutes later they were all seated around the kitchen table with Kirri sitting on Marama's right and Sean, very conscious of her proximity, on Marama's left. As Mere began dishing portions of the steaming pie, amidst the mouth-watering aromas Sean was also aware of the faintest trace of a scent Marama had been wearing that magical night down on the riverbank.

All set to with gusto. Talk was abandoned briefly, other than short comments thrown at the cook complimenting her on her culinary expertise. These Mere took with the merest of smiles but was clearly pleased with the enjoyment her cooking was giving. As cutlery was laid down and chairs pushed back, Tama topped up the glasses of lager. Kirri was excused to play with her toys prior to the arrival of the dessert.

Hemi was meanwhile eyeing up the remnants of the crayfish.

'Sean, would you like some more?' asked Mere.

'That was fantastic, Mere, but I'm full as a tick at the moment.'

'You don't need to ask old hollow legs, Nana,' said Marama nodding at her brother. 'You'd think he'd never eaten.'

'Working man burns up a lot of energy, Sis. You sure Sean,' asked Hemi already moving towards the remainder of the pie.

'I'm sure, Hemi. Your need is greater than mine,' smiled Sean. And the pie was almost on Hemi's plate before Sean had finished speaking.

'Say, Gramps, you know anything about this new quarry?' asked Hemi pushing his empty plate slightly away from him.

'Funny you should ask, Hemi, I had Jack Maitland bending my ear about it yesterday afternoon. How did you hear about it?'

Hemi went on to describe the conversation he'd had with Vic down at the pub. 'Thing, is, Gramps, I told Vic that the old burial site is Maori land. And Vic said he thought so too, but he also added that Jack and cousin Michael were saying it's Maitland land.'

'He's wrong. That land is Maori land and it's tapu. But it looks like we might have a battle to prove it. That's why Sean and I are going down to see a lawyer on Tuesday about it.'

'What's this, Sean? You taking up Maori land rights now?' asked Marama quizzically. 'I don't understand. What do you know about all of this?'

'Hey, girl, cool it,' said her brother.

'No, it's alright, Hemi.' Then turning to Marama Sean continued, 'I don't know anything about Maori land rights, Marama. It's just that the topic came up when I was meeting with Professor Parata at the museum in Dunedin last week and he mentioned that he had a cousin who specialized in this field and would be in Dunedin next week. When your granddad was telling me about the quarry development, I suggested he might want to speak with Tupe Parata's cousin. So, we've arranged a meeting.'

'But what in heaven's name were you talking about that raised the question about who owned the old burial site?'

'I think that's Sean's business, Marama,' said Mere.

'That's OK, Mere,' then turning to Marama he added, 'I was meeting Tupe Parata to discuss something I'm researching that might give me background material to the story I'm hoping to write. It involves an incident that happened way back during the gold rush days. It also involves a Maori chief of that period. That's how the subject arose. But I didn't know anything about the quarry development that Hemi was talking about or that there might be some contesting of who owns the burial and cave area.'

'Sean was telling me about the story the other day. I told your grandmother about it. The background to it is quite fascinating, Marama, and could well involve some of our relatives from away in the past. And it turns out that I was able to fill him in on some information that Professor Parata couldn't give him.'

'You   didn't   tell   me   anything   about   this,

Gramps. Why not?'

'You've been pretty pre-occupied with other things lately, Marama. I would eventually have got round to telling you about it. But what about the quarry, has Michael Maitland not told you anything about their plans?'

'We don't talk shop to each other,' answered Marama, rather quickly. 'He doesn't discuss his business affairs and I don't discuss school.' She didn't add that when they first started going out, Michael was forever telling her about his plans and ambitions for the future, nor the fact of his apparent disinterest in all matters relating to her teaching work. And on two occasions when she happened to extol the virtues of Sean as a teacher, she thought she detected in his attitude not just disinterest but something approaching resentment.

'Well, given the fact that the quarry issue involves the old burial site, I'd have thought he might mention it to you,' said Hemi.

'Don't see it's a big deal,' answered Marama somewhat defensively.

'Come on, Sis, you know that it's got to be a big deal with a lot of folk'.

'Old folk, yes. Young ones, not really. It's just an old burial site. Is putting a road beside it going to wake up the spirits of our ancestors?'

'That's being disrespectful, Marama,' said Mere.

'But,' began Marama becoming more heated in her argument, 'what about the fact that the Maitlands will donate money towards a new community hall at the marae, is that not taking a more positive step to promoting our culture?'

'Who said anything about donating money, Marama? Sounds like you did know a bit about this development,' added Tama.

'Michael did say something about it a while ago,' answered Marama, flushing slightly. 'I did mean to mention it to you when you came back. I guess I forgot.'

'Forgot!' said Hemi, raising his eyebrows.

'I'm surprised you didn't say anything to us, Marama,' said Tama.

An awkward silence hung over the room for a few seconds before Sean interjected, 'Hey, Folks, I saw Hemi's guitar in the sitting room. How about treating me to a few songs.'

'OK, Sean,' said Hemi picking up on Sean's change of subject matter. 'But, Hey! Where's the pudding?'

'It's in the fridge, Hemi. We're going to have it in a little while. Some of us are quite full at the moment!' said Mere.

'OK, let's all go through to the fireside. Kirri, will you sing Only A Little Kiwi for us?'

'Yes,' said Kirri clapping her hands, 'Only Little Kiwi. Come Gramps,' she said pulling Tama by the arm.

'Marama and I will clear up,' said Mere.

'No you won't, Nana,' said her grand-daughter. 'You made a lovely meal. Go through with the others. I'm happy to clear up.'

'If you insist, dear.'

All adjourned to the sitting room where Hemi twiddled with the guitar tuning before getting Kirri to sing about a lost kiwi bird.

It was around ten o'clock when Sean said good night to Tama and Mere and thanked them for a great meal and evening. Kirri had long been tucked up in bed and Hemi had excused himself earlier to go off to the pub. Rather to Sean's surprise, Marama had said she'd walk him to the end of the road with Turi the border collie who'd been lying by the fireside for most of the evening.

As they walked along the road together Sean felt his pulse begin to quicken. 'Hell,' he thought, 'how does she always have this effect on me?'

'So, Sean, tell me about this story of yours that has brought you all the way back to little old New Zealand.'

Sean thought, If only you knew, Marama, the real reason for me coming back. But instead, he began, 'Well, it was a visit from an old crofter in my village of Applecross that started things off. I seem to have told this story a hundred times in the last few weeks.' He then proceeded to give her an abbreviated version of Calum's story.

Focused on telling the story and with the full attention of Marama, who interjected with the odd observation or question, Sean began to relax. It was like old times. Observing her mannerisms close up, the depth and intensity of those beautiful eyes, the faintest changes of expression as she listened to his account, it was all he could do to stop himself reaching out and kissing her.

As he concluded with Tama's confirmation that he was aware such an event had occurred – but omitting the details that he'd been sworn to secrecy about - Marama stopped and turned to him. 'That's fascinating, Sean, I did wonder at you coming all this way just to write a story. But I can see now why you needed to. You know, I've read both your books and I really enjoyed them. You've got a natural talent. What! A great teacher, a singer and now a writer!'

'Bit of an exaggeration! I've been lucky so far. Whether I continue to be so, remains to be seen. But I do enjoy writing.' Then tentatively he added, 'I always wanted to come back. When I came across the story, it gave me a reason to do so.'

'And how did you get on with sexy Annette last weekend?' said Marama changing the subject. 'Didn't realize you two were that friendly.'

'We're not. I was at the dance with friends. I gather Annette and her buddies gate-crashed the place. I believe they do this quite often.'

'Sounds like Annette alright.'

'Annette found me and decided to stay with me all night.'

'All night?' asked Marama quizzically.

'I took her home. That's all. Some of her friends arrived for a party and I decided it was time to make tracks. Annette's OK. I quite like her.'

'You certainly made a handsome couple. Anyway, Sean, Turi and I had better get back. It was nice to see you. They've all missed you. Kirri likes you too.' To Sean's surprise, Marama stepped forward and kissed him on the cheek before quickly moving off.

Dazedly Sean called after her, 'Night Marama.'

'What was all that about?' Sean asked himself as he headed down the path to the bridge. 'First she's the old Marama listening to my story then she reverts back to the cool arms-at-length Marama querying me about Annette. Then she gives me a good night kiss!'

Sean switched off the bedside light and lay on his back, blankets pulled up to his chin. In his heart of hearts he felt there was still a connection between himself and Marama. He deliberately hadn't asked anything about Michael Maitland. But she had asked him about Annette. And she had kissed him good night. He fell asleep with the glimmer of a smile still on his lips.

23

Julia was excited. It was Tuesday morning and tomorrow couldn't come quickly enough for her. Tomorrow was the start of a new phase in her life.

'Oh, by the way Jack, I'm going to be up in Oamaru a few days a week from now on, starting as of tomorrow. I'm going to be running a shop there.'

'You taking on running a shop! What are you on about, woman, you don't know the first thing about running a business.'

Julia was sitting at the kitchen table, holding her tea cup in both hands. Jack was facing her, leaning back against the kitchen sink, a mug of coffee in one hand and a cigarette in the other. He took a long draw then exhaled. His eyes narrowed, 'This has got something to do with the Rose dame, Gail Munro's sister, hasn't it?'

'Yes, it's got a lot to do with my friend Rose. It so happens, Jack, that I'm taking over her florist shop and delivery service. Rose has decided to take things easier.'

'Don't tell me she's just going to give it to you,' sneered Jack. 'I know the outfit. It must be worth a bomb. Unless you've come to some cosy arrangement,' he smirked.

'What do you mean?'

'Well, she is a bloody lesbian, isn't she? You know, batting for the other side and all that. So, you batting for the other side too, Julia? Wouldn't surprise me. You don't seem to be offering it around to anyone else.'

'Get your mind above your belt, Jack. We've come to a financial arrangement. I've got the money from Mum and Dad's house in my own account as you well know. I won't be touching our joint account, though putting up with you all these years I should be perfectly entitled to do so.'

'So, you've spent most weekends lately in Oamaru. Now you're going to be up there during the week too. Where does that put me? Folks will wonder.'

'It puts you right where you are at the moment, 'cept you'll have to do a bit more cooking. And I reckon folks won't wonder any more about us than they do at the moment. And I don't give a stuff anyway. I've given the best years of my life to you and the family. Now, whilst I've the chance, I'm going to live for me.'

'Suit your bloody self,' said Jack banging his mug down on the worktop. He strode to the back door and slammed it behind him.

Julia grimaced and said to herself, 'Oh well, that didn't go too badly. Step one completed.'

The constant ringing of the phone in the adjacent office made Michael Maitland sigh in exasperation and get up from his desk. His desk phone was out of order and he'd forgotten that Judy had a doctor's appointment and wouldn't be back for the rest of the day. He strode through the doorway connecting the two huts that made up the admin block for the quarry and picked up the phone.

'Maitland Limeworks, Michael Maitland….'

'Michael,' his father cut in. We've got problems. Old Te Kanawa and some smart-assed young lawyer have just been at the planning department. They've succeeded in raising an injunction that blocks any movement on the new road until appropriate legal proceedings are instigated and there's been a court hearing. I just got a call from Trevor Hall. He seems to think we could have trouble.'

'I don't understand, Dad. I thought Trev said it was all sewn up.'

'He did. But things have changed. I'll see what else I can find out at this end. But I'll have to meet up with you and Jack. I want you down this weekend. This is all we bloody need. According to Trev, this Maori guy knows his stuff – very professional, very articulate and not the type we'll be able to buy off, that's for sure. Oh, and another thing, Trev said that they were accompanied by a third guy – the Campbell boy that used to teach at the school. What the hell would he be doing there?'

'Don't know. But I'll find out,' answered Michael feeling an inner tension start to build up.

'Do that, Michael. Be in touch.' Grant Maitland hung up and his son thoughtfully placed the phone back on the receiver.

As he walked slowly back to his own office he thought

about Sean Campbell. He'd had very little contact with him. But when he'd met him at the party way back, he'd taken a dislike to him. Admittedly this was in part due to the fact that Campbell and Marama seemed to get on so well together. He'd got the impression that the Scot fancied her. But even then, he, Michael Maitland, had had his own plans for Marama, despite the fact that she was engaged to his cousin Rob. He thought about cousin Rob. What a no-hoper! Well, he was eliminated from the competition, as would anyone else be if foolhardy enough to get in his way.

He clenched his fists tightly. He could feel the anger coming to the surface. He felt the tension increase and his head begin to throb. He took several deep breaths, just as he'd been instructed to do.

Jack woke with a start to the sound of a car engine. He listened for a moment and recognized it as Julia's Mini. Glancing at the clock he saw it was just before seven. Throwing back the covers, he walked over to the bedroom window. He watched the tail-lights of the car winking down the drive in the greyness of near-dawn. Where the hell was she off to at this time on a winter's morning? he wondered. Normally Julia wasn't up before eight at this time of year. He himself, never later than a six o'clock rise for most of the year, could allow a bit of a lie-in for a few weeks over the winter period. Stretching his arms to touch the ceiling he yawned and then got dressed. He'd have a shave after breakfast.

He went downstairs to the kitchen and flicked on the light. Everything was spick and span, but if he wanted breakfast he'd have to get it. The miserable bitch hadn't even put as much as a cup out for him. He then saw the note on the table. As he lifted it up, he suddenly recalled she was going off to Oamaru. He held it up to the light and the note confirmed his thinking.

Jack – I'm off to Oamaru for the rest of the week. Might be back on Saturday, don't know yet. I officially take over the shop this afternoon.

Julia

He crumpled up the note in his fist and felt a surge of resentment come over him. 'Hope she makes a right balls up of it,' he thought. 'And I won't be missing her sour-puss expression around here.' But he was also suddenly aware of another inner feeling, a dawning that this was the way it was going to be, that he was on his own. And he felt a twinge of emptiness. Shaking off the feeling he said to himself, 'Must pop down and see Mary tonight.'

Julia hummed to herself as she took the road into Palmerston. In contrast to the darkness of the morning and the promise of a wet dreary day weather-wise, she felt excited and happy. And she was relishing the challenge ahead of her. Despite a tingle of nerves and some trepidation, she knew she could handle taking on the new venture. And, of course, she had the support of Rose and Merv – good friends who'd given her encouragement and loads of practical advice.

She thought of Merv. She could see the possibility of them becoming closer friends, or even more. But she would take things slowly and see how they developed. For the moment she was happy to have his friendship. The shop and its possibilities were more than enough to fill up her life for the foreseeable future. She'd had a long chat with Annette about her plans and had received her daughter's whole-hearted backing. She'd been surprised too by Vic's reaction. She'd thought he might have queried her being away from Jack but Vic had smiled and said, 'Go for it, Mother.' Driving along she began to focus on the initial priorities she had planned for the next few days.

24

Michael Maitland looked at Marama thoughtfully. He flicked the ash off the end of his cigarette and said casually, 'You know Marama, with me working up here during the week I thought I'd be seeing a lot more of you. But, if anything, I'm actually seeing less, especially as you don't seem to be managing to come down to Dunedin at the weekends.'

'Look Michael, as I've told you before, my first priority is Kirri. During the week she gets my full attention. I don't mind the odd weekend away, but not too often. I've also got my job which involves me doing preparation at night as well.'

It was a Thursday evening and they were sitting at a table in the Glenbeg Arms lounge bar. Marama had agreed to go out as she couldn't manage the weekend in town. And Michael had said that he and Jack would be spending most of the weekend with his father in Dunedin working on a business project.

Maitland took a sip of his gin and lemonade then gazed at the glass. 'Have you seen much of this Campbell individual lately?'

'Sean? No. Not since last week anyway. Why do you ask?'

'Where did you see him last week?' asked Michael ignoring Marama's question.

'Well, he was round at my grandparents' for a meal one night. But what's that got to do with anything? Sean's always been friendly with them. He and my grandfather get on well together.'

'So I hear. So well in fact, that he was down with Tama and a lawyer at the planning department. What the hell has that got to do with Campbell?'

'I wouldn't know, Michael,' said Marama looking him straight in the eye. 'You'd have to ask him that.'

'I might just do that. Look, I had my father on the phone the other day. We could be facing trouble getting this quarry started on time. It seems your grandfather is causing problems. Things could get nasty. It's putting me in an awkward spot. I need to know where you stand in all this.'

'You mean with regards to the road by the caves?'

'Of course.'

'Well, I don't have strong feelings either way. But the old folk regard the land as tapu and that's important to them. And if it belongs to the tribe then your lot will just have to fork out the money to take the road the long way round. I don't think it's going to bring Maitland Products to its knees. Can't you find a compromise?'

'That's the trouble, there's no bloody compromise. We're signed up with contractors and they're due to come in and start work on the road in two weeks' time. If this is all held up by legal injunctions and the like, that will cost us money, and big bucks too.'

'Not my problem, Michael, and I don't plan to get involved.'

'But you are involved. If you're going to be my future wife I expect your support.'

'Whoa! Hold on. Where does marriage come into all this? It's news to me. And, for the record, I am not intending to take sides. So don't push me, Michael.'

Maitland could feel anger welling up. Try as he might he couldn't stop himself, 'It's this bloody Campbell character, isn't it? I thought it was just him attracted to you but it's mutual, isn't it? You've fancied him all along!'

'Don't be ridiculous,' said Marama feeling the flush spread from her neck to her cheeks.

'I saw it at the party that night. You were all over him. Poor old Rob might have been dead drunk but he could see it too.'

'You're talking nonsense. Don't tell me you're jealous of Sean!'

'Jealous! That'll be right. What's he got that I haven't got ten times over. He's just a bloody primary teacher.'

'Correction. *Was* a primary teacher, and a very talented one. Now he's a successful writer. And in case you've forgotten, I'm a bloody primary teacher too.'

Maitland put his hand firmly down on top of Marama's wrist and held it there on the table top. He took two deep breaths and spoke in a low but controlled voice, 'I don't want you seeing him anymore. Just keep away from him.

'Well, that's going to be rather difficult as Sean's working in school tomorrow. And he'll be taking Bryn's class for the next week. What do you want me to do, wear a blindfold?'

'He's going to be working with you again?' said Maitland, taken aback.

'Yes, Bryn's got a conference in Wellington,' said Marama pushing her chair back and standing up at the same time. Maitland was forced to let go of her arm. Marama raised her voice, 'I'm seeing another side to you, Michael, and I don't like it. I won't be threatened. And I won't be told what to do. I'm going home, alone. Don't make a bigger fool of yourself than you've done tonight already.' Marama grabbed her coat and headed for the door.

'Marama,' he began. But she was already gone. He noticed a few faces looking across at him. He stared defiantly across the room searching for any lingering looks. Bloody cockies, he thought to himself, you can see the sheep shit sticking to their boots. He endeavoured to look unconcerned, smiled and then threw back the rest of his drink. He walked over to the bar with his empty glass.

Lyn looked at him thoughtfully. 'What's it to be, Michael?'

'A double,' he replied.

Marama walked quickly down past the Store and petrol pumps and then turned into the cul-de sac. She was angry but also a little shaken. 'What did I see in that arrogant sod?' she thought to herself. She'd known before that Michael had a temper and heard from Hemi about him roaring and shouting at the workmen. According to Hemi, some of the guys were wary of him but her brother just seemed to find it amusing. Hemi hadn't had any bother with him. It could have been because Michael wanted to keep in with the family. Then again, thought Marama, if there had been no family link it would be highly unlikely that Michael messed with Hemi. Hemi was good-natured but he could handle himself well, very well!

But Michael had always kept his temper in check with her. In fact, he seemed always very calm and composed, and, in control. *Control,* yes she thought, control was a word that you would very much associate with him. He liked to be in control of everyone and everything, and of her. He'd always been quite possessive when they went out together but tonight, observing him, she had seen an almost manic look in his eyes. She had felt just a little scared when he grabbed her wrist. His grip had hurt her, but it was the way he had looked and spoken that had worried her. No, this was a situation she needed to get out of fast.

She'd been going out with him for the past year. They'd certainly indulged in a bit of heavy petting but she'd so far resisted sleeping with him, despite his protestations. And when they'd gone to Dunedin, she'd mostly stayed with an ex-university colleague in her flat. A couple of times she'd stayed at Michael's parents' home up in Maori Hill. But she'd always had a bedroom to herself.

As she passed the school, Marama noticed a light on in the senior classroom. It was too dark to make out the time on her watch but she remembered the clock above the bar showing nine-thirty, just before she left. Must be Sean she thought, making sure he's fully prepared for the day ahead.

That's dedication for you. She opened the metal gate and walked along the concrete path that wound round the side of the building. She tip-toed over to the windows and peeped through. She felt a sudden pang as she saw Sean sitting at Bryn's desk studying some papers and intermittently taking notes. The blackboard displayed the new day's programme. Everything looked orderly and organized. Sean looked up from what he was doing and over in her direction, but Marama had quickly pulled back into the shadows. Reluctantly she turned away and made for the swing bridge. Crossing it, she thought back to the magical night by the river. Later she was still thinking about it as she climbed into her bed and switched off the bedside lamp.

Lyn had just seen the last of her customers off the premises. She bolted the first half of the main door then turned and called over to Michael Maitland where he sat staring morosely at his glass. 'Mike, are you going home or what?'

The sound of her voice served to jerk him away from his thoughts. 'U-uh. Yeah, yeah. I suppose I'd better be off.'

'You don't need to you know,' she said standing up and placing her hands on her hips. 'Mum's off for the night. You can come through to the flat and have a nightcap with me if you want.'

Michael's attention was now focused on the curvy Lyn, suddenly aware of the sexy barmaid and the hint of something more than just a nightcap.

'Sure, I'd like that,' he said getting up unsteadily from his seat and following her through to the private back sitting room.

The room was small and cosy. The subdued lighting came from a converted brass oil lamp perched on the right-hand side of the stone mantelpiece and a small table lamp set on a mahogany desk at the back of the room. Lyn gestured to him to take a seat on the sofa facing the fireside. She placed another log on the fire. 'Another gin, Mike?'

'Whatever you're having, Lyn.'

She poured two substantial measures into crystal tumblers, topped them up with lemonade and carried them over to the sofa. Leaning forward she handed one to Michael, her ample cleavage moving perceptively with the motion. Taking the glass but not moving his eyes from the enticing bosom, he whispered, 'Nice, ve-ry nice.'

'You like?' she asked rhetorically and knelt down in front of him.

'Very much,' he croaked placing his glass on the occasional table at the side of the sofa. He leant forward and clasped each of the orbs.

'Mmmm,' she said, closing her eyes. 'That's nice.' Then putting her own glass beside his, she placed her fingers on his thighs and began massaging from knees to crotch, teasingly stopping just short of his genitals.

'That's even nicer,' he replied. He slid his hands under her light woollen top, pushing his fingers up and under her bra and lifting it over the top of her breasts thus freeing them to be clasped in the palm of each hand. Moving his forefingers and thumbs to hold the aroused and projecting nipples, he then began to move the thumbs in a circular motion that stroked them lightly.

'Oh,' she sighed. Then getting up from the floor, she straddled his thighs and began to unzip his trousers.

With her skirt almost at waist level, he slid his hands down the back of her skimpy pants and squeezed her firm shapely buttocks.

She lunged forwards and thrust her tongue deep into his mouth. Clothing was urgently thrown off and they became entwined on the sofa. He was about to enter her when she pushed her hand down on him. 'Wait a minute. You were in the Boy Scouts?'

He looked blankly for a minute then gave a lazy grin of understanding. 'Uuh..Be Prepared. I, a-ah.'

'It's OK. I've got one here,' she said taking a condom from the table and handing it to him.

He hurriedly put it on and immediately thrust himself into her.

She gasped, 'Hang on, Mike, I want you to shag me hard.'

But he ejaculated quickly and suddenly became limp. 'Sorry about that,' he half laughed as he pulled himself out and away from her. 'Just couldn't hang on. Guess I'm out of practice.'

She lay back and closed her eyes. God, she thought, that wasn't too impressive. I thought this guy would be really experienced.

They lay there for a few moments, each with his own thoughts before Lyn broke the silence and said petulantly, 'Well, Michael, what's wrong, you not getting it from Miss Te Kanawa?'

Michael tensed. 'What do you mean?'

'Well, you said you were out of practice and you certainly jerked off pretty damned fast. Marama putting you on rations?'

Michael raised himself off her and slapped her twice, forehand and backhand, hard and across the face. 'You cheeky slut. What I do with Marama is none of your bloody business.' He then grabbed her by the throat and squeezed roughly. Lyn let out a choked squeal and he eased the pressure a little. 'Listen, you ignorant bitch, you say nothing of this to anyone. Nothing! And if I hear of any gossip that suggests things are not right between Marama and me I'll fucking kill you. Do you understand?'

Lyn looked at him fearfully. The crazed look terrified her. This was someone she didn't want to cross again, someone she didn't want to see again. She was suitably scared.

'I..I won't say anything to anyone, honest,' she whimpered.'

'You'd better bloody not,' he said removing his hand from her throat. He then ran the back of it gently down the side of her cheek, relaxed and smiled. 'Good. We understand each other, Lyn. Not a word then.' He got up and pulled on his clothes whilst she lay on the sofa, too frightened to move. The manic look had suddenly gone. He appeared calm and even sober. 'Don't get up, I'll see myself out.' He left the room.

When she heard the slam of the outside door she ran over sobbing and quickly locked it.

25

'Please Sir, this kelpie creature sounds a bit like our taniwha. What do you think?'

'I think you're right, Nik, smiled Sean. 'They certainly didn't look alike but there are a lot of similarities in the way they lived– or should I say live,' he added with a laugh.

'You mean the kelpie's still there?' asked Jenny Mains wide-eyed.

'That's right, Jenny. A lot of people believe that,' answered Sean, at the same time thinking to himself, Heavens, a subtle change of tense and this kid gets the point right away.

Sean was in the senior classroom at Glenbeg Primary which, like all small rural schools, was a composition – in this case of Standards 4, 5 and 6 pupils. It was near the end of the school day and the pupils had been listening raptly to the story of the Kelpie's Pearls, written by the acclaimed Scottish novelist Mollie Hunter. After a day's teaching it seemed to Sean as if he'd never been away. Bryn had collared him a few days previously and explained that he would be attending a conference up north. It meant him being off school for a week and there were no supply teachers able to cover. He desperately needed the favour. He'd cleared it with the Otago Education Board that Sean could be employed, if available to do so. Sean couldn't refuse his old friend and as a bonus he knew that he'd be in close proximity to Marama. To get up to speed with programmes of work, he'd spent the last two days in class alongside Bryn. It was just like old times.

'It's just like the Loch Ness Monster. People believe in that too, don't they Sir?'

'Yes Nikora, they certainly do.'

'Well, I don't know about the kelpie, but stories about the taniwha certainly kept little kids away from deep pools and other dangerous places. And I suppose that's what the grown-ups wanted.'

'You're right. And tales of the kelpie would have achieved the same objective.'

'What about the Loch Ness Monster, does it come into the story Sir?' asked Billy MacDonald.

'It does indeed. Remember, this story takes place in Abriachan, a tiny little village in the hills above Loch Ness. I've been there and it's just like Molly Hunter describes it in the book. The lake, or loch as they say in Scotland, is just a walk down the hill. Right you lot, it's just about home time. On Monday we'll read a bit more of the story and during art time you're going to sketch or paint your own fantasy creature or, if you like, your impression of a kelpie or taniwha.'

'Yeah! Great!' chorused the class.

'OK. A quick tidy up before we leave. Check your desks and the floor around you for any rubbish. Put it in the bin and then we'll see who's sitting up, arms folded and ready to go. I'll count to 10. Go! One – two – three….'

With all hands to the task everything was cleared up quickly, eager young bodies sitting up straight, keen to please their teacher.

'Stand everyone. Good afternoon boys and girls.'

'Good afternoon, Mr Campbell,' they replied in unison.

'Off you go,' said Sean with a smile, at the same time thinking, what great kids. He headed towards the staffroom and caught Marama's eye as she ushered some younger pupils towards the exit. 'Coffee? he inquired raising his eyebrows.'

'Wonderful,' she replied. 'Be right with you.'

He felt buoyant. It was clear that Marama was happy for him to be back in the school.

When Marama entered the staffroom Sean was in conversation with Bryn's wife Pam. Pam did the school cleaning to help supplement the family income.

'Hi Marama,' said Pam as she lifted her cup and then swallowed the remnants of her coffee. 'Isn't it great to see Handsome Harry back here with us,' she exclaimed, leaning over to ruffle Sean's wavy mop of hair. 'Anyway, must dash. I'll get the cleaning done double quick. Due to take the kids into Palmerston for a swim and then we have our Friday night ritual of a visit to the chip shop. See you later.' And she disappeared along the corridor.

'That woman is perpetual motion,' said Sean shaking his head.

Marama sat down on one of the easy chairs and leant forward to take a biscuit from the tin. 'Cheers, Sean. So how did your day go with the biggies?' she asked.

'I'd a good day. Everything went more or less according to plan. The kids were great. I reckon I'll survive till the end of next week.'

'That's good, I didn't think it would take you long to get back into the swing of things.'

'Yeah, it was OK. But tell you what, this teaching lark is tiring. And the kids are with you all the time. Writing is quite a disciplined occupation and if you're writing towards a deadline, it can be quite intensive. But boy, folk who haven't worked as teachers have no idea just how demanding it can be. By the way, where's Sally?'

Marama laughed, 'Can't but agree with you about teaching, Sean. Sally had to get off really smartly. I think they've got the in-laws coming from Waimate for the weekend and she's still got a dozen things to do before they come.' She crossed one long shapely leg over the other. Sean, though focused on her face, was quite aware of the movement. 'Anyway, what are your plans for the weekend? Don't tell me you're going to spend it all on school work?'

'Not at all. Bryn's got everything well planned out. So it's not as if I'm starting from scratch. I'll need to do a bit of preparation to keep ahead of the game, but it won't be a big deal. I actually thought of going for a walk over to the old caves up beyond the quarry at some stage. What about yourself?'

'Nothing really planned. Katelyn Cameron was asking me on the phone last night if I'd like to take a run up to see her. Might just do that. Want to come?'

Marama's invitation surprised Sean. 'Eh… yeah, I' d like that. But are you just going yourself?'

'Just Kirri and me. Oh, and if you're wondering about my dear friend Michael Maitland, well forget him. He's history and I don't want to talk about it. OK?'

'OK. Fine by me,' said Sean. 'When were you thinking of setting off?'

'Oh, reckon about ten. We'll take my car. I'll give you a toot. We'll go and see Katelyn first and then take a run into Ranfurly. Don't be surprised if she insists we stay for lunch. After that we can have a wander about and take Kirri to the icecream parlour.'

'Sounds grand. I'll look forward to that.'

'And so will I,' she replied with a twinkle in her eye. Anyway, Nana and Grandad will be due back from the pa with Kirri at five. I'd better tidy up and get on my way. Till tomorrow then.'

'Tomorrow it is.'

26

He caught sight of the Zarkov kid as he sat in the hide. The boy was watching him from further up the bank. Vic put his finger to his lips indicating he didn't want any noise. Jakob stared intently and then nodded in understanding.

Despite his gruffness, Vic had always made a point of acknowledging this strange silent kid when he saw him around the village. Some said he wasn't the full quid whilst others gossiped that he'd been dropped on his head as a baby. He knew the boy was a loner and that he didn't communicate with anyone, didn't seem to be able to speak to anyone outwith his family home. For this reason, Vic would always give a nod of the head or a wink, an acknowledgement that he was sure Jakob picked up on. If anything, it established a distant connection between them. Vic could recognise a response in the boy's eyes even though his face always seemed to be devoid of any expression.

Yeah, the kid was a loner. And Vic empathized with this fact. Though not a loner as such, he'd grown up in the shadow of Rob. He'd always been in the background. Rob had been the pretty one, the outgoing one, the footie star, the guy that had all the sheilas running after him – always the centre of attention. Sure, when they'd got older and gone out on the piss Vic would play up in front of the group and usually do something outrageous and fairly stupid. But it would get a laugh from the group – and from Rob, the one he'd always wanted to please and impress. If there was the threat of a punch-up, Vic would always be to the fore, launching into the fray head-first, often literally. But other than that, Vic was background, he tagged along and was tolerated, accepted partly because he was Rob's young brother. His capacity for rage and his not inconsiderable physical strength also stood him in good stead with the others, feeling they'd do well to accept him as a member of the group.

Vic gestured to Jakob to come down, at the same time repeating the sign to do so quietly. Surprisingly, the boy responded and came silently to the hide. Vic noticed one hand clutched a pad which he held close to his chest.

'Hi, Jako,' he whispered. You like watching birds too?'

Jakob nodded. Vic handed him his binoculars and said softly, 'Look over to the right of the big weeping willow. There's a kingfisher sitting on the bank.'

Jakob raised the binoculars. Screwing up his eyes he waved them erratically.

Vic stood behind him. 'Not like that, son. Take it slow. He gently guided the boy's hands until they were directed at the point where he reckoned he'd clocked the bird. Jakob stiffened then excitedly gave a sharp nod.

'You see him?'

Another nod.

'Good boy. He's a handsome little bugger, isn't he?'

Eventually Jakob handed the binoculars back. As he did so the bird flew off.

'Well, reckon that's him away to hunt for his dinner, Jakob, and I guess you and me better be doing the same.'

The boy still didn't say anything but shyly he lifted up the pad he'd put on the ground and began turning over several pages. Vic got a glimpse of several vivid sketches but his eyebrows rose in wonder when Jakob held the pad up to him.

'Jesus, Jako, you didn't draw this did you?'

Jakob nodded and stared intently at Vic.

'But that's bloody marvellous, son. That's wonderful. Have you shown this to anyone else?'

The boy shook his head.

Vic looked at the sketch of a kingfisher in flight and resplendently coloured. He shook his head slowly, in disbelief.

'This is good, Jako. You're an artist and no mistake. You've got to show this to other people.'

The boy started to look alarmed and pulled the pad to his chest fiercely. His eyes became watery.

'Hey, boy, it's OK. Look if you don't want anyone else to see this just now that's OK. It'll be a secret. Is that what you want?'

Jakob looked up and nodded, sniffing slightly.

'Right, son. Guess I'm really privileged to see your beautiful drawing, so thanks for that. I take it there are others there?' asked Vic, and taking care not to push things he added, 'Maybe you'll let me see them some day?'

Again, Jakob nodded.

'Good boy. I'd like that. Meantime you come down and use this hide any time you like though I guess maybe you use it just as much as me. Sometimes I see little bits have been added. Was that your good work Jakob Zarkov?'

The trace of a smile formed on Jakob's lips.

'OK, Jakob, I'm off now.' Vic patted him on the head and set off back along the river path.

Jakob scrambled up to the top of the bank and disappeared over the other side.

They'd knocked off work at four o'clock, a practice Vic had got going a year before. He'd arranged with Grant Maitland that the men cut their lunch hour down on a Thursday and Friday and got away early for the end of the working week. His cousin Michael didn't seem too chuffed about the arrangement but so what! In fact, he'd noticed that the bugger had taken off at around three o'clock himself and without a word to anyone. But that was Mike, a strange character. No. More than strange. Odd.

Vic had told the boys he'd something to attend to and wouldn't make the pub till later on that night. He was curious to see if the little kingfisher was still around and had made for the river instead, not that any of them was aware of his interest in wildlife. In fact, if that came out over a few jars they'd all be pissing themselves, he thought with a smile. He parked the jeep at the side of the old homestead and got out. He climbed the steps up on to the weather-beaten veranda and thought, Hell I'd better give the old place a coat of paint before the weather gets much colder. Maybe I should start tomorrow.

Pushing the door open, he dumped his tucker bag and binoculars on the chair by the door and went through to run the bath. The water was piping hot and steam began to billow as he opened the window. He stripped off his dust-covered outer clothes and dropped them on the floor, then, taking a key from a hook just above the bathroom door, he padded through in his underwear to the back room. Unlocking the door released a little light into an otherwise completely blacked-out room. He flicked on the light switch and the room came to life underneath the fluorescent tubes.

Vic looked around and thought of the pleasure and satisfaction that this place gave him. It had been the main bedroom in the old homestead, the one his grandparents would have used. Now it was a workshop and veritable gallery. A huge and ancient pine table covered with tools, glues, cardboard and photo prints, sat in the middle of the room with a stack of empty frames and glass leaning against one of its legs. A solitary pine chair was tucked under one end of the table. Heavy black curtains covered the window on the back wall, below which was a small bookcase, its top shelf holding three cameras and its other shelves filled with hardback books. Apart from what looked like a walk-in cupboard in the far right-hand corner, the room was devoid of any other furniture. But all the walls were covered in framed and unframed photographs depicting wildlife and landscapes – stunningly beautiful shots of birds, deer, leaping fish, snow-capped peaks and glass-like lakes. All had been taken with a skilled and sympathetic eye. Vic Maitland's eye.

It was almost dark as Marama began to cross the old swing bridge. She felt good, better than she'd felt for a long time. She took several deep breaths, inhaling and holding the cold night air in her lungs before exhaling what looked like miniature puffs of smoke into the still atmosphere. She also felt a tremor of excitement at the thought of going off with Sean and Kirri in the morning. But her elation suddenly dropped as she recognized the faint outline of Michael Maitland's black Austin Cambridge parked at the end of the avenue. Fallen leaves rustled and crunched under her feet as she approached the vehicle.

Maitland got out just as she reached the car. 'Marama, I was hoping I'd catch you before I set off.' Unbeknown to Marama, he'd been sitting there for the past hour cursing the school and the thought of her in close proximity to Sean Campbell. He stretched out a hand to her shoulder. She flinched and he immediately dropped it. 'Marama, listen, I'm sorry about last night. I've just been under a bit of pressure lately. So,' he said, a tight smile forming, 'is all forgiven?'

Marama looked at him coolly though she was aware of an inner anxiety. 'Let's say we'll leave the past behind, Michael.'

'Good,' he interrupted, visibly relaxing. 'Will I see you on Sunday night then?'

'I don't think so, Michael. Let's just leave things for now.'

'For now! What do you mean for now?' His voice had lost its conciliatory tones and his face had hardened. 'You're not by any chance giving me the brush off are you,

Marama? It would not be a good idea. Not for you and not for your family.'

His words chilled her. 'What do you mean?'

'Your secret. I know about it.'

Marama felt as though she'd been punched in the stomach. Momentarily she was lost for words, panic-stricken. But he continued, 'Listen, I plan to marry you. I can provide all that you need and all that your little girl needs. You'll want for nothing. You won't need to work. You'll enjoy a good life.'

She rallied and tensely responded, 'I'm enjoying life at the moment thank you. And I enjoy my work. Threatening me and telling me you'll marry me is not going to work. In fact, it has the opposite effect. Go and find somebody else, Michael.' She had deliberately ignored the remark that had totally thrown her, hoping against hope that she'd misheard him, that his comment referred to something else, something trivial. She started to move off but she paused and turned to look at him as he called after her...

'I know you were in the truck that night.' He continued, 'I'm sure the police would be very interested. Think about it, then think about what I'm offering you. I'll be in touch,' he said as he got back into the car.

Marama set off, quickening her pace. A feeling of despair enshrouded her as thoughts of the past flooded her mind.

Maitland got into the car. He clenched the wheel, knuckles gleaming white in the dark interior. A cold rage surged through him. The bitch was trying to give him the brush off. We'll see about that, he thought. If she knows what's good for her, she'll stick with me. And if she didn't, he'd be a laughing stock. Plenty of the locals round here didn't like him, not that that bothered him. But the thought that they'd learn he'd been dumped, that was not something he could entertain. No, he Michael Maitland did the dumping, not the other way around. And this bastard Campbell, he was sure he was at the root of Marama's change of mind. He had to be sorted out.

He started the car and revved it harshly, the roar of the engine reflecting his mood. Flicking on the lights he drove off, spinning the vehicle into the backroad turning. The headlights picked out Marama's white trench coat as she walked towards the Te Kanawa cottage. He quickly went through to third gear, his foot hard on the accelerator. She didn't turn around but moved onto the grass verge at his approach. He moved the car closer to the verge and slammed it into top gear, shooting past her with inches to spare. He looked into the mirror and smiled at her now stationary figure, 'Let that be a little warning to you dear Marama.'

Marama knew he would be passing her. Initially she thought he might stop to talk further. She had felt the full force of the slipstream as the car whizzed past her so close that it almost put her off balance. 'What a crazy sod,' she'd thought angrily. But he had frightened her, reached and touched that hidden worry spot that lurked within her.

27

It was Saturday morning. The air was crisp and the blue sky gave the promise of a fine day ahead. Sean was leaning against the school boundary fence, hands in tracksuit top pockets and eyes closed enjoying the morning sun's rays on his face.

A cheery 'Good morning, Sean,' delivered in a thick guttural accent caused him to open his eyes and focus on the speaker. It was Istvan Zarkov, Jakob's dad. Istvan, like many of his countrymen, had fled Hungary during the 1956 uprisings. Around a thousand Hungarian refugees had settled in New Zealand at this time.

'Hi, Istvan,' said Sean with a smile. 'What a beautiful day.'

'Indeed. I can see you enjoy the sunshine. Not so likely to get autumn weather like this in Scotland, yes?'

'Well, we can get crisp sunny days, but certainly a few degrees cooler. How is Jakob getting on these days?'

'Jakob. He is OK. He talks about you at home. He thinks Mr Campbell is great!'

'Well, I'm glad to hear he is getting enjoyment from school. It's strange, I mean the fact that he won't – or doesn't seem able - to say a word in school or the wider community and yet he'll communicate with his family. I've never come across this before. Bryn was saying that he'd heard of a similar case when he was teaching in Wales. I gather he'd talked about this with you.'

'Yes, he has given us hope. The doctor in Palmerston sent us for special help in Dunedin but no-one has any answer. Jakob had meetings with psychologist who travelled up to see him. But Mr Jones sees psychologist and tells him about case in Wales. It is decided that we carry on as normal in school and don't demand any response from Jakob. We don't put pressure on him. We just let him listen and do the things the other children do. Then maybe, like happened with the child in Wales, some day he will begin to speak. Over last year Jakob is giving some response to other children. He will nod his head for 'yes' and shake his head for 'no'. That is progress, not much, but still progress.'

'Well, I hope we get a break through soon. He's a nice little lad and he seems so focused on listening to all that's going on. He's still drawing and sketching at home?

'Oh ja. Always drawing. I think he's pretty good.'

'I've had the privilege of seeing a couple of his private sketches. He's really talented. But so far, he doesn't really seem to display his ability in school. But we'll keep encouraging him. Anyway, Istvan, nice talking to you. Must go, here's my transport arriving,' said Sean nodding towards Marama who had pulled up just past them and was manoeuvring her little Morris Minor to head back out of the cul-de-sac.

'Hi, ladies,' said Sean climbing into the front passenger seat. 'How are you this fine day?'

'We're good,' smiled Marama, determined not to let the events of the previous evening spoil their day out.

'And we might be going to the ice cream parlour, after we visit Katelyn,' added Kirri excitedly from the back seat.'

'You don't like ice cream do you Kirri?' asked Sean teasingly.

'Yes I do, I really do. And Mum said as a special treat we might sit down and have an ice cream sundae!'

'Don't you think it should be an ice cream Saturday?'

'Sean, you are silly,' giggled Kirri.

A happy day began with games and songs on the journey to Naseby. Driving into the grounds of the new bungalow built on the outskirts of Naseby, they were met by Barney carrying three-year old Jack, a heavily pregnant Katelyn and six-year old daughter Meg. With introductions over, Marama adjourned with Katelyn to the kitchen to catch up on all the news whilst the men went for a tour of the property with Meg, Jack and Kirri. The children's tour stopped at the miniature house Barney had built for Meg. Complete with furniture and trappings, it drew Kirri like a magnet. Leaving the children to play, Barney continued the tour with Sean.

'Gee, you made some job here, Barney. Marama tells me you built the whole house single-handed. I know you're a surveyor but did you do an apprenticeship as a carpenter?'

'Nah. Making things has always been a hobby of mine. My old man was the same. Guess I inherited the building knack from him. Come on, there's beer in the fridge, let's go up to the veranda and have a glass.'

Sitting on an old sofa on the veranda and clutching a glass of cold beer, Sean said, 'This is the life, Barney. I could get used to this.'

'Yeah, mate. From what I hear you've got a pretty interesting life as it is. So, this writing lark, you're doing OK at it aren't you?'

'Yes, well I've had a few lucky breaks and I must admit I'm enjoying life.'

'You and Marama, I don't want to be nosy but are you sort of going out together?'

'Not really but…'

'But you might?' asked Barney with a smile.

'You could say that,' grinned Sean. 'I knew Marama from the last time I was in NZ. But things are a wee bit complicated.'

'Well, she's a great girl and you could do a lot worse. Come to think of it, reckon she could too'. Barney raised his glass, 'Cheers mate.'

'Cheers,' said Sean returning the salute.

A call for lunch saw them all gathered round the table in the Camerons' large kitchen with much animated chatter and laughter. Sean recognized in Katelyn and Barney the sort of people you meet for the first time and feel immediately relaxed and comfortable with. He caught Marama gazing across at him. As their eyes met she smiled and he gave her a wink.

With the children back out playing and the adults sitting over a cup of tea, Barney asked, 'So what's the plan for the afternoon?'

'We thought of taking the kids into Ranfurly for a walk around and an ice cream,' said Marama. 'Maybe Katelyn would like to have a peaceful rest while we did that.'

'Tell you what. Sean, you been to Naseby before?' asked Barney.

'Only passed by. Always meant to have a look.'

'Well, how about you and I take the kids along to Naseby, have a walk around and then go back to the milk bar in Ranfurly for an icecream?'

'Sounds good to me. Do you want to come, Marama?

'I don't mind. If Katelyn wants a snooze I'll leave her to it.'

'I'm not sleepy, Marama. Just lazy! I'd be happy just having a good chat with you. If the boys take off with the kids that'll be a good enough rest for me.'

'Settled then,' said Marama, 'but take yourself off to the sofa whilst the rest of us clear up here.'

The sun continued to shine brightly as they wandered around the small township. Barney explained to Sean that in the 1860's Naseby was one of Central Otago's thriving centres for the gold mining industry. Since then it had shrunk in population terms to the category of a 'one-horse town'. But it was literally now a living museum attracting growing numbers of tourists, particularly in the summer time, to view the old buildings left over from the gold rush heydays. These were now well preserved and of great historical interest. Sean made a mental note to revisit the little township when he was on his own. He thought it would be worth further absorbing the atmosphere and utilizing it as a location in the story that was beginning to take shape in his head.

Much to the children's delight, they finally finished up in Mackenzie's Milkbar in Ranfurly where orders were taken and appetites indulged in some exotic-looking ice cream sundaes.

As they drove back down to Glenbeg with Kirri sound asleep in the backseat, Sean said, 'Well, Marama, that was a really enjoyable day. And I think Barney and Katelyn are a great couple.'

'Yes, I like them a lot. 'Course, Katelyn and I go way back. We were pals even before we got to primary school. They like you too, by the way,' she said smiling but eyes still focused on the road ahead. 'So, what's on your programme tomorrow?'

'Still have a hankering to visit the old caves up beyond the Works. Might have a leisurely leisurely morning and do the walk in the afternoon. What about yourself?'

'Well, I'm due to drop Kirri at Julia's around two. It's a routine we established once she'd become a toddler.'

'How do you get on with them, the once-to-be in-laws I mean?'

Marama seemed to freeze for a moment and Sean could see his question had caught her off guard. 'Hey, sorry Marama. That was pretty insensitive of me. I didn't mean anything by it.'

Marama's shoulders visibly relaxed and she gave a rueful

smile, 'No, that's OK Sean. It's all water under the bridge but when I think about it, it makes me realize just how close I was to becoming Rob's wife. And that would have been a big mistake, no question about it. Actually, Julia's OK and we get on fine together and she loves to see Kirri. Don't think she has much of a life with Jack. They live together but seem to do their own thing. Julia spends quite a bit of time up in Oamaru with her friend Rose, Gail's sister. Jack, Jack's a funny bugger. I never know quite how to take him and I must admit I prefer it when he's not around. He dotes on Kirri alright and always makes a big fuss of her.'

'Well, she is their grandchild and I suppose she is a tangible connection with Rob for them.'

'I suppose,' said Marama frowning and feeling an inner anxiety cloud her demeanour.

Sean steeled himself for a moment and then blurted out, 'Don't suppose you'd feel like a walk tomorrow afternoon then?'

Marama felt herself brighten. Yeah, I'd like that, Sean. I could do with the exercise and time won't be a problem. Julia always drops Kirri back at Nan's after her visit.'

'Great. How about I meet you over at your Nan's around two fifteen? I'll bring a flask of tea and some biscuits.'

'If Nan's been baking, I might be able to do better than biscuits,' grinned Marama as she pulled up beside the Glenbeg store. 'You said you'd some messages to get so here we are.'

'Thanks, Marama. It's been a great day. I really enjoyed it.'

'We enjoyed it too, Sean. Won't waken Sleeping Beauty in the back till we get to the house. See you soon.'

'See you,' said Sean climbing out of the Morris and closing the door. He went into the store, only vaguely aware of the motor cyclist and passenger parked on the opposite side of the road.

'G'day Sean, what can I get you?' asked Bill Hargreaves.

'Hi, Bill. Don't need much just now. I'll just take this loaf and milk for the mo',' he said placing them on the counter.

'So, I hear you're still doing these runs up to the Limeworks.'

'Yeah. Got to try and keep in shape. In fact I'm just off to do one now. You coming with me?'

Sonny Te Hurunui just caught Sean's response before Bill answered, 'You must be joking, mate. My running days are well and truly over.'

'Never say never, Bill,' laughed Sean, as he carried his purchases past Sonny with a nod and a smile.

Sonny gave him a friendly grin.

28

They jumped him halfway up the road to the Limeworks. Sean had just rounded a blind bend. The bike was lying on its sided and the stocky Maori boy with the long black hair and bandana was leaning over his mate who was lying on the ground groaning. Sonny looked up and said, 'Hey, man, can you help me? My mate seems pretty crook. Took the corner a bit fast. Bike went into a skid and we came off. He cracked his head. Think he might be concussed or somethin'.'

'Well I've done a bit of first aid but I'm no expert,' said Sean as he moved to lean over the casualty. Sonny straightened up and took a pace back.

Sonny suddenly grabbed Sean from behind, wrapping his muscular arms around him tightly. The grip increased and he struggled to breathe as his chest cavity felt the force of the increased pressure. He desperately tried to hook a foot behind his attacker to throw him off balance, but as he did so the fellow on the ground got up and punched him twice in the solar plexus. At the same time Sonny released him and Sean collapsed in a heap, gasping for breath.

He tried to speak, 'Listen you guys, what…….?' But

he didn't get a chance to complete his question. A black boot suddenly slammed against the side of his head and he gave a yelp of pain. As further kicks rained upon him, he automatically curled up into a foetal position with his arms clutched around his head.

The assault continued in relative silence, the only noise being the grunts of his attackers as they laid into him and Sean's gasps and groans of pain. Finally, they stopped. Sonny knelt down beside Sean, 'You hear me fella?'

Sean managed to murmur a faint, 'Yes.'

'Nothin' personal. We're just the messengers. But the message is you've been pissing some people off real bad. They think you should go back to Scotland real soon and don't get into matters that don't concern you, like with old Te Kanawa. Oh, and the message is, keep away from Miss Te Kanawa too. Her boyfriend doesn't like you. OK?'

'Fuck off.'

Sonny chuckled. 'Just be a good boy and do as you're told. Next time we might break something and you won't be doin' any more runnin'. See you Scottie boy.'

Sean heard the bike start up and Sonny yell out, 'Let's go.' A cloud of dust puffed over him as the bike roared off.

He lay still for a few moments longer before trying to move. He ached all over but knew he was going to feel a whole lot worse. Slowly he uncurled and got to a hands and knees position. The least little movement made him wince. This is ridiculous, he thought, at this rate, I'll never get home tonight. Eventually he got to his feet, dazedly swaying as he tried to keep balance. The right side of his face felt the size of a house. He touched it gently and looked at the blood on his hand. Feeling further up, he found the cut that was the source of the blood.

Yes, he'd been given a right doing and no mistake. But it could have been worse. These bastards had seemed quite cool about the whole thing and quite detached. Lucky for him that they'd not been told to do further damage. He started to walk down the road, but each step made him gasp. God, I'm in a bad way, he thought. He gritted his teeth and gingerly moved on.

By the time he got to the junction, daylight had almost gone. Wearily he stopped and let himself slowly sink down onto one of the limestone rocks that sat on each side of the road, marking the way up to the quarry. 'Bugger it, I'm sore,' he said to himself.

He was caught in car lights as they swung round from the direction of the main road. As the car passed, he heard its brakes screech and saw the brake lights glow red. Annette threw open the door of her new Mini, climbed out and ran towards him, high heels clacking on the tarmac. She called out anxiously, 'Sean, what happened?'

'Annette, I'm glad to see you. Get me home will you.'

'God, Sean, look at you. You've got blood all over your face and head. Stay there a minute.' She went back to the car and leant into the back seat. Returning with a new white fluffy towel, she knelt down and placed it against his wound. 'Right, keep that pressed hard against your head. Now, up you get.' She helped him get to his feet and round to the passenger door. She could tell from the effort it took for him to get into the car that he was in considerable pain. She slammed the door shut and ran round to the other side, stuck the Mini into gear and slammed her foot down on the accelerator.

'Annette, where are we going? You'll have to turn back round to the main road to get me back to the cottage.'

'You're coming home with me, Sean. We're going to fix you up, and get a doctor.'

'No, no. I can't go to your place. Your dad….'

'My father's not there. He's in Dunedin for the night and Mum's in Oamaru. I just came up tonight to bring more of my things down to the flat.'

'But I….I…'

'No buts about it,' she cut in. 'You're not in a fit state to help yourself. So hang on, we're just about there. And keep that towel tight. It's new, but more importantly, so's the car!'

The Mini bounced up the tree-lined track to the main homestead, passing Vic's house which was in darkness. One final bounce before the car drew up alongside the Maitland residence caused Sean to let out an involuntary grunt of pain.

'Sorry about that,' said Annette. 'Now just wait there,' she ordered. She got out of the car and hurried up the steps, got the door unlocked and put on the hall and veranda lights. She went through to the kitchen, filled the kettle and switched it on. Next, she checked that the immersion heater was on and then hurried through to the downstairs bathroom and started to fill the bath. Opening the small window to let out the steam, she then closed the door and got back out to the car.

As she opened the door Sean said, 'Annette, this is not a good idea. Your folks…'

'Sean, shut up. Now just do as you're told and let's get you out of the car.' She leant forward. 'Put your left arm round my neck and shoulder and we'll haul you up. But keep that bloody towel on the wound.'

With a bit of manoeuvring and encouragement she finally got him out of the car and up the steps to the house. Though he wasn't saying anything, she was aware that he was suffering given the amount of weight he was relying on her to support. Once she had him sitting on a kitchen chair, she ran through to check on the bath and turned the taps off.

Returning to the kitchen she looked at him. 'Sean, I should call a doctor.'

'No, listen Annette, I'll be alright. I can tell nothing's been broken. If you can clean me up a bit I'd be most grateful. Then just give me a wee run home.'

'Well, we'll leave the doctor for the moment but you're not going home tonight. I'll clean you up, you'll have a bath and you'll sleep in the guest room tonight. Mind you,' she smiled, 'you're welcome to share my bed – if you feel up to it!'

'A kind offer, Annette, but I must admit I'm not up for anything at the moment other than sleeping.'

'Still that's promising, Sean. I'm taking it that that's not ruling out a maybe in the future!' she laughed as she poured water from the kettle into a bowl and sprinkled in a dash of dettol.

'Right, shirt off,' said Annette in a business-like tone. Gently she helped him pull his tracksuit top over his head followed by his t-shirt. 'Jeee-sus, Sean, what happened to you?' she gasped as she saw the angry red weals on his body, already beginning to spread further into what would become ugly bruising. 'Who in heavens name did this?'

'Forget it, Annette, I just had a wee accident. That's all I can say for the moment.'

'Wee accident my foot! This should be something for the police.'

'No. Just leave it. Ouch! That's hot,' he said as she started dabbing his cheek with a wad of cotton wool.

Annette quickly added some cold water to the bowl and then began to efficiently clean up his wounds. 'Nothing there that looks like it needs stitches.'

'Thank goodness for that.'

'But that side of your face is going to be black and blue. How's the head feeling?'

'Could be worse, but I wouldn't mind a couple of aspirin.'

'OK, let's get you into the bath and I'll bring you through a cup of sweet tea with some pain killers.'

'Sounds good. Let's go.' He struggled to get up from the chair and waved her off as she moved forward to help.

'I'll go and check out the water's not too hot. Just follow me through, it's first on the left.'

The bathroom was still quite steamy but Annette pulled the window over. Right Sean, are you going to need help to get into the bath. You don't need to be modest. It might surprise you to know that I've seen a few male bodies before.'

Trying to smile, Sean responded, 'I'm shocked Miss

Maitland. I'll be OK, thanks.'

'Right, I'll get you your tea.'

It proved a bit of an operation to get into the warm water but he made it and lay back. 'What is it with this place?' he thought to himself, 'I seem destined to get knocked about and then have people patch me up.'

Annette actually knocked before bowling into the bathroom with a tray. At the knock Sean had strategically placed his hands over the area soccer players cover when lined up in front of free kick specialists. 'Why, Sean, what big hands you've got!' she smiled. She placed a tumbler of whisky and two aspirin on the flat edge of the bath and the tray with the tea on the toilet seat. 'Dad's best malt whisky. I think you need it.'

'Thanks, Annette. I'm sure he'd be delighted to know I'm drinking it.'

'Just think, what a laugh it would be if he came in now and saw you in the bath knocking back his whisky!'

'Yeah. I 'm sure he'd kill himself laughing.'

Half an hour later Sean was tucked up in bed, some older towels strategically covering the pillows to catch any blood residue. He quickly fell into a deep sleep.

The barmen in the Palmerston Royal were working flat out. At nine o'clock the bar was packed and under a thick semi-blue haze of cigarette smoke. A band from Dunedin was set up on a slightly raised platform on the far side of the lounge, belting out a variety of '60's numbers.

Perched on a bar stool and holding a cigarette, a rather

inebriated Sony Te Hurunui was listening through semi-closed eyes to the chatter of a leggy young blonde perched on the stool beside him. He nodded languidly, giving the impression that she had his attention as he took the occasional sip of his rum and coke.

'Sonny, phone call for you,' shouted George, one of the barmen. 'You can take it round the back.'

'Thanks, chief,' said Sonny getting up slowly from his stool. He put his hands on the bare thighs of the blonde whose skirt just about covered her modesty. 'Keep it warm for me Honey,' he smiled and moved off to the office where the manager was doing some paperwork. He handed the phone to Sony.

'Hi, Sonny here.'

'Yeah, Sonny. It's me. Did you manage to get that little job done for me?'

He instantly recognized Jack Maitland's voice. 'Well and truly, Boss. Everything done according to instructions. Our boy was given the full treatment. Anything else I can do for you?'

'No, that's all for the moment. But there will be more to come. Hopefully our fella will not require further treatment.'

'I very much doubt it, Boss. I think he's received all he requires.'

'That's good with me. Be in touch.' Maitland put the phone down and turned to his brother Grant and Michael. 'Seems our friend Campbell got roughed up a bit. If he knows what's good for him he'll bugger off back to Scotland.'

'Don't know, Jack,' he might be a bit tougher than you

think,' said Michael.

'Well, he'll be an even sorrier case next time – a hospital case,' he said chuckling at his own witticism.

29

Sean opened his eyes. A ray of sunlight from a slightly parted curtain slanted across the room. It puzzled him. He didn't get sunlight in his room first thing in the morning. He lifted his right hand to rub his eyes and focus better. He flinched as he touched his face and suddenly remembered where he was and how he'd got there.

He pushed himself up onto his elbow, groaning at the effort involved, and gazed around the Maitland's guest room. The door opened and Annette breezed in carrying a cup of coffee. 'Morning sleepy head. How you feeling this morning?' She put the coffee down on the bedside cabinet, strode over and pulled the curtains wide. The rest of the sunlight came flooding in, causing Sean to screw up his eyes.

'What time is it Annette?'

'About ten-fifteen. Thought I'd better let you sleep in. I checked on you about two hours ago and you were sleeping like a baby.'

'Ten–fifteen! Hell, I'd better get moving,' he said grabbing the top of the quilt.

Annette placed her hand gently on top of his, 'You'll

stay right where you are, have the coffee and we'll see how you are after that. And don't worry, no-one's going to be around here until after lunch, so there's no rush. Mum rang to say she'd be back around two and Dad won't be back till late afternoon. Would you like some bacon and egg?'

'Very good of you Annette. Don't think I could face anything just now.'

'OK, you'll take some toast. I'll be back in a minute'

'Thanks, Annette.' Sean was seeing a side of Annette totally new to him. She seemed far removed from the party-loving girl he'd previously come across.

Annette was just entering the guest room with a plate of toast when the front door swung open and her brother Vic entered. 'Hi, Sis, saw your car and reckoned I'd come up.....' he paused as he noticed her carrying the plate of toast. 'You got company?'

'Sort of – it's just Sean Campbell.'

'Sean Campbell! Christ, the Old Man will flip his lid. What are you thinking about, Girlie?' And he's in the guest room. Is this your latest conquest?'

'Calm down, Vic. It's nothing like that.' Annette proceeded to explain how Sean happened to be in the house.

Vic followed her into the room and looked at Sean who'd got himself to a seating position in the bed. The top half of his body told its own tale.

'Hell, man, somebody been tattooing you with a sledge-hammer?'

Sean grimaced, Something like that, Vic. I didn't intend spending the night here but your sister insisted and to tell you the truth I wasn't in much of a state to argue with her. She certainly looked after me. A real Florence Nightingale.'

'You must've annoyed someone really badly, boy.'

'That would seem to be the case, but I'm not sure what I'm supposed to have done.'

'Any idea who's responsible?'

'Not really.' And then endeavouring to change the subject he added, 'Anyway, I should be making tracks. I'm grateful for Annette's hospitality but I'm not going to outstay my welcome and I certainly don't intend being around when your folks get back home.'

'Relax, Sean. I told you they won't be here till later in the day. Look, have a bit more rest. I'll make you a sandwich for lunch and take you back down the road at one. How's that?'

'Sounds a good offer. If I were you I'd take it,' said Vic. 'Tell you what, if Annette gets that sandwich shortly, I'll have one as well and drop you off at your place. I'm heading up the valley anyway.'

Given Vic's approval, Sean nodded. 'Thanks, folks, that'll be great. I'm still feeling a bit delicate. Don't know though whether I'll have room for toast and a sandwich.'

With his running gear back on and, at Annette's insistence, an old duffle coat thrown over his shoulders, Sean said his farewells and thanks to Annette and gingerly made his way down the driveway to Vic's house.

'Come on in for a minute and take a seat,' said Vic as he took the two steps onto the veranda. 'I've got a coupla things to get and then we'll be off.'

Sean slowly followed him into the hallway. He sat down on a small wooden chair positioned beside a low table on which were a pile of magazines and a telephone. Vic went along the short hallway and into a room on the left. Opposite Sean a half-open doorway led into the sitting room. From what he could see, he was surprised at how tidy and orderly the room was. Though usually dishevelled and unshaven, Vic was obviously quite domesticated.

Sean's attention was drawn to a room directly at the end of the hall. The door was open and the light had been left on. He could make out a large coloured photograph on the far wall. The picture looked spectacular. Despite his injuries, he eased himself out of the chair and shuffled over to the doorway. At that moment Vic appeared.

'Hey, fella, don't go in there!' Vic, slightly red in the face, pushed past him and pulled the door shut.

'Sorry, Vic. I guess I was being nosy but that picture looked fantastic. I could see it from my chair and just wanted to see it a bit closer up. I wouldn't have been rude enough to go into the room. Honest. But where did you get it from?'

Vic relaxed and sighed. Then he blurted out, 'It's mine. I took the photo.' It was the first time he'd ever confessed to anyone that that he took photographs and he had surprised himself that, on the spur of the moment, he'd admitted the fact to this Scots guy.

'You took the photo, Vic? I didn't know you were into photography. Really, it looked amazing.'

Again Vic surprised himself. He opened the door and jerked his head. 'Come on in.'

Sean's jaw dropped as he took in the room - the mounted photographs, the table top with its materials and equipment and what seemed like a darkroom tucked away in a corner. All in all, not a room but an artist's studio. He walked slowly across to study the photograph that had initially caught his eye. It was a stunning view, taking in the little Church of the Good Shepherd perched in front of Lake Tekapo, with the snow-covered Southern Alps providing a spectacular backdrop. He turned to Vic, 'Gee whiz, Vic, I didn't know you were an artist!'

Vic looked down at the floor self-consciously. He mumbled, 'Well, I'm not a painter. I just take a few photographs.'

'No, what I mean is you're an *artist*. You're a talent. You're obviously a bloody brilliant photographer!' Sean shook his head, 'I had no idea. What do the family think of all this?'

Vic shrugged, 'They don't know. Nobody knows. You're the first person that's ever been in here, well, since I turned it into a workroom that is.'

'But Vic,' said Sean glancing around the walls, 'don't you realize how good this stuff is? I'm no expert, but any clot can see these pictures are great. You should be selling them. They should be seen in magazines. They are good! What do you plan to do with them?'

Vic suddenly changed the subject. 'Dunno. Anyway, better get you down the road. Let's go.'

Sean thought of saying more but took the hint. In around ten minutes they were back at his cottage. 'I've a couple of beers in the fridge, do you fancy one?'

Vic paused for a moment then said, 'Why not. It's not too early in the day.'

Sean eased himself out of the car. He could see the key sticking out of the lock. 'That's strange. Don't remember leaving it there. He opened the door. There was a fire glowing in the hearth. It had been banked up with some dross on top to keep it from burning away. A scuttle full of coal and a basket of logs sat on one side of the fireplace. He was totally nonplussed. 'How in the hell…'

Vic grinned. 'My sister. She nipped down when you were in the land of Nod. Got the door key out of your pocket.' He walked over, removed the fireguard and started poking at the caked top. Flames began to spring to life. 'How about that beer, Scottie.'

'Sure thing,' smiled Sean. You Maitlands are certainly surprising me today.'

Seated by the fire and nursing a glass of Speights, Sean was beginning to feel a bit better though still very sore. He hesitated a moment then said to Vic, 'Vic, all those shots you've taken. Surely you realize they're good? I mean, how long have you been doing this sort of thing?'

Vic half smiled. 'I bought the camera from a joker in a pub in Dunedin a few years ago. He was off a ship and I think he picked it up duty-free somewhere. Took a few quid for it. I must have been a bit shikkered at the time 'cause I didn't have the first idea about cameras and photography. Anyway, I went to the library and got a few books on the subject and discovered the camera was a really good one. Although my mates don't know it, I've always been interested in wild-life and the countryside. So, I started taking photos and I guess I just got the bug and carried on and on. Ended up buying gear and even doing my own developing.

'As to what I'll do with the pictures, I've never thought much about it. I just like taking photos of animals and landscapes. And it's been a kind of secret with me. I've found something I actually enjoy doing. I do get some regular photographic magazines sent to me from Oz and Auckland and I had thought of maybe submitting something but have never got around to doing anything about it.'

'You should do, Vic, your stuff is really good. No bullshit.'

'You think so?'

'Too true, you're hiding your light under a bushel.'

Vic jerked his head back and snorted and then took a swallow of his beer but Sean could see he was quite chuffed with the praise.

'Anyway,' said Vic changing the subject again, 'who the hell gave you the doing? You must have got on someone's tits real bad.'

'I honestly don't know. There were two of them and they totally took me by surprise. One was lying on the ground beside their motorbike. I went over to see if I could help them and I was jumped. Didn't even get a chance to land a punch or a kick. Mind you, they made up for it. One was a Maori boy, a powerfully built guy. Both of them had black leather jackets.'

'Maori boy have long black hair and a bandana?'

'Yeah.'

'Sounds like Sonny Te Hurunui. He lives out by the old Pa at Waihemo Point. He's a bad little bugger. But why would he have a go at you?'

'Not really clear. He was acting for someone. I was told to go back to Scotland and to stop getting involved with old Tama.'

'This all to do with the quarry thing?'

'Possibly. Well, probably. Being as it could involve your relatives I didn't like to mention the fact. '

'No skin off my nose, mate. I've bugger all to do with their business schemes. But giving you a doing like that isn't on. What do you plan to do about it?'

'Ach, I'll leave it in the meantime. But that doesn't mean I won't do something about it in due course.'

'OK. You be alright then?'

'Yeah. Thanks Vic. I'm grateful to you and your sister.

'No probs. Think she fancies you a bit.'

'Yeah, well, she's a beautiful girl but a bit young for the likes of me.'

'Right, I'm off. Plan climbing a hill before dark. See you around.'

'Yeah, see you Vic.'

The fire was still going strongly. Sean put his feet up on the small coffee table and closed his eyes. He thought about Vic. He was certainly a complex character and obviously one with hidden talents. He had taken him by surprise when he'd revealed his secret hobby. Vic was the sort of guy who could be loud and pretty coarse when in a crowd and especially when drinking. But he never really gave away anything about himself. Today it was as if he needed to open up to someone about his art and to seek their approval. Approval! Hell, he didn't need approval. His talent stood out a mile. But obviously it didn't to Vic. Sean felt humbled that Vic had actually confided in him of all people. And he also felt humbled that his previous impressions of Vic were so well off the mark.

He switched to thinking about his attackers. And then he fell asleep.

30

Marama Te Kanawa was angry, angry with Sean Campbell but more with herself as she strode along the track that led from the old caves back to the Limeworks road. And she was hurt and bewildered too. She had been quite excited about the idea of going on the walk with Sean. The old feelings she'd had for Sean, and held in check, were beginning to take over again. And this had not been perturbing her too much. Being with him and Kirri on Saturday had been a perfect day and she'd gone to bed that night thinking about what could be - what might be - for them in the future.

And now she was feeling what a bloody fool she had been. She'd gone up with Kirri to Julia's just before two and after seeing Kirri settled, she'd had a word with Annette who was out front washing her car. When asked what she was up to for the rest of the afternoon, Marama had mentioned that she planned walking up to the caves with Sean. Annette had paused then stated that she doubted Sean would be up for it. When asked why, she had smiled coyly and said he had spent the night with her and had gone off home very wearily that morning. Marama had flushed but refrained from commenting and had bade Annette a curt good-bye.

As she had driven back to her house she puzzled over Annette's statement. After Sean's previous comments on Annette, she couldn't figure how on earth he would have allowed such a situation to arise, unless he had wished it. Still, she thought she'd wait to see if he turned up and then confront him with the facts. Sean had not turned up so she set off by herself in an extremely angry state of mind.

Marama was half-way along the track when she met Vic coming towards her. 'G'day Marama, how are things?' Vic asked.

'So, so, Vic,' she replied.

'See you've got another holiday tomorrow.'

Vic was always moaning (or was he pulling her leg?) about the number of holidays teachers got. 'Not exactly a holiday, Vic. It's an in-service day. Kids are off but teachers are working. There's a big meeting in Palmerston about changes to the maths curriculum. OK, it's a change from working with the kids but it's still work.'

'Well, your supply teacher will be getting a holiday anyway. Can't see him being fit to go.'

Marama suddenly became alert. 'What do you mean, Sean won't be fit to go?' asked Marama anxiously.

'Got duffed up yesterday by two guys when he was out on a run. Saw him at Annette's this morning. He was black and blue and pretty crook.'

'But what was he doing up at the house? Is he OK?'

'Yeah, he'll live. Annette found him lying on the road. She took him home and put him to bed and I took him back to the cottage late this morning. He's pretty sore but he's quite a tough cookie for a Pommie.'

'Scots don't regard themselves as Pommies, Vic. Anyway, think I'll drop in and see him. He was supposed to come walking with me this afternoon and didn't turn up. Annette never let on that he was ill. In fact, she gave me the impression that……Oh well, never mind what.'

Vic grinned, 'That's our Annette. Always out to stir things a bit – especially where affairs of the heart are concerned,' he added pointedly. 'Anyways, I'm heading for Digger's Bluff,' said Vic pointing to a smaller track cutting off to their right.

'See you, Vic,' said Marama taking off down the main track at an increased pace.

Vic watched her for a moment then turned and walked on.

That scheming little bitch, thought Marama as she made for the roadway. Then she felt guilty about her earlier thoughts on Sean. She had doubted him and should have known there would be an explanation. It suddenly came to her that her thoughts and feelings had been driven by jealousy. But her prior anxieties had been superseded by a new one, a concern for Sean and his present condition. She reckoned that if she kept up her present pace, she could reach Sean's in forty minutes.

Sean woke with a start to the sound of the door opening. By the time his eyes had focused in on the arrival, Marama was over kissing his forehead and then kneeling by his chair.

'Sean, what's been happening to you? Lord, what a state you're in!'

'God, Marama, I was supposed to be over at yours for two o'clock. Once Vic left I'd meant to go over to Bryn's to phone you but I fell asleep. What's the time now?' he asked looking at the clock and then answering himself, 'Heavens it's after four. I've been asleep for more than two hours. Now if that phone had been installed, I could've rung you. Did I tell you that the phone company is due to link us up next week?'

'No, you didn't. That's good to know. But it's OK, Sean. I actually went up the track myself and met Vic on the way back. He explained to me that you'd been attacked and were in a pretty bad way. You seem to spend your life getting into such situations.'

'Don't I just!'

'But what did happen and how and why?'

'I'm not really clear.' Sean began to relay the events as he recalled them. He didn't speculate on why they'd occurred.'

Marama listened attentively until he'd finished then said, 'You know, this is serious, Sean. The police should be involved. You can't have characters making threats, beating people up and then getting away with it.'

'I'm not planning on them getting away with it. But I don't want the police involved, not yet at least. I didn't enjoy my last experience with the police and will keep them out of things as far as possible.'

'Well, if you ask who has motives for what's taken place the finger rather points towards a certain family in the neighbourhood.'

'It certainly does, Marama. Mind you, two members of that family were very kind to me. But let's not speculate for the moment. I'm pretty tired and not thinking too clearly. You think it'll be OK for me to pass on tomorrow's meeting?'

'Of course. Don't be daft. As a relief teacher there's no need for you to be there, although I know you like to keep up with any new developments. Anyway, how about me making you a snack for tea or are you feeling hungrier than that?'

'No, I'm fine. I'm not particularly hungry at all.'

'I'll get you something anyway. I dropped into Nan's on the way home and said it might be after tea-time before I was back. She sends her love by the way.'

'That's nice.'

'So, would you like something to drink?'

'There's a bottle of Malt in the cupboard to the right of the cooker and glasses there too. But I'll get them,' said Sean making a weak gesture to get up.

'No, Mr Campbell, stay right there,' said Marama lifting her right hand. I'll manage fine.'

Marama appeared back with a tumbler displaying a sizeable slug of whisky and a small jug of water. 'There you are, a wee dram as they say in your part of the world. I see the bottle says fifteen years old.'

'Well looking at the glass, can't say it looks wee for its age!'

Marama returned with a glass of a similar level but already diluted with water. 'Slainte, Sean. Here's to a quick recovery.'

'Slainte, Marama, and thank you.'

After giving the fire a poke and adding a log, Marama disappeared with her glass to the kitchen where she began to rummage around. Sean listened to the noise of crockery being moved, grill pan being taken out and fridge door opening and closing. He sipped his drink and closed his eyes. Just having Marama here made him feel better.

In next to no time, Marama was back with a delicious cheese and egg mixture grilled on toast and topped with sliced tomato and salad cream. She laid it down on the coffee table, poured the tea and said, 'Right, Sean, enjoy!'

By the time they had finished eating it was quite dark. The lamps were still off in the room. The glow from the fire gave an intimate cosiness and the room a cavern-like quality.

'Sean, I've a confession to make. I was really hurt when Annette led me to believe that you'd stayed the night with her under rather different circumstances.'

'Yeah, she's a proper little bizzum alright. She likes stirring things up. And yet she looked after me really well.'

'I know but I think she's holding a candle for you.'

'Marama, there's nothing going on between Annette and me as far as I'm concerned.'

'I know. It's just, I may as well admit it, I was pretty jealous. There, I've said it!'

'Really?' said Sean with a smile. I guess that's a good thing from my point of view.'

'That's alright then.' Marama moved across and leant over the chair to give him a long and lingering kiss.

Sean responded with rising passion but an involuntary gasp from him made Marama pull back. 'Here, boy, you're an invalid remember.' She knelt by his side and held his hands, 'This is nice but it would be a lot nicer if you weren't carrying all these injuries.'

'Marama, to have you here, they were worth it.'

31

Michael Maitland sat at his desk and morosely gazed at the framed photo on the office wall. It portrayed him clutching a large silver cup to his chest and staring unsmilingly in the direction of the camera. Underneath was the caption, 'Michael Maitland, School Sports Champion 1964'. Essentially, he'd got the reward for his prowess on the athletic field. Long jump, high jump and middle- distance running were his specialities. He was an individualist, not a games player, not a team player.

Deep down he was aware that he didn't relate particularly well to his peers. He knew that he was superior to them and was quite happy to openly acknowledge this fact. That was probably why he wasn't very popular with them. Not that that bothered him too much. He was driven to achieve success. He hated being 'bettered' by anyone. Academically he'd been quite successful though he'd had no qualms about resorting to cheating when the opportunity arose. In sport, running and jumping were his strengths. In rugby and other ball games his co-ordination wasn't particularly good and, frustrated by this fact, he avoided such activities wherever possible. In school PE sessions he'd had to participate in these and other disciplines and it was there that he'd found great difficulty keeping his temper when a more adept pupil waltzed past him.

His thoughts turned to his cousin Rob. Rob had been good at all sports. And the bastard had never seemed to try or to work on his skills and techniques. He'd just been naturally good but with no ambition whatsoever. He treated everything as a bit of a joke. And he was so bloody popular with everyone! But what had got up Michael's nose more than anything was the realisation that Rob was faster than him on the athletic field. Not that he'd had to compete with Rob at high school or Uni. Rob was a drop-out. He'd gone to Palmerston High and left as soon as he'd reached fifteen to work with his dad on the farm.

Bloody bumpkin. Michael frowned as he recalled racing Rob out in the playground at Glenbeg. Before Sports Day the boys would have mini- races around the field. Both he and Rob would leave the others behind and he'd be straining with every ounce of effort he could summon and hissing, 'I'm going to beat you, you bastard, I'm going to beat you.' And Rob would start giggling and occasionally double up with laughter thus giving Michael victory. But at other times he'd grin and say, 'Come on then Mick, let's see what you've got,' and effortlessly draw away from him. Michael smiled grimly and said out loud, 'But I got you in the end, Rob. I got you in the end.'

His thoughts switched to Marama only to be immediately deflected back to Rob. What the hell, he wondered, had Marama seen in the prick? Maybe "prick" held the clue. Rob was a big attraction to the female sex and obviously had no problem getting his leg over regularly. But with Marama? She was intelligent, educated. She would have known his reputation. Maybe she was gasping for it and once she'd got it wanted more. The bastard!' When they'd gotten engaged it had nearly driven him crazy. And he'd vowed then that he'd make sure they never got married. He'd been mad about her since the end of primary school. Even all the years he's spent in Dunedin, he'd thought about her, fantasized over her. And she had never looked at him, not till later, much later. He closed his eyes and inhaled deeply a number of times, just as he'd been told to, gradually letting his tension subside. Then he smiled, 'But I got you in the end, Rob, I got you in the end.'

Momentarily he thought of the "shrink" he'd had sessions with in his final year at Fieldings. It had been after the incident where he'd dropped the weights on top of Jones' legs. He'd feigned innocence and claimed it had been a total accident. But he reckoned old Macintosh, the Rector, had read (correctly) between the lines. Macintosh had still wanted his dad's financial input into the school and this cash promise had caused him to draw the line at expulsion. But he was obviously shit-scared that he, Michael, might do something even more drastic. It had taken all his father's persuasive skills to assuage his fears, assure him that his son would get through the rest of the session trouble-free and that, for good measure, he'd have him attend a series of temper management sessions with a local psychiatrist.

And, whilst he'd picked up a few stress-calming techniques from the guy, he'd basically played along with the role of the anxious and willing patient – ensuring a positive report went back to the school.

He intertwined his fingers and pressed the thumbs of each hand against his eyes. Now, what to do about dear Marama, he thought. And this Scottish prick!

Marama had cut across the hayfield behind the house and down to the river path. The course in Palmerston had finished early and she felt the need to get some exercise and fresh air. Turi was lolloping along the path, stopping here and there to sniff at a scent, cock a leg and then turn his head back to check on her whereabouts before dashing into scrub in search of some creature presence, real or imaginary. For the time of year, the weather was mild but despite the pleasantness of the day and the surroundings, she suddenly felt a cloud of despondency envelop her.

She had been looking forward to cutting along by the river and up to see Sean at the cottage. But the river was bringing old memories back and with them the feelings of guilt. The feelings had haunted her dreams and daytime thoughts for a long time after Rob had died. She'd worried that her actions had caused his death. Had she driven him to killing himself? If she'd stayed with him, it wouldn't have happened. Afterwards she'd been in shock and terrified of being blamed for Rob's death. And how could he have driven the truck? She'd taken the keys to ensure that he wouldn't be able to drive it and he'd been totally out for the count anyway. He wasn't in any condition to blow his nose let alone find the keys and drive off.

And she had the worry of Michael and his threats. She was beginning to realize that there was more than just an intensity to him. His behaviour was becoming quite irrational. She was certainly shocked when he mentioned knowing she was at the scene of the accident that night. How did he see her there? What was he doing there? Why hadn't he mentioned anything to the police at the time? Did he have anything to do with Rob's death?

God, it was all coming back again. This time she would speak to Sean. Maybe he would be able to put things into perspective for her. But she'd wait till he was feeling better before bothering him with it all.

As she followed the path round to the bridge, she heard Turi growl and a sharp voice snap, 'Leave it.' She felt a tightening in her chest and her pulse quicken. She knew that voice. She looked upwards to where the path met the road.

He was leaning on the railing near the end of the bridge. The highly-polished brogue of one foot rested nonchalantly on the lower iron work. True to form, he was dressed immaculately, sharply creased grey slacks and black polo neck jumper under a suede jerkin. His thick blond hair was brushed back from his forehead. Turi was looking up at him, hackles slightly raised. He'd never taken to Michael and the feeling was mutual.

'Why Marama, what a pleasant surprise.'

The sarcastic tone was clearly discernible and had the effect of increasing her anxiety. 'Hello, Michael, unusual to see you walking anywhere.'

'I was up at Jack's and thought I'd walk down to the shop and hopefully see you coming out of school. But they told me at the shop that it was an in-service day. But amn't I lucky. Here I am on the way back and here you are too.'

'Why would you want to see me? I thought it was clear we were going our own ways.'

'Clear to you, maybe. Not to me.' He made to move from the bridge and the big collie began to growl again.

'No, Turi. Heel up!' The dog came round behind Marama.

'That's better. Bad enough your dog being antagonistic towards me without having to feel the same vibes from you.'

'That's nonsense, Michael. I don't feel anything towards you. But I don't want anything to do with you either.'

'Ah but you see Marama, dear, that's not possible. You and I had, correction "have", a relationship whether you like it or not. And if you don't return to it very soon things could get bad for you, and consequently for your family.' He raised his head and tauntingly asked, 'You do understand, don't you?'

Marama tried to hold her composure and said, 'No, I don't.'

Michael smiled. 'You remember I mentioned something about the scene of Rob's accident. I know you were there. I saw you there. No-one else knows about it. I think the police might be interested. Don't you?'

'Yes, I was there before the accident. But I don't know what happened. Do you? Could you have saved Rob? What were you doing there? Wouldn't the police like to know about that too?'

Maitland laughed. 'Whoa! Typical Marama, going on the attack. Don't worry about me. If I were ever to be questioned I can explain away my presence quite easily. You're the one who would have trouble. Not coming forward to explain you were near the scene of the accident, not mentioning that you'd been with Rob and were quite possibly the last person to see him alive – these issues pose serious questions. You might even end up with a jail sentence. What impact would that have on Kirri and your family?'

'But I'm telling you I don't know what happened. Yes, Rob did drive along to the house that night, though how he managed to drive there in the condition he was in I don't know. I heard the truck and went out to see what was going on. He was crying and telling me how sorry he was. I got him to move over and said I'd drive him home. Just near the turn-off to the river he got me to stop. He started blubbing again and telling me how sorry he was. When I told him we were finished he started getting abusive but he was so drunk I could hardly make out what he was saying. And then his head dropped and he started snoring. I took the keys out of the truck and left him there to sleep it off. I thought he was quite safe. How the truck landed up in the river I don't know.' And then she paused for a moment, 'But maybe you know what happened, Michael?'

He shook his head. No, I don't know. Let's just say I was passing by. I saw you both in the truck. You were both arguing. It was none of my business. I left you to it. But you might have a job convincing the police of your story.'

'What about you? You could be accused of holding back evidence as well.'

'My situation is a lot less serious, believe me. I've a few explanations up my sleeve that would get me out of any serious bother.' Then in a more conciliatory tone he added, 'But listen, Marama, I don't care what happened. That's why when the news came out I didn't say anything to the police. All I cared about was you. You're all I ever cared about. And admit it, once we got together things were going well for us. They just seem to have fallen apart since all the business about the new road arose. Not to mention too, the arrival of this Scots character Campbell. But, hey, I'll leave you to your thoughts. You've got plenty to think about.'

He turned to make for the avenue but then stopped and looked at her again. 'And where are you off to just now?'

'Not that it's any of your business, but I'm going to see Sean.'

He frowned then said, 'I hear your friend had a disagreement with some bikers. Maybe I should send him a get-well card.' Chuckling he made off.

Marama inhaled deeply in an endeavour to reduce the pounding of her heart. 'Come on, Turi. Where's Sean, where's Sean?' The dog let out a bark and bounded across the bridge.

As Michael made his way back to his uncle's homestead, the bluff confidence he'd displayed in front of Marama evaporated. There was no way he wanted the accident business revisited by the police or anyone else. It was one thing putting the frighteners on Marama. He didn't think he could be fingered in as a suspect in Rob's demise but it would not be prudent to have the police sniffing around. And he could do without trying to explain away his presence at the accident scene.

Yes, things had worked out well that night and much better than he could have hoped for. As it said in the report, he'd taken Rob and Annette home and after Annette had gone to bed, he'd driven off leaving Rob sitting on the veranda steps, almost legless. But he'd driven only as far as the woolshed when a sudden idea had come to him – an inspired thought.

He'd swung the car in between the woolshed and the bunk-house and then walked back to where Rob was still sitting and mumbling away to himself. There'd been no sign of anyone around. He'd guessed Vic would be sleeping it off up at Nick Munro's. He'd helped Rob up and steered him down to where his truck was parked beside the tractor shed. Rob had been rabbiting on about how sorry he was for upsetting Marama and Michael had told him to drive along and see her. Even in his drunken state, Rob was aware he wasn't in any fit state to drive but Michael had assured him he would be fine and that there were no cars around anyway. His reasons for encouraging his cousin were two-fold. One, with a bit of luck he'd crash the truck and maybe break his bloody neck. Secondly, if he did get as far as Marama's, he would likely rile her all the more which in turn would not help their relationship.

Once he'd got Rob underway, the truck weaving erratically all down the track to the road, he'd followed in his own car. The truck appeared to be chugging along in second gear. He'd tracked it from some distance behind and then turned off at the avenue heading down to the bridge. There he'd turned the car round and pulled it off the road onto a soft verge of leaves and pine needles. The over-hanging branches of the firs growing at the corner pretty well concealed him from view.

He wondered what the outcome with Rob would be. He didn't have long to wait before the truck passed by at a much faster speed than before. He'd spotted Rob in the passenger seat. Marama was driving. He was about to pull onto the road when he saw the truck had stopped just a hundred yards or so ahead at the inset where an old track led down to the river. Its lights went out. Were they making up or having an argument he wondered? He got out and jogged down to the river path intending to approach the truck from below road level.

He was making his way up the slope to where they were parked when he heard a door slam. Through the trees he caught sight of Marama moving alongside the vehicle and placing her arm over the tail-gate. He paused and watched as she stepped onto the road and began striding out in the direction of her home. He waited a few moments and then went quietly up to the vehicle and looked through the passenger window. Rob was slumped across the bench seat, head twisted sideways and mouth wide-open. Sound asleep.

He walked round to the roadside and could just faintly make out Marama a few hundred yards away. Looking back inside the cab he noticed the keys were missing. He guessed

Marama had taken them to ensure Rob couldn't drive. She'd obviously thought he was safe enough to sleep it off where he was. Then his face broke into a smile. He moved around to the truck's tailboard and scanned the wooden floor base. He was right. He spotted the keys lying in the corner where she'd dropped them, no doubt figuring old Rob would never find them until he'd sobered up. Picking them up, he moved back to the cab and climbed in. He had the opportunity he'd been looking for.

Pushing his snoring cousin over to the left, he started the truck up. He manoeuvred it forward a little and straightened the wheels so it was on the level part of the track but facing the downhill slope. Putting it into neutral, he kept the handbrake off and gently let his foot off the brake pedal. It didn't move. He switched on the headlamps. He had difficulty hauling the limp and totally comatose body of Rob over to the driver position where he draped his arms over the wheel. He got out of the cab, closed the door and moved round to the passenger side. Leaning across the floor he managed to get Rob's foot onto the clutch pedal. Holding his ankle, he pushed the foot down. But as soon as he moved his hand away Rob's foot limply slid off. He tried again and this time the foot stayed in position though the clutch wasn't totally to the floor. Rob hung over the wheel, still sound asleep.

Then came the tricky bit. Making sure the door was wide open, he reached across and tapped the gear lever into first and moved back quickly. The vehicle remained stationary. He then leant forwards, pulled at Rob's knee and thrust himself backwards and clear of the cab. The truck moved forwards and rocked to the right, the passenger door fortuitously slamming shut.

Once over the slope, the vehicle careered downwards to the pool below, engine whining in complaint at being stuck in first gear. It gathered momentum. Panting, he watched it crash into the pool and the tail end rear up. It was then he saw a figure running towards it. It looked like Sean Campbell. There were a few bits of old fence posts lying around the parking spot. He picked one up and headed down to the river. Campbell never knew what hit him as he dropped like a stone into the water. Michael moved quickly back along the river path, throwing the post up into the wooded embankment.

Yes, it had been a fruitful evening. On reflection, however, it would have been a lot more fruitful if Campbell had ended up like Rob. Dead.

32

The dark louring sky and a rushing wind gave promise of a rain-lashed day ahead. Already a few heavy spots had splashed upon his face. The two collies, free of their chains, were haring around the hillside completely oblivious to the weather. But as Jack Maitland strode up the old track that skirted the burial caves, his mood was as bleak as the elements. He thrust his hands into the pockets of his parka, hunched his shoulders and increased his pace. He'd just heard from his brother that the judge in Dunedin had ruled the burial area should be considered to belong to the Maori community of Waihemo. Their solicitor's argument that there was no written proof, had cut no ice with the judge who based his decision on the fact that under normal circumstances, such areas of land inevitably were in Maori custody.

His brother Grant had been bloody angry but this in no way compared with the pent-up rage felt by Jack. This was his land. The Horis were never around it. He felt he should be able to do anything he wanted with it. He felt like getting some dynamite from the quarry and blowing the whole so-called tapu area up.

There was chink of hope, however. On being pressed by their solicitor, the judge had agreed that provided a majority of the Maori community was willing to sell the land then this would be legally acceptable. So, Tama, you old bastard, he thought, you've not won yet. They had plans afoot to convince the Maoris to sell, plans that consisted of some enticement and some threats. He would be ringing his friend Sonny later in the day.

Sean arrived home mid-afternoon just after dropping Tama at his house. They'd gone down to Dunedin early that morning. Sean had left Tama at the court-house with Nikora, Tupe's lawyer cousin. He'd then gone on to the Otago Daily Times where he'd done the interview he'd promised with Bill Spiers. Like the good newsman he was, Bill's questions had kept Sean on his toes. He'd been interested in how Sean had made the transition from teacher to writer and then gone on to inquire about the successful televising of his first book. When asked about his reasons for returning to New Zealand, Sean had not gone into detail but said that he was working on a story set partly in Scotland and partly in New Zealand. After a photo shoot they'd adjourned to Bill's office for coffee and fresh doughnuts. A grateful Bill had told him they'd run the article in their Saturday's Arts section. He'd left Bill with a promise that he'd keep in touch regarding progress with his research.

Tama had been in good spirits and delighted with the court ruling which he'd recounted to Sean on the drive home. He knew that the matter was not yet over and that the Maitland team would be making moves to persuade the community to agree to the road. He thought he could rely on most of the elders to vote for the status quo and also some younger members committed to Maoritanga, Maori culture. There were other elements with a different outlook, however, and enticements from the quarry company might persuade them to vote in its favour.

Sean made a coffee then sat down at his desk and took off the typewriter cover. The storyline he had in his head was beginning to sharpen. He began to type.

The day after the court decision saw Jack Maitland enter the Royal as the grandfather clock in the foyer struck two. He glanced through to the public bar where a few blokes were sitting at the counter on bar stools and a couple were playing darts. Good, he thought, the place is dead quiet. He went through to the lounge bar. Sonny Te Hurunui was stretched out on a small settee set in a window alcove across from the bar. The place was otherwise empty. A glass of beer sat on the table next to him. Sonny looked up from the ODT sports page and waved. As Jack approached, he swung his feet onto the floor, placed the paper on the table and stood up. 'Hi, Boss, how are ya?'

'Could be better,' grunted Jack taking a seat opposite Sonny.

'You want a beer, Boss?'

'Could do with something stronger, but better settle for a beer.'

With no sign of life behind the counter, Sonny went

through to the public bar and returned with a jug of lager and another glass. He filled the glass and handed it to Jack, placing the jug on the table. 'There you are, Boss, get that down you.'

Jack nodded and took a swig. 'I need your help, Sonny. I've got problems that need sorting.' He proceeded to tell Sonny about the recent developments and the outcome of the judge's decision. They then went on to discuss how the community at Waihemo Point could be persuaded to vote in favour of selling part of the burial site land over to Maitland Products. They spent around an hour and a half mulling over what strategies and pressures might be brought to bear. Sonny was able to identify individuals in the community who would likely be for or against Jack. He also came up with some interesting thoughts on how people might be *encouraged* to change their points of view.

At around three-forty, Marama drove past the Royal on her way to pick up Kirri from the kindergarten. Normally this was done by Mere but both she and Tama were off to spend a couple of nights with relatives near Waihemo Point. Tama was keen to talk to as many folk in the community as possible about the Maitland development prior to a meeting of all interested parties scheduled for the following week. As she passed the front of the hotel, she caught sight of Jack Maitland coming out accompanied by a stocky Maori boy with long black hair and wearing a bandana. She glanced up at her rear vision mirror. Jack hadn't seen her. He appeared to be engrossed in conversation with the younger man. The bandana suddenly clicked with her and she thought of the bikers that had jumped Sean. This was obviously one of them. And pally with Jack Maitland. Why didn't this surprise her? She wondered if she should mention it to Sean or not. Maybe she'd let Hemi know.

But her mind quickly moved from Maitland to cooking. She'd invited Sean over for a meal with herself and Kirri and was mentally planning what she had to get at the shops – pork chops from the butcher, kumara and silver beet, a bottle of gin (stocks were running low) and some more ice cream.

With purchases made and Kirri chatting animatedly about her kindergarten day, Marama headed for home. Sean was due around five thirty. She reckoned she could have everything just about prepared by then, the fire blazing away and herself dolled up a bit. After Kirri was packed off to bed, they would have the house to themselves as Hemi was off for a few days pig hunting up Kurow way. A glimmer of a smile came to her lips as she thought of the perfume she would put on. She wondered if he'd recognize it.

'Mum, Mum, you're not listening to what I'm saying,' said Kirri bouncing up and down on the back seat.'

'Course I am, Miss Mischief, you were telling me about little Jack Black trying to get the goldfish out of the tank and nearly tipping it over. So there! And stop bouncing about on the seat.'

Kirri sat down and began to play with Gretta, her doll.

Marama glanced at her daughter in the mirror. 'We've got a visitor coming for dinner tonight.'

'A visitor. Oh I know who it will be.'

'Who will it be Miss Clever?'

'Sean!'

'You're right, it is Sean. But how did you know that?'

'I don't know. I just know'd it would be Sean. I like Sean, I love Sean! Do you love Sean, Mum?'

'Yes, I think I do, darling.'

'I don't like Michael.'

Marama tightened her hands on the wheel. 'Why don't you like Michael? He hasn't been bad to you has he?'

'No-ooo. But he doesn't play games with me or even talk to me. Sean does. I wish Sean was my daddy.'

Marama's swallowed hard and her eyes misted. 'Sean's our very good friend, Honey. And I think he loves you too.'

'I think he might love you too, Mummy. I think he might want to kiss you!' Kirri began to giggle.

Out of the mouths, thought Marama. But she answered, 'Don't be silly, Kirri. And don't say anything like that to Sean!'

With the car unloaded, the messages dumped in the kitchen and a match to the fire that Mere had already set, Marama and Kirri went out to the back to unchain Turi from his kennel. The usual lively welcome ensued with Marama laughingly trying to unleash a dancing bundle of fur and Kirri squealing at the big dog's antics. Marama left them to play in the garden and made for the kitchen. Inside she smiled as she listened to her little daughter's calls and Turi's excited barks. She hummed as she got the meal preparations underway. She was happy. She was looking forward to the evening with Sean. For the moment, her worries and anxieties were distant shadows.

Sean lay back on the armchair with Kirri curled up on his lap listening to yet another tale of Benjamin Bunny. He had the little girl's rapt attention. One moment she would be sitting thumb in mouth and the next the thumb would be out as she excitedly predicted what the next page would reveal. Occasionally she would ask him a question.

Marama shouted out from the kitchen, 'Kirri come and get your hands washed. It'll be ready in five minutes Sean, so drink up!'

Kirri ran off calling to Sean, 'I love Benjamin Bunny and Peter Rabbit,'

Sean smiled. He sipped his gin and lemonade and thought about Kirri. She certainly was a beautiful and animated kiddie. Definitely took after her mother and there was no mistaking the mother/daughter link. But there was something else about Kirri. Some look or expression in her face that reminded him of someone else. Was it something to do with when she smiled?

Come and get it,' yelled Marama.

The delicious aroma emanating from the kitchen diverted Sean's thoughts. He put another log on the fire and placed the fireguard on the hearth.

Marama tucked her legs up on the sofa and laid her head on Sean's shoulder. Kirri, high and excited after dinner, traded off going for a bath with the promise of a bedtime story from both adults. Sean had washed up whilst Marama bathed her daughter. Drooping eyelids just made it to the end of the last story before the Sandman totally ensnared her.

Sean sat on the sofa, legs stretched out and feet just touching the edge of the hearth. 'That was a fabulous meal, Marama. I'll have to do another couple of miles tomorrow to work it off. I'm as full as a tick.'

'M-mmm, I rather enjoyed it myself.' The fireside glow gave the darkened room a cosy and intimate feel. She put her hand on Sean's stomach, 'Seems pretty flat to me, Mr Campbell. Maybe just a slight bulge!'

'Hey, that's relaxed muscle, Miss. Let's feel your tum,' he chuckled and tickled her sides.

Marama squealed and wrapped her arms around Sean's neck and began to blow in his ear. A short wrestling match ensued before lips and mouths and tongues met eagerly and hungrily. Clothing was hastily removed and bodies thrust against each other urgently and passionately. They came quickly but in unison, striving to satisfy unfulfilled longing and need. Afterwards, Marama lay on her back, legs still wrapped around Sean as she stroked the nape of his neck. Sean, chest heaving, lay on top of her, head leaning over her shoulder and cheek against hers, his arms pressed into the sofa taking most of his weight.

They lay like that, not talking but in a contented peace, enjoying the proximity of the other and the wonder of the moment. Sean opened his eyes, realizing he had dozed off. Soft fingers were gently caressing his back from neck to buttocks. He was still between Marama's legs and could feel himself stirring. He leant his weight onto his left arm and began to stroke her breast. Marama moaned and pressed herself up against him.

Sean rolled to the outside and leant his head on his elbow, 'I've dreamt of this for so long. But I never thought it could happen. I love you Marama Te Kanawa.'

'And I you, Sean Campbell.'

They kissed, a long and lingering soft kiss that expressed all that they felt. This time there was no rush.

Together they lay back. Above them the ceiling was now almost one dark shadow. Only glowing embers remained of the last log.

Marama took Sean's hand in her own and turned to him, 'Sean, what does the future hold for us?'

'Anything you want it to, my darling. But I hope it's all about us being together.'

'Yes. But I mean where will we be? This is my home. Your home is in Scotland. I don't know if I could live anywhere else.'

'I understand that. I hope you will come with me to Scotland to see it – and with Kirri! But I will live wherever you want to. As far as I'm concerned, home will be wherever we all are together.' He sat up and looked down upon her, 'And I will treat little Kirri as my own daughter and love her just as I love you.'

Marama's eyes misted. She sat forward and put her arms around Sean. He could feel her body trembling and suddenly realized she was crying. 'Marama, Honey, what's wrong?'

Marama tightened her hold on him and sniffed, 'Oh, Sean, it's just that…..there's something I have to tell you…I should've told you before but I just couldn't.'

'Couldn't tell me what?' he asked, concern in his voice.

She lifted up her tear-stained face to look directly at him, 'It's about Kirri. Kirri is your daughter, Sean.'

Two small logs, strategically placed, had given the fire a new lease of life. They sat close to it and on the rug, facing each other. Sean was dressed and Marama in her dressing gown, each holding a cup of hot cocoa. Sean had been shocked by Marama's revelation, but shock had turned to incredulity and then wonder at the news. He was a dad, Kirri's dad and the father of Marama's child! Whilst he was bewildered that Marama had kept this information from him, much to Marama's relief she could see his reaction was one of delight though he then bombarded her with questions.

'But Marama, if you'd told me at the time, I wouldn't have left you all on your own.'

'I know you wouldn't have, Sean. But I was in a bad way and in no position to make a reasoned judgment. I'd fallen out of love with Rob and I thought I'd fallen in love with you but I didn't know if this was just a reaction to the way things had gone with Rob and I. And then the shock of his death, the funeral, Jack Maitland blaming you. I just couldn't face doing anything. And so I told you to go. But I can tell you now, I cried and cried after you'd gone. And you've never been far from my mind in all the time you were away.'

'You should have got in touch with me. I never stopped thinking about you.'

'I realize that now but I would hear from Bryn how you were doing and I kept thinking you must have got into a new relationship. I imagined that your success with your writing and all that, you'd probably forgotten all about me.'

'The very opposite. I never stopped thinking about you. It was like in that song Willie Nelson sings, You Were Always On My Mind! Bryn kept telling me to contact you but I just didn't believe you would have wanted that and then I sent you the Christmas card and you replied. That was what motivated me to come back. I was pinning my hopes on your wording and on the photograph, although I feared I might be reading too much into them. And the taiaha, well that was really my cover story for coming back.'

'I'm so glad you did my darling.'

33

'I've got problems, Sean,' said Tama. 'The meeting for the community vote on the quarry development is a week today. I've talked to a number of my friends. They're listening to me but not saying much. And I've just discovered why.'

It was Thursday, mid-morning. Sean and Tama were sitting in Sean's cottage. Tama had a worried look on his face. 'What's the problem, Tama?'

The Maitlands are the problem but via another source. I learned from my old friend Billy Tamaki that a boy called Sonny Te Hurunui has been visiting certain families and telling them that if they don't vote for the Maitland road to go ahead then they, or their children, will lose jobs at the Katiki Freezing Works or MacKenzies Canning. It would appear that the Maitlands have connections with these businesses and could cause them to lose their jobs. Many of the people living at the Point work for these companies. This is serious, Sean. Workers need to provide for their families. We can't have folk losing their jobs.'

'Isn't there any way we can prove the Maitlands are blackmailing people into voting for their road to go ahead?'

'Not really. If anyone spoke and explained that Te Hurunui was delivering a threat from the Maitlands, they'd just deny it. As would the boy of course.'

Sean thought for a moment and then said, 'But what if this guy Te Hurunui's threats were recorded?'

'You mean like some James Bond spy trick? If only we could do something like that,' said Tama wistfully.

Sean smiled, 'Actually I think we can. I've got an idea and I think it just might work. Do You know if Te Hurunui is due to make any other visits?'

'As a matter of fact, he told Billy he'd be around to see him and a few others on Friday night.'

Sean and Tama arrived at the Tamaki house at eight in the evening. Tama switched off the engine of his old van and clambered out. Sean sat in the darkness and watched as Tama knocked on the door. There were lights on in the neighbouring houses but no-one visible outside. When the door opened, a splash of light spilt onto the doorstep. Tama spoke to the huge figure filling the doorway then beckoned to Sean. Sean got out, carrying the box that had been sitting on his knee and followed the two men inside.

The sunlight streaming through the cottage window and falling on the table where Sean and Tama were seated was a good omen for the start to the weekend. Sean was in good spirits. In an hour's time he was leaving with Marama and Kirri to go down to Dunedin where they would spend the weekend with Andy and Cara Bell. He was keen for his friends and Marama to meet. But he was also feeling a little apprehensive for he was about to play the reel tape sitting on the school's tape recorder.

It had been Sean's idea that they set up the recorder in the Tamakis' sitting room, suitably concealed along with its external microphone. They had experimented with the machine on the Thursday evening and Sean had instructed Billy's wife Anni how to use it. After a few attempts, Anni seemed to have the hang of it and the dummy runs they'd tried out had recorded quite clearly. The recorder had been placed on the floor behind the sofa and the microphone, which fortunately had a length of wire some twelve feet long, had been hidden in a magazine rack on the far side of the sofa. The mike was pointing towards an armchair opposite that they had planned for Sonny to sit on. It was agreed that whilst Billy answered the door, his twenty -year old son Weeni would sit at the sofa end nearest the mike and that Anni would press the record/play buttons on the machine.

Tama had collected the machine earlier that morning. After Sonny left, Anni had stopped the machine but they'd been unwilling to try any rewinding or playbacks, worried that they might accidentally damage the recording. So now it was crunch time. Tama had watched anxiously as Sean rewound the tape to the beginning and pressed 'PLAY'.

There were a few seconds of silence before some clunks and bangs intimated the opening and closing of doors. Voices that were initially muffled began to increase in strength and become audible as bodies entered the room and sat down. Sean leant forwards and turned up the volume knob. He gave the thumbs up to Tama as Sonny began to speak.

'Look, people, I'm not here to threaten you, I'm here to do you a favour. The Maitlands want to take the new quarry road alongside the old burial site. Now you know, and I know, there's virtually nothing there. Leastways, not where the road's going to go. And the Maitlands have promised a handsome donation to the new community hall if a majority give the vote for it to go ahead. Fifteen thousand dollars! Now that would help the hall fund and no mistake.'......... And so the tape went on, Sonny first praising the Maitlands' generosity and all the positives of a new hall. Then came the veiled and not so veiled threats........'You know, there's young Weeni sitting there. You've got a good job I hear up at the freezing works. Good money. Good prospects. Now you wouldn't want to lose that would you?'

Then Billy's voice came in with, 'I don't understand what you mean. Why could Weeni lose his job?'

Sonny sounded like he was pleading, 'Look fellas, I'm on your side but business is business. The Maitland Group is becoming big time. They'll be bringing more work to the area. They can help us but we don't want to cross them. If you turn up and vote against the road then a lot of young fellas like Weeni could lose their jobs. Like I said, the Maitlands are powerful people.'

'You mean they could arrange for Weeni to lose his job?'

'Yes. That's what they told me to tell you. I'm just the messenger, but hey, these people are tough. It won't do to cross them.'

Tama and Sean smiled at each other and then listened

to the rest of the tape. Sean then pressed the STOP button and rewound the reel.

Tama grinned, 'We've got them, Sean boy.'

'You bet,' said Sean.

34

After a late morning snack at the Te Kanawas, Sean, Marama and an excited Kirri, set off for Dunedin in Marama's Morris. Kirri was excited about meeting the Bells' children, daughter Jill and little George. An hour and a half later, they were pulling into the driveway on the hill above St Clair beach. The excited and chattering Kirri had become shy and subdued as they got out of the car and greetings and introductions were made. Whilst it was a bright breezy day, the cool wind had Cara ushering them into the house and Andy helping Sean with their belongings.

Within a few minutes, the girls were off to Jill's bedroom with George toddling in tow. Marama went into the kitchen with Cara to sort out some hot drinks and eats. Andy and Sean made for the lounge to catch up on their respective news.

As they settled down on the armchairs on each side of the fireplace, Andy said, 'So that's Marama. I remember her from the night at the dance. What a smasher. Too bloody good for you, Campbell,' he joked.

Sean grinned, 'Don't know if it was my good looks, fatal

charm or all-round intelligence that attracted her. Probably all three.'

'Aye, possibly,' smiled Andy. 'Seriously, though, she does seem a lovely girl and her wee lassie, what a wee beauty.'

Sean cleared his throat, 'Andy, keep this to yourself for no-one else knows yet, but I've just found out, Kirri's my daughter.'

'You're joking! But how...I mean, I know how...but...'

'Ach it's a long story, but briefly...' Sean commenced to explain to Andy why he'd suddenly departed from Glenbeg on his last stay and why he'd come back and Marama's eventual revelation to him about Kirri. 'I'm still getting used to the idea...,' he stopped as Cara entered carrying plates of sandwiches and home-baking and Marama a tray with mugs of tea prepared to order.

'Getting used to the idea of what?' smiled Cara.

'Well,' said Sean a little lost for words.

'It's alright,' laughed Marama, 'I think I've been having the same conversation with Cara as you have had with Andy.'

'I think it's wonderful, Sean,' added Cara laying the plates on the coffee table. 'I've just met Marama but frankly the two of you seem made for each other.'

'Thanks, Cara, we're kind of feeling that way ourselves. Kirri isn't aware yet but we think she'll grow into the idea of me becoming her dad in due course.'

'And she absolutely adores Handsome Harry here,' said Marama putting the tray down and grinning at Sean.

'I'd better nip up and get the kiddies down to the kitchen. We've got juice and buns out on the table for them.'

'Och, leave it Cara. Have your tea then Sean and I'll go through with them,'. Wee George's already had a bottle. He'll be fine for a bit.'

An hour of chatting, reminiscing and blethering ensued. The children had their snack, the little girls returning to play again whilst George lay sound asleep on the sofa between his mother and Marama.

Later, all wrapped up warmly, Andy drove them down to the beach for a walk along the shore front with little George ensconced on his dad's back in a bag carrier. On their return, the girls made a bee-line for Jill's bedroom, the women prepared a cup of tea and, at Cara's suggestion that they might wish to adjourn to the pub, the two men departed with alacrity.

As they drove down the hill Andy said, 'Where do you fancy, the Criterion or the Beach?'

'I'm happy either way. I take it Alec and company won't be at the Criterion?'

'I know Alec won't be. There was a bye today and I know he had something planned with the family. But he'll be up at the house tonight with a few others.'

'Sounds good. Let's make it the Beach then. But not the Park. It brings back bad memories,' said Sean recalling the funeral reception.

Andy drove to the parking area at the back of the Tahuna Beach Hotel. Both got out and entered the lounge bar area.

'I'll get this. You grab a table,' said Sean heading over to the busy bar counter. It was around three forty-five and the bar was filling up rapidly. Carrying a jug of lager and two glasses, Sean spotted Andy waving to him from a table beside a bay window that looked onto the hotel's back garden. He filled the glasses up and gave the Gaelic toast, 'Slainte!'

Andy lifted his glass in acknowledgement, 'Slainte. It's grand to have you and the family here, Sean.'

Sean smiled, 'That's going to take a bit of getting used to. But keep it under your hat in the mean-time. Not another soul knows yet.'

'Mum's the word. Anyway, how's this story of yours going?'

Sean relayed what he'd been up to so far on the working front but then explained how his attention had been diverted to the road development issue and what was currently happening regarding this.

'Strewth, Campbell, you don't half get yourself involved in difficult situations.'

'Well, can't say I look for trouble. It just seems to find me.'

'And this Michael Maitland guy, he's the prat we saw Marama with at the dance?'

'Yes, I gather he's been pretty keen on her for the past couple of years but she gave him the heave-ho recently. I don't think I'll be flavour of the month with him. He's a strange guy. From what Marama's said of him he can be pretty irrational.'

'You mean a fucking header.'

'You've got a way with words, Mr Bell. But yeah, you're right.'

The two friends continued chatting, considered another jug but decided there'd be plenty of time at home to further indulge – Andy reminding Sean that the bottle of duty-free Talisker he'd brought him had to be broken into before dinner-time. They were just about to go when Sean spotted a leather-clad Sonny Te Hurunui disappear into the gents' toilets.

'Here, Andy, one of the jokers that gave me a going over has just gone into the toilets I've got a bone to pick with him.'

'The one on the motorbike?'

'The very same,' said Sean as he stood up and strode across the lounge.

Sonny was laughing as he turned from the urinal, zipping his fly up. His greasy-haired biker friend, still wearing his leather jacket with an eagle emblazoned on the back, stood on Sonny's left peeing away. 'Well blow me down, it's the Scotchman,' grinned Sonny as he recognised Sean. 'I thought you'd have pissed off to Scotchland by now.'

'Naw,' Sean smiled, 'I couldn't leave without saying cheerio to you, Sonny.' Sean made as if to walk past Sonny's right and to the adjacent urinal.

'Is that a fact, Scotchman?'

Almost alongside Sonny, Sean half-turned and in a seamless movement grabbed the lapels of Sonny's jacket and pulled it off his shoulders and downwards, thus trapping his arms. At the same time, he forcibly head-butted Sonny on the nose.

Sonny let out a yell of pain and bent over clutching his

hands to his face as blood gushed forth. The speed of the action had taken Te Hurunui totally by surprise.

'Shit, you've broken my nose,' he yelled.

'Come on, you didn't think I'd leave you without a wee Glasgow kiss.'

'Jeez,' he moaned staggering towards a hand basin, 'Trev get the bastard.'

His lanky friend hastily zipped up and moved towards Sean.

'Hey, Greaser,' said Andy. 'You forgot to wash your hands.'

Trev hesitated, 'It's more than a fuckin' Glasgow kiss you'll get if you don't piss off now,' warned the normally mild-mannered Andy.

Trev took one more look at Andy and holding his hands up said, 'Right, right, I'll just attend to my mate.'

Turning to Sonny who seemed to have all the stuffing knocked out of him, Andy added, 'You got off lightly, Sonny Boy. Just steer clear in the future if you know what's good for you. My mate here might seem like a pussy cat but he's a fuckin' nutter when you get him angry.'

They left Sonny still bleeding like a stuck pig. 'Oh well,' said Andy, 'that was fun.'

'Do you have your guitar? We could do with a wee sing-song,' said Andy quietly.

'No, but I've got Marama's'

Andy raised his eyebrows, 'She sings?'

Sean raised his finger to his lips and said in a low voice,

'She doesn't know I've got it.'

The party was in full swing. After an early meal for the little ones and baths and bed-time stories over, Marama had given Cara a hand with final supper preparations which included Bluff oysters and freshly cooked crayfish, compliments of the Te Kanawas. A few family friends had arrived just after eight, including the MacKays. Chat and witty banter ensued, the Scots present progressively losing their New Zealand twangs as the evening unfolded and becoming more pronounced in their native vernacular. The Kiwis present, including Marama, joining in and affecting Scots accents that made the exiles laugh.

Sean slipped out of the room and went out to the car. Before they'd left Marama's he'd got Hemi to put the guitar on the floor below the back seat. It was covered with an old rug and un-noticed by Marama when she sat Kirri in the back. He returned to the hall-way and handed the guitar to Andy.

'You not going to give us a tune?'

'Later. Go in and get Marama to do a number. She's good!'

Andy grinned. 'A girl of many talents.'

'Too right.'

'OK, folks,' said Andy entering the lounge and holding up the guitar. I'm reliably told that there's a certain lady amongst us who can warble a bit.'

This was met with a cheer. Marama looked over to Sean who was standing behind Andy. He winked and she grimaced but he knew she'd be up for a song.

'Come on, Marama,' Andy smiled at her. The rest of the

party cheered encouragement. Marama shrugged and made a face at Andy as he handed her the instrument. She strummed a couple of chords then launched into Puppet On A String. Everyone loved it. Maori songs, old Scots refrains and songs of the sixties followed.

The party was over, guests departed and the room quickly tidied up with dishes and glassware stacked in the kitchen for the men-folk to tackle in the morning. The four adults sat half asleep – Marama and Cara sipping coffee, Andy and Sean finishing off a malt night-cap.

'Well,' said Andy yawning, 'that was some night.'

'We loved it,' said Marama. 'Thank you for making Kirri and me so welcome.'

'We loved meeting you, Marama,' said Cara, 'and the kids adored Kirri. We hope this will be just the start of many visits to come.'

'Aye, and you can even bring Handsome Harry with you,' said Andy.

They all laughed.

35

'Right, everyone, it's gone seven thirty, I think we'll start.'

Tama, as Chairperson of the Waihemo Maori Community Council, looked around the sea of faces in the old dilapidated community hall. This was the largest turnout he'd seen for many years. But he hadn't been surprised given the circumstances and the impact the outcome would have on many of the people. Sonny Te Hurunui had been busy, he thought grimly.

He'd been speaking to a few of his old friends prior to the meeting and all thought that the result would be a foregone conclusion, a victory for the Maitland brothers. The meeting was closed to all but residents of Maori descent living in the Waihemo district and the two planning officers who were there to report on the meeting's outcome. He could see Mere and Hemi, Sean, and Marama with little Kirri perched on her knee, sitting two rows from the front. Mere raised her hand slightly as they made eye contact. Tama nodded. He had also spotted Sonny Te Hurunui standing at the back of the hall, leaning against the wall and wearing dark sun glasses.

'People of Waihemo,' he began, we all know why we are here tonight. We are here to vote on whether a road should be built in the area sacred to us, the burial site of our ancestors. Make no mistake, this is Maori land. It always has been Maori land. Other land areas nearby were sold to the pakeha last century. But we are not here to debate that. I know many of the young people here feel we have to progress, that the older folk are living in the past. But that has always been the way of things. And I understand that many believe to keep our customs and culture alive, we would be better taking the substantial offer from the quarry company that will help us build a new community hall and cultural centre. But I promise you, that whatever the result of this vote, we will have a new hall. How grand it might be may depend on the result of tonight's vote, but we do, at the moment, have the basic funding to start the building of a new centre. I also know that many of you feel coerced into voting in a certain way. I will not try to influence you. You all know my views. But, before you give your vote, I want you to listen to a tape recording that was made last Friday evening. It might cause some of you to think again on how you decide to vote.'

Sonny was jolted to full attention at Tama's last words. He took off his glasses, displaying the heavy bruising around his nose and under his eyes, to watch as Tama's friend Billy Tamaki came onto the small stage and moved towards a box-like object sitting on a table at the back of the stage. Billy's son Weeni appeared with a microphone and stand and positioned it in front of the tape-recorder. Sonny's heart began to thump faster. As the words echoed around the room he knew he was in big trouble. He slipped out of the hall as his own words resounded in his ears……

'Like I said, the Maitlands are powerful people. They know a lot of people in other businesses. He could lose his job.'

'You mean they could arrange for Weeni to lose his job?'

'Yes. That's what they told me to tell you. I'm just the messenger, but hey, these people are tough. It won't do to cross them.'

Tama nodded to Billy and he stopped the tape. Tama looked at those gathered in the hall. 'I promise you, with this evidence you will have no worries about any of you losing your jobs. If there is the least hint of any such threats, you will have the whole community behind you and this evidence and expert legal support to ensure that nothing of the sort happens.'

A buzz began in the hall as folk began to discuss what they had heard. Those who felt they had been coerced into voting for the quarry access, were now feeling relief that this pressure had been taken off them and renewed indignation that the pressure had been put there in the first place. Heads turned round to look at Sonny Te Hurunui but he had slunk off. The majority of people seemed to be conferring and nodding in agreement, and smiling! And then a spontaneous clapping commenced and rose and rose in volume.

Tama smiled, 'Well then, I think we will vote now unless there is anything else anyone would like to say on the matter.' There was silence at first and then a young teacher, Katerina Tauroa stood up.

'Mr Te Kanawa and people of Waihemo, I for one truly

believed that giving the quarry road the go-ahead and thus bringing essential funding to our long-overdue meeting centre, was a good idea, and a justified one. I was not, however, aware that some of our members had been – how did Mr Te Kanawa put it? – *coerced* into voting for the road. I am horrified and I am angry that such a thing has taken place. New hall or not, we cannot be blackmailed into giving our consent. I have certainly changed my mind about how I wish to vote. Thank you.' Katerina sat down.

'Thank you, Miss Tauroa. Now, would everyone who believes we should vote for the Maitland Company quarry road to go ahead as shown in the current plan, please raise their hands.'

Not a hand was raised.

'And all those who are in favour of rejecting permission for the road to go by the burial site please now raise their hands.'

A forest of hands shot up.

'Then, as Chairman of the Waihemo Maori Community Council, I hereby declare that we, the People of Waihemo, reject any applications for a road development on our ancient ancestral site. I will have this result recorded and passed onto the Authorities herewith. Thank you for your attendance and support.'

As one, everyone stood and began applauding. Cheers, whistles and foot-stamping ensued. Tama and Billy embraced. Mere dabbed her eyes and looked proudly up at her husband.

The Maitlands were going to have to find another access

route for their quarry.

Jack Maitland sat at his usual table in the Glenbeg Arms lounge bar. He morosely gazed at his half empty glass, not seeing it but instead reflecting on the events of the past few days.

His mind was still reeling from the way things had unfolded.

Vic appeared in the passageway through from the public bar, spotted his father and called out, 'Hey, how's tricks?'

Jack looked at him. 'You're lookin' pretty pleased with yourself. You win the Golden Kiwi or somethin'?'

'Nope. You want a drink?'

'Got one,' said Jack nodding at his glass. He'd been spending most evenings down at the pub. It was something to do and he had to admit he was missing Julia being around.

Vic got a drink and came over to sit opposite Jack.

'Here, what's this about you doing photos and stuff?'

'Aw, you know, just an interest I've got. Anyway, who told you about it?'

'Your sister of course. She said you've got a whole bloody room full of photos. Said they were pretty damn good too. You never told me.'

'Yeah, well Pop you never were very much interested in what I did.'

A feeling of guilt passed through Jack's mind but he let it go. He sat silent.

'Hey, did you see the article in the Times about Ma?'

'No.'

'Hey, Mary, you got a copy of today's paper there?'

'Sure, help yourself,' said Mary lifting the paper from under the counter and slapping it down on top.

Vic took the paper over to his father and laid it open. 'There, look at that. Ma's doing good and looking great, don't you think?'

Jack looked at the paper. A large picture of a smiling and glamorous Julia gazed out at him. Her arm was perched on Merv's shoulder.

'Who's the joker beside her?' asked Jack.

'Read the article. It's Merv MacLean her business partner. Good lookin' bloke, i'n't he.

Jack snorted and glowered. 'Maybe it's her new fancy man. She looks pretty happy. In fact, ev'ry bugger seems extra happy just now.'

'Ma deserves some happiness. She's not had a lot to make her smile round our way for a long time.'

'What's that supposed to mean?'

'I'm just saying. Anyway, why the long face? Grant and you might have lost the battle to get your way with the road. But you've got the dough to put it round the back. If it's of any interest to you, I'd be inclined to run it up the track behind the old house, knock down the hay barn up on the top field and Bob's Your Uncle – you've by-passed the cave site by two hundred yards or so.'

Jack stared at Vic in wonder. When did you think that up? Why didn't you mention it before?'

Vic shrugged. 'Nobody asked. Anyway, it's no skin off my nose.'

'But it's our family business,' retorted Jack beginning to get red in the face.

'Correction Jack. It's your business and Grant's and Michael's. It doesn't include me at all. Remember, I'm just Vic, thick as two planks.'

Jack's eyes narrowed. He was beginning to see a side to Vic he wasn't aware of. But he couldn't get away from what was really galling him. 'Another route is not the point. The bloody point is that the land is mine, and the bloody Horis have won the legal rights. We've got to back off. I don't take kindly to losing. And to make matters worse my brother has decided to make the donation to their bloody community hall. He reckons it might get us off the hook after the balls up with the Te Hurunui revelations.

'Yeah, well tough. Seems there's a few things not going your way these days.'

'Like what?'

'Well, I hear it was Sean Campbell that helped Tama's crew set up the recording that scuppered you jokers.'

'I suspected he'd have something to do with it, but I'm not finished with that Scot's bastard yet.'

'You going to get that little hooligan Te Hurunui to rough him up again? You seen Sonny's face. Word has it that he ran into Sean in Dunedin. Mind you, looks more like his nose ran into a brick wall.'

'I didn't hear that.

'Oh, talking of noses, cousin Mike's must be well out of joint too.'

'How's that?'

'Seems Sean and Marama are an item. They spent last weekend down in Dunedin with friends of his. They took Kirri too."

'Did they now?' Jack's countenance darkened.

'Well, nice talkin' to you Pops. You have a good night now.' Vic left his father moodily picking over the information he'd given him. But Vic didn't feel any sympathy.

Nearer closing time and several whiskies later, Jack, rather unsteadily, went over to the bar where Mary was polishing glasses. 'You on for tonight, darlin'?' asked Jack winking at her.

'Something wrong with your eye, Jack?' said Mary, her face expressionless. Then she added, 'No, Jack, I'm whacked. Lyn's off tonight and I've had a heavy day. 'I'm off to Dunedin early tomorrow. You'll just have to save it up.'

'Suit your bloody self,' said Jack bad-temperedly and made for the door.

Unusually for him, he'd walked down to the pub. As he headed down the lane towards the old bridge it started to rain. This did not improve his mood. Passing Sean's cottage he could hear laughter, a woman's and man's voice. The rain got heavier and aided by increased gusts of wind began to drive against him. He gritted his teeth and lowered his head.

36

The phone was ringing in Kerrs' Mornington pharmacy as Ricky Kerr saw his final customer off the premises. He quickly shut the entrance door and flipped the OPEN sign to CLOSED. He strode to the counter to silence the relentless ringing. Normally he'd be cursing the phone encroaching upon his lunch hour break but today was Wednesday and therefore half-day closing. He lifted it to his ear and politely intoned, 'Hello, Kerrs the Chemist. Can I help you?'

'Richard, my friend, how are you?' boomed out the voice of Michael Maitland.

'Mike. Mike Maitland? Christ, it's a surprise to hear from you. What have you been up to, apart from making money, you pecunious bastard?'

'Pecunious. Now that's a good word, Richard. My, but your vocabulary is improving by leaps and bounds.'

'You are a sarcastic prick, Maitland.'

'And a busy one, Ricky boy. And a busy one. Lots to do these days and no time to waste. Really must try to meet up with you soon. In fact, how about tonight?'

'What you after Mike?'

'Me? Why, I just want to see your happy smiling face. But, as it happens, you could also do me a big favour.'

'Now that sounds more like the Michael Maitland I know,' said Andy grimacing at the phone. But he listened as Michael cut in and began outlining what he required.

'Jesus, that's a bit dodgy, Mike. We're not supposed to dish out stuff like that. I could land in hot water if I was caught. What the hell do you plan doing with it?'

'Relax, Ricky. It's just for a bit of a laugh. We're having a stag do up here for one of the local farmers. He'll just get a whiff of the stuff, enough to put him out for a couple of minutes max. There'll be no danger I can assure you.'

'It's not on, Mike. Really. More than my job's worth.'

'Remember that little red-head Laura that works in my father's office? How about I set you up for a date with her? She's really hot stuff. A great shag and always up for it. How about it, Andy?'

The vertically challenged and, when it came to women, self-conscious Ricky, paused for a moment and mentally pictured the sexy typist he'd seen arm-in-arm with Maitland about the town. 'You sure the individual you're going to play this joke on is quite healthy? And you sure you'll give him a minimum doze of the stuff?'

'Look, he's a cocky for God's sake. He's got the constitution of an ox. Course I'll be careful and follow your instructions to a T. But I left this thing a bit late. The do's on Friday. Can I meet you in the Ambassador at six tonight?'

'Yeah. Well OK. But what about this date with Laura?'

'Look, tell you what. I'll phone her now and give you

the arrangements when we meet up. How's that?'

'Yeah, but…..' Ricky paused and listened. The phone was dead. Michael had hung up. All thoughts of the packed lunch sitting in the back shop had vanished. He was picturing the red-head in the back seat of his Standard Vanguard in a little cul-de-sac he knew of up on the Flagstaff road.

As Michael put the phone down the hooter sounded for the lunch break. The damp and dust-caked figure of Vic entered the office. He grinned at Judy who was sitting at her desk applying fresh make-up. 'Hell, Judy, you don't have to do that just for me.'

She smiled back and fluttered her eyes, 'Always try to look good for you, Victor. You looking for His Nibs?'

'Yeah, he around?'

Judy nodded her head in the direction of the other office and Vic walked over and opened the door. He looked at his cousin, apparently absorbed in the paperwork lying on his desk. 'Ross says you wanted to see me.'

Michael looked up and focused on Vic. 'Yes, I've got some personal business to attend to in Dunedin this afternoon. I'm leaving after one. Won't be back today, so consider yourself in charge.'

Vic nodded, 'Out there, Mike, I'm always in charge but on a day like today when it's pissing down and beginning to blow a gale, I must admit swopping places with you has its attractions. Mind you, if this weather gets any worse, reckon we might have to hole up in the shed.'

Unfazed, Michael replied, 'Ah yes, Vic. But the world

needs administrators, people with foresight, people who can plan ahead. Your place is definitely outside.'

'Yeah, *doing*. Those who can, do. Those who can't *administrate*. Have a good afternoon, Mike.' Vic slammed the door behind him, winked at the receptionist who was now filing her nails. Strange guy, thought Vic as he headed over to the shed to join his mates for a sandwich and a smoke. Never could figure him out. And he'd seemed to be on edge all week, snapping at the men, complaining about order deadlines and the like. Something was definitely bugging him but dear knows what – not that he gave a stuff. Cousin Michael was the last person to give a toss about anyone other than himself.

Michael sipped his coffee as he contemplated his plan of action.

'Rain – Rain – Rain; Rain – Rain – Rain…..oh- oh, oh-oh, No-ah, Noah said it would rain. ….Good evening all you Dunedin residents, this is Gerry MacLaren on your very own 4ZB Radio Station. Couldn't resist the little ditty. It might be raining now but looks like this is nothing compared to the wild stuff we're going to get over the next few days. I guess…'

'Yeah, I get the picture,' said Michael Maitland sourly as he switched the radio control knob to OFF, cutting out the jaunty presenter's bouncy prattle. Headlights on and wipers working overtime, he changed down as he approached the end of the motorway, braking slightly and swinging onto Cumberland street. He peered through the murk of a late Dunedin afternoon and the oncoming lights of home –going commuters making for North-east Valley suburbia. Hope this little bastard's got the stuff for me, he thought.

Richard Kerr looked at his watch. The sod's late he thought. Mind you, he always did tend to turn up after drinks had been ordered, and paid for! Two glasses and a jug of lager sat on the table beside him. He filled a glass and took a sip of the chilled beverage. He thought about Michael Maitland. He'd known him all through secondary school and had gone through uni at the same time as him. At school Mike had carved out quite a name for himself on the athletic field and he'd done OK academically. So it wasn't too big a surprise that in sixth year he became a prefect and captain of his House.

But for all that, Mike wasn't that popular with the other boys. He was a big-head and totally up himself. And he had a helluva temper. He wasn't too great on the footie field, or any team games for that matter. He couldn't stand being out-classed by other opponents and he'd been reprimanded quite a number of times for lashing out at players when they got the better of him.

Yeah, he was a bit of a strange bugger, Maitland. And yet he'd got on alright with him. Maitland didn't seem to mind him, probably because he was pretty useless sports-wise anyway. And probably because he was easy going and quite popular with the other boys and teachers. Ricky had come to the conclusion that Maitland saw him as a useful ally. He was someone convenient to have around in a mediating capacity when there was a bit of hassle, usually caused by Maitland himself. And of course, he, Rick , was very conscientious –

and successful for that matter – with all academic studies. Maitland frequently cribbed a lot of his homework and assignments.

Yes, they'd got on OK together. They belonged to the same House and ended up prefects. They'd been drunk together on many occasions and got up to some fairly hairy escapades. But for all that, he didn't ever feel that he knew the real Michael Maitland. Behind all the brashness and bull-shit, he got the feeling there was a shady and darker presence. Sometimes he would gaze at you and there was a look about him, a cold calculating look. And at the same time a remoteness.

Ricky recalled their upper sixth year. There'd been a whisper going around amongst the seniors that if it hadn't been for Maitland's father's connections and money that Mike would have been a dead cert to be expelled. He'd overstepped the mark on a number of occasions but each time got away with it and even, amazingly enough, retained his prefect status. Two incidents towered over the rest of his misdemeanours.

The first had caused hidden laughter, and probably a degree of envy, from his peers. It concerned Barbara Mathers, the janitor's seventeen- year-old daughter. Babs was a day pupil at St Hilda's and a good-looker. Given the fact that she was old Mathers' daughter and that Mathers was a big, tough, no-nonsense ex-paratrooper, Babs was regarded as a no-go area to the Fieldings boys. One evening when the parents were off out, Michael had visited her, equipped with a bottle of vodka. They both got drunk and had it off in her bedroom. When the parents arrived home in the early hours of the morning, they found them sound asleep and smelling heavily of booze. Old Mathers was livid and it was all his wife could do to stop him half killing Maitland there and then. Mike had laughingly told him later about being on the mat in the rector's office. Barbara Mathers, mysteriously, was away from home a couple of months later. Word had it that she was 'up the duff'.

The other incident, which was never mentioned in Maitland's company, was of a more sinister nature and certainly didn't raise him up in the estimation of his peers. Indeed, it gave many a feeling of unease around him. It had resulted in Ivor Jones, captain of the first fifteen, ending up with two broken legs. That morning there'd been a punch up between Ivor and Maitland during a seven-a-side in PE time. The two of them had been in the gym that evening and, according to Maitland, had made up and shaken hands over the morning's encounter. Ivor had been using some light weights and Mike had said he'd act as support if he wanted to try some heavy stuff on the bench press. This was strictly forbidden unless there was a master present. Ivor had agreed and somehow or other Michael had dropped the bar carrying one hundred and fifty pounds onto Jones' legs. Later he claimed he'd tripped on a curled end of the bench mat. Jones remained tight-lipped and didn't dispute the claim. But given Maitland's record of animosity towards the rugby captain, the whole incident was regarded with suspicion by many.

Ricky was jolted out of his thoughts as a figure loomed up in front of him. Speak of the devil!

'Ah, Richard my friend. Good to see you. And you've got the drinks in too. But it was going to be my shout. You shouldn't have arrived so early.'

'Cut the crap, Mike. You're late. But there's plenty of time to get another round in.'

'So, you got the stuff for me?'

'Yeah, but I'm not too happy about it. Anyway, I'm going to give you some rules about what you don't do with it. So, listen well.'

37

'Hi, Nan, just me here.' Marama had the school phone tucked into her shoulder, freeing her hands to sort out the papers on the staffroom table. 'You still going to see Aunt Kat this afternoon?'

'Yes, Honey, I'll drive down to Waikouaiti after I drop Kirri. You'll pick her up?'

'Sure. Thought I'd check you're still going down the coast. It's pretty wild out there. Kirri fine?'

'Yeah. She's good. She and Turi seem to have invented some strange game between them. They were dashing round the field half the morning until the rain started again. Wish I had their energy.'

'Good-oh. Drive carefully and give Katerina a big hug from me. See you at tea-time.'

'Will do, dear.'

Marama put the phone down and absent-mindedly bit into her sandwich as she marked some morning maths work. The rain was chucking it down and the children were all confined to having their packed lunches inside, supervised by Sally for the first part of the lunch hour. Marama was scheduled to take the second half. It was Bryn's turn to be free and he'd gone over to the house to have lunch with Pam.

In the cottage, Sean was bent over the typewriter composing a piece describing 1860's gold-fevered Dunedin. A slight emptiness in his stomach reminded him it was quite a bit past lunch-time. The clock on the mantelpiece was showing two o'clock but he'd no intention of interrupting the Muse whilst the words were flowing. Food could wait.

The spattering sound of rain on the window increased as the wind strengthened. The sky outside was dark, necessitating the glow from the table lamp. The fire was banked up and the room felt cosy. Sean paused and pictured for a moment the reconstructed street scene in Dunedin's Early Settlers' Museum that he'd viewed earlier in the week. It had been excellently depicted. Now he closed his eyes and imagined it all brought to life, the vitality and sheer vibrancy of it all…the smells and shouts and sounds of people and carts and animals; the hammerings and sawings of carpenters putting up new buildings and extending others; the dashings and squeals of youngsters chasing and dodging around pedestrians and horse-drawn vehicles on the dusty and wheel-rutted streets; the miners in the hardware stores and drinking dens. Dunedin, a town expanding by the day and imbued with an almost tangible sense of excitement. All attributable to the discovery of gold in the hills and rivers of Central Otago.

The shrill ring of the phone took him out of his reverie. He moved through to the kitchen, 'Hello, Sean Campbell.'

There was a pause and then a voice responded. 'Campbell, I need to meet with you. It's Michael Maitland here.'

'Why would you want to see me?'

'That's the thing. It's a very delicate matter but something you need to know about. It's about when Rob Maitland was killed and it very much concerns Marama.'

'You're not making sense. I…'

Maitland cut him off. 'Listen, I know Marama was there that night. No, don't interrupt. I've got definite proof of that. Meet me up at the Works office at seven and I'll explain it all and why I think you need to know. Otherwise, the police will be informed instead.'

'That sounds like a lot of bull-shit, Maitland.'

'Your choice. Meet me and hear me out. But one thing, don't bring anyone else and DON'T say anything to anyone else, especially not Marama. If you're not up at the office by seven the police will be informed, and, I can guarantee Marama will be getting a visit from them.'

'But…' The phone had gone dead. Sean listened for a moment and then put it down. Michael had hung up.

His writing for the day was well and truly over. He knew he had some serious thinking to do. Not that he believed all the rubbish about Marama being at the accident. If there was any truth in it she would have told him, wouldn't she? He would find out from her in due course but firstly, should he go up and find out what this clown was on about? From the first time he'd met him he'd taken an immediate dislike to the guy, bemused by his supercilious airs. No doubt the feeling was mutual! Marama had recently given him some idea of what Maitland was like and how he'd become more intense and even irrational in his behaviour. Bryn had suggested he was someone to be wary of and even Vic, his cousin, hadn't had anything positive to say about him.

He made a coffee and took it back through to the fireside. He took a sip and then nursed the cup between his palms. Why would this character be giving him such information? What was his motivation? From what he'd heard from Marama, Maitland was obviously still smitten. So why would he threaten to see her in trouble? Was it just a case of Maitland trying to put him off Marama? He clearly knew they had developed a close relationship. But he was barking up the wrong tree if he thought anything he could do would break up that relationship. Sean knew without a doubt, that if – and it was a big if – Marama had been at the scene, there would be a rational explanation. And in no shape or form could it even be contemplated that Marama had anything to do with the demise of Rob. But why hadn't she told him anything about it?

'Jeez, what should I do?' he said to himself. 'Either the bugger is going to try to put me off Marama, or maybe he's got it in for me in some other way. But hell, it's the local limeworks. Nothing's going to happen there. Maybe I should do as he suggested and refrain from saying anything to Marama till later.'

A sudden knock on the door and Marama sailed in, ably assisted by a rain-filled gust of wind. She pushed heavily against the door to slam it shut. 'Hi Honey, you having a break from the typing?'

'Yeah, something like that.' Sean checked the clock. It was just after three. Then he remembered, 'You off to pick up Kirri?'

Yes, it's such a lousy day, thought I'd nip in early and get her home as soon as possible. Nan's down at Wakouaiti. Hope she doesn't get blown off the road. It's wild out there and they say there's a storm brewing up. Just thought I'd get a quick kiss from my handsome man before I set off.'

Marama knelt down in front of Sean, took his cup and put it on the little table beside the chair. She put her hands round Sean's. 'Sean, what's wrong? You're looking a bit worried. Anything bothering you?'

'Yes. Don't know if I should say but I've just had a phone call from your friend Michael Maitland.'

'He's no friend of mine!'

'No, he didn't exactly sound friendly on the phone. He wants me to meet him. He was on about Rob's accident.'

Marama's grip tightened. 'Oh Jeez. He's been telling you I'm involved, hasn't he?'

'Yeah, but I know it's a load of balls.' Sean looked at Marama and added, 'And if you had been at the accident scene, I know there would be a perfectly good explanation for it.'

'Oh Sean, thank you darling. I should have talked to you ages ago about this. It was a nightmare at the time for me and it's been the subject of many nightmares since. I was down near the river that night. And I've thought so often about telling you. And there have been times when I've been on the verge of doing so. Then I'd get cold feet and feel I just didn't want to rake up the past again. I've just wanted the past to be past. I certainly don't know anything about the actual accident. But I was there that night before anything happened to him.'

Sean pulled his hands out of Marama's grip, slid them under her elbows and stood up, lifting her to her feet at the same time. He kissed her on the forehead, 'Talking about it is probably the best thing for you. Come on, I'll come with you to get Kirri and you can tell me all about it on the way and I'll give you the gen on our friend Michael's call.'

Sean drove Marama's car as Marama explained to him the events of the night after he'd left her and then added, 'The shock of Rob's death traumatized me. I hadn't been able to think rationally and felt I was in some way responsible for his death, even although I eventually came to the conclusion that somehow he'd killed himself. But I reckon it must've been accidental. Rob was not the suicidal type. But then I couldn't understand how he got the truck to move. When I left him, he was totally incapable of doing anything and sound asleep. And of course, I'd dropped the keys into the back of the pick-up. He seemed to be quite safe to me. You might recall that the final report concluded that the truck had been driven down into the river. That has always bothered me. I don't think Rob could have crossed his hands together let alone get out the cab and find the keys.

'At the same time, I was fearful that if I confessed to the police that I was the last person to see Rob alive, then they might doubt my word and even implicate me in some way. I really needed someone to confide in. I should have gone to you or Bryn, or both of you together. But I just couldn't face it.'

Sean nodded, 'It's all in the past, darling, and should stay there. But if you have to report what happened to you that night, then don't worry. Your story is perfectly believable and acceptable. Given the trauma of it all, I'm sure you would get plenty of medical back-up regarding your situation should it be required. But what about Maitland? What the hell does he know about it all? And how does he know? If he was there – and he's got to have been if he's saying he knows you were – then the chances are he's in some way implicated himself. Is he likely to go to the police? I doubt it. I think he's bluffing.'

'Yes. I think you're right. But he was so adamant that he had a rational explanation that would satisfy the police should he need to do so. You're not going up there, Sean. I don't trust him.'

'I think I should. It's worth finding out what he's up to – what's going on in his mind.'

'Well, I'm coming with you.'

'No chance. He was emphatic that I didn't speak to you or anyone about it. It could possibly be dangerous for you.'

'Sean, he scares me. I'm beginning to think he's unbalanced. It might be you who's the one that'll be in danger. If you decide to go up there then I'm going too.'

38

Fed, bathed and in her pyjamas, Kirri sat on Mere's lap by the fireside. Sean and Marama sat on the sofa in front of the fire. It was just after six-thirty. Marama had explained to her Nan, Sean's decision to meet with Michael Maitland and his reasons for doing so. On learning of the worry Marama had kept to herself over Rob's accident, Mere had expressed concern that her grand-daughter had not shared it with her, though she understood her reasons for not doing so.

They'd been sipping tea by the fire and discussing what they were going to do. No-one had felt like eating. Outside the wind had risen to gale force and rain lashed the old cottage.

'OK. Are we agreed on the plan of action?' Sean looked to Mere and Marama.

'I understand what you plan doing, Sean, but I'm not happy about it – for both your sakes. From the sound of things, Michael Maitland is more than a little crazy. You could be in danger. Both of you.'

'I think it'll be alright, Mere. You know if we're not back, or if you don't hear from us by eight, to phone the police.' Sean glanced at Marama. She looked tense. 'I'm still not keen on you coming.'

'I'm going and that's that. But I promise I'll keep out of sight.'

'Right, we'd better get the waterproofs on.'

Marama looked at Kirri. The toddler had fallen asleep. 'No story tonight, Nan. I'll carry Toots up to bed. She's not going to waken by the look of her. I'll be right down.'

Adrenalin had given Sean a buzz. The hands on the clock were now showing a quarter to seven as he donned his parka and a cow cocky's hat Mere had found for him. Marama came down dressed in a waterproof anorak and wool hat to go under its hood.

With Tama and Hemi out and not expected until later in the evening, Mere would have to go through the anxiety of waiting for news on her own. Despite the weather, she insisted in coming out to the car with them. Sean's heart went out to her when, with lines of worry showing on her normally placid face, she said, 'Be careful the two of you. Come home safely.' She turned to Marama, 'Take this, grand-daughter. You may need it.'

'Oh Nan, for goodness sake!' Marama looked at the softball bat that Mere was holding out to her. She tried to smile as she took it. She kissed her grandmother on the cheek and said, 'Get inside out of this rain. Don't worry, we'll be back soon.'

Mere watched as the tail lights faded into the distance. It was just on ten to seven.

The windscreen wipers were struggling to compete with the strength of the wind-driven rain as Sean approached the bridge spanning the shallow gully just below the cattle grid entrance into the Limeworks. The car's headlights spotlighted the white foaming water racing under it and sheets of water cascading across its surface as large waves hit the bridge supports. In fact, it looked as though there were several inches of water on the crossing itself. 'God, it's not going to last long at this rate,' he thought. He accelerated hard and felt the car jolt as it hit the bridge.

As planned, he parked the car alongside the boundary fence with the driver's door facing the office huts. He thought it strange that they were in darkness. Then he wondered about Marama making the crossing, but his thoughts were cut short as a powerful torch beam immediately shone on the car and became stronger as the holder approached. Sean got out.

'Stay there!' Maitland's voice could just be heard above the shrieking wind. He stood still as Michael walked around the car, shining the torch inside it and around the fence perimeter. Seemingly satisfied, he yelled, 'Right, let's go over to the office.'

Maitland led the way, torch illuminating the ground ahead and alarm bells went off in Sean's head as he noticed the rifle being carried in his other hand. Maitland climbed up the steps and pushed the door open with his torch hand. He then flicked on the light and gestured for Sean to go in. Sean entered and the door was slammed behind.

'Right, sit.' Maitland ordered gesturing to a chair placed

a few feet away from he reception desk and with its back to it.

'Sean nodded towards the rifle. 'This is a bit dramatic, isn't it?'

'Just sit down.'

Sean shrugged and sat down. His nostrils twitched as he caught the scent of something that reminded him of the dry cleaners. But his thoughts were diverted as Maitland began to speak.

The wind continued to whistle and howl, sweeping across the hillside and attacking anything standing vertically on it. Carrying the softball bat, Marama bent forwards, struggling against the rushing air.

Sean had dropped her off at the last bend, some two hundred yards before the road reached the bridge crossing. She had never witnessed the stream in such a torrent. The water level was just above the bridge surface but flowing rapidly. She wondered how Sean had fared going over in the car. She wasn't relishing the prospect of going over on foot.

The whole gully seemed to be a cacophony of noise, of shrieking wind and thunderous roaring waters. She could feel the ground tremble around her. The bridge spanning the narrow ravine was little more than twenty feet across. Though old and constructed mainly of wood, it had been reinforced a few years previously to withstand the weight of the larger trucks being deployed by the company. But the structure was now groaning and shuddering under the tremendous pressure of the flood waters.

Marama took a deep breath, heaved the bat over to

the other side and then stepped down to bridge level and into the ankle-deep swirling and foaming water. She lunged forwards to grab a hold of the right- hand rail as she felt the force of the current. With both hands clutching the rail and the structure continuing to tremble and shake, she pulled herself as quickly as she could across the gap.

At last she was over. Climbing up the bank she lifted up the bat and made for the cattle grid. She was suddenly aware of the numbness in her legs from the knees down. The danger had made her totally oblivious to the freezing cold water. A shrill crashing sound caused her to stop and turn round. Part of the railings that had supported her move across the bridge had snapped and been driven against those on the other side. How long the rest would stay was anyone's guess.

Maitland sat on a chair facing Sean, gazing at him with undisguised hostility, 'OK, here's the story. I know for a fact that Marama was at the scene the night Rob died. I've asked myself on a number of occasions why she was there. If she had an innocent reason for being there, why didn't she come forward and tell the police of this at the time? Seems strange, don't you think? Even suspicious.'

'I don't know what you're getting at, Maitland. Marama would never have harmed Rob or anyone else. If she'd been around at the time that Rob had died, there's no way his death could have been attributed to her.'

'I'm not so sure about that. But listen, I couldn't care less about Rob being dead. He's no loss to anyone. He was a no-hoper with no ambition whatsoever.'

'I don't get it. What are you on about then?'

'Point is, Campbell, I don't care about Rob but I do care about Marama. Things were going well between Marama and me until you came along. I planned to marry her. I still do. But to do so, I need you out of the scene.'

'I think Marama's made it perfectly clear to you that she's not interested. In fact, I can tell you that she and I are committed to each other and that you're just going to have to live with that.'

'I don't think so. You see, you won't be doing her any favours by hanging around. If you do, the police will be informed, anonymously, of the fact that she was at the scene of the so-called "accident". This would result in her being interviewed by the police. Could lead to a court case and a lot of stress and problems for her and the family.'

'And you're prepared to put her through all that?'

'If you don't bugger off, sure!'

'You're a nasty bastard, Maitland. But if you think your threats will work on us then think again. And, by the way, I already know that Marama was at the accident scene. But when she left Rob, he was sound asleep in the truck and quite safe. The thing is, where were you when all this was happening? Were you the last person to see Rob alive? What happened to him? Do you have the answers?'

'Alright. Try this for size. Not only are the police anonymously informed that Marama was there that night. They're also informed that you were both in a relationship and that it was in both your interests to have Rob removed from the scene. The bang that you got to the back of your head could easily have been administered by Marama. It might have exonerated you before and seemed genuine enough, but bringing a new twist to the tale raises a lot of other questions'

'I think you're bull-shitting, Maitland. If the police become involved, you'll become involved too whether you like it or not. I think you'd have quite a bit of explaining to do.'

'Well, tell you what. There's a copy of the letter the police will receive lying on the desk behind you. Why don't you have a read of it and then think about its implications. On you go, pull your chair up and read it.'

'It won't make any difference but I'll look at it.' Sean stood up and turning the chair around pulled it up to the desk. He sat down and began to read.

As Marama cautiously walked over the grid, she could see the light in the office block. She ran across and stopped underneath the window. The prefab building sat on concrete piles and she needed a couple of feet of extra elevation to see what was happening inside. She looked around and spotted a wheelbarrow lying face down in the mud and half under the building. She thought it just might do the trick. Leaving the bat on the ground, she picked up the barrow and pushed it alongside the wall. Gingerly, she climbed onto it, keeping her hands on the hut wall for support. Gradually she straightened her body to its full height. Her eye level was just above that of the bottom of the window. She looked through.

They were sitting side-on to her, Michael facing Sean and Sean directly opposite him with his back to the office desk. Her eyes widened in alarm as she noticed the rifle lying across Michael's knee. He suddenly got up and laying the rifle on his chair waved his hand towards the desk. Sean stood, turned his chair around then pulled it up to the desk. He sat down and began staring at something on the desk. He seemed to be reading. Maitland had moved out of vision but Marama tensed as he came back into focus. He had something in his right hand. It looked like a piece of cloth. He suddenly bent over Sean, put his left arm around his throat and thrust the cloth into Sean's face. Sean half stood and began to struggle then slowly his legs appeared to give way. He fell backwards, the chair and Maitland going with him, Maitland still clinging on tightly. Sean had stopped struggling and lay still. It looked like he was unconscious. Michael let go of the cloth and stood up. His chest was heaving with the effort of holding Sean. Then she saw him grin. He bent down and grabbing hold of Sean's ankles began to pull him along the floor toward the back corridor. Marama jumped down from the barrow and taking the bat made for the rear of the building.

Maitland had the office back door open. The pool of light from the corridor faintly illuminated the gap between the office and the squat concrete structure built into the earth bank behind it. It was the explosives store. Sean's inert body lay half in and half out of the open doorway. Maitland disappeared into the office and then returned with his torch and the rifle. Though they were sheltered from the full force of the wind, strong gusts swirled around the gap between the buildings.

Holding the rifle and torch in his left hand, Maitland took out a large key from his pocket and unlocked the heavy door. Pulling it open, he moved in to switch on the light A dark shadow appeared behind him and a baseball bat landed heavily on his back causing him to fall forwards. Marama slammed the door shut and as Maitland cried out, she turned the key in the lock. Maitland began to hammer and throw himself against the door. His yells were muffled by the thickness of the door and the shrieking wind as Marama rushed over to Sean and cradled his head in her arm. 'Sean, Sean, wake up!

Sean opened his eyes and tried to focus. He saw Marama and smiled. Groggily he asked, 'What happened?' Then with a look of consternation he struggled to sit up. 'Where's Michael?'

'Don't worry, he's locked up in the storeroom. But he's still got his rifle. Sean darling, are you alright? I was looking in the window and I saw him put a cloth over your face. I think he drugged you. Can you managed to stand up? Come on, I'll help.'

Unsteadily, Sean managed to get to his feet and Marama supported him back into the building. Once back in the office she got him into a chair and knelt down to hug him. 'Are you sure you're, OK?'

Yeah, just a bit groggy. The sod caught me by surprise. I went out like a light. I'm sure it's chloroform he had. Where the hell he got it from, dear knows. Anyway, thank goodness you were around. You saved my bacon.'

'Told you I had to come.' Marama smiled and kissed him on the forehead. I'm going through to get you some water. Then we'd better decide our plan of action.'

Marama returned with a glass of water and pulled a chair up alongside him. Sean took a long drink then said, 'We'll phone your Gran right away and let her know we're fine. Then the police. We'll keep that nutter locked away until they arrive. If anyone opens the door, he's likely to shoot them.'

Marama went over to the desk phone and picked it up. She listened for the dial tone. There was no sound. 'Sean, the phone's dead. Could be the storm's put the lines down.'

'I think we should get back down the road as fast as we can.'

'Can't go over the bridge. Half of it's been washed away.'

'Well looks like we'll have to go up by the track to the caves.'

'No, Sean. On a night like this it'll be too dangerous. It's extra steep and with some precarious drops and the track will be like a torrent. But there's another route up by Taylor's Ridge. It's longer but a more gradual climb. You go up by the old quarry excavations on the right and eventually link up with the main track just before the caves. Don't worry, I know the route well. The thing is, are you fit enough to do it?'

'Yeah, I'm feeling better. But we should leave a note. What if anyone manages to get up here? They'll wonder where we are. And we'd better warn them about not letting Maitland out of the store.'

'OK. You're the writer. Make it quick but to the point.'

Sean made to get up but Marama pushed him back onto the chair. 'No, wait here. We need you to recover. I'll get the paper and stuff from reception.'

With the note made out in clear block letters and taped to the manager's door by Marama where it would be clearly visible to anyone coming in, Sean said, 'Button up tight. But be prepared to get soaked.'

'What's new! But are you sure you're up to it?'

'Yeah. The fresh air should clear my head. Mind you, it's so bloody wild out there it might blow my head off altogether!' At the back door Sean picked up two torches from the shelf beside the coat hooks. He handed one to Marama. 'Just a minute. Look, are these leggings hanging there?'

'You're right. I might have to roll the cuffs up, but if they keep us a bit drier and warmer it'll be worth it.'

Taking off their coats, they quickly got into the waterproof trousers, strapping the braces tops over their shoulders. Then they redonned their coats.

As Marama opened the door a gust of wind blasted down the corridor. Switching on the torches and with Marama in the lead, they set off into the storm. Unbeknown to either, the wind force had flung open wide the door displaying their notice.

39

Vic jammed on the brakes of the jeep and swung the wheel over to the right. The old vehicle rattled and screeched and finally skidded to a halt.

'Jakob, move over son,' Vic shouted over the drumming of the rain on the hood and bonnet.

The passenger door swung open and Hemi climbed in and slammed the door shut. 'Thanks, Mate. What a bloody night!'

As he peered through the misted windscreen, Vic had spotted Hemi coming out of the pub and guessed he wouldn't say no to a lift. 'This is your lucky night ,Te Kanawa. By the time you got over the bridge you'd've been soaked. It's fair pissing down. Jako and me were up at Naseby. A joker up there's been promising to sell me a new fly rod he didn't want.'

'Any good?'

'Yeah, it's a real beaut. Got it for twenty-five bucks. It's worth four times that'.

'Strewth, sounds like a bargain. Anyway, how's young Jakob here?' said Hemi ruffling Jakob's hair. 'Night like this, Jakob, I should've stayed in the bloody pub, what d'you think, eh?'

Jakob just grinned. Vic had seen quite a bit of the little lad since the first time he'd talked to him down at the hide. After that Jakob seemed to pop up any time he was down at the river. The kid was very shy but obviously had a fascination with nature and a wish to share his interest with Vic. Vic had had a word with Istvan Zarkov, to let him know what was going on. It turned out that Jakob's folks were just pleased that he was in a situation where he was communicating even if not actually talking. They'd been advised to take advantage of any such opportunities, the hope being that he'd eventually be able to talk to others out-with the family circle.

'Right, fellas, it's Home, James, and don't spare the Horses!' Vic released the brake, slammed down the accelerator and they roared off.

'Is Jakob not going down to his house?' Hemi asked as they passed the entrance to the cul-de-sac.

'Nah. Istvan's round at Roy MacLean's. I said I'd drop him off there on the way home.'

As the Te Kanawa homestead showed up in the headlights, Hemi frowned. 'Hey, that's Nan standing on the veranda. What's she doing out in this weather?' The jeep came to a standstill and Mere waved frantically to them. 'Come on, Vic, let's see what the trouble is. My Nan doesn't get excited too easily. Looks like there's something wrong.'

They all got out and ran over to the veranda. 'What's going on, Nan?' They followed Mere into the hall and Jakob pushed the door shut. The faces of Hemi and Vic grew grim as Mere explained the events of the last few hours. Without alluding specifically to the accident night, she related how Michael Maitland had contacted Sean and wanted to meet him at the Works but that no-one else was to know about the meeting.

Hemi looked at his watch. The time was seven forty 'I'm going up. I don't like the sound of this situation. I find Mike Maitland a strange geezer at the best of times. All sounds very weird to me.'

'I'll come with you,' said Vic.

'Thank boys. I feel happier knowing you're going up. But be careful.'

'No worries, Nana,' said Hemi looking at her strained face and hugging her. 'Things will be fine.'

'Jako, you be all right to run along to the MacLean's from here?' asked Vic.

'I can take him,' said Mere.

Jakob shook his head, pointed to himself and the door and went out.

'He'll be OK, Nan. It's only fifty yards down the road. When's Gramps due back?'

'He said he hoped to be back before half-eight but that it would depend on the weather.'

'I'll get some waterproof gear,' said Hemi going out to the hall.

Mere called after him, 'Take the big torch. It's in the cupboard. I put a new set of batteries in it yesterday.'

Hemi came back with the torch, two oilskin mustering coats and sou'westers. He passed one set to Vic, 'Here, Mate, get these on you.' Then he kissed Mere on the cheek, 'Right, we're off. Don't worry, we'll get them back safely.'

Mere watched from the doorway as they ran over to the jeep. Her lips were moving in prayer as Vic drove out of the driveway and headed back along the road to the turn-off.

40

There was no let- up in the weather. The rain continued to lash against the windscreen. As they reached the junction Vic asked, 'We got a plan here?'

'Not really. Nan said Marama was going to get out before the run-up to the cattle grid. Reckon we'd best do the same and leave the jeep beside the old gravel pit. We'll walk up to the huts from there. What d'you think?'

'Sounds good. Be prepared to get wet.'

Vic grunted in response. The old jeep shook and shuddered as it became more exposed to the full brunt of the wind. As they got closer to the stopping spot, he switched off the lights and took the jeep down to a slow crawl. Whilst he knew the road like the back of his hand, he knew too that in these conditions it would be easy to become disorientated. He suddenly spotted the black gaping hole that had been cut into the hillside. He pulled the vehicle over. Zipped up and hats tied tight, they got out to face the elements.

Coming out of the comparative shelter of the pit, the full force of the wind hit them. Heads bowed against the driving rain, they leant forwards and started walking up the road.

'Bloody hell,' said Hemi as he caught sight of the bridge, 'I don't like the look of that.' He took the torch out of his coat pocket and shone it on the gully crossing. They paused and gazed at the havoc. There were no railings or posts left on the right-hand side. On the left, some debris and a few posts and bits of broken railing were all that remained.

'Sure as shooting, the whole bloody thing's going to go. We gonna chance it? Water's about knee high. Reckon there's enough to hold onto if we're quick.'

'Come on. Best not think about it,' said Hemi striding forwards. He waded into the torrent and immediately struggled against the force of the water. Working his way across and trying to support himself on parts of the shaky structure, his muscular figure bull-dozed its way to the far bank. Vic, similar in bulk, did the same.

'Jeez, that was fun,' panted Vic as they both walked up to the cattle grid. I tell you what, the old bridge is not going to be there for much longer.'

'You're right,' shouted Hemi as they again became exposed to the howling wind. Don't think we'll be getting home that way, that's for sure.'

Once over the grid they moved to the admin block. All the lights were on. Where the pool of light spilled into darkness they stopped. Vic pointed to the hut window and then to Hemi. Hemi nodded. They crept over. Vic indicated to Hemi he'd give him a leg-up but Hemi shook his head and pointed to the wheelbarrow. He climbed onto it, supported by Vic, and looked in. He shook his head at Vic. They moved along until they were below the reception window.

The ground was higher here and both of them were able to look inside from ground level. Hemi put his mouth up to Vic's ear, 'The place seems to be empty. I don't think there's anyone around.'

'Right, let's go in.'

They climbed up the steps and into the reception area. Vic moved through to the manager's office. The door was wide open. The gust of wind encountered by Sean and Marama as they left the building had blown it back almost flush with the office wall. In his haste, Vic completely missed Sean's note. 'No-one here.'

Hemi went through to the back hallway to check the toilet. It was empty. He went back into reception where Vic stood looking puzzled. 'Did you try the back door?'

Hemi shook his head. Vic moved past him and along the corridor. Hemi followed Vic turned the door handle. The door was unlocked. He opened it.

'That's strange. They must've gone out the back but why?'

'Listen!' said Vic. Was that a voice?' They stood for a moment and above the roaring of the wind they heard a faint shout.

'I think it's coming from the store,' yelled Vic.

They moved across the short space. 'I think he's got them locked in here. See if the key's still in the lock. Hemi felt for the key. 'I can't see a bloody thing.'

'That's 'cause you're blocking the light.'

'There's bugger all light out here. Wait. Got it.' Releasing the lock, he swung the big reinforced door open with a smile. His smile froze. He couldn't make out the figure in the darkness of the store's interior but he could make out the rifle barrel pointed at him. As he turned to move away the rifle went off with a resounding bang. Hemi fell backwards and onto the ground.

'Christ. Bloody thing just went off,' exclaimed Michael Maitland.

Vic looked in shocked disbelief at his friend and then at the emerging figure of his cousin. 'You stupid bastard, you just shot Hemi!'

'Shit!'

Vic dropped to his knees beside Hemi. He put his fingers to Hemi's neck and his ear close to his face. 'He's got a pulse and he's still breathing,' he croaked. 'We've got to get help. He looked up at his cousin.

Michael gestured with the rifle, 'Get him inside.'

Vic got his hands under Hemi's arms and began to pull him backwards into the office building. Michael followed.

In the light of the back office, Vic gently laid Hemi down and leant over to examine him. Hemi had been fortunate. His natural reaction in turning away from the pointed weapon had resulted in the bullet creasing the side of his head. But the wound looked messy and blood oozed down the side of his face.

'He's out for the count,' said Vic, 'but his breathing's OK. You've just creased him but he needs hospital treatment. Jeez, Mike, you could've killed him.'

Maitland sat on the edge of the desk. He held the rifle loosely across a knee and had calmly lit a cigarette whilst Vic was examining Hemi. Any initial agitation he'd expressed had vanished. He exhaled a plume of smoke. He'd got himself back in control. He knew what he had to do. 'Right, Vic, so he'll live. Now stop playing doctors and sit on the chair over there.'

'What you on about? Hemi needs treatment and he needs it now.'

'Shut up.' Pointing the rifle at Vic's chest he added, 'He's bloody lucky. No doubt he'll get help sooner or later. Now sit on the bloody chair.'

Vic sat down but immediately retorted, 'What d'you think you're doing Mike? Where are Marama and Sean?'

'Didn't you see them when you came up here?'

'No.'

'What do you mean? You must've passed their car on the road.'

'No. The bridge's flooded and breaking up. We just made it across on foot and no more. I doubt if it's still standing.'

'They must've gone up the track, heading for the Valley. Bugger it. Won't catch up with them.'

'Why would you need to?'

'A bit of unfinished business.'

Vic inwardly cursed giving Michael information that might endanger Marama and Sean. 'What unfinished business?'

Michael glared at Vic, steely-eyed. 'Some facts, Vic. And quickly. How come you and Hemi are up here? I want the truth otherwise I'll put another bullet into your pal here and it won't just crease him this time.'

Vic looked at his cousin. 'What in heaven's name are

you talking about? You lost your marbles or something? Why the hell are you threatening us? I'm your cousin. Hemi works for you.'

'I'm asking you again, 'Why are you up here?''

It was suddenly dawning upon Vic that his cousin was quite off his trolley. This wasn't someone he could rationalize with. He sighed and shrugged, 'I was dropping Hemi off at his house. Mere told us Sean and Marama were coming up here because you'd said you urgently needed to see Sean. For some reason, Mere was worried that they might be in danger and that you might do something stupid. Looks like she was right. We decided to come up and see what was going on.'

'Who else knows about this?'

Vic paused. Maitland pointed the rifle at Hemi's head.

'No-one else knows anything to my knowledge. Looks like you're quite safe for the moment,' he added bitterly.

'Good, cousin. I believe you're telling the truth. Now get off your backside. We're going to lock you up in the cell out back then I'm going after the lovebirds.'

'Let me put Hemi through to the other office. It's smaller. I'll get the heater on there. It'll warm up faster.'

Michael paused then relented, 'Right, you've got one minute. Move.'

Vic dragged the still unconscious Hemi through, placed a jacket hanging on the coat-rack under his head then switched on the wall heater. The lights were flickering. He wondered how long the power would stay on. He looked at his friend then closed the door.

'What's this? Maitland motioned Vic to move over to

the side when he spotted Sean's note. He walked over to Seans's note and ripped it off the door. Still pointing the rifle at Vic, he scanned the note and his lips twitched into the beginnings of a smile. 'Well, well. Looks as if I've got time to catch up with your friends. Because of the weather they're going up Taylor's Ridge. If I go up the gully track I can catch them. They also say that they locked me up in the explosives store. Pity for you you didn't read this before,' he laughed scrunching the note up in one hand and sticking it into his pocket.

Dismayed at not having seen the note before and even more so at the fact that Michael could potentially catch up with Marama and Sean, Vic tried to stall for time. He turned towards the office door. 'Look I'm going to have to help Hemi.'

'Bloody well move. Now!'

'No, listen.'

Maitland smashed the rifle butt against Vic's head. Vic dropped to his knees.

'Get up!'

'Get stuffed.'

There was a deafening noise of the rifle going off and almost simultaneously Vic's scream of pain as the bullet smashed through his boot.

'Oh, Jesus, Jesus, Jesus.'

'You dumb bastard. Now get up or I'll put another one into you,' yelled Maitland his face livid with rage.

'Oh, Jeez,' gasped Vic pushing himself up onto his one good foot.

'Now MOVE!'

Vic hopped along the corridor using his hands on each wall to keep his balance, his injured foot dragging uselessly behind. A dark red stain was oozing from his ankle and flowing down over his boot. Awkwardly he hopped down the two outside steps, holding the door jambs for support. He paused in front of the explosives store.

'Not there. Outside. I want you over by the conveyor. Do it!'

Mind numbed with pain, Vic did as he was told and hopped across the pathway to the left of the building. The force of the wind and the effort involved caused him to collapse in a heap beside the fence bordering the path. Four feet below ran a long, galvanized trough containing a metal conveyor belt. Chunks of quarried stone filled the trough.

Michael came over and kicked the gasping Vic. 'On your feet.'

Swaying as though in a drunken stupor, Vic got up and balanced on his good leg. Behind him Maitland reversed his grip and holding the rifle barrel in two hands brought it crashing across the back of Vic's head. Vic toppled forwards over the fence and fell unconscious onto the rubble below.

Michael smiled grimly, 'Right, cousin, you're due to go on a little journey and for you it's a one-way ticket. He headed up to the Engine House that operated the conveyor and rock pulverising system. Arriving there he flicked the lights on. Outside two large arc lamps came on simultaneously, illuminating the area around the hut and part of the conveyor system nearby. He laid the rifle on the table positioned in the middle of the room, zipped up his parka and pulled the hood over his head. He then patted his pocket to check his ammunition was still there. Moving to the window that looked down on the belt, he pressed the START button. There was a whine and a slow rumble that vibrated across the floor. The rumble increased to a roar. He pushed forwards the giant lever rising up from the floor. With the gear engaged the machinery went into action and the belt began inching ahead.

Maitland gave a satisfied grunt, took a torch from the tool shelf, lifted up his weapon and left the room, seemingly oblivious to the fact that the lights were still on.

41

Vic groaned and opened his eyes. Consciousness brought with it acute awareness of the excruciating pain in his foot. He felt himself moving forwards and his body shaking in time to a juddering noise. His head was aching and he wondered at first whether he was having a god-awful nightmare. But the screaming wind along with the clanking of metal and rain lashing against his sodden clothes made him realize this was no dream. Realisation suddenly hit him that he was on the conveyor belt leading to the 'crushers'.

He sat up quickly and then let out a cry of agony, the movement reminding him in no uncertain way of his shattered foot. He placed his hands on the surrounding rubble and tried to push himself backwards. Again, an intense pain caused him to yell out. He discovered he couldn't move. In the dark he could faintly make out that a sizeable slab of rock was trapping the lower leg of his injured foot. This bloody brute of a thing was crushing his leg and the rest of him was going to be totally pulverized by machinery in a few minutes time. How the hell the rock had landed on him he didn't know. He guessed he must've dislodged something when he fell.

Pulling his free leg up and under his buttocks he frantically leant forward to put his hands under the edge of the stone but because of his seated position he couldn't utilize his strength to any effect. He closed his eyes and roared in frustration. He was almost at the gateway where the quarried rock dropped into the crushing chamber. And then the conveyor came to a sudden halt followed by a series of judders and screeches. The wind continued to howl and the rain drummed down but these sounds were music to Vic's ears. Who'd turned off the machinery? He craned his head backwards to the engine shed and spotted a slight figure with fair hair moving quickly alongside the conveyor rail. As it got closer, he recognized it was little Jakob and he was overcome with emotion, 'Jeez, son, am I glad to see you.'

Jakob smiled and lifted up a crowbar he'd picked up from outside the shed.

'Good boy! Give us it here,' said Vic stretching out his hand. Vic placed the end of the bar out alongside his boot and pushed until he got a little of it under the rock. Now he had purchase and with a concerted pull on the bar he dragged his injured foot out. 'Here, take this, son,' he said handing the bar back to Jakob. Then swinging his leg over the edge of the rail, he gingerly lowered himself down to the ground, taking care to land with all his weight on his good foot. But the pain he was suffering almost made him pass out.

'Oh, bloody hell, Jako, I'm in a bad way here.'

Jakob handed him the crow bar. Vic nodded and shouted, 'Thanks cobber, this should help take some of my weight but I'm still going to have trouble walking. If I put my arm round your shoulder d'you think I could lean on you a bit?'

Jakob pushed himself up against Vic and put his arm around Vic's waist

With Jakob supporting him, Vic began the arduous struggle back to the quarry buildings. They eventually made it to the back door of the offices. Jakob opened the door. Once inside Vic stopped, heaving and panting. 'Just give us a minute sport, then we'll go through and see how Hemi is. You saved my life, Jako. But how did you get here and how the hell did you know how to stop the belt?'

'I-I've been up h-here before wh-when there's been no-one around. I-I've looked at the buttons before and I knew the red one stopped everything. And I knew you were going to help Mr Campbell and Miss Te Kanawa so I jumped into the back of your jeep.'

'Did you now! Lucky for me that you did!'

'I-I waited in the jeep for a while then went up to the huts. I heard the gun go off so I hid under the building. I was v-very frightened when I heard the gun go off again. I thought someone might be dead. Th-then I saw Michael Maitland knocking you over the edge. When I saw him go up to the engine room and start the machine I kn-knew I had to stop it. I waited for a couple of minutes after he left and then I stopped it. With the noise of the wind, I don't think he could have noticed anything.'

'Well,' then suddenly aware, Vic paused and exclaimed, 'Blow me down, Jako, you're speaking!'

Jakob grinned back, 'I- I know. I don't know how but I just can.'

'Right son, let's see how Hemi is. We'll phone the police and warn them about this maniac. Let's hope he doesn't catch up with Marama and Sean. 'Get the door, cobber.'

Jakob opened the inner door and helped Vic through. The room was warm. Hemi still lay on the floor but his eyes were open and he seemed to be breathing normally. He smiled and then frowned as Vic staggered past him and collapsed into a small easy chair beside the desk. His brow was beaded with sweat from the pain and effort of his walk. His chest heaved as he gulped in quantities of air.

'You OK, mate? Hemi asked. Then he spotted Jakob. 'Hey Jako, how in heaven's name did you get here?'

'He saved my life, Hemi. I'll explain in a minute. Jako, get me and Hemi some water from the kitchen, would you.'

Vic gave Hemi a quick summary of events then lifted the phone, paused, dialled, paused and then hung up. He lifted the phone again. 'Shit!' He slammed the phone down onto its cradle. 'It's dead.'

'So what are we going to do? said Hemi, eyebrows raised.

Vic looked at Hemi. The glass of water Jakob had given him seemed to be helping him revive. He was now sitting with his back against the hut wall. His head wound looked nasty with blood now congealed and crusty. 'You don't look in a fit state to do anything old chum.'

'I'm feeling better. I might look bad but you're the one in real pain. You need help, and soon.'

'Yeah, it's bloody painful alright.' He looked over at

Jakob, 'Hey Jako, go through to the kitchen again. There's a medical cabinet underneath the sink. See if you can bring some scissors and a bandage and anything else that might help us. Oh, and bring some more water. There's a pot or something on the cooker shelf you can carry it in.'

Jakob came back with a variety of ingredients. Vic struggled up from the chair and let himself down awkwardly onto the floor, hissing through his teeth as he did so. 'Right, son, see if you can get this bloody boot off my foot for starters and then try to cut my trouser leg up to the knee.'

Following Vic's instructions, Jakob managed to access the wound, though Vic's roar when he took the blood-soaked sock off almost frightened the daylights out of the youngster. Despite the renewed flow of blood, Jakob was able to place a clump of gauze over the foot and wrap a long length of bandage around it. A roll of surgical tape was used to keep it in place.

'Thanks, Jako,' Vic whispered and closed his eyes.

'Well done, cobber,' said Hemi in admiration. 'You're a brave little fellow.'

Vic opened his eyes and looked at Jakob. 'Listen, son. We can't get help because the bloody phone is down and we might wait long enough before anyone appears here. If you take one of the torches over there, d'you think you could get back down the road and deliver a message?'

'I d-don't know if I'll be able to speak to anyone else, Vic.'

'No worries. I'm going to write a note. If you can get it to Mere, she'll be able to get the help we need. What d'you think? Could you manage? It's quite a way down and a wild night.' Then he remembered, 'Jeez, what am I saying? You won't get across the bridge. In fact, how the hell did you get over it in the first place?'

'I-I went further up the hill. I was up there for a walk with my dad a while ago, up by the pine plantation. Someone's put a big rope between two big trees on each side of the creek.. It's quite easy to swing over on it.'

'But listen, fella. The creek must be flooded there too. It'll be far too dangerous.'

'No, it's OK. It's the b-bit before the other two creeks join the main one.'

Hemi looked at Vic. What d'you think?'

'Dunno.'

'Where have Mr Campbell and Miss Te Kanawa gone?'

'They're going the long way round back to Hidden Valley.'

'Does Michael Maitland want to hurt them?'

'Yeah, you're right, son.' Jakob's questions helped Vic make his decision. 'Listen, kid, they'll be OK. But we really need to get help as soon as possible. Do you think you get back down by yourself? It's a long way for a little fella on a night like this and I really hate asking you.'

'I can do it.'

'You sure you want to do this son? You don't have to.'

Again Jakob nodded.

Vic dragged himself to the desk. He quickly wrote out a note for Mere, folded it up and said, 'Right, Jako. Put this in your anorak pocket. Now listen. If there's any danger crossing further up the creek then you come right back here.

You don't take any risks. Right?'

'OK, smiled Jakob. Then he lifted the torch sitting on the shelf by the door.

'Good luck, kiddo,' said Hemi. 'Be very careful and as Vic says, don't take any chances.'

Clutching the torch, Jakob set off. Outside the torch beam cut a swathe of light through the darkness. The wind was mainly coming from behind him, the strong force of it pushing him forwards.

42

Sean and Marama were breathing heavily as they reached the highest point on their trek over to Hidden Valley. Just below them and hunched in a dip in the hillside, the vague outline of a building could be seen through the murk. It was a trampers' hut. The higher they'd climbed the stronger the wind had become. Despite their waterproofs, water had succeeded in penetrating parts of their clothing. A sudden fall of heavier rain mixed with hail made Sean grab Marama's shoulder and yell in her ear, 'Stop at the hut. Let's get out of this for a bit.'

Marama nodded and made off down the track.

The hut was situated at the foot of a cliff-face on a fairly level piece of rocky ground. They went round to the entrance which was on the far side of the building, sheltered from the prevailing wind.

'The key's on a nail just below the window sill,' Marama shouted and flashed her torch towards the window just to the right of the door.

Sean found the key, unlocked the door and both stumbled inside. In the initial climb their adrenalin levels had been high after the confrontation with Michael Maitland.

Despite the effects of the chloroform, Sean had recovered remarkably – a recovery ironically contributed to by the wild weather they'd had to endure during their ascent. But now they were beginning to tire.

Sean's torch picked out the fireplace and the semi-circle of seat benches surrounding it, the bunks along the back wall with their straw palliasses, the old wooden table set against the window wall that overlooked the hillside below. Outside the wind continued to howl and the hail to rattle against the hut and its corrugated roof. 'What a night,' said Sean. 'Could do with a big fire and a cup of something hot.'

Marama smiled weakly. 'I'm tired. I just want us to get back home.'

Sean put his arms around her. 'I know, Honey. Let's give it five minutes or so and then we'll get going. Sit on the bench here. Sorry there's no food or drink.'

'Just a minute!' Marama unzipped her anorak and fumbled around in an interior pocket. She fished out a bar of dark chocolate. 'Look what I've found. Just remembered I had it when I was going to meet you for that walk up to the caves.' Marama divided the bar into two. 'This'll give us some energy.'

They sat munching the chocolate and listening to the storm. Marama cocked her head then said, 'It's not hailing anymore. Time to go. I just hope Michael is still safely locked up.'

'Sure he is. Don't worry. And Mere will likely have called the police by now. Right, we're off.'

The gradient was steep and despite the light from the

torches, it was difficult to keep their footing as they stumbled and slid their way downwards, Sean in the lead. Where the path took a sudden steep turn down to their right and dropped below the projecting shoulder of the hill on their left, Sean stopped to get a clearer picture of how precarious their descent would be. Marama looked down from behind him. With the increase in the slope, the rivulets of water they'd encountered before, now joined together to become a small rushing stream. They did have the tiny bonus at this point, however, of being protected from the wind and the comparative shelter enabled them to negotiate the path without the added danger of being blown over.

Arriving at the bottom of the drop, Marama grabbed Sean's arm and shouted in his ear, 'I'll lead the way now. We're going to be out in the open in a minute. Where the track splits, we're going to fork to the right. Once we're round into Hidden Valley it's an easy route down to the Maitland homestead.'

'OK. I'm sure they'll be glad to see us. Let's do it.'

As they emerged from the shelter of the shoulder to walk along a level ridge, the wind and rain attacked them with renewed vigour. They reached the spot where the tracks diverged, the one back to the quarry falling steeply away down the hill-side, the other a more gentle slope, dropped down to the cave site at the foot of a rock escarpment. Marama waved her torch in an arc indicating they were moving to the right. Sean moved to follow her. Another more powerful arc of light from below suddenly swept across them and then back again, wavering but seemingly intent on holding them in its beam.

Sean grabbed Marama and both turned to look down at the source of the light some fifty yards below them. Excitedly Sean yelled out, 'I think it might be the police.'

Automatically he pointed his torch in the direction of the other beam. It immediately switched off and his own light revealed a dark shape fumbling with something in its hands. Sean shouted, 'Get down!' and launched himself sideways, pulling Marama down with him. Two loud bangs could be heard above the sound of the storm.

'Jeez, I hope the kid makes it down alright. We're expecting a helluva lot of him.

'I know. But I know this kid too. He's something special. He'll get there.'

Both Vic and Hemi were half sitting, half lying on the office floor, backs against the wall. Vic had his eyes closed. Spasms of pain were causing his face to contort.

'You in a bad way?'

'Not too good. The pain's pretty bad. What about yourself?'

'I'm actually feeling better,' said Hemi getting onto his knees and then onto his feet. 'Whoa, just a bit dizzy.' He steadied himself, putting his hands against the wall. 'I'll be right in a minute.'

Hemi shuffled through to reception and the kitchen galley tucked away in a corner. The continuous dull pain he was getting in his head flipped to more needle-like attacks as he moved. He filled the kettle and switched it on, got cups, sugar and tea from the cupboard above the sink and a half-full bottle of milk from the small fridge. He then rummaged in the first-aid cupboard, taking out a blanket and a packet of aspirin. With the kettle boiled, he infused the tea, put three spoons of sugar in each cup. Leaving the spoon in one cup he added some milk to both. Holding the blanket under one arm, he managed to carry cups and aspirin in one hand and teapot in the other.

Hemi put the tea things on the desk top and went back through. There was something else he knew was kept for special customers and occasions in the small cupboard above the fridge.

'Vic, this is strictly medicinal,' he said pouring a generous slug of whisky into each cup. He followed this by topping up each cup with tea. 'Tell you what, mate, after hearing about the note stuck on the door, I feel like downing the whole bloody bottle.'

'Yeah, we wouldn't be in this situation now, that's for sure. I remember the door was folded right back. Must've been the wind. Just our luck.'

'Anyway, get this down you, cobber,' said Hemi, kneeling beside Vic and handing him three pills and a cup.

'Vic shoved the aspirin into his mouth and took a swallow of the hot drink. Despite the warmth in the room, he began to shiver and put both hands around the cup for extra warmth.

'Oh, forgot this.' Hemi grabbed the blanket from the desk top and put it over Vic. 'Thank God the power's not off.' Taking a couple of tablets for himself, he then carried his cup to one of the chairs and sat down. He took a few sips and then looked at Vic.

'Got to get you to hospital as soon as poss.'

'I'll be OK. What you got on your mind?'

'Who said I've got anything on my mind?'

'I know you, Te Kanawa. Come on, spit it out.'

'Yeah, well. Reckon I've got to go up the hill, Vic. That's my sister up there with that loony on the loose. I've only been creased and I feel a bit better.'

'You look like hell with all that blood on your head and face. But listen son, get going. I'd be doing the same if it wasn't for this bloody foot.'

'You be OK?'

'Yeah. Should be help coming soon. Just put that bottle down beside me. Medicinal purposes, of course.'

'Of course,' grinned Hemi.

Hemi got up, swallowed the rest of the cup contents and began to fasten up his coat.

'Hemi, go get some bandages from the cupboard and some tape. I'm going to wrap some stuff round your head.'

'You're in no fit state to help me.'

'Just do it.'

'With Hemi kneeling beside him, Vic was able to place a piece of lint over the wound area and wrap a quantity of bandage around his friend's head. 'That should help a bit. It's a mess underneath but that's a job for the medical folk. Now get that sou'wester tied tight and go and sort the bastard out.'

'Thanks, Vic. I wish I had a weapon with me. Just hope that if I come across the bugger I'll have the chance to surprise him. Anyway, time to go. You just take it easy.'

'Be careful, mate.'

The beam of light came on again, searching, sweeping. 'Come on,' shouted Sean pulling Marama to her feet and pushing her below the ridge line. Marama needed no persuading. They ran down the track to the cave, Marama in the lead. Where the path dipped and levelled out at the gaping cave mouth they stopped, gasping for breath. Streams of water were cascading down the cliff face and falling in sheets from the cave roof onto the depression at the cave entrance. But where there was normally a dry gravel and shingle bed, there was now a large pool of water.

'It must be Michael,' yelled Sean. 'How the bugger got out of the store I don't know.'

'He's mad, Sean,' cried Marama. 'God, he's trying to kill us. What should we do? If we go round the back and down the Valley he's going to get a clear view of us. The hillside's totally exposed there.'

'Best to hide in the cave and hope he thinks we're going down the hill. There's no way he'll think we'd be mad enough to go into the cave and be trapped there. If he doesn't appear in the next ten minutes, we can assume he's gone on. We can then double back and go down the quarry track. Hopefully, by the time he realizes what we've done, we'll be far enough away to be out of danger.'

'But remember, there'll be no bridge crossing.'

'We'll worry about that later. At least we'll have put some distance between ourselves and this head-case.'

'I don't know. It's a big risk.'

'We don't have any choice. Come on, let's do it.' Taking Marama by the hand, Sean pulled her with him and they waded through the pool and under the falling torrent.

'You know these caves. Where do we hide?'

'This way.' Marama directed her torch beam to the left of the entrance and headed towards a narrow gap about two feet in width. The outside pool had spilled into the front of the cave floor and flowed along the downwards-sloping crevice. 'At least there won't be any footprints to follow. This passage runs for about twenty yards and ends up in a small chamber. But there's no other way out. Let's just move along halfway and wait. If he comes in, we might spot the light from his torch without being seen.'

'If he comes in it'll only be to check the entrance. I'm banking on him thinking we won't be stupid enough to hide in here. And he won't want to waste time. There are other passages if I remember rightly?'

'Three. Further back.'

Sean flashed his torch around the passage. The ceiling seemed to be a long way above them. Despite the noise of the falling water at the cave mouth and a deep but distant roaring sound from a nearby underground stream, Sean dropped his voice to a whisper, 'Better put the torches out.' He looked at the luminous dial of his wrist watch. 'We'll give it another five minutes. If he hasn't come in by then we can assume he's headed for the back track. Then we'll make a move.'

They stood still, close to each other, ankle-deep in water, saturated, hearts thumping. Sean put an arm around Marama. Her teeth were chattering, as much from fear as the cold. He squeezed her waist reassuringly though assurance was not something he was feeling at that moment. After all, there was a mad bastard out there with a rifle. He'd already taken a couple of shots at them. There was little doubt as to what his intentions were.

'Right,' said Sean, it's eight forty-six. Come on, we'd best move.'

'God, Sean, he might be just around the corner.'

'I know. We'll just have to chance it.'

They edged back along the passage, Sean in the lead. At the cave mouth everything appeared as it was when they entered, except for the fact that looking out, the water cascading from the roof had produced the effect of a roaring waterfall.

'Right, Honey,' Sean yelled. 'We go straight through and make for the quarry. We'll keep the torches off. Ready?'

'Yes.'

'OK. Let's go!' Holding hands, they began wading and then quickly burst through the falling water. Coming up from the pool, they had just reached the track when Marama looked to her left. She froze and her stopping broke Sean's grip on her hand.

'Look Sean!'

Sean looked to his left and saw the faint bobbing pinprick of light some considerable distance away but heading towards them. 'Quick, back into the cave. He can't see us. He's using the torch to follow the track.'

They dashed back through the water, splashing and crashing, desperate to escape being spotted.

43

Tama entered the house, his face showing alarm and worry. Mere got up from the sofa where she'd been talking to Sergeant Braithwaite and his two colleagues. She moved over to Tama, 'Oh Tama.'

'Mere, what's wrong? Are you hurt? Where are Hemi and Marama? I saw the two police cars outside.'

'I'm alright, Tama. I was just beginning to explain to Sergeant Braithwaite and his officers why I called them.' She then proceeded to relay what had happened. As she finished there was a thumping at the door. Before anyone else could move, Mere hurriedly went through to the hall and opened the door, Tama following her. A thoroughly drenched little figure looked up at her.

'Jakob, what are you doing here? You're supposed to be with your dad at the MacLeans. Come in out of the rain. I'll get someone to take you along right now.'

'No, I..I've got a note for you. It's from Vic.'

Mere was taken aback. The sound of the boy's voice was a shock to her. She knew Jakob and his family well. She had never heard him speak before. Aware of the sharpness in her voice, she took Jakob by the hand. 'Come,' she said gently, 'we'll see what the note's all about.'

Jakob looked at all the grown-ups in the crowded lounge and dug his hand into his anorak. He handed the note to Mere.

Mere unfolded the sheet of paper and began to read. She paused and gasped, 'It is from Victor.' And read out to them all…

To Mere or whoever gets this note……

I'm sending Jakob down with this letter. He's a brave little bloke and I just hope to God he gets down safely. Please get the police if you haven't already done so. Hemi and I are injured. Michael Maitland shot us both. We need hospital treatment but we're OK. We're still in the office at the Works. The bridge is down but Jakob says you can get across further upstream. Sean and Marama have gone off up the long track to Hidden Valley. Michael has gone after them. He's got a gun and is likely to use it. He's already creased Hemi and shot me in the foot. He seems to be off his trolley. Please warn the police that he is dangerous and armed.

Vic

Sergeant Braithwaite said quietly, 'I'd better have the note Mrs Te Kanawa,' and he took it gently from Mere's shaking hand.

'Dear God, this is terrible.' She looked at the police officers, 'Please bring Marama and Sean and the boys back safely,' she whispered.

'We promise we'll do everything we can, Mrs Te Kanawa.' And then in a more strident and businesslike voice he said to his two young colleagues, 'Right, fellas, call for an ambulance and reinforcements immediately. The ambulance can go up as far as the bridge and meet you there. Get yourselves and the crew across to the Works somehow or other and tend to Hemi and Vic.

'I'll go up to the Maitland homestead and wait for support to arrive. You'd better tell them to be armed. They can ring me when they're on their way. We'll be on the lookout for Sean Campbell and Marama.'

'I'd like to come with you, Sergeant,' said Tama.

'Right, Tama. Mrs Te Kanawa, will you stay with young Jakob, we'll get back to you as soon as we can?'

Mere nodded and the police officers left the room. Tama put his arm around his wife, guiding her over to the sofa and sitting her down. But Mere suddenly remembered Jakob and immediately got up. 'Jakob, take that soaking wet anorak off and come and sit by the fire. I'm going to get us both a hot cup of cocoa. Tama, go with the sergeant. Go now!'

Tama kissed Mere on the cheek and followed Braithwaite and the officers. He was relieved that Mere had Jakob to keep her occupied.

44

'God, Sean, he's going to find us. We're going to be trapped in here.' They were back in the cave, fear fuelling the rapid pounding of their hearts.

'I can't understand how he got back so quickly. He must have been really moving. He's guessed we were hiding here but he'll probably think we've made a dash back down to the quarry. He'll have to go to the top of the track and check we're not on our way down. So, we've probably got a little more time. You say there are four different passageways.'

'Yes, but they're all dead ends. He just needs to explore each one systematically to find us.'

'Yes, but whilst he's in one he doesn't know if we're coming out of another. With a bit of luck, this might drive him mad.'

'No madder than he is already.'

'So, none lead anywhere else?'

'No. Well, there's the taniwha tunnel at the end of the back cave but it'll be full of water.'

'What d' you mean? Is it a way out?'

'Hemi and two friends once went through it one summer

when they were teenagers. It's a very short underground creek that comes out at the back of the hill into the Valley. I believe it's only about fifteen yards long. But even in summer it was almost up to their waists. They all did it as a dare and no-one wanted to chicken out. But they said it was completely black and scary. The fact that there's a story of a taniwha living there didn't help. Afterwards, Hemi said he'd never go through it again.'

'Let's make for it. If we have to go through, we'll do it.'

'But in this weather the creek will be roaring through. The tunnel might be totally full. We could drown.'

'We could also get shot. Come on, Marama. Lead the way.'

Marama pointed her torch directly ahead into the cave's blackness whilst Sean, close behind her, shone his torch on the floor to guide their footsteps. They moved tentatively and unsteadily ahead, the ground sloping upwards. Eventually Marama located the passage entranceway. It was much wider than the previous one they had been in. They stopped and swung their torches around. Water dripped from the gleaming walls. Small stalactites hung from the roof and the floor was caked with their accumulated residue, stalagmites in their pubescence.

Carefully they edged ahead, Sean now in the lead. Their path now began to slope downwards. They were well away from the cave entrance and a new sound of rushing water reached their ears. The lower they descended the louder the noise became. The passageway suddenly narrowed and they squeezed through a rock fissure and found themselves in what appeared to be a fairly level chamber. A high vaulted roof rose into the darkness above them. Ahead the source of the noise revealed itself. A foaming creek charged through from a tunnel on their right and disappeared into another gaping hole on their left. Alarmingly, the gap between the tunnel roof and the level of the water seemed to be little more than eighteen inches.

'Jeez, Sean, we couldn't go into that!'

'Tell me again. Where does it go?'

'It comes out in the Hidden Valley hillside, out over a flat rock and falls into a pool where we've sometimes swum as kids in the summer. But that's not what frightens me. If we go into that tunnel we might end up under water.'

'But you said it's only about fifteen yards long. It's clear of the roof at this end. Chances are it'll be like that all the way. Even if it's not, we can hold our breaths long enough. The force of the water will push us through in no time.'

'I'm scared.'

'So am I, darling. But I'm more scared of the nutter with the rifle than getting a soaking in the creek. Come on, let's do it.'

Sean climbed down to the level of the stream. Seeing the force of the water close up worried him. 'Listen Marama, he yelled above the noise of the water. 'When we get in, we'll be swept off our feet. The creek bed is obviously dropping downwards. We'll just have to go with the flow and keep our heads up. Will I go first?'

'No. If we're going, I want us to go together.'

'Stick your torch inside your anorak then wrap your arms around my waist. I'll carry my torch and keep my arms free. The force of the water will sweep us along. If your feet touch the bottom just keep pushing off in a running motion. It'll be like giving you a piggy back in the water.'

Sean sat down at the water's edge and gasped as he placed his lower legs in, feeling the cold and the pull of the current. Turning back to Marama he shouted, 'Kneel behind me and hold on. When I yell GO, I'll slide in. Just hold on as tightly as you can.'

'OK.' Marama wrapped her arms round his midriff.

'Ready – GO!' Sean shouted. He slipped in, his feet momentarily touching the creek bed before he was lifted up by the sheer force of the current and thrust forwards, Marama clinging to him like a limpet. They were in the mouth of the tunnel in a flash. Apart from the initial shock of being immersed in freezing temperatures, the struggle to keep their heads above water focused their adrenalin-fuelled bodies. Sean's torch faintly exposed the top of the tunnel walls and roof as they moved along. Ahead Sean suddenly saw the black water surface merge with the roof. Marama spotted the danger and inhaled quickly. The next moment they were under water, Marama still holding on to Sean. A couple of bumps against the tunnel ceiling and suddenly they were out of the tunnel and being unceremoniously dumped into the pool below. Disentangled and half swimming, half walking they fell panting at the pool's edge.

'Oh Sean, I've never been so frightened in my life,' gasped Marama between coughs and splutters.

'Me neither. God that was scary. Where to now? We didn't drown but we might bloody well freeze to death.'

45

Michael Maitland cursed as he stumbled and lurched back along the track beside the caves. He'd been so sure they'd have taken the route round the back and into the Valley but there'd been no sign of them. Miraculously the bloody rain had stopped and the wind lessened. He should have been able to spot them on the exposed slope. The tussock would have given them little cover, if any, and he didn't think for a minute they'd have risked lying amongst it knowing he was coming after them. The bastards must have gone into the caves. He hadn't thought they'd be so stupid considering there was no way out.

His rage increased as he hurried back to where the path descended to the quarry. He reasoned they must have allowed time for him to follow the track past the caves and then made a dash for it. Again, the hillside here was similarly exposed, offering no cover until the track twisted out of view much further down. And given the conditions he'd come up in, there was no way they could make fast time in the descent.

He gazed below him, pointing the powerful torch into the darkness. The beam didn't show up anything. His vision was suddenly enhanced as a shaft of moonlight slanted through a break in the clouds. Switching the torch off, he again scanned the drop. There was definitely no movement. Momentarily puzzled, he wondered where they could possibly be. Then he smiled and clenching the rifle turned back towards the caves.

Sean helped Marama to her feet, supporting her as they climbed up the embankment surrounding the pool. Both of them were shivering with the cold and the shock of their ordeal. 'Look, the rain has stopped and the wind has dropped. There's actually a bit of moonlight peeping through the clouds. Come on Marama, I'm lost. Get us out of here.'

'The track is further over. Can you make out that small group of pine trees away down to our left?'

'Yeah.'

'We'll hit the track if we make for that point. The burial site is in the small hill just behind them. Have to be careful though. Crossing this tussock in the dark won't be easy.'

'Right. Want me to lead the way?'

'No. It's OK, I will. We're not that far away. The moon's coming out even more. Best put the torches off. We might see better without them.'

They were almost at the valley floor when Marama gave a sudden yell and fell to her right. She began crying out in pain. Sean, a few feet behind her, moved quickly to help. He spotted the problem. Her right leg had slid into some sort of pot-hole and she had crashed over onto her side, landing painfully on a low-lying rock.

'Oh, shit! I'm hurt. My leg, it hurts like hell.'

'Keep still, Honey. Let's get you out of there for a start.' He tucked his hands under her arms and shoulders. 'I'm going to pull you out. I'll do it gently. Just yell if it hurts too much.'

'Right.'

Sean began easing her backwards. He stopped as she began to moan. 'Just keep going. It's sore but bearable.'

He finally got her clear. Panting, he moved alongside her. 'Whereabouts does it hurt? Can you move your leg?'

'It's around the knee area.' Marama tried to pull her knee upwards and let out a yelp. Ouch! That's sore.'

'Right. Let's see if we can get you onto your feet. We'll get your arm around my neck and lean on the good foot. Then we'll see what weight you can manage on the injured leg.' He finally got her into a standing position and gingerly she straightened her right foot on the ground and then put a little weight on it.

'That's not too bad but I don't know what'll happen when I put the whole weight on it.'

'Let's try. Slowly!' Keeping her arm around his shoulder and supporting her with his arm around her waist, he helped her take a step forwards. As her full weight came onto the right leg, Marama grimaced in pain.

'It's sore but I think I can move. Anyway, we've got to move. But I'm going to need your help, Sean.'

'That's OK, darling. Let's make for these pines. I reckon they're only about sixty yards away and the ground's flattened out here.' He glanced up at the sky. 'The moon's shortly going to be covered in cloud again. We'll be needing the torches soon.'

'OK. Trust me to go on about the terrain being dangerous and then putting my foot into a bloody hole.'

Maitland had waded through the pool at the cave entrance. Where the floor sloped upwards, he'd managed to locate their footprints at the water's muddy edge. It looked like they'd gone to hide in the far back passage. He pushed the safety catch off the rifle. It had been years since he'd last been here but he remembered the room and the creek at the end of the tunnel. He proceeded cautiously with the torch in his left hand and the rifle barrel resting at an angle over his left wrist.

They weren't there. Where the hell could they be? They'd been there. The torch beam had shown partial footprints by the edge of the roaring creek. Then he recalled Rob once telling him that he'd gone through the underwater tunnel with Hemi and that it had taken them out to the Valley behind. He hadn't believed him at the time and even now he wondered if anyone would be mad enough to contemplate it. In these conditions it would be crazy to try. Surely they hadn't attempted it. But they could have. There were no signs of footprints going back out. Well, he wasn't going to try it. Hopefully they'd drowned.

He raised his head to the vaulted ceiling and yelled above the water's roar, BAS-TARDS! Then, turning, he scrambled back up the passageway.

He exited the cave entrance and half ran back along the track that would take him to the top of the Valley. If they had got out without being drowned, he might just catch up with them. Ten minutes later he reached the spot where the track dropped down into the Valley. He paused. The moon had gone again but he thought he could see a pin-point of light further down. It looked to be quite close to the back of the burial site. It seemed to barely move. His heart quickened. It must be them. But what were the chances of catching up with them?

46

Sean was worried. It had taken an age for them to reach the pines and the track. He was exhausted but more concerned for Marama. Their move over the short distance had been painfully slow and obviously very difficult for Marama. She'd shown a lot of guts to get this far. But the cold, their drenched condition and the injury had piled up the odds of her getting any further.

'Marama, you can't go on. We've got to get up to the caves and find some shelter and then I've got to get help. We're not that far away from the Maitlands' homestead.'

'I know. I'm sorry, Sean. I should have been more careful. But I'm not too sure about the caves. The site's tapu. I'm not particularly superstitious but it worries me having to go in there.'

'Come on, girl. The wind's getting up. I know you can't get much wetter but we've got to get you out of the wind chill. And as far as superstition goes, remember we're the good guys. I'm sure the spirits will look after their own.

Maitland was hurrying. Being on the track he was making

good progress even although the moon had disappeared and the wind force increased. He'd elected to keep his torch off. He didn't want to be spotted. He wanted to catch them off guard. He stopped again to check if they were still visible. Yes, there it was. The pin-prick of light was moving across to the burial caves and at an extremely slow rate. But why? Why weren't they heading along the track to Jack's place. It looked like he still might have a chance of catching up with them after all.

'We're nearly there, Marama,' said Sean half carrying her to the tunnel entrance. Is this the only way in?'

'From this side, yes, as far as I know. I remember Gramps telling me about the back entrance from the Valley and how it leads to the large cave at the front. And I've spotted it when we were playing over here. But we were always warned to keep well away from it. At various points there are supposed to be little vaults that have been hollowed out of the rocks for the ancients to be buried in.'

'So, if anything, this will be a short-cut to Jack Maitland's steading?'

'Well, sort of.'

'That's even better. It means I can get you to the front and then get help. Let's move just a few more yards in and rest for a moment. As Sean moved slowly along supporting Marama, his foot collided with something that caught around his foot. 'Jesus Christ!' he yelled and then shone his torch downwards. The strap of a large rucksack was wrapped around his calf. A variety of tools lay beside it on the cave floor on top of what looked like a canvas sheet. 'What in heaven's name is this?'

'I'm just remembering. A while back when all the legal stuff about the road build was going on, Gramps and big Billy Tamaki were up looking at the proposed road route. Some weird bearded fellow came out of the cave entrance carrying some artefacts. Billy must have scared the life out of him because he dropped everything and made a dash past them. He ran all the way down to a van parked on the back road and took off. It is, of course illegal to raid places like this.'

'This must be the stuff he left behind. You don't think it could have been Harrison Ford?' said Sean trying to lighten the situation. 'Here sit down, Marama. Let's see what's in his rucksack.' Helping Marama down and getting her to shine her torch on the rucksack, he pulled it forwards. 'Hey,' he smiled, 'look what's behind it.'

Behind the rucksack was a billycan, bottle of water, a pile of small broken-up tree branches, a few magazines, a small pot and an oil lamp. The rucksack's contents included a sleeping bag, a jumper, a lumberjack-style shirt and a pair of thick wool socks. There were also several cans of beans.

Sean sniffed the clothes. 'They smell OK too. The spirits are definitely with us, Honey. I'm going to get you set up with a bit of warmth before I go for help.'

'No. You'd better just go. We don't know if Michael's picked up our trail.'

'I think we're safe. He wouldn't think there'd be any point in us coming here. Come on. Let's find a sheltered spot nearer to the other entrance and then I'll drag this other stuff through.'

Sean moved fast. Within quarter of an hour, he had the shivering and exhausted Marama zipped up in the sleeping bag, her soaking clothes discarded and wearing the shirt, jumper and socks. Beside the glow of the oil lamp, he had constructed a ring of stones inside which a fire blazed cheerfully. Though it would take time for their chilled bodies to warm up, the psychological effect of the fire had lifted their spirits.

Sean knelt beside Marama and took her face in his hands. 'I won't be long. You'll be OK.' She gave a small smile and nodded.

'I love you.'

'Very touching. Very bloody touching!' The voice froze them. Michael Maitland came closer and into the lamplight.

47

Sean eyed up Michael Maitland. The effects of the lamplight in the cavern accentuated the demonic expression on his face. He looked cold and wet, dishevelled and exhausted – just like themselves. But there all similarities ended. His eyes were wild and staring and he was struggling to hold the rifle steady. It quivered and shook, an extension of the tremor in his arms and body. He seemed to be clutching it harder in an endeavour to stop it moving.

'This is not the way it was going to be,' he said hoarsely, spitting the words out. 'We could have had a good life together, you stupid bitch,' he said waving the weapon at Marama. 'But you chose him instead,' he added moving the rifle from Marama to Sean.

'You know, it's quite funny,' he said with a bitter laugh. 'All this fuss about the bloody site. Well, you got your wish. It'll remain untouched by any development. And you'll be able to share in its preservation because you're going to be PART of it, cooped up with the bones of the other horis lying here.'

'Right, Marama, get out of that bag and lift up the lamp.'

'She's injured, Maitland. She can't walk.'

'Ah, so that's what slowed you down so much. What a pity!'

'Michael, please, just let us go. You're not well. You can get help.'

'I don't want any bloody help. Come on, Marama. Up. Now!' Maitland's voice cracked out like a whip.

'Listen, I told you…'

'Shut up or I'll shoot you now,' said Maitland pointing the rifle at Sean.

'No. No! Panic-stricken, Marama struggled to unzip the bag with shaking fingers. 'It's alright, Sean. I'll manage.' She struggled to her feet. The large shirt appeared nightgown-like on her, stretching almost to her ankles. She hobbled over to the lamp and lifted it up by the handle.

Sean lifted his torch up but Maitland immediately snapped at him, 'Put it down, Campbell. Then walk ahead of us, over towards the entrance.'

Sean laid his torch down and with Marama's lamp casting some light ahead, he walked forwards, alert and tense but trying to look subdued and cowed. Marama followed. He knew he would have to have a go at Maitland. At the very least he had to create a chance for Marama to escape, though in the condition she was in he wondered just how much help this would be.

The mouth of the cave was around twenty yards wide but surprisingly low, the roof sloping steeply down to a gap of not more than four feet at its highest point. Maitland suddenly called out, 'Stop! Move over to your right.'

In the flickering lamplight, Sean could see a small chamber blocked with stones up to a height of around four feet. Between this and the tunnel roof was a gap of about three feet, the original stones of which were lying on the cave floor, either dislodged or purposely removed.

Michael had picked up Sean's torch and he shone it into this corner. He kept back from them and slightly to the left.

Desperately trying to stall for time, Marama said, 'You seem to know your way around here. Have you been here before, Michael?'

Maitland blinked and shook his head, as if struggling to concentrate on what she'd said. 'What? Oh. Of course. Rob and I explored these caves as teenagers. Never let on to Hemi. He would've gone mental. Even old Vic didn't approve and thought we might be tempting providence. But I guess the spirits have got used to me. They don't seem to mind my presence,' he laughed mirthlessly.

But then he gave Sean a spark of hope. 'You're going to clear more of these stones. Marama, stand over there and hold up the lamp so as it shines on the wall,' he said pointing to the right side of the chamber's entrance.

'Why in heaven's name do you want more stones shifted?' Sean asked though he feared it was quite clear what Maitland had in mind.

'I'll leave you to work that out for yourself. Suffice to say, this is a burial tomb. Right, Campbell, start making the hole bigger.'

With the flickering light from the oil lamp and the beam of the torch on the tomb, the scene was like something out of a horror movie. Macabre. For a moment Sean experienced a feeling of unreality. He looked at the gap. He reached up and pulled at one of the top stones. It rolled off and fell with a thump at his feet. He bent down and lifted it. It was about the size of a football and heavy. He heaved it over to his left. He was aware that Maitland was standing behind him. He turned to look.

'Don't turn round. Just concentrate on the job.'

Having Sean in front of him and Marama to his right, he'd made the mistake of having two angles to cover. Sean figured that the best bet would be to find a rock light enough to throw at him. But he needed an opportunity to do so. He was dislodging stones and throwing them to the right and left of the entrance. When he found the rock he was looking for he let it fall at his feet and left it there.

As the wall became lower and the gap got bigger, Marama's heart beat faster. She had noticed the rock that had fallen by Sean's feet. She knew that at any minute he would try something and racked her brains to think of how she could divert Maitland's attention. She had to do something. She had to do it now!

She lowered the lamp a little and throwing out her arms took a few stumbling steps towards him sobbing, 'Please, Michael, please let us go.'

The new set of wildly dancing shadows created by the swinging lantern momentarily confused Maitland and he moved backwards. But then he pointed the rifle at Marama. She dropped to her knees and began to sob louder. Sean grabbed the rock with both hands and still in his bent position, spun round to his left and with all the force he could muster delivered a scrum-half pass directly towards Maitland's chest.

Spotting the movement at the last moment, Maitland tried to move further left to avoid the rock, at the same time swinging the rifle back to point at Sean. But the stone caught him on the shoulder and the weapon went off with a deafening bang, the bullet ricocheting off roof and walls and miraculously missing everyone. Sean followed the throw with a dive forwards in an attempt to tackle Maitland.

His success in hitting his target, however, had done him no favours. Michael Maitland had been knocked off balance but also out of Sean's reach. Managing to keep his feet, he crashed the barrel down on Sean's back.

Maitland booted him in the ribs and began screaming, 'Right, that's it. You asked for it.' He pointed the rifle at Sean's head.

A roar resounded around the cave and a flashing taiaha staff hit the side of Maitland's head, twisted in a semi-circle and then the bladed edge crashed into the back of his neck. As he was falling the weapon descended again, this time the broad flattened surface landing with great force on the top of his skull. The limp body of Michael Maitland collapsed in a heap on the cave floor. Hemi kicked the rifle away from the fallen body. Chest heaving, he dropped the taiaha and went over to kneel by his sister. Marama fell into his arms and began to cry.

'Hey, Sis, it's alright. We're all OK. Everything's going to be fine.'

Sean got up and joined them. He was shaking but he put an arm around brother and sister and hugged them. 'Hemi's right Marama. Everything's going to be alright.'

48

Sean tip-toed into the room signalling for the others to wait at the door. The room was bright and the winter sun though low in the sky was shining directly onto Vic's face. He looked surprisingly peaceful. Though sound asleep and sporting his usual few days' stubble, he had a benign smile on his face.

'Wake up Sleeping Beauty,' said Sean.

Vic opened his eyes and focusing in on Sean grunted, 'Oh it's you, Haggis. What brings you to this neck of the woods?'

'I come bearing gifts,' said Sean plonking down a bottle of juice and bag of grapes on the bed-side table. 'I've also got some visitors for you.' Turning to the doorway he called out, 'Kirri, come and see your Uncle Vic.'

Kirri came in and ran over to the bed, 'Hi Uncle Vic, I've got sweets for you,' she said holding up a box of chocolates.

'Thanks, Honey,' said Vic with a smile. 'What say we open them now? Will you do that for me? You know how much I like chocolate.'

Kirri excitedly tore at the wrapping paper as Vic winked at Sean. When she got the box open, she lifted it up to Vic.

'I like the orange-flavoured ones, do you?'

Vic smiled, 'Get Sean to pick a coffee one for me and an orange one for you.'

'Oh, thank you Uncle Vic. But Mum said they're supposed to be for you.' Then she added, 'Jakob's here to see you too.'

'Is he?' Well you tell him to come in and have a chocolate.'

Kirri ran to the doorway and called out, 'Jakob, come in.'

Jakob came shyly into the room carrying a parcel wrapped in brown paper. He brought it over to the bed. 'This is for you Vic, I thought you might like it.'

'Gee, Jako, you shouldn't be bringing me presents. I'm the one that should be getting something for you. But here, take a chocolate and then will you open it for me?'

Jakob picked a sweet and then began tearing at the sellotape on the back of the parcel. Vic could see it was rectangular in shape. Jakob pulled the rest of the paper away and held up the contents for Vic to see.

Vic's eyes misted slightly. 'Aww Jeez, Jakob, that's beautiful son, and it's in a glass frame too. I'll keep it up on my wall always and it'll remind me of my cobber Jakob, the boy who saved my life and who became a famous artist.'

Jakob beamed proudly as he looked at his kingfisher picture. Sean chipped in, 'We asked Jakob if he would like to come down with us and he wondered if you'd like to have the picture. We all knew you'd love it. And you might recognize the frame. Annette thought it would be a good idea to set it off. She got into your workroom and framed it herself. Quite a capable girl your sister. Oh, I was to tell you that she and your Mum will be along shortly.'

'How the hell did she know about my room?'

'Well, a couple of days after her Florence Nightingale stint, I met her at the shop and we got to talking about you. I might have let it slip that you had a hobby no-one else seemed to know about. You know Annette, she doesn't mess about. Found the key and was straight in. Might add, Vic, she was mightily impressed by her big brother's talent.'

Vic sighed.

'Oh, I've got one more person to see you before we go up town. I think he should be here by now. Sean left the room and came back with Tupe Parata.

Tupe walked over to the bedside, 'Hello, Vic,' how are you feeling now?'

'Not too bad I guess,' said Vic looking puzzled.

Tupe stretched out his hand to shake Vic's and explained, 'I'm a friend of Sean's. I work down at the museum. We have an area there where we do art and photographic exhibitions. We'd like to do one displaying your work. What do you think?'

Vic raised his eyebrows, 'You must be joking. I mean how…?' Then he looked at Sean. 'I suppose this joker Campbell's been telling you about me taking photos? You don't mean to tell me that based on this you're going to exhibit my stuff. Pardon the expression, Tupe, but are you taking the piss?'

Amused at Vic's bluntness, Tupe smiled. 'No reason to do that, Vic. Sean got your sister to drop by the museum with the Lake Tekapo shot. It's magnificent. I haven't seen any of your other work but based on that picture and Sean's assurances that you've got a pile of good stuff – and I rate Sean's opinion highly - when you're fit and well we'll certainly want to display your work.'

'Well, I'll be damned.

'You've got the talent, mate,' said Sean grinning. 'No sense in hiding your light under a bushel, or in your case, behind locked doors.'

'Vic looked stunned. 'I don't know what to say.'

'Anyway,' said Tupe, 'I must go. Sean asked me if I'd pop round and I've been delighted to do so. We'll be in touch with you in due course, Vic. Get well soon.' He shook hands with Vic again and gave Sean a smile. 'Bye everyone.'

Sean couldn't stop grinning. Vic looked at him, 'Bloody haggis-eater.' And then he started grinning too.

It was good to see Vic on the mend, thought Sean. Fortunately, there wasn't going to be any permanent damage to his foot and he was due to commence physio soon.

It was the first Monday in June, Queen's Birthday weekend, and therefore a public holiday. Sean had taken Marama, Kirri and Jakob down to visit Vic at Dunedin's General Hospital. Marama had gone off to visit Vic firstly whilst Sean took the children on a trip to the museum and to check on whether Tupe was still available to pop around to the hospital. Marama was then due to meet up with an old college friend before meeting the others in the town centre later in the afternoon.

Sean could have spent all his time studying the Maori exhibits and artefacts and the exhibitions featuring Polynesian and Melanesian cultures. But apart from being amazed by the size of the Maori war canoe, the real treat for the children was wandering around the Victorian- inspired zoological gallery with its amazing assortment of animals and birds.

From the hospital they headed for George Street. 'Where are we going?' asked Kirri.

'We're due to meet your Mum at four o'clock,' said Sean.

'When will it be four o'clock?'

'Very soon. And you know what that means?'

'What does it mean, Sean?'

'It means icecream time.'

'Oh good. Isn't that good, Jakob?'

Jakob grinned and nodded.

49

As he drove back to Glenbeg, Sean felt a warm sense of contentment flow over him. Marama had fallen asleep and Kirri and Jakob were chatting happily in the back. In fact, for a boy who hadn't said a word to the majority of the people he'd met during his young life, he was doing a brilliant job of keeping Kirri entertained.

Jakob's break-through seemed nothing short of remarkable. The whole business with him saving Vic from imminent death and then getting help had totally confounded everyone. Before his return to school, Bryn, Marama and Sean along with Jakob's parents, had discussed how best to deal with his transformation. There was an underlying concern that he might revert to his previous state when back in the school context. It had been decided to keep everything low-key and to treat Jakob as before. They would leave it to him to take the initiative to speak in class and with the other children.

On the first morning of Jakob's return Sean had popped across to the staffroom at lunch-time to learn how he'd got on. But Bryn had reported no change in his normal class demeanour. Jakob seemed to have resumed his normal role. And then in the afternoon it had happened. It was library reading time for the middle school class. During this period Bryn would sometimes send a group of volunteer senior pupils through to 'pair read' with the younger children. Jakob had put his hand up when Bryn had asked for volunteers. Jakob had been great. He'd been paired with little Mervyn White. It was clear that Jakob had known the story. He'd listened to Mervyn read, helped him with one or two difficult words and asked appropriate questions. He'd also praised Mervyn in the manner a teacher would adopt. The silent Jakob of the classroom may not have said anything in the past but he'd certainly been listening, observing and absorbing all the time!

Indeed, as the days passed by, Jakob was beginning to actively participate more and more in classroom life. He would still always be more of a listener but there was nothing wrong with his ability to communicate. Needless to say, his parents were overjoyed at his transformation.

All seemed to have gone quiet in the back of the car. Sean checked the mirror. Kirri was sound asleep, her head against Jakob's shoulder. Sean caught his eye, 'You OK, Jakob?'

Jakob smiled and nodded and then continued to look out of the window.

A glance at Marama filled Sean with a rush of tenderness. She looked so serene, so peaceful. Just over a week had passed since the fateful night on the hill. The trauma, the horror of it all, could be with them for a long time to come. A nightmare that had really happened.

Thank God for Hemi. And thank God for the taiaha. Good old Hemi had tracked them down. Despite the elements and his injury, he'd pushed himself hard and reached the Hidden Valley track in time to see Maitland enter the burial caves. And by some very strange co-incidence – or was it fate? – he had stumbled across the taiaha staff. When they'd been discussing it later, they'd come to the conclusion that the guy fossicking around in the burial site must have taken it from the vault where the old chief had been buried. Given the fact that it had saved a direct descendant of his, Sean didn't think he'd have minded too much about it being used to lay out Michael Maitland. Poor sod. The blow hadn't killed him but he'd ended up in Cherry Farm, brain-damaged, and would likely stay there till the end of his days. Well, what was worse? If he hadn't ended up in that condition then he'd have been locked up in a secure part of the hospital set aside for the criminally insane.

The story had created quite a stir in the local press. He'd given old Bill Spiers an exclusive. Bill had come out of retirement just long enough to write the piece himself.

His mind went back to thinking about the taiaha again. The spearhead had come home after all these years. And he'd learned from Tama and Tupe that some very important elders in the Otago Maori community were going to arrange a special ceremony for the return of the repaired taiaha to the burial tomb. He wondered what old Calum MacKenzie would have thought of that. He guessed he would have been pleased.

It had come home. *It had come home*! Strewth, of course!

'What are you thinking about Sean?' asked Marama sleepily. Sorry I've been so out for the count.'

'No problem, darling. Think you needed the rest. No, listen. I was thinking about the taiaha. Remember I told you about Calum's account of the encounter between the old chief and Beardie O'Neill?

'Yes, Sean. I'm not likely to forget it. The taiaha's had a big influence on a number of people's lives, not least our own.'

'Right. True. But listen, you know about Takarua being your forebear. There's something I'd totally forgotten about. Remember when I'd left you the night of the accident and ended up upriver, falling asleep on one of the giant rocks?'

'Ye-ess.'

'Well, there was one thing I never mentioned because it seemed to have been blanked from my mind. I'd had this strange dream. A dream that seemed so real. I was on a big rock by the river…'

'Which you were,' Marama interjected.

'Yes. But in the dream there was a mist swirling around me. And yet as I looked in the direction across the river, the curtain of mist parted, revealing a young girl in Maori traditional costume. I could hear some chanting, in Maori. The girl was kneeling at the feet of an older man, a heavily tattooed man. He wore the cloak of a high-ranking warrior. Wisps of mist floated around them both but I could see them clearly. I thought the girl was you, Marama, but I realize who it was now. And the man. I didn't know the man, but I can guess now who he might have been. He had one hand on the girl's shoulder. His other hand stretched out towards me and he seemed to be speaking to me. Although the words were in Maori I could understand what he was saying…… *BRING IT BACK, PAKEHA. BRING IT BACK ACROSS THE GREAT OCEAN OF KIWA TO ITS RIGHTFUL HOME* . At the time I didn't know what he meant. I do now!'

Marama shivered. 'That's scary, Sean.'

'It's eerie when you think about it now and how things turned out. I guess you could say his wishes were fulfilled. I don't think it's something we need to feel frightened about. Remember the taiaha brought me back to you. And the taiaha, through Hemi's hands, saved our lives.'

50

Despite the sharp early morning frost, Sean could feel a warmth on his back from the slanting winter sun's rays. He stood, formally dressed in suit and tie, some twenty yards below the entrance to the burial caves. Above him a group of Maori elders and dignitaries, many of them wearing traditional korowai – Maori cloaks – over their funeral attire, were gathered at the cave mouth. They stood in a semi-circle facing the burial site and Tama. He could hear the karakia, the prayers or incantations, being intoned. Behind him and at a respectful distance from the ceremonial group stood Bill Spiers and a photographer along with a small group of interested onlookers.

The chanting stopped and Sean lifted his head. The semi-circle had divided into two parallel lines. He could see Tama standing facing him. A tall erect figure moved from the group and walked down towards him. When Tupe reached him, he gave Sean a secret wink and brief smile. Then he stood beside him and looked up towards Tama.

Tama stretched out his arms and began calling out in his native tongue. Tupe translated for Sean as the old leader spoke. 'Welcome Sean Campbell from across the great ocean of Kiwa. Welcome our friend who has brought back the sacred taiaha of Takarua Potaka. Now we can return it to its resting place. It will rest with the bones of this great warrior and those of our ancestors.'

Tama inclined his head and Tupe touched Sean's arm. Sean, who had been cradling the carefully repaired weapon, moved forwards, stretching out his hands, palms facing upwards and with the taiaha lying horizontally. Tupe followed him. As he arrived in front of Tama, Tama smiled and placed his hands on Sean's shoulders. 'On behalf of our people, I thank you Sean Campbell…Tena rawa atu koe.'

Sean bowed his head then passed the taiaha over to Tama. The emotion of the moment came over him as Tama turned and walked into the cave, chanting as he did so. The others, including Tupe, followed, responding to the chant. Sean turned and walked back towards Bill.

The Te Kanawa home was bulging at the seams. Late in the afternoon after the burial ceremony, some relatives plus Tupe Parata and Bill Spiers and their wives, Bryn and Pam and Sean and Vic, had gathered there.

A huge array of food covered the table in the dining room and the guests were making regular forays there to try out the multitude of delicacies provided by the women folk.

'Hey, Sean,' said Hemi as he devoured yet another chicken leg, 'you going to include all this cave stuff in your story? They might televise the story. They wouldn't need an actor, I could play myself. What d'you reckon?' said Hemi grinning. 'You know, big hero and all that.'

'Big skite,' said Marama winking at Sean as she passed by carrying a tray of replenished drinks.

Sean laughed and as Hemi moved off to pull the leg of some other unsuspecting visitor, he leant against the wall and looked around him. He felt very privileged to be amongst these friends and Marama's family members. And thinking of the recent past, he felt very grateful to be alive.

Later that night they lay together in bed in the cottage, tired and contented. Marama raised herself to rest on an elbow and looked down at Sean. She tickled him under the chin and he opened his eyes. 'Hey, I've got news for you.'

'News. Good news?'

'Of course, what else! Bryn got a call from the Board. They've Okayed me getting absence from work from the end of June till the fourth term start in mid -October. That gives us three and a bit months free to travel. We can go over to Bonnie Scotland and visit your Mum. And it'll be summer time!'

Sean's eyes lit up. Then he paused, frowning, 'Better warn you now. Summer in the north-west of Scotland is not always warm. Smiling, he added, 'But I'll keep you warm!' He put his arms around Marama and kissed her, a long lingering kiss.

As they lay back, side by side and hand in hand Sean said, 'That's wonderful. Mother will be over the moon and I'm so desperate to show you and our beautiful daughter off to everyone at home. I think we'll keep it a secret that Kirri's her grand-daughter until they meet. What do you think?'

'Well, it might be a bit of a shock to her.'

'It'll be a delightful shock. Believe me.'

'Talking about shocks. I've got more news for you. I met up with Julia in Palmerston yesterday. I'd arranged to have a coffee with her. We had a long chat. I've always got on pretty well with Julia. Seems she's doing great in her new business venture and loving the work. I wouldn't be surprised if she moves up to Oamaru permanently.'

'What about Jack?'

'Jack's going to have to fend for himself. I get the impression that things are pretty well over between them. In fact, Julia seems to have a new lease of life altogether. I think there could be a new man in her life. But my main reason for our meeting was to tell her about Kirri and about you being her dad.'

'Jeez, that must have been difficult.'

'Not really. When I told her I don't think she was that surprised. In fact, she said she'd never managed to see any resemblance in Kirri to any of her family. Not that that in any way stopped her loving our daughter, or will stop her in the future.'

'And Jack?'

'Yeah, he's a different kettle of fish. But Julia said she'd deal with informing Jack in due course. Oh, and it appears that Annette, your femme fatale, has a new man in her life – a young trainee physiotherapist who's been working with Vic in the hospital.'

'Hell, he doesn't know what he's in for.'

'Julia likes him. Seems to have his head screwed on and

to be a good influence on Annette. Quite a hunk evidently. Plays for the varsity first fifteen.'

'Oh well, there's all my chances with Annette dashed.'

'Don't even think about it,' chuckled Marama as she rolled on top of him.

EPILOGUE

Sunlight danced and sparkled on the waves. Across the Sound of Raasay the truncated cone of Dun Caan stood green and proud against a light blue sky. Further west, the pointed peaks of the Cuillins were clearly visible above a few scattered clouds that had been shepherded as far as their lower slopes by the brisk south-westerly.

Below the garden wall Sean snoozed in the sheltered warmth of his mother's garden. Three weeks ago he'd been experiencing the wintry temperatures of Otago. Now he was back home, the garden a riot of colour as the flowers sought to take advantage of the warm front covering the north-west of Scotland.

He could hear Kirri's voice chatting animatedly to his mother as she raked the soil with her fork and his mother's patient replies. He stifled the sob of emotion that suddenly rose in his chest. He'd not just brought a future daughter-in-law home to his mother, but also a grandchild. And Kirri was calling his mother 'Grannie' as if it was the most natural thing in the world to do. He could tell his mother was delighted – her first grandchild. She'd fallen for Kirri the minute she'd set eyes on her and, likewise, the apprehensive Marama whom she'd greeted with a great hug and a kiss at their first meeting.

And it was Marama who'd worked out the connection he'd been trying to figure out in the Te Kanawa cottage. She'd pointed out to him how alike Kirri's smile was to that of his mother's. They hadn't told Kirri yet that he was her real dad. They'd decided to let her keep calling him Sean and as his paternal role in her life grew, they might put it to her that she could call him dad if she wished. They would look for an appropriate time when she was older, but not too old, to explain that he was in reality her actual father.

'Tea everyone,' called Marama as she carried the tea-tray down the garden steps to the sun-bed spot by the sea wall.

'Oh goodie,' squeaked Kirri. 'Come on, Grannie, we're going to have the pancakes I helped you make after lunch. And with the new raspberry jam!' She helped her Gran up from the flower bed and then ran over to Sean. 'Come on Sean, it's pancake time.'

Sean opened his eyes. He looked at Marama and smiled. Marama smiled back.

The End

Printed in Great Britain
by Amazon